11:59

David Williams

A Wild Wolf Publication

Published by *Wild Wolf Publishing in 2010*

Copyright © 2010 David Williams

ISBN: 978-0-9563733-5-9

www.wildwolfpublishing.com

This book is dedicated to the memory of Robbie, who was looking forward to reading it when it was finished. I'm sorry I didn't make it in time.

I

Ambient noise on the talkback line, then Marni's words come through. "IRN's standing by." I smile at her through the glass and she presses slender fingers briefly to her throat, acknowledging the catch in her voice. Still getting used to the speaking parts. I wink and glance at the studio clock as I ride forward on the fader to the mike.

"Exactly ninety seconds to midnight and the news. Less than two minutes to dig yourself out of a hole, guys. And women too, of course..." grinning at Marni. "We're not the only ones who forget. Quick as we can, let's see how many more relationships we can rescue before we all turn into pumpkins." I fade in a driving music bed for urgency and look up at the first name flashing on the screen. "Graham on line 3, do you have a message of undying love for your partner?"

There's the usual startled pause before a hesitant Scots voice says, "Aye, I have, Marc, yes. I'd like to say Happy Valentine to Chris, please."

"Chris. Is that a man or a woman?" Marni looks quizzically through the glass at me and I shrug, mouthing 'Whaa?' as Graham answers. "Oh, she's a woman, aye. Christine. My girlfriend - fiancée actually. Christine Proud."

"And is she proud of you, Graham?"

"She will be now, I reckon, with speaking on the radio."

"Well, Graham, be sure to come back on when we've a little more time to chat. Thanks for your call, and give my best to your lovely lady Chris. We have another lovely lady on line 1."

"Is that me?"

"I don't know, is it?"

Line 1 squeaks to someone next to her. "Ee, I'm not sure if I'm on or not." I shake my head and look across to share the wind-up with Marni but she's turned away at her keyboard, logging names and numbers as more green lights flash at her elbow demanding attention. Marc and Marni, it's a perfect fit. My eyes stay on the sheen of her blonde hair as I talk to line 1.

"How many Valentine cards did *you* get today?"

"Who, me? None. Is that Marc Niven?"

My eyes flick back to the screen. "Is that Emma?"

"It is, yeah. I'm a first-time caller, Marc."

5

"And who's that with you, Emma?"

Giggles. "Oh, it's just my friend Julie."

"And who's the friend you'd like to give a message to?"

"Well, he's not really a friend. Not yet anyway. Just a lad I know from work."

"What's his name?"

"Daniel. Dan."

"And where do the two of you work?"

"Tescos in Long Valley."

"Oh, I was in there the other day." Trying to picture Emma at the checkout. Dan stacking shelves probably. "You know, they had a whole aisle stuffed with Valentine cards. Hey, Daniel from Tesco in Long Valley, where's Emma's card?" More giggles from line 1. Marni looks round and smiles, peeling her headset off, strands of hair still clinging to it. "What do you want to say to Daniel, Emma?"

"Well, just to let him know I like him an' that, and if he wants to go for a drink or whatever he only has to ask."

"There you are, Dan, you only have to ask, cos Emma's gagging for it. Can we fit a couple more in before we go to the news? Let's talk to Hassan on line 2." Marni's making cup-tilting signals at me as I'm doing the cross-fade. I nod back. "Who do you want to give your heart to, Hassan?"

His voice is steady and serious. We get all types. What possesses these folk to call up radio stations when they should be tucked up in bed? Or while they're in bed. "I should like to send all my love to Amina. Amina Begum Khan." Marni leans over the desk to draw big letters with her finger on the glass. *T* followed by a *C*. She draws her *C* the wrong way round from my point of view. Then she straightens up and poses with her palms out, questioning. Cute.

"Amina, is it? Nice name. Wife or girlfriend?" I trump Marni's mime with one of my own, standing to make the little teapot shape, gay as I can make it. Marni cups her chin in her hands and does a stage school pout, then turns to leave the ops room. Our little bout of theatrics has left a vestige of a wiggle on her bum, sexier still as she's unaware of it.

"Wife, yes," says Hassan. "My widow. Mother of our darling child." I'm watching Marni out of the room, still standing as I cross-fade to line 4 and lean into the mike again.

"Excellent, thanks for calling. Now we've just got time to squeeze in…" peek at the screen "…Jed. Who's the last lucky lady tonight?" Silence. "Jed?" and 'Shit' nearly out loud when I glance down to see my hand resting on the wrong fader.

6

I guess the thing I'm most famous for (well, some of the nationals covered it, not just the local boys) is that I once talked somebody down from a suicide attempt. It was Friday night, loony night, and he'd managed to get himself right up in the arch of the Stephenson Bridge before he phoned us on his mobile. The police told me later he even had our number on speed dial so either he was a regular (not one on my radar) or he'd planned it all out before he went up there.

To tell you the truth I usually get the girls to heave anybody who calls from a mobile. It's not just that reception can be dodgy, more that you're laying yourself open to all sorts of abuse when people are ringing off the street or from god-knows-where. Same goes for withheld numbers, I won't be having them. I like the security of knowing you can always track people down if push comes to shove, and more importantly *they* know it as well so it keeps them halfway sensible. Most of the time anyway.

This one was so obviously different, though. Sam was still with us then and she got the vibes straightaway when she took the call. She tapped the glass and I could see her jabbing at the talkback switch so I knew it was urgent before I heard her ask me to pick up 5. And there he was, perched a hundred feet over the river, crying on the phone to me before I even knew his name.

To be perfectly honest, I couldn't tell you now what he was called. I mean I found out at the time – god knows I said it often enough while I was calming him down, acting like I was his best mate - but I'd have to go back to my press cuttings to remind myself. My short term memory for names is OK but beyond that I'm a disaster. I reckon it's talking with strangers night after night that does for it. The worst part is they expect you to remember them, say if they ring twice in the same week, and they can get quite shirty if you don't, so I usually play along. I have it down to a fine art now, and I rarely get caught out.

Half the time it seems as if you're there to offer some kind of free therapy, open session. I'm not saying fifty percent of my listeners are mental cases but I do get more than my fair share. Our controller Meg Reece once had the bright idea of calling my show *Nightwatch with Niven* but she dropped it when I asked her if I was in charge of a radio show or a psychiatric ward.

So I guess it was no real surprise when this poor bloke picked me to tell his troubles to. Not that it was a specially interesting story. Usual thing, really. Wife left him (join the club, pal), tried to stop him seeing the

7

kids, in trouble at work for hitting the drink… blah, blah. It does wonders for your concentration, though, knowing that one word out of place, one hint of sarcasm or blame could send this fragile soul over the edge, literally, into the cold, dark river. I felt as if I was up there with him, and even while I was really listening to him, and really listening to my own responses, sieving them for anything he could misinterpret or take offence to, I found myself thinking about how he would die if he slipped off the bridge. Would the impact kill him? Would he be drowned? Poisoned by the mucky river? Could he even survive it, maybe, supposing he *did* fall? I was having this conversation with myself at the same time as I was talking to him, and both of us in the moment, forgetting we had thousands listening in and more joining all the time.

Which there were. I don't know how these things get about so fast. I suppose one person rings another going, 'You've got to listen to this,' then another, and so it spreads like a fire or the plague. There were people turning up at the bridge apparently, rubbernecking – so many, the ambulance and the firemen had a hard job getting through. That would have been an ironic ending, wouldn't it, DJ's suicide rescue foiled by his own fans.

Would he have jumped? Not sure. All I could do was keep talking to him, trying to bring him down mentally while the real rescue workers got their act together. Sam did as much as me to help – she had the presence of mind to tip off the emergency services – but she got no praise for it, not even from the station. Or from me actually, come to think. I was the star of the show and I got the publicity. That's the way of the world. There was even talk of a bravery award, which gave me quite a buzz until Sam gave me the hint about how stupid it would look, me accepting a medal for sitting in a warm studio while a fireman with a proper job was shinning up girders at the Stephenson Bridge in the rain. I put the word out that I didn't think it appropriate, just glad to do my part etcetera.

The incident did wonders for my listening figures for a few weeks at least. Whether people were tuning in every night expecting some other nutter to put himself on the line I don't know but we didn't have any more real-life dramas, not as intense as that one anyway. No more suicide watch. Not until tonight – and I didn't even notice it.

I grab a quick cuppa with Marni and about three minutes' flirting time before we're on again after the news, sport and weather. At the weekend especially the board's lit up like a star ship just after midnight so I usually kick in with some back-to-back tracks while Marni's working on the queue. When we're not doing what I call message board stuff – dedications, quick competitions, that sort of thing – we normally ring the punters back if we decide to bring them on the show. That way I get to pick and choose a little, weed out the obvious drunks, block off the bores.

Tonight I've teed up a couple of 70s classics, a mover and a groover. *Devil Gate Drive* followed by six-and-a-half languid minutes of your night owl favourite *Hotel California* - plenty of time to stick my head round Marni's side of the suite to see what's coming in.

"Nick says Valentine's Day is just another rip-off. Same with Mother's Day, and you're pandering to commercial interests."

"Did *he* say pandering? We have an intellectual on the line. OK, that's good continuity, happy to start with Nick."

"Lee wants to know was Hassan making a sick joke or was he not right in the head."

"Hassan being…?"

"Mmm, one of the Valentine calls, just before the news."

"Oh, yeah." I remembered the low, serious voice, no detail. Seemed OK to me. "Don't know where Lee's heading with that, but I smell racist. Better ditch him. Next."

"Simon…"

"Aggh. Too many boring bloody blokes. Where are all the women? Night like tonight, we need to get a bit of sexual chemistry going."

Marni smiles and pinks up a touch, the way blondes do. "We have a Lynn from Towngate."

"Hooray. What does she want to chat about?"

"Knives on the street." My forehead thuds on the door frame. "No, but there's a kind of romantic element," Marni says, lifting her hand towards me in such a comforting way I have to resist crumpling at the knees and putting my face in her lap. "Seems the trend is for the lads to get their girlfriends to carry their knives for them cos they're less likely to be searched. Lynn found one in her daughter's bag tonight."

"Well, leaving aside what she's doing rooting about in her teenager's handbag, that sounds quite promising. Tell you what, I'll trail the urban violence thing for a while, get some steam up, and we'll have Lynn first on after the break."

Twenty minutes later and I'm well into my stride. Nick turns out to be fair game – a bed-sit tree-hugger on a guilt trip because he's just out of private school and into university. He'll be back for more until he finds himself a girlfriend who can pretend to be listening to him without letting

9

her eyes glaze over. After Nick it's Joseph blatantly plugging some charity bike-athon he's organising. Cheeky bugger even tries to wangle a promise on-air that I'll come along and start the bloody thing. On your bike, mate, is what I want to say, but I can't be caught dissing a do-gooder so I have to go in for some swift ducking and diving instead. If I ever pack in this job maybe I should try politics. Or boxing.

I've cued the commercial break and am about to check we've got Lynn from Towngate on hold when Marni's voice honeys my cans. "Sorry, Marc, I have an Oliver Dunn on the line. Claims he's been on redial nearly half-an-hour. He needs to talk to you urgently, he says, but off the air."

Marni watches as I roll my eyeballs up, then she flicks the switch again. "He sounds quite desperate," she says but I'm already shaking my head. Ollie Dunn is my train spotter. He knows more about the show than I do. He listens every night without fail, as he never tires of telling me, and he often pops into Reception between times, so I guess he only lives a few miles away. What else do I know about him? Not much. He's probably roughly the same age as me, though it's hard not to think of him as almost a child. I doubt that he has a job or if he does he must enjoy the ultimate in flexi-time since he always seems to turn up wherever I'm booked for a PA, taking pictures, queuing for autographs and giveaways. He must have some sort of brain to store all the trivia he trots out every chance I give him, but he has a special needs look about him and sounds, frankly, a shade retarded. For all his obsession with the programme he has been on-air only twice to my knowledge and both times got himself so tongue-tied it was painful. Whether he lives alone or still with his mam I'm not sure but I'll bet you a pound to a penny there's no other woman in his life. He must change his clothes occasionally - sometimes it's the red and sometimes the white - but I've never seen him without one of our freebee tee-shirts stretched over his considerable paunch. Fashion statement, not.

"I haven't time for him, Marni. Tell him thanks for calling and can he put his question on an email. I'll get back to him as soon as I can."

"He said be sure to tell you it's really important."

"Everything's important for Ollie," I tell her. "But only for Ollie. I'll fill you in on him later. Have you got Lynn standing by?"

And I'm rolling again, righting the region's wrongs, dishing out top-of-the-head advice and just generally taking the piss out of people in the nicest possible way.

We're off-air and ready to leave when Marni says, "Where's the best place for me to get a taxi this late? I should probably have ordered one, shouldn't I?"

"What's happened to your little Polo?"

"My flatmate borrowed it to go to Edinburgh for the weekend. Her boyfriend's working up there just now." She flicks her hair over her coat collar with both hands, then looks up and smiles at me watching. Is this a come-on?

"Don't bother with taxis. I'll give you a lift, no problem."

"Oh, I wouldn't want to put you out of your way," she says, but takes very little persuading otherwise and soon we're heading towards Reception, practically arm-in-arm, when I spot somebody chatting to Ron the security man at the entrance. I pluck at Marni's sleeve and we step out of sight around a corner. With her back against the wall and her coat half-open she looks primed for a snogging session.

"What's up?" she says, eyes wide, ready for mischief.

"Ollie Dunn's out front. My personal stalker. We'll be here another half-hour if he sees me."

"What was his email about?"

"Didn't open it. Come on, let's slip out the back, Jack."

"Eh?"

"Nothing, just the jukebox in my head. Blame my parents. This way." Marni and I sneak down a short corridor and through a fire escape at the side of the building. We manage to get to the car park and off into the night while our Ron's still occupied with Oliver Dunn. Some security bloke he is.

I had imagined Marni's flat would be somewhere in town near to the bright lights but she directs me down the coast road and we're soon five or six miles from the city, travelling in exactly the opposite direction to my place. Still, I'm not expecting to be heading back anytime soon.

"So, am I lot different from Sam?" she says, nestling in and turning to watch me as I drive. This is potentially dangerous territory. I don't know how much if anything Marni knows about my relationship with Sam or what made her leave when she did. I try some fishing of my own.

"Did you get to meet Sam when you were appointed?"

"No, she'd already gone. I think you had somebody from the morning shift temping."

"Debbie, that's right."

11

"She called Sam the queen of the switchboard."

I smile, thinking about the description, and smile again, thinking about Sam. "I guess she was, yeah. She kept us all in order."

"So why did she pack it in?"

Killer question. She either knows and is looking for my reaction, or she hasn't a clue about us. I'm not going to fill her in on the details. Don't want her supposing I'm supposing she'll fill the void left by Sam in more ways than one. Even if I am. Not really. Well, not exactly. Nothing like. "Dunno, maybe she wanted a fresh challenge. Left to explore new career opportunities, isn't that the line?"

"What's she doing now?"

I really don't want to pursue this. "No idea. We've kind of lost touch. Anyway, to answer your question, you're not a bit like Sam."

"You mean I'm hopeless, don't you?" She turns on her side as if we're talking in bed. I can feel her eyes on me as she waits for what I've got to say.

"That's not what I meant at all. You're learning the job really quickly. No, I mean you're different in all sorts of ways. Physically, for example. If you don't mind me saying so, you're a very attractive woman…"

I glance across as I say it to make eye contact and check out her body language. Marni's left hand caresses her own face and her long fingers push back her hair. She's ready to hear more.

"I'm not just talking about superficial pretty-prettiness. Lots of young girls, women, have that… it's more, I don't know, there's a depth about your beauty that I noticed the very first time I set eyes on you…" And that's me away, freewheeling down bullshit boulevard while Marni snuggles into her seat beside me, lapping it up. She's so engrossed that she nearly forgets to tell me which slip road to take and I have to swerve hard left at the last second, back tyres screeching and the ESP kicking in. One advantage of driving at two-thirty in the morning is you can usually get away with daft moves like that and we manage to get to Marni's place in one piece, bonded by the thrill of our dangerous moment. She blows her cheeks out as I pull up to the kerb as if we'd just finished a roller-coaster ride, and we lean into each other slightly, engaged. I all but put my arm around her right then, but I decide to bide my time. We contemplate the street lights in silence.

"Well, Marc," she says at last. "Thanks for the lift. You shouldn't have, honestly, but it was really sweet of you." She unclips her seat belt and slows the movement down, letting the belt play gently through her hands as it's reeling in.

I glance up at the building we're parked beside. "Are you upstairs or down?"

"Second floor, actually. Left at the top of the stairs. It's OK, quite spacious. That's our window up there, see?"

"Our window?"

"Claire's and mine. She's the girl I room with."

"Who's in Edinburgh at the moment."

"Mmm. I'm all on my ownsome."

I recognise my cue. "Aren't you going to invite me in, then? Cup of coffee?"

She smiles to herself, still looking up at the window, and I can feel my arousal. Furtive adjustment required, I'm thinking. I'll do it while we're getting out of the car.

Except I don't get out of the car. Marni flops back on the headrest and turns to face me slowly, still smiling. "Oh Marc, I'm sorry, but I'm really tired, you know? Just not used to these late nights yet. I'm going to have to roll straight into bed, if you don't mind."

For a second I'm taking this as another come-on and it's on the tip of my tongue to suggest I roll straight in there with her, when Marni suddenly goes into prim mode, closing her knees and reaching to bring her bag up from the floor-well to her lap. She already has her hand on the door catch when she turns to me again. "See you tomorrow, Marc. Today, I should say. Thanks again for the lift." In one smooth movement she is out of the car, passenger door efficiently shut without slamming, bag over the shoulder, heels clicking up the path to her three front steps.

I sit sulking in my car, tracking Marni's journey as single lights go on and off again - in the downstairs lobby, the stair-head, her room on the second floor – and I wait another quarter of an hour for her bedroom light to go out before I ram the gear-stick petulantly into first and finally drive off.

I'm dropping off the coast road to skirt round the city, still cursing all cock-teasers I have known and not loved, when the illuminated Tesco sign catches my eye in the distance and, without particularly thinking about it, I direct the TT to the mostly-deserted car park of Long Valley's Retail World.

Tesco is open 24 hours but as far as I can see I'm their sole customer and the only reason I'm here is my hitting on Marni has made me restless and prickly. Everyone else seems to be stacking shelves. What was the name of the girl who called the show tonight, in love with a shelf-stacker? Emily? Emma? Emma, I'm pretty sure. Can't remember the guy's name. Like a bored detective on a slow day I go mooching around the aisles in vague pursuit of likely suspects.

One that might fit the male profile is a tallish, twentyish lad with streaked hair and not many spots, stamping sell-by dates on milk cartons with a certain deliberation. I sidle up, pretending to consider my options on long-life cream while I sneak a look at his name badge. Andy. She *might* have said Andy. I watch him working for a few moments then ask casually out the side of my mouth, "Is Emma on tonight?"

"Sorry?" He looks across and I'm waiting for some flicker of recognition but what I see is a faint look of disgust. It suddenly occurs to me that he thinks I'm on the pull.

"No, I'm... I just know this girl Emma that works here. I just wondered if she's on tonight, that's all." I must sound adequately disarming in a lame Hugh Grant sort of way, wiping some of the suspicion off Andy's face. Now he looks quietly baffled. "Dunno, this is my first week. I don't really know anybody yet." He peeks anxiously past me as if Emma might pop round the corner of his aisle to announce herself, then, when she doesn't, "You should maybe try Customer Services," he says seriously enough, so I give him a thumbs-up and head off in a show of doing that. Where I really end up is at wines and spirits, picking out a screw-top bottle of red that I pay for without looking at the girl on the till in case Andy's put the word out.

I'm too pissed off to suffer the tedium of the drive home before I apply myself to the booze, so as soon as I'm back in the car the cap is off the wine and I spend the next twenty minutes alternately tilting the bottle and staring listlessly through the windscreen across the car park. In fairness to myself I have to point out I'm sipping not swigging, taking careful stock of the fuddle factor. Don't want anybody supposing I'm some kind of reckless drunk.

At the far side of the square is a row of huge lorries and transporters parked up for the night. My mind is idling - playing with the notion that these truckers might be fans of mine, our station on pre-set for easy tuning as they rumble through the region around midnight – when the offside door of a DAF container swings open and a pair of decidedly untrucker legs come into view. An arse-hugging skirt rucks up further as it scrapes past the footplate. I sit up and take notice as the figure slips below the door of the cab and lands short stilettos precariously on the tarmac. She has to duck slightly, stumbling away from the rig as the door swings shut over her head. A fair-skinned woman, a girl really, as she looks barely eighteen, appearing even more frail against the backdrop of the giant trucks.

She wobbles slightly as if there's a wind sweeping across the car park and she looks about, unsure of her bearings. Then, unexpectedly, she takes off in the direction of the petrol station, running as fast as those unsuitable heels will let her. After a few yards she pauses to tear off her shoes, then takes flight again, carrying them in one hand like a baton.

It's clear she's in some sort of panic. I'm hurriedly screwing the top back on my wine bottle intending to drive across and offer her help, but someone else is quicker off the mark. There's a screech of wheels and a silver BMW loops round from behind the line of trucks. It accelerates past the girl then cuts in front of her, braking hard to block her escape route. As she switches direction a big bullet-headed black guy springs out from the front passenger seat and grabs at her. The girl, wailing, tries to beat him off with her shoes, but she's no match at all for this guy who simply swamps her with his great arms, tugs open the back door of the car and bundles her inside, following her and hardly getting the door closed before the driver starts up again.

I have no idea what I'm about, but I lob my bottle onto the seat beside me, fire the engine and roar after the Beemer as it hurtles towards the exit. The bad guys are easily ahead when they reach the main road but I keep my eye on the direction they're taking and I'll swear I'm gaining on them when *smack* - my wheels hit a vicious speed bump. There's a bang as the car stalls and a crash as the bottle launches off the passenger seat and hurtles into the dashboard. "Shit!" as I look down on the red stain spreading across the floor-well. By the time I raise my head the BMW is out of sight.

My first instinct is to reach for my cell phone to let the police know what I've witnessed, but even as I'm unlocking the keypad I'm watching the wine seep into the carpet and trying to calculate how much of it I'd actually poured down my throat before this thing kicked off. The car stinks of alcohol fumes. Besides, those guys are well away by now. I put the phone away, turn the engine over and drive carefully home.

I suppose you'd call where I live now a bachelor flat, though I'm not strictly a bachelor and I'm still helping to pay off the mortgage on the three-bedroom semi I used to share with my wife Linda until she left me. Well, that last part is not strictly true either, since it was me who did the leaving, though it was more in the way of an eviction after Linda found out for definite about Sam. These days there's no Sam either, of course, and my best friend in this place is the fridge.

Once I get back I'm too wrecked to do more than pick out the larger bits of broken bottle from the mat of the TT and drop them noisier than I mean to in the bin outside. Then it's through the door and collapse face-first on the bed-settee in the darkness without bothering to take my shoes off.

Tired or not, sleep doesn't come easily. I have long periods aware that the frame of the settee is rubbing against my scalp, there's an ache in the small of my back and my feet are heavy and uncomfortable. But I'm as helpless as a cripple tipped out of his wheelchair. I have a troubled, fleeting dream of children scampering away as I lie in a dark alley. I have to catch up with them, but first I need to just stretch my hand to reach this broken glass and put it in the bin beside me. But I can't get any closer to the glass. I'm trapped in the fug of the bin, wrapped in its stench. Then I'm awake again, still unable to move an inch to find relief. M.E. must be like this.

Daylight is pushing in past the curtains and my bladder is straining like a prisoner beating at his cell door before I summon enough energy to roll away from the sofa and totter to the loo. By the time I'm shaking off, Pavlov's dogs have barked and the rest is routine Marc morning except I don't have to go through the bother of washing and dressing since I'm still in last night's clothes.

My habit is to fire up my laptop and open Windows while the curtains are still drawn. I resist the daily temptation to google my own name and instead download my personal emails as I sip at a breakfast drink – there's no orange juice left in the fridge so I have to make do with San Miguel. I'm foolishly nurturing the hope that Sam might have responded to the hangdog apologetic Valentine message I emailed her yesterday, but of course there's no reply from her. As far as I know she might have changed her email address.

The usual lurkage of weirdoes and petty criminals from the dark corners of the globe have been spewing their slime into my cyberspace through the night - illiterate inducements and offerings of penis extensions, orgasm multipliers and other assorted lechery. Zapping them clears my in-tray completely, so I key into my work email, looking for contact that might be at least halfway human. Whether Ollie Dunn qualifies I'm not altogether sure, but I clock that his name appears three times on the sender list, one of his busier nights considering he'd shown up at the station in the middle of it. I double-click to open his first message.

Marc,

Tried to call FYEO but your new girl wdnt let me thro to you. Coud you please tell her? (FOR FUTUR REFRANCE). Coud be Emmergence call like now what am suppost to do? Reason been really woried that the Indian man I think he was is doing the same as James Watson. Maybe you need call him back help him you like did James. PLEASE PLEASE let me know youve recd this Marc. Even just to say it on the radio if havent the time to call back, I'm all chirnd up about it. They shoud leave you alone as far as that sort of thing is conscern'd. Go to the doctor if they are feeling like that or a banker if its money worrys. Its not your job is it or SHOUD'NT be. What do they expect?

Yours truly, Oliver Dunn (Mr)

FYEO? James Watson? Isn't he the guy who discovered DNA? Mental double-take. James Watson was the bloke on the bridge, the suicide caller. What's Ollie saying? The Indian man is doing the same as James Watson. What Indian man? What is he on about? I point the mouse at Ollie's second message, and click.

Marc,

Its Oliver (Dunn) writing again sorry but youve not replyd yet to mssge sent 12.36 or said on radio I dont think, havent even been to the toilet for listening. Does your new sam KNOW about she shoud be checking your emails during the prog or if you dont, seeing as youve not menshd anything coming in or eyther on text even. I mean not just from me anybody. Thing to remind to her, make a LIST is good for remembring. Thats one for top of the list specialy tonite when matter of life and death posibly. Its over 1 hr since he was on any way so maybe too late posibly, but its always worth a try. I've put URGENT on this one in big so she will know to open it when she checks hopefully or you to.

Yours truly, Oliver Dunn (Mr)

I scroll back to the top of his email to check the time he sent it. 1.03 am, during the news when it was safe to break off from listening for whatever message he was expecting me to give him on-air. So this Indian guy he's talking about was on over an hour before that. Which would have been the Valentine dedications... oh, the Asian bloke, good radio voice. Somebody else mentioned him after. Marni. No, she said somebody had called asking if he was joking or insane or whatever. Ollie's picked up the same vibe. What? He was just a normal bloke making up for not sending his girl a Valentine. What have I missed? She had a nice name, I remember, I'm sure I commented on it. He said her full name, very rich and romantic. Nothing wrong with him at all, he was spot on.

Ollie's final message is timed 2.52 am, subject box blank. I double click and read.

Marc,

17

I came round to see you but youd gone well your car was still there when I wark past befor. I nerly was going to wait next to it so we coud speak not for other ears but all of a sudden I thorght maybe theyd think I was trying to NICK it insted went to front door. Security man knew who I was any way. He said you was still in the bilding which I knew any way as had my earphones in. One in only when I was talking to the Security man plus I could see the clock. But we waited till 2.21 and then he said hed go and see were you were I waited by the door then he came and said you were'nt in the bilding. Then I saw your car had GONE. I dont know how I missed you but I did sorry about that. Then I thorght maybe you rushed round to this mans house to stop him from killing himself or the police station cos sometimes it might be say just a cry for help isnt it, so there might be more time or if he just took a few pills or HOWEVER he was going to do it. I know its not my bizness poking in nothing to do with me but PLEASE let me know what happend and everything alright or not. I dont mean all the goory details. Its not for that like some peple, its just about being woried is all about with it happening on your show and like the last time which turnd out alright thankfuly. So hope to hear from you SOON Marc. We wont forget THIS night in a hurry Forteenth Feb (and) 15th Feb. Both as he spoke to us before 12 only just. Last time was also Forteenth (pm) but of course September also a Friday Thank you Marc if you see.

Yours truly, Oliver Dunn (Mr)

I open each of Ollie's messages again one by one, reading them more carefully, trying to mine the meaning out of them, then again, my anxiety growing each time. Ollie may not be able to string a sentence together but nobody listens to my programme more carefully than he does. And at least one other person must have picked up on whatever I've missed. My mind slips back to last night's show. The run-up to midnight. I was skittish, showing off to Marni. Christ, somebody might have *died*, just through me not taking enough notice of them. I don't think this is just Ollie bleating; the evidence is pointing at some sort of balls-up. And it's pointing right at me.

I shift the mouse to the reply button, ready to pump Ollie with questions, then, with a sudden shudder of guilt, sweep across to close down instead. Grabbing the keys for the TT, I hurl open the door and half stumble down the stairs in a panicky rush to make up for seven lost hours.

II

"Get the garlic out, Dracula's woke up early." Jim the technician breaks off from browsing through the sports pages to grin at me. "Tell you what, Marc, mornings don't suit you, pal. You look like shit."

"Yeah, well you look like this all the time." Trying to act casual. "Can you do me a quick favour, Jim?"

"No, you can suck your own."

"You're not my type anyway. Seriously though, can you dig out last night's ROT file and set it up for me?"

"Eh, can't you see how busy I am?" But even as he's saying it he's swivelling his chair round and propelling himself across to the Perspex cabinets that house the gubbins only Jim and his like ever delve into. As he's searching for my programme recording I'm skimming anxiously through the headlines of the local paper he's left on his desk, a pointless thing to do since anything that might have happened would have been too late for the morning editions. I'm just stoking my paranoia.

"There y'are," says Jim, pulling his head out of the cabinet. "I've put a feed into Studio Two. That's free until eleven if you want to go in there."

"Cheers, Jim."

"What did you do? Say *fuck* on the radio?"

"No, I just wanted to check something. Thanks for your help, mate."

There's some perfectly good speakers in Studio Two but I shut them off and put the cans on to listen to the recording, feeling furtive, praying nobody from upstairs randomly decides to indulge in a spot of management-by-walking-around and noses into the studio to ask what I'm doing.

I cue the in-point at 11.58 on the timeline then nudge the bar a few seconds on to the end of the music track for my pick-up. 'Exactly ninety seconds to midnight and the news...' Chirpy old-fashioned stuff, but it fits our demographic as they say upstairs. Besides I can't do it any other way – DJ-wise, I'm cryogenically preserved. Here's the dedication sequence. Graham the Scotsman, inoffensive, zip it on. The Tesco girl next, I was right about her name. Daniel her boyfriend, not Andy. I'm sending Emma up for Marni's attention. Look at me Marni, aren't I the dog's bollocks? Ah, here he is. Hassan. Hassan, he's called. Doesn't sound Indian, Middle East maybe. British Asian, I don't know.

'I should like to send all my love to Amina. Amina Begum Khan.'

'Amina, is it? Nice name. Wife or girlfriend?'

Through the earphones I can just hear the slight sigh of my chair. That's me standing up to mime the teapot thing.

'Wife, yes. My widow. Mother of our darling child.'

What? I jog the audio back, too far left on the timeline, and I'm hearing Emma's nervous giggles again. Nudge forward and Hassan is so calm by contrast.

'I should like to send all my love to Amina. Amina Begum Khan.'

'Amina, is it? Nice name. Wife or girlfriend?'

'Wife, yes. My widow. Mother of our darling child.'

'Excellent, thanks for calling. Now we've just got time to squeeze in… Jed. Who's the last lucky lady tonight?'

Fuck. Fuck, fuck and double fuck. I wasn't listening to a word he was saying. Basic fucking error. *My widow.* The guy's about to end it all and he's sending a message to me as well as his poor wife. And I ignore it. What did Ollie say about a cry for help? I could fucking *scream*.

My instinct is to wipe the file, get rid of the evidence, remove me from the scene of the crime. But my rational mind is already kicking in with a few objections – like I couldn't do that on my own, like it's illegal, like it wouldn't make a damn bit of difference to the facts – and there's even a runt of conscience trying to make its feeble voice heard in all this din, suggesting that maybe I should spare a thought for Hassan when I'm through with the self-pity. Maybe he's still hanging on, like James Watson, on the off-chance I might actually come and rescue him.

Yes, yes, there is still that chance. I could try his number, see what happens. Come to think of it, there's all sorts of possibilities. He might have changed his mind, be happy as Larry this morning. Or maybe he never meant to top himself at all. If English isn't his native language he might have just chosen the wrong word, said *widow* thinking it meant, whatever, *soulmate* or something. And suppose it's the worst case scenario, say he *is* dead. At least I can honestly say I made an effort to contact the guy. Just a few hours late, that's all.

I close down in Studio Two and make my way along the corridor to the main suite, trying not to run. On air it's Simon on Saturday. In the ops room Debbie has her back to me, filling in programme returns. As I walk towards her my eye catches a glint of epaulette behind the studio glass and I can't suppress a "Jesus!", startling Debbie, before I realise it's just some fire officer being interviewed by Simon Barnes.

"God, Marc," says Debbie. "What a fright you gave me."

"Sorry."

"Got a hangover?"

"No, no, I'm hunky dory."

"Thought you maybe hadn't been to bed. What brings you in so early?"

"Just a meeting. Mind if I use this computer for a minute?"

"Help yourself." I can feel her eyes appraising me critically as she makes room for me to sit down in front of the screen. She says, almost under her breath, "Hope your meeting's not with anybody important," then, aloud, "How's Marni settling in?"

"OK, good." I notice Marni has replaced Sam's Celtic logo with a flower on the desktop. I click through. "What's the password for our Call Log?"

"WHAMBAM. One word, all upper case."

Debbie says it nonchalantly, but I can't help colouring slightly as I'm keying it in, reminded of past bedroom sessions and my ritual post-coital whisper that gave my ex-lover the idea for her password. "Wham bam, thank you, Sam." Yeah, it sounds macho, but trust me, I'm the tender type.

Password not recognised. Try again?

"Is it spelt with an H or without an H?"

"With."

"That's what I thought." I type it a second time.

Password not recognised. Try again?

"Hmm. Won't let me in."

"Shift over, let me have a go," says Debbie, and she settles her ample frame in front of the screen to demonstrate my incompetence. Except she has no more success than I had.

"I know what's happened," she says at last. "Marni's changed the password."

"What's she gone and done that for?"

"Well, if she's like me she'll use the same one for everything she does. Makes it easier, dunnit?"

"Not for me, no. How can we find out what the new password is?"

"We can't. Not until Marni comes in."

"But that's not till tonight. I can't wait that long."

"Can't help you, sorry," says Debbie, going back to her programme returns.

"Shit!" I bang the desk so hard it hurts. "Bloody idiot!"

"Missing Sam, are we?" says Debbie sweetly, with a touch of gratuitous malice. I scowl and walk out into the corridor.

I'm stalled now for hours. There's nobody in from HR to tell me Marni's home number. Not that they'd be likely to in any case – they wouldn't give me a sniff when I tried to get back in touch with Sam. I suppose I could find my way back to Marni's place and ask her for the password in person. But she'll see that as my excuse for turning up on her doorstep, flatter herself I'm still after her body. No way. Or she'll start asking questions I'd rather avoid. Chill out, Marc, the guy's probably fine. I'm just looking for reassurance about that without bringing the world's attention to it. Then again, maybe those extra hours could make all the difference. Or not, how would I know? Fuck.

I wander along to the newsroom. Kate Foreman's in there, working on her script for the midday bulletin. I do a couple of little drumbeats on her shoulders to alert her as I lean over, scanning the screen. "What's the latest, Scoop?"

"Death and disaster."

"Really?" Slight quickening of the pulse. "Where?"

"Indonesia."

"Oh. Nothing local?"

"Not in the way of earthquakes, no."

"I mean, people stuff. Who's been… anything interesting come in?"

"Look, do you mind? Some of us have a deadline to meet. If you've got nothing better to do can you do it somewhere else, please? Don't mean to be rude, but I'm really pushed, you know."

"Sorry, sorry." I'm already backing off. "Carry on, Kate." I retreat into the corridor and, with nothing but time to kill, keep walking right out to the car park.

As it happens there's nothing to worry about in Kate's news bulletins all afternoon, nor in the evening paper which I pore over in the Eldon Arms, so I'm breathing a little easier by the time I come back into work to prepare for the show. I'm relieved to find some things aren't password-protected. While I'm waiting for Marni I check the handful of emails and texts that came into the programme last night, deleting those from Oliver before I scan through the others. There are four from listeners who have heard or think they heard Hassan referring to his wife as a widow and

22

asking what that was all about. I agonise over these – should I zap them without reply or respond? Which is more likely to come back and haunt me? In the end I decide that no news is good news on the suicide front and I send the same cheery message to each of them before I remove all traces of the correspondence.

That's what's known as a 'blooper' in radioland! I'm guilty of them all the time (as listeners regularly remind me!) so I think we can forgive Hassan his little slip of the tongue. I believe he was a first-time caller. Thanks for getting in touch with the show and keep listening.

Best wishes

Marc

For once I'm glad that Marni's lack of routine has meant that I've got to the emails before her. I'm still irritated by the password business, though, and she's hardly got her coat off before I'm at her about it.

"Why the hell did you change the password on the Call Log file?"

"What? Oh, I didn't think it would make any difference. I'm the only one who uses it, aren't I?"

"Of course not. Whose show *is* this, anyway? There's all sorts of things I might want to… analyse. Fine tune, sort of thing."

"Sorry. I'll get it up for you." As she seats herself at the computer her mouth swells into the faintest of pouts that I would have found sexy twenty-four hours ago. She logs into the machine, then lifts her eyes coyly and says, "Sorry, Marc, I hope I didn't upset you last night. I mean, when I said I was tired…"

"It's got nothing to do with that. This is purely a work thing. I'm not getting at you. Just… oh, forget it, all part of the learning curve. Could you get me a printout of the Call Log, please? Not reams of it. Just from, say, eleven o' clock last night."

"No problem." She gives me a brave-little-girl smile. "I know I've got a lot to learn still. After all, I have a lot to live up to."

Maybe it's me being over-sensitive but I can't help feeling the softest bite of sarcasm in that remark, though whether it's meant for me or for Sam I'm not sure.

Anyway she manages the printout efficiently enough and I sneak off to what used to be known as the smoking room before government prohibition. On the second page of the list I find the name Hassan Malik and a landline number. He's definitely a local; by the look of the area code probably not far from the city centre. I suppose I'd expected him to be called Khan since that was what he said was his wife's last name, but there again different cultures have different rules about names, so what do I know? Well, what I *do* know is that I have to call this number.

23

There's a prehistoric extension phone parked on top of some old papers and laminated notices in the window corner, as if they're all waiting to be thrown out. I lift the receiver and press 9 to check I can still get an outside line, then pause for a beat, forming an opening sentence in my head as I do when I'm about to go on-air, before I dial Hassan's number.

From here, away from the studio, I can see right across the city. I find myself wondering if I'm facing in the direction of the home where the phone is ringing, even, surreally, trying to locate it, placing the throb of the phone in a room with a high ceiling in a terraced house. The longer the phone rings the emptier the room in my head becomes until it seems quite desolate. A room deserted. I put the receiver down and stand motionless at the window, held by the trance of this image.

The extension next to me rings loudly, making me jump. I stare at it, trying to get my head round the strangeness of it ringing right now, then pick it up hesitantly. "Hello?" For some odd reason I'm expecting it to be Hassan. It's Marni.

"Oh, is that you, Marc? I have an outside call for you."

"How did you know where I was?" My paranoia rising again.

"I don't know where you are, that's the thing. So I pressed this All Call button. Was that wrong?"

"Who is it?"

"I think it's the man who rang in last night." (Christ, it *is* Hassan.) "Should I try to put him through?"

"No, I'm not… Put the phone down." I don't mean to sound so brusque, but I'm fazed by what's going on.

There's a click, followed by silence. But the line's not dead. In her panic or huff Marni must have hung up her end and connected the call by mistake. I listen quietly to what at first seems emptiness from the other end. Tuning in more intently I can make out the sound of laboured, snuffly breathing, as if the person at the other end has a cold. Hassan is alive at least, if this is him.

Alive and now, it seems, eating crisps. I don't immediately place the noise of the packet opening, but there's no mistaking the crunch and damp munching that follows. Graze while you wait. I can't help a trace of a smile at the bathos of this after all my melodramatics with the phone call.

"Is someone there?" I ask, cautiously.

The hurried rustle at the other end is of an animal disturbed, but the voice is human, suddenly urgent.

"Marc? Is it you speaking?" A pause with a slight panting underneath, like a dog waiting for you to throw the ball back, then a noisy, phlegm-filled swallow. "This is Oliver Dunn on the line. Are you there, Marc?"

"I am. Sorry, I was expecting... another call."

"From the policeman?"

"What?"

"About the man on the phone. That's who I'm ringing about. Is he saved or... not saved?" Without waiting for me to answer he plunges on in that headlong way he has. "Only I sent you some emails then I thought he'll not be bothering with them if he's busy with the man and the police and everything, right enough. I mean *you* won't. Only couldn't help worrying so I rang. Same if you've got somebody in hospital, innit? Even if you can't do anything and you're just a bother, you can't help it. Stands to reason when you've got your hands full already without having me to think about. Never mind Joe..."

"Joe?"

"Public. That's like a thing, innit, Joe Public, like people say?"

"Look Ollie, I'm sorry, but I'm really busy, you know. I've got my programme to prepare..."

"Are you going to mention it?"

"Mention what?"

"About the Indian man. Hassan, remembered his name. Only, after the thing about James Watson, I mean the day after, night after pardon me you said, thanks for all your emails and calls, I'd just like you to know that everything is sound. Everything is *sound* is what you said, which was a relief for everybody hearing that. You know, with wondering. You kind of hang on till you hear everything is sound. Competitions is bad enough, never mind this."

"Eh?"

"I mean waiting for the results just. Say if you've entered. Or not, even."

In Ollie's world every listener is on the edge of their seat, poised for the next exciting shift and turn of my thrill-packed programme. Would it were true. No, scratch that, one Oliver Dunn is more than enough to cope with.

"Look Ollie," I say, trying to put some perspective on this for both of us, "Don't go overboard about one word you hear on the radio. Probably a slip of the tongue. It could mean anything, it could mean nothing..."

25

"Have you not found out yet?" He doesn't intend it as an accusation, saying it more like a child seeking certainty from the adult, but it pricks me.

"Hey, I'm on the case, OK? I'm in touch with Mr Malik…"

"Is that him? Mr Malik. Oh, that's good you've talked to him…"

"I didn't say I've talked to him, that's not what I said. I said I'm *in touch* with him. I have his number. I was just dealing with… the issue when you rang as it happens. Bit of an interruption, to be honest."

"Oh." A shocked pause. "Really really sorry, Marc. Messing things up…" He sounds so forlorn my tetchiness drains away, leaving my shittiness exposed.

"No, don't…" I start, then, "No, really, I'm glad you rang… Appreciate your concern, Oliver. We all do. Just, don't worry, OK. It's being sorted. Everything will be fine. I promise."

"Yes, Marc," he says. A child scolded, forgiven, and off to bed. "Love your show."

"Know you do. Thanks."

As he's putting down the receiver his end I hear him repeating faintly "Everything will be fine," as if he's speaking to someone beside him, but I guess he's just talking to himself.

It's catching. "Everything will be fine," I say as well, seeking my own solace from an empty room.

What is certainly not fine is tonight's show. Blame it on Marni and me losing the rapport we'd been building up, or the strange sense I have of being judged on every word I speak on-air – whatever the reason, we manage to combine amateur hour in Hicksville with the cheerlessness of a get-together with the Plymouth Brethren. I miss cues, garble links and snuff out any spark of life from callers, with weary responses that emerge from a dead area somewhere behind my eyes. Usually as the programme rolls along I cut down on the music, harnessing energy from what flows in through the phone lines, riding it more or less spontaneously. Tonight I don't want the calls, I'm half-afraid of what might come in. Instead I spend much of my air-time taking refuge, you could call it, behind the work that other people have produced in studios far away and long ago. I just cue the music and sit for long minutes, brooding through the glass while Marni leaves punters on hold and tries to keep up with logging my unplanned selections from the play list.

After the show she doesn't dally or drop hints about a lift, just gives me a half-wave as she gathers her coat around herself and clacks off down the corridor. I slouch off to the non-smoking smoking room and stand apathetically looking down at street lamps defining the ways out of the city. In the middle distance a police car or an ambulance with its lights flashing slicks silently onto the ring road.

The Call Log printout is where I left it on the window sill. I pick it up and turn again to the entry for Hassan Malik. Near the foot of the same page my eye is caught by Oliver Dunn's name and number, recording the first attempt he made to contact me off-air. I feel almost duty-bound to call him, to report back. About what, exactly? The only thing that has happened since we spoke earlier is that I've presented probably my all-time worst radio programme, and Ollie will know that better than most if there's a gnat's-worth of critical faculty in among the super-fan mush. Maybe the compulsion to call him is driven more by my need for reassurance than his. Anyway it's well after two in the morning. I imagine even Ollie will be cuddling into his teddy bear by now. Somehow he seems like the kind of person that might go into an epileptic fit if I dragged him out of a deep sleep.

Drag him out of a deep sleep. On impulse I lift the receiver and start dialling. It's not Ollie I'm phoning; I'm trying the number for Hassan Malik. The ring tone feels different from earlier, not louder but more insistent, not searching but drawing someone in. It's still ringing, longer than before, but I'm not giving up this time. I know it's going to be answered. I'm conscious of my breath matching the rhythm from the phone, supporting the effort. There's a click from the other end. My breath holds.

"Who is this?"

The voice is female, sleepless. I can feel blood draining from my muscles.

"Is...? I'm sorry for calling so late... matter of some urgency. Would it be possible to speak with Hassan Malik?"

Pause.

"Hassan Malik?" I give it more of an *ee* sound this time. "Am I talking to Mrs... Khan?"

"Who is this?" she says again. "What do you want?"

"I'm... It's all a bit complicated, actually. The thing is... I just wanted to check that Mr Malik is all right."

Her voice is suddenly curt. "Hassan Malik is dead. Please don't call here again."

My mouth opens but the words won't come. In any case there's nobody left to hear them. We're disconnected long before I can say I'm sorry to the widow Amina Begum Khan.

III

I've never been Neville Crawcrook's blue-eyed boy – he's flirted with the idea of sacking me a couple of times when we've had those my way or the highway kind of conversations – but he'd be the first to admit I'm one of his best turner-ups. One of the compensations of starting your shift so late is that you can get over most hangovers by the time you need to come in. Over the years the only nights people have sat in for me have been planned vacations, except for the one time I ended up in A&E for fifteen stitches when I tried to break in through the window after Linda locked me out of the house. And the only reason I was so anxious to get in was to rescue my car keys so I could go to work. Plus I made it for the final two hours, bandages and all.

I'm not saying I've never been ill. Some nights I've had to run to the Gents between links with the shits or throwing up my guts with some bug I've caught. But I've been back in place to open the pot right on cue and not missed a beat. Doctor Theatre.

This is altogether different. I suppose my GP would say there's nothing wrong with me physically (not that I've been to him to find out), but I just can't move out of my room. It's something similar to the feeling I had after my night on the settee, but far worse. I feel trapped, like Gulliver in an illustration I remember from a book I used to have as a kid. Gulliver wakes to find that hundreds of little people on the island have tied him down with thousands of tiny ropes, so many all over his body that he can't move, big as he is. Or like Samson after all the strength has sapped out of him.

It takes me until halfway through the afternoon just to pick up the receiver and call in sick. Even though I leave the phone on the floor not three feet away from me I can't rouse myself to answer it when it rings an hour or so later; the station, probably, calling me back with some question or other. By teatime I drag myself to the tap for a cup of water and on my way back to bed I'm at least able to switch on the radio. I drift in and out of sleep as it plays in the background, awake enough by ten o' clock to register that Simon Barnes has been drafted in to babysit my show.

Even while I'm feeling this bad there's a part of me demanding to know why I'm indulging in such self-centred angst. It's as if I've somehow discovered an unsympathetic twin brother inside myself, angry with me, bullying, insisting I snap out of it. I can't explain myself to this brother. I don't know the cause, except that it's obviously related to the death of Hassan, even though with a bit of effort I could rationalise my way out of responsibility for that one – *I* didn't turn the gas on/shove the pills down his throat/tie the rope round his neck/pull the trigger... or whichever way he went. It was his act, his choice. Just as it was his choice to call me and leave a sort of crossword clue about it. It's no more my fault than, well, happening to be in the car park to see that girl run away and get caught again.

She's somehow part of this weight on me as well. She must be – the symptoms came on just after it happened. Or maybe before that. Maybe it's been tugging on me unnoticed for a while. Perhaps it's to do with Sam, or Marni, or Linda... There's a whole queue of women I can blame, and I will once I can think straight, once these damn hooks lose their grip on my nerve fibres.

Around midnight the telephone on the floor rings again. I must have been drifting away as I have the sensation of being pulled back, not into the room but into the sound. It's taken on that relentless tugging job from the little men on ropes. My brain is sucked into the vortex of it, the insistent, echoing spin of it. I fall in so deep that after its first assault the tone loses its sharpness. I'm enveloped, submerged, folded in so thickly that the sound blankets me from itself, dulls, anaesthetises.

How long it rings I haven't a clue. At some point I must have fallen back into a cocoon of sleep. The next time I feel anything like consciousness I can sense the daylight at the curtain through my eyelids, and after a while I notice that the late morning show is playing in the room, Kelly Coyle sitting in for Simon Barnes so he can recover from sitting in for me. I still have no inclination to get up. I put a pillow over my face to shield me from the damp light that's seeping through from outdoors and stay prone on my back for an hour or more, waiting for enough energy to return so that I can spend some on assessing my precise level of crapulence. Rain starts outside, beating against my window.

I'm still lying there motionless when from nowhere a thought strikes that jars my attention. I grab the pillow away from my face and stare wide-eyed at the ceiling. Hassan Malik is a terrorist. He is a suicide bomber. He wasn't just saying goodbye to his wife; it was a signal, something others were waiting for. That's why he was so measured, so calm. That's why he didn't just send her a fucking Valentine card.

I have absolutely no evidence for this but the certainty of it goes through me like an electric charge. I throw the covers off and leap out of bed, accidentally sending my telephone spinning across the floor. Having jumped up so readily, I've no idea what to do next, and I stand unsure and stupidly naked in the middle of the room. I'm not about to run bare-arsed down the high street like Archimedes shouting *Eureka!* Eventually I do make a move, searching under the furniture for my phone, but can't find a use for it once I've fished it out from under my desk, so I stick the phone back in its cradle, switch my laptop on and start to get dressed.

While the screen splutters into life I peek through a chink in the curtains at the rain, and register my second small shock of the day. Oliver Dunn is standing beneath the bus shelter on the other side of the road, looking straight up at my window. I dive out the way as if I'm being sniped at, landing on my backside between the bed and the wall. From there I creep up to the window-sill and lift the bottom of the curtain a fraction. It's definitely Ollie. He's wearing a cheap yellow waterproof, so thin I can still see his red tee-shirt underneath, and he's holding a limp carrier bag with both hands in front of him. His being there can't be a coincidence. Anybody waiting for a bus would naturally be watching for it coming, not peering directly, deliberately up at the building like this. What's he playing at? How did he get my home address?

When I told Marni that Oliver was my stalker I wasn't uneasy about it. I was showing off a bit, truth be told, bigging myself up for her benefit. Ollie's attentions have never really been a bother. I've tolerated him, liked him even in a stray puppy-dog sort of way. But finding out where I live, parking himself outside my door... he's beginning to worry me, and it's not *his* welfare I'm concerned about. I'm starting to feel closed in. Or closed in on.

Still crouching on the floor I'm at eye level with the telephone sitting on the base unit, with the display reminding me of the two calls I'd ignored. I reach out for the phone and scroll through the menu for the missed numbers. The late afternoon one is from work as I'd surmised. The call that came through the night was also from a local number, and I'm pretty sure I recognise it. The jeans I was wearing yesterday are lying on the settee. I make sure the curtains are pulled to before I stand up and walk over to take out the crumpled paper I'd stuffed in my back pocket before I left the station. The log entry for Oliver's telephone matches the second missed number on my display. So that's my address and home telephone number he knows, along with everything else he has in his Marc Niven compendium. He's not as green as he's cabbage-looking, Mr Oliver Dunn.

To complete the set he has another message waiting for me when I log on to my work email. This is a strange one, sent 12.38 am.

Marc,

Sent incase you see tho I know your ill not like YOU and pray its not a CURSE like you here about. I dont like useing the other way's for reason of privasy evryones intitled to same as Joe public, well more even cos of rest needed speshally if sick or overtyed. Im the one shoud have rememberd that SORRY Marc about phone ringing Only one to blaim ME but forgetin and with been desprit to tell you about (sumthing FYEO about you know WHO we talkd about soon) Reason been for secrise for the NEWS Ive found to tell you been very very strainged indeed and NOT for others. (ie new sam &setra) Only BAD coud come only thing Im sure of that. So desprit what to do so IF I dont here from you PLAN is to be aroundabout but TO NOT DISTURB. Also to bring EVERDENCE inc as well DATE/S for beleiveing as I woudnt not if not in BLACK AND WIHTE wich youll know more than me about cheking for. And what to do with. A PREIST maybe, coud be one thing, or the same like in there religuin. For the SOUL to Rest In Peece (RIP). To me thats the IMPORTANT thing. And no need for panic or scarrd about it. So hope your feeling a bit better Marc and not too wory I will just wait and not to nock (or not ring if a bell) or disturb.

GET WELL SOON!

Yours truly, Oliver Dunn (Mr)

I can't figure all this babble about religion and priests (the SOUL for Christ's sake), but it takes him a few points up the nutter scale in my opinion. What's this guff about praying and curses? About not getting scared? For me this is definitely edging into psycho territory.

I creep back across the floor to have another peek through the curtain. There's a double-decker bus parked at the stop, obscuring my view, but when it moves off I see Ollie in the same place as before, only now he seems to be eating what looks like a Mars Bar. From the hem of his waterproof to his trainers he's showing spatters from the wet road. How dangerous can a guy be who doesn't have the nous to stand back from the edge of the pavement?

I look through his email again without making any more sense of it, before logging onto the BBC News website. I'm almost disappointed to see no reference to terrorist strikes or suicide bombs. Not domestically, anyway. They are so common in Afghanistan and Iraq these days they barely rate a mention. Maybe that's where Hassan was off to. Another recruit for Al-Qaeda or the Taliban or whoever. There's no shortage of British Asians prepared to be cannon fodder, apparently. Often they don't even tell their families. Was Hassan copping out of confronting his wife about his decision? Leaving his farewell message with me instead? Where was she when he called me? At her mother's? Upstairs in the bedroom?

No, the timing doesn't support the notion that he went abroad. He was already dead by the time I spoke to the woman, not much more than 24 hours after he talked to me. The whole suicide bomber thing doesn't wash, just me jumping to conclusions based on foreign names and... well, prejudice if I'm honest. I should be reassured. If he had turned out to be a terrorist I'd have more than one death on my conscience. But somehow the idea was energising me, and now I'm back to square one. I've got to find out what happened to this guy, if only to ease this clamp off my brain.

I try googling Hassan Malik. The name seems to be the Asian equivalent of Smith – I get more than 132,000 hits from the UK alone. I'm just thinking of keywords to refine my search when the telephone rings once at my elbow. I answer it automatically, realising too late it could be Oliver Dunn. But it's Meg Reece calling from her office.

"Marc, that was quick. You're up and about then?"

"Oh, hello Meg. Just testing myself out, yeah. I'm hoping to get in tonight."

"Don't worry, don't rush yourself," she says breezily. "I've asked Simon Barnes to sit in again. He did a good job last night."

"Yes, I heard a bit of it. Sounded fine, yeah."

"So I'd rather you make sure you're one hundred percent before you come back in. Don't want you under par on-air, do we?"

"No, really," I say, my antennae beginning to twitch, "I'm sure I'm going to be OK to come in. I'm not one to ..."

"It's fine, honestly," she insists. "There's nothing spoiling. That's what I was ringing to tell you. It gives us a chance to give Simon a good try-out."

"What do you mean, try-out? Simon's had his show the best part of a year now..."

"On a different slot, I mean. It's always best to keep your options open, isn't it, keep things fresh. You know we like to try things differently now and again. Good shuffle of the pack sometimes doesn't go amiss."

"What you saying, Meg?" My hackles rising now. "Nobody's said anything to me about a reshuffle. Leaving aside the breakfast show I've got some of the best figures on the station..."

"Slipping, though. You've got to admit that."

"All the ratings are down, it's an industry thing, it's not just me."

"Simon's are up, actually," Meg comes back.

"Well, bully for him. Best to leave him where he is, then."

"I'm not saying anybody's moving anywhere for the moment," Meg says. "Look, I don't want to get into this right now, with you not well..."

"You started it."

"Cool it, Marc, will you?" There's a steely pause, then she continues. "I just rang to check how you were and to let you know the ship isn't sinking without you. OK?"

"OK."

"Right. There's a time and place for conversations about the future." I can hear her gathering herself before she switches into agony aunt mode. "Marc, I know you've had some... personal issues lately. I fully understand why you're feeling a little tense..."

"I'm not tense."

Her sigh is almost graphic in its impatience, her hand crushing a glass. But she maintains her forced calm. She didn't get to be Neville's lieutenant without mastering that full range of management skills. Or skill set, I think they call it now.

"Well, whatever. Enough said." She signals the end of the round. No knockouts, no submissions. I put one in after the bell.

"So you don't want me to come in, then?"

"Come in when you're one hundred percent, Marc. Not before. We're cool with that." And she rings off.

Meg's call has left me thoroughly antsy. For the next couple of minutes I walk randomly around my flat knocking the heel of a hand against bits of the furniture, the fridge and door jambs. Every so often I pass one or other of the two hanging mirrors, never failing to stop and scowl at my reflection, leaning forward as if I'm about to head-butt myself, then staring transfixed for a while at the anger, maybe madness, in my eyes. I only stop when I mis-hit a swipe at the wash-basin, punch a tap and finish scrunched up, tears welling, squeezing the pain out of my ravaged knuckles.

One day off and they're trying to unload me. I'm going to get down there now, lug that box file stuffed full of fan letters from my drawer and plonk it on Neville Crawcrook's big shiny desk. On the way out I'll stuff my Sony Award up Meg Reece's tight arse.

I really mean to do this. I finish dressing in a state of urgency and even snap a shoelace by pulling on it so vigorously, fired up with a sense of purpose that's been lacking in me for weeks. It's only when I reach out for my car keys that I remember Ollie.

I sneak another look through the curtains. Four people have joined him at the bus shelter and they're all standing – Ollie dead centre –

as if they're forming an identity parade. Only he looks so conspicuous among them there might as well be a huge arrow above the line pointing directly down on his cartoon head. I do hope for his sake he has thermals under that tee-shirt; he must be freezing.

It's going to be next to impossible to get out of the apartment and into the car without him spotting me. What should I do, take him along? Neville, meet Oliver Dunn, prime representative of my huge fan base. Perhaps not. In terms of a fit with Meg's target audience profile he's more square peg than round hole. Come to think of it, maybe there are too many of Ollie's ramblings in my box file for it to be the killer tool in my Save Marc Niven campaign.

A double-decker comes along, once more obscuring the view between the building and the bus shelter. By the time the people in the queue get on board I could be doing a runner, gone before he knows what's happening. But I'm still watching through the window as the bus rolls away, leaving Oliver to his solitary vigil. I couldn't do it to him twice in one week. He's smiling to himself down there now, as if he knows what I'm thinking, but I guess it's just because the sudden rush of activity has relieved the monotony a little for him.

To be fair, the last time I avoided him he actually did have something important to say, so I should give him this second chance. He's not coming up here though – he knows more than enough about me already, and I'm still harbouring a notion he might turn out be the male version of Annie Wilkes. Trouble is, I don't really want to be seen with him in public either, not just the two of us, not round here where I'm pretty well-known.

Ollie, however, seems to have it all quite well planned. As soon as he sees me crossing the road towards him he beams broadly and immediately dives into his crumpled carrier bag. Just for a second I'm thinking John Lennon, Dakota Hotel, but what Ollie pulls out is a little red zip-up purse, the sort kids and old people keep their money in. He waves it happily at me. "Bus fares," he announces.

Bizarrely, a couple of minutes later I find myself sitting next to Ollie on the top deck (his choice) of a bus on its way to the city centre, having had my fare paid for the first time since my mother took me through to buy my first school uniform.

"Like Rolo, Marc?" he says, offering one, though I notice his good manners don't extend to giving me first refusal; he's already working his mouth round a couple he popped in earlier.

"No thanks. How did you know where I live?"

34

"Marcmobile," he says, using the same childish DJ-speak I'm prone to when the mike's open. "*Sure* I saw it on the bus, me on the bus I mean, was… day after New Year. Not the night New Year, not with Big Ben, the day after the day after that, has that got a name? Just through the window I *thought* it was but I had to come all the way back and it was right. With NIV, innit, that's how I knew for sure. Then I saw it another day, an' another day, and I thought does Marc live round here, then I *knew* it cos another day was fifteenth of January, a Wednesday, and I was on the top deck and your light was on in the window, your window upstairs, and I saw you opening your curtains, and I waved, but you didn't look like you was looking. You know the stupid thing? I knocked on the glass, like this, right…"

He demonstrates by shuffling across the aisle and along an empty double row of seats to tap on the opposite window, then turns to grin at me from there. "Cos I was sitting on this side, that's how I saw you through the window. But fancy me tapping, eh, Marc? How stupid's that? Like you could hear, eh?" He chuckles to himself and shakes his head, then comes lolloping back to his seat, searching my face for a reaction, like the eager puppy he so often seems to be. "How stupid's that?"

I'm reluctant to agree that he's stupid, even at his invitation (he must have plenty of people telling him that for free), so I nod in an ambiguous way, a nod that says something like how wise you are to recognise that temporary stupidity in yourself, then I follow up with, "What about my phone number? I'm not in the book."

He chuckles again, and slaps the carrier bag on top of his knees. "Shouldn't write it on people's hands, then, should you, don't want people to know."

"Eh?"

"At the Arena, when you done the Christmas show, remember? When that lady came up after."

"What lady?"

"The one what came up when you were signing my programme. The one who asked if you did charity dos. You said she could call you to talk about it and you wrote your number on the back of her hand. With my pen."

"Oh, right. Yes, I vaguely remember." Actually, now Ollie's jogged my memory I can easily picture the 'lady' he's on about. Busty blonde lass. Probably just out of university. I think she said she was doing some voluntary work to get PR experience. Not a stunner, but quite attractive. Don't get me wrong, that's not why I gave her my number. Just a get-out clause really. She never called anyway. Or hasn't so far.

"I wrote it down as well, on my programme," Ollie continues. "Had to keep it in my head all the time you were talking to her, cos you still had my pen. I remembered it right, anyway. It was just for having it, that was all. I wasn't gonna ring you up, honest. Only now, which couldn't be helped, could it? Lucky enough I keep things, eh? I'm a hoarder, Mam said. But she's the same one always said you never know when things might come in useful, so you can't have it both ways, that's right, innit, Marc? You can't have it both ways."

That's the first time Oliver has mentioned his mam directly. Is she still around, I wonder? If so I have to tell you, Mrs Dunn, good job in the circumstances, but maybe you could just have a word with your boy about personal hygiene. I mean, I'm not overcome by fumes or anything, but he is starting to remind me why I never use public transport these days. Fortunately there are only the two of us in the upper deck, so the embarrassment factor is not as high as it might have been. I just hope we don't meet anybody I know when we finally get off this bus. I look out of the near window instinctively as that thought occurs, then turn to ask a question, and find Oliver with a little Sony digital pointing at me.

"Smile, Marc," he says, squinting down at my image on the screen. I give him an offhand one that's supposed to mean I don't want particularly want to play but hey, if it pleases you... He shows me the result and all I can see is my face in shadow against the light from the window behind. The subtlety of the smile is lost along with all the other detail. He seems satisfied with it though and he replaces his camera carefully in a pocket of his waterproof as if he has captured a great treasure.

"Where we going, Ollie?"

"We have to look for the man in the moon."

"Excuse me?"

"*A good night guaranteed.* Then count three more stops and we have to get off. You know what's best to do? Count to twenty after two stops, just slow, then stand up and go where the man can see you in the mirror. That way you won't miss the stop."

"And once we get off the bus?"

"Easy after that," he says, rubbing an itch, or maybe a snot-flake from his nose. "Walk away from the bus, not the same way. Keep walking till you see the sign pointing. Then you walk where the sign says and you're there."

"Where?"

"It's called the Central Library. That's the sign to look for. The walking sign, not the man in the moon sign. That says *A good night*

36

guaranteed. Have you never been to the Central Library? It's good. You don't have to pay to get in or anything. It's for Joe Public."

It must be nearly twenty years since I've been in the library building. I feel strangely guilty about that, not least because one of my regular rants is about the way public services seem to be disappearing because the government's too scared of the electorate to put taxes up to save them, and how we only start to respect what we had once they've gone. I'm pleased Ollie's feeling the benefit, but I'm still not clear why he wants me to share it with him, until he drops another clue.

"You gotta have a ticket to take the books home," he says. "You can't keep them, though, just for a lend. Or you can read them there. They've got tables and chairs for it. And the papers. They've got all the papers for you to read if nobody else has already got it out to read before you get there. And you know what's good? They hoard them. They're all in the drawers so say if you missed reading one one day you could get it out of the drawer next time. Or you could get them from a long time ago. So I thought, hang on what if this date's wrong? Or maybe they've got some names muddled up. So what's the best thing for us to do, is to go and check, innit."

"Check what?"

"Check what if it's wrong what they say on the internet. They say all sorts sometimes. Doesn't always make it right, does it? Well, for example, you. Say, if you type Mark Niven different from your proper Marc. You can still get things about you and sometimes Marc with a *cee* Niven and sometimes Mark with a *kay* Niven."

I know he's right. I might be the only person in the world to type my name in a search engine more often than Ollie does. "But you still haven't told me what we're supposed to be checking at the library."

"To see if these is right," Ollie says, lifting up his carrier bag.

"What do you have in there?" I ask, and Ollie is about to open the bag to show me when he gets his eye on the Premier Inn sign and won't take his attention away from spotting the rest of his landmarks until we've left the bus and are safely inside the library building.

Nothing much looks to have changed since the days I would occasionally visit this place for the purpose of copying out large chunks of information verbatim from one huge encyclopaedia or another in the reference section to hand in later as homework. The only immediately obvious difference is the number of computer terminals ranged around the walls, each of them with either a student or an oldster sitting in front on the trail of whatever happens to be important to them, while the huge reading desks in the middle are largely deserted except for the odd semi-vagrant browsing through one of today's papers, or just tapping a hand on top of it, possibly contemplating its value as an extra layer of underclothing if they could manage to smuggle it out.

Oliver takes me to a large empty table in the far corner, partly screened from the main section by the positioning of a couple of microfilm readers and several sets of wooden drawers where back-issues of the more recent local newspapers are kept. He takes a seat at one end, still in his yellow waterproof, his carrier bag on the table in front of him, while I hang my coat around a chair and sit to one side, waiting to have the mystery of the bag revealed.

Ollie had been jovial, excited, on the bus, earnest as he tracked his way to the library, obediently silent as we made our way through to this corner. Now, in spite of his comic appearance, he looks troubled, and he's passing that on to me. He bobs up for a moment, checking that no-one is in the vicinity, then sits down again and bends towards me, confidentially.

"That man. Hassan Malik. He's dead."

"I know." My voice is low too, matching his. "I spoke to his wife. His widow. The night before last. How did you find out?"

"Put his name in my computer. Found out about him."

I remember my own hurried Google effort, one hundred and plenty hits, which I didn't get the chance to refine because of Meg's call. I have my doubts about how sophisticated Ollie's search could be. Then again, he'd already proved himself surprisingly resourceful in uncovering all things Marc Niven, so maybe I shouldn't judge the book by its cover. "How did he do it?" I ask.

Ollie looks at me meaningfully. "He didn't kill himself," he says.

"Oliver, what are you talking about? I already know he went through with it. I told you, I spoke to his... partner."

"He didn't kill himself," Ollie says again. "Look."

From his carrier bag he slowly draws out a couple of sheets of paper, printouts in black and white. They are obviously from website pages. The top one I recognise as a page from the online version of the *Chronicle*.

"What's this?"

Oliver pushes it across. It looks like a typical *Chronicle* news story, with the headline *Death driver named*. I start reading the story underneath.

Police have formally confirmed the identity of the driver who died when his car left the road and hit a bridge rampart on the A191 near Townhead late last Sunday night.

The dead man has been named as Mr Hassan Malik, 31, from the Springhill area of the city. Mr Malik died at the scene after his vehicle burst into flames on impact. There were no other passengers in the car at the time of the accident, which is believed to have been caused by a tyre-burst.

I glance up at Oliver, who has been watching me intently for a reaction, and I shake my head, smiling in what I hope is a reassuring, not a patronising, way. "This isn't our man, Ollie. Look, I've already found out that Hassan Malik is quite a common name. Probably more common than, say, Dunn is in... our culture. I bet you've come across a few people with the same name as you now and again. I know I have. And if I'd been called Mark Brown, maybe, or Mark Smith, I'd be bumping into them a lot more often."

Ollie's expression hasn't changed. "This is the same man what called you, Marc. The man on the radio."

"No, Oliver, you're wrong. And I'll prove it to you. You're somebody who remembers dates, aren't you? What date was it when Hassan called the show?"

"Fourteenth of February. Valentine's Day."

"Correct." I turn the *Chronicle* piece towards him and point to the top of the page. "And what's the date above this story?"

I notice his eyes don't stray to the page, but they widen a little as he says, "Thursday twenty-first of November."

"Right. And the accident happened the Sunday night before, so that would have been the..." I do a quick calculation on my fingers. "Something like the seventeenth, yes?"

Ollie nods, still watching my face. I'm assuming he just hasn't thought this through. "So you see what I'm saying?" I explain as patiently as I can. "*This* Hassan Malik died, what, nearly three months before *our* Hassan Malik, if I can call him that, before the night our man rang my show."

Instead of responding directly Oliver reaches across to the printouts in front of me and slides out the second sheet from under the *Chronicle* article, placing it on top for me to see. It's another report of the police announcement – it even has the same headline – but this one is from the archives of the local BBC news site. Near the bottom of the page someone, presumably Oliver, has ringed part of the story with biro. My eyes go straight to that paragraph.

Hassan Malik's widow Amina Begum Khan was being comforted last night by relatives and members of the close-knit Muslim community in the Springhill area where she lives with her two-year-old son, Tarik.

This time I can hardly bring myself to look up and be caught in Oliver's gaze. He knows I had him down for a fool. "Is that the name he said, Marc?" Ollie asks, almost as if he's signalling that he's still prepared to put his trust in me, however dismissive I've been of him.

"It is, Oliver, yes." There is really nothing else I can say for the moment. I'm dumbfounded. We sit in library silence for I don't know how long. Everything seems suspended for me around these five separate names on one line of print. Hassan Malik Amina Begum Khan. How can this precise combination be a coincidence? How can these two couples, from the same locality, marked out by a death, *not* be one couple? Because to reject the coincidence is to invite in a ghost.

At last I say, more to myself than Ollie, "There must be some explanation for this."

Ollie replies, "Library's the place to find out things."

For the next half an hour the two of us busy ourselves pulling out back-copies of newspapers from the drawers, checking that the dates of the originals match with the online versions (they do) and building up a picture of the accident using a few other accounts we come across. We can't find anything at all in the national press and even the regionals don't have a great deal to say about the incident – another car crash, another fatality, ho-hum. Certainly it hadn't registered with me before now. The only thing that slightly lifts it out of the ordinary is the fact that there was no-one else involved. Hassan was travelling alone in the early hours of the morning when a front tyre blew and he must have lost control, hitting the bridge. By the time the emergency services were alerted he and his car were burnt out, which is why it took a little while to come up with a positive ID.

But it's our man, right enough. Hassan Malik. British-born Pakistani, graduated at the city university, ran his own IT business. One of the papers even has a picture of Amina, snapped in the street somewhere with one of the policemen in the case and an older man who could be her father, I suppose, or maybe Hassan's, dressed in what I would call the full Asian. She's half wrapped up as well, the way they often are, and obviously keeping her head down, but she seems to be a good-looking woman, early thirties maybe, attractive figure.

After we have checked all the sources we can find, Ollie and I lapse back into silence. I'm still brooding on the pages of news-sheet spread out on the large table. Ollie is watching me carefully once more, waiting, it seems, for me to somehow solve this conundrum for both of us. The perplexed look that's scrawled onto his otherwise blank round face reminds me so much of the Charlie Brown character that in a different context I would have found it funny. At the moment it gives me a sense of melting sadness, just as I sometimes feel for Charlie, in fact, when the world or Lucy has bested him yet again.

All I can think of saying is, "I don't believe in ghosts, Oliver." He shrugs, and I reach sideways to put a consoling hand on his shoulder. Just then a woman library assistant walks around the cabinets with an armful of newspapers for filing, and I withdraw my hand quickly as if I've been caught in some guilty act. Ollie and I look on without speaking as she labels, smoothes and places the papers in the appropriate drawers. When she's finished that job she turns to the table and contemplates our scattered news pages.

"Are you still busy with these?" she asks, pleasantly enough.

"Oh no, I think we're through, thanks," and as she starts tidying the papers away I say, "Do you keep telephone directories in the library?"

"Just the local ones, is that what you're after? You should find them in the Local Reference section on the other side of the reading area."

Oliver follows me as I skirt round the library furniture to the shelves the assistant has pointed out. I pick out the city directory and start browsing through the residential pages under M. Despite what I had told Ollie about how common the name is, I only come across three entries for Malik, and only one H. Malik, which is in the Springhill district, 110 Prince Albert Road, so that correlates. The telephone number could easily be the one I rang the other night but I can't be sure without referring back to the printout, which is still in the flat.

"Do you have a pen with you?"

Oliver dives into his carrier bag for a biro. I write the number from the directory on the back of my left hand and wink at Ollie, as I give him back his pen, to remind him of the back-of-the-hand story he told me on the bus. His face lights up and I find myself saying in the afterglow, "Come on, I'll buy you a sandwich."

The library is not that far away from the Eldon Arms, where I would normally go for a pie and a pint in the city centre, but I'm keen to avoid it with Ollie in tow, so we end up down a side street in one of those dingy pubs that always seem to have a couple of ex-miner-types spending the afternoon with one elbow by their drink at the bar, looking down past

41

their feet as if maybe they've lost 10p or are following the progress of a very slow-moving cockroach, while a telly bracketed into a corner broadcasts horse-racing endlessly to no-one in particular. Ollie seems quite oblivious to these surroundings by the time he's been served a run-of-the-mill sausage bap with a few oven-ready chips and three sachets of tomato ketchup. He does act mildly alarmed when I suggest buying him a beer, but settles in comfortably once he has a large Coke in front of him, served in a glass with, apparently, added slurp factor.

"Usually I'd just be getting up around now," I say, not so much to start a conversation as to give me some sort of baffle against Ollie's noises. He stops and considers this for a while.

"D'you have breakfast or dinner?" he says at last.

"When I get up? Oh, some variation of breakfast, depends what I can be bothered to make, really. A bacon sandwich is about my upper limit. More likely toast and marmalade, or toast without marmalade. Sometimes I just stick my mitt in a packet of Sugar Puffs and eat them dry."

"I do that as well," Ollie grins. For some reason I find that information deeply depressing. We lapse into (relative) silence while I get over it, then try to pick up from where we left off.

"So you live... look after yourself then, do you, Oliver?" (Please say no; I can't take any more parallels.)

"Nnn, sort of. There's my mam." (Thought so.) "But she's not very well. She's got catsracs."

"Cat's rash?"

"Catsracs. In her eyes. Waiting for the operation."

"Oh, cataracts. Right. Shame."

"She likes listening to the radio. Likes you, Marc."

"Tell her thanks. What's her name? I'll give her a dedication next time I'm on." (If they haven't sacked me first, that is.)

"Vera. Mrs Vera Dunn."

"What about Mr Dunn?"

"That's me."

"No, I mean your dad."

Oliver's bottom lip juts out a touch. "No. Just me and Mam." Whether that means his father is dead, or left home, or was never around for Ollie to get to know, I can only guess. It doesn't seem fair to pursue the subject.

"*Could* be a ghost though, eh, Marc?" says Ollie, and it takes me a second to realise he means Hassan Malik, not his dad.

"Eh, no, I told you, Oliver, there's no such thing as ghosts."

"Is that for definite?" Another one of those damn child-like sucker punch questions, more expectant than challenging, Oliver counting on me to have the right answer. How the fuck should I know?

"Absolutely. Science has proved it. No, we've got to look for other explanations. First thing I'm going to do is check this number," turning my wrist to show him the number printed on the back of my hand, "See if it matches with the number we've got on record at work. I mean, it could have come from anywhere in town couldn't it, that call, and from anybody pretending to be Hassan."

"What for?"

Aggh, enough already with the sixty-four-thousand-dollar questions. I'm working on it, OK?

"I'm working on it. I'm going to sit down tonight and write out all the possibilities."

"Like, make a list?"

"Exactly. Ever heard of Sherlock Holmes?"

"Yeah, Sherlock Holmes and Doctor Watson," he says, catching me out being patronising yet again. How can I possibly know what he knows and what he doesn't know? Sometimes he seems to have as much of a clue about the world as a new-born chick, other times...

"Anyway, Sherlock Holmes said something like, when you have excluded the impossible, what remains, however improbable, must be the truth. And..." I add as Oliver gazes at me blankly, "Ghosts are impossible. Sherlock Holmes didn't say that last bit, I did."

Ollie waits until he's sure I've finished before he beams encouragement at me then leans forward in his seat and says, "Do they have ice creams in here, Marc?"

The sky looks a bit brighter when we step outside, though that might be a trick of the eye caused by the gloominess of the pub. Back on the high street Oliver takes on the job of pathfinder to the bus stop, but he does it without moving ahead of me, rather he stays close at my side, almost with his hand under my elbow, which I guess is how he walks along with his mother on their rare trips out together. He's in such an effervescent mood now you'd think he'd had something stronger than a couple of Cokes over lunch.

"You know what, Marc? Know the place you live? Guess how far it is from our house? Should I tell you? It's only two stops from our house. I told Mam, I says your favourite lives just two stops away, Mam. You know what she says?"

"What?"

"She says he's dead. I said he isn't."

"Why did she think I was dead?"

"She thought I meant Inspector Morse. At first she did. Then I said I mean your favourite from the radio. And she said Marc Niven. She cottoned on. Cottoned on you say, innit? Mam cottoned on when I said radio."

As he chatters away we cut across the pedestrian precinct. There's the usual crop of deadbeats and toe-scuffers hanging around the benches and lounging malevolently against the plinths of the civic artworks. Out the corner of my eye I notice a couple of youths watching us from under their hoodies. Not sure if they recognise me, but I'm thinking they're more likely to mug us than ask for an autograph. As we get nearer to them one nudges his mate quite forcefully in the back and they turn to each other, sniggering. Ollie doesn't seem to pick up on this at all - maybe he's inured to people taking the piss out of him - and he burbles on as we pass.

"Thing is, you could even come for tea with us if you want. I mean whole tea, not just drinking tea. Or coffee we've got as well. Mam said that, it was her idea when I said it was just two stops. You should ask him round for tea sometime, Oliver, she says. Hot chocolate we've got as well, that's not what Mam said, I'm just thinking that now. Thinking aloud. Do you do that, Marc? Thinking aloud?"

"Sometimes, yeah."

"I do as well. Here's our stop, look. See, 19, 19A, 21, 22. 19 we need, but sometimes I see 19A and I don't know whether it's really the same, or not, so I don't get on if I see 19A on the front. Will it be the same, Marc, 19A?"

"I've no idea. Listen, Ollie..."

"Mam says best not to chance it if it's 19A. Anyway, you don't get them that often. You could work it out if they came a lot, but they don't. Anyway, there'll always be a 19 if you just wait for it. Patience is a virtue." He takes his camera from his pocket and carefully unzips the cover. "See that man coming along? I'm going to ask him if he'll take a picture of the both of us."

"I was going to tell you, Ollie, I've just remembered, I've got a thing to do in town. So I'll catch you later, OK?"

Ollie, camera in hand, looks momentarily perplexed, but he quickly brightens up, "I'll come with you if you like, nothing spoiling for me, Marc. Nothing that's spoiling. We can get the bus back later."

"No, really. It's a work thing. Quite an important meeting actually, I nearly forgot it, so I'm going to have to dash. Listen, I'll give you a ring as soon as I find anything about, you know…"

His deflation is so obvious as I turn away that I nearly change my mind, but that doesn't stop me being irritated when I hear him come panting up behind me.

"Marc?"

"What!" through my teeth as I look back over my shoulder. He is holding a bus ticket out to me like a relay baton.

"Don't forget your ticket, or you'll have to pay again. I got returns."

"Thanks, Ollie," I say, hating myself as I'm taking the ticket from him. "That's really good of you. Give my love to your mam, eh?"

Five minutes later I'm at a taxi rank well out of sight from the bus stop, giving my address to the first driver in the queue.

Halfway through the taxi journey I'm wishing I'd stuck with the option of having Ollie for company on the way home. Or that I'd stayed quiet in the back instead of coming out with the old taxi-cab favourite, "Busy today?"

"Busy? I'm never busy these days, pal. Know why?"

"Not enough fares?"

"Too many flamin' Poles. And bastard - pardon my French - Lithuanians."

"Ah, right." I slink down in my seat and hope that my lack of positive feedback will be enough of a hint to persuade him to shut up, but he's already into his flow and subtle body language sure ain't gonna stop him.

"Makes no difference whether you're on days or on nights, they're always there like a rash. Like a flamin' rash. And it's not just mini-cabs. What gets me is the Council handing out licences to every Tom, Dick and Slobachops so they're on the ranks an' all. They've already put them first in the queue for houses, now they've given them our jobs as well. That's not right, is it?"

If this guy had been a caller on my show, I'd have made mincemeat of him. But that would be him in my territory; right now I'm in his and I'm not about to risk getting clubbed.

"I mean, don't get me wrong, I'm not a racist," he continues, half turning round to reassure me of his liberal credentials. "Far from it. Some of my best friends… it's just they're letting that many in, man. And I

45

know they say it's a free country, or European thingy, freedom of labour and that and we could go and work in their countries, but who would want to go there, eh? You know, seriously? Why do you think they want to get out? And if there was any flamin' jobs in their country they wouldn't be over here nicking ours, would they? I mean, they wouldn't would they?"

He pauses as if expecting an answer. I just purse my lips and shrug in a non-committal sort of way, then look sideways out of the window, so he continues the argument on his own.

"And the fact of the matter is they don't even know *how many's* coming in. Cos you can guarantee that for every one that comes in on a passport there's ten more comes in the back of a lorry, know what I mean? And that's not even counting the asylum seekers, never mind the blacks and the A-rabs an' that, don't get me started on them."

I try not to, but he does anyway. "I mean what gets me about these Muslims, these terrorists, is they'll take all the benefits and the education we give 'em and that, then what do they do, they go and stick a few bombs in the London Underground, what's that about? And half o' them that does that was *born* here. Supposed to be British. Till it suits them to be Muslims instead and they'll say fuck you, mate, I hate your country, bang. Only good thing, at least there's one more of them gone an' all, know what I mean? Plenty more where they came from, like." And on that tender note he draws up gracefully behind my parked TT and rolls his window down, his winning smile already auditioning in expectation of a tip.

I'm carefully counting out the exact fare to hand through the open window when I have to press close to the body of the cab to avoid being swept off my feet by a passing bus. It halts briefly at the stop a few yards along the road for an old woman to get off, then carries on, but not before I've clocked the number 19 on the display at the rear and either caught or imagined a glimpse of yellow material among the passengers seated nearest the pavement. There's no doubt that he would have seen me if it was Ollie. "Shit!" I say under my breath as I dive back into my pocket for an extra pound or two for the taxi driver. The last thing I want to do now is make another enemy.

46

IV

Of course the first thing I do once I've let myself into the flat is to check the number I'd written on my hand in the library against Hassan's number on the printout from the Call Log. The numbers match. Even though my general recollection of the number sequence had led me to expect this, I'm surprised at how much the confirmation of it spooks me. I find myself gazing through the window down at the bus stop as if I might see the ghost of Hassan (pictured in my mind like a son of Osama bin Laden complete with white robes) looking up at the apartment from the spot where Oliver was a few hours ago.

In need of a soother, I prise myself away from the window to seek out an opener for the first of only two bottles of San Miguel I have left in the fridge. For the best part of the next hour I'm propped up on the sofa, all but lost in reflection, with a bottle tilted just enough now and again to keep my lips moist with lager.

The same arguments and counter-arguments keep running through my brain. Hassan Malik could not have made that call since he was already good and dead. The possibility of it being mistaken identity - that the caller was another Hassan Malik altogether – is more or less eliminated by the fact that the call was made from the home of the Hassan Malik who had died in the car crash, and his widow Amina Begum Khan. The caller referred to his wife as *my widow*, casting himself as the ghost of Hassan, but even allowing for the existence of ghosts the idea of one choosing to communicate from the grave to his partner using a BT landline and a commercial radio station is just too ludicrous to contemplate – but then again, no more ludicrous than the notion of a dead person talking platitudes through a medium in a trance or on the stage of a spiritualist church.

The strongest possibility seems to be that someone made the call as a cruel joke, but over the years I've got to be pretty adept at sussing hoax calls. Yes, I was distracted when it was broadcast live, but having heard the recording two or three times I'd swear that whoever this Hassan might be he was serious in his purpose, whatever that purpose was. Besides, what hoaxer could be making the call from the widow's own home? I'm beginning to discover the flaw in Sherlock's method;

47

once I've eliminated the impossible there doesn't seem to be any possible left to latch onto.

A large part of me wants to leave this alone. Let it rest in peace. From my point of view it doesn't look as if I was in any way responsible, directly or indirectly, for somebody taking their own life, or failing to do my best to stop them taking their own life. I've also managed to avoid any awkward questions about that peculiar phone call on my shift, or at least I've been able to fob off those who were both awake enough to notice it and could be arsed to follow it up. Whatever the truth behind the call it's hardly likely to make any positive difference to my life or anyone else's in the future; in fact trying to investigate it is more likely than not to cause hurt, especially for the widow, which is why I'm avoiding trying her telephone number again. All in all, best to forget it.

Then there's another voice nagging at me not to let this go. Partly it's to do with feeling some sense of responsibility to Oliver to get to the bottom of the mystery. Mainly though, it's my own ghost. I don't even know what I mean by that except that I have this strong sense of a self inside of me (maybe not so much a ghost as some imagined superhero, somebody who doesn't have my terrible habits and wicked, selfish thoughts) who's telling me that I'll let myself down badly if I give up now, and that I'll never forgive myself for not having the strength to see through something worthwhile. Which is weird because at the same time this ego-ideal of mine can't define what would be *worthwhile* about any outcome it/I/we could possibly imagine. But it's the voice that's compelling.

So, what am I supposed to do now? I've no plan of action, but whatever I do I can't risk upsetting Amina or her child. On a selfish note (same old Marc), I've got to keep a low profile. Meg has already made it obvious I'm in the firing-line at work and I'm bound to be shot at if I'm seen to put my head above the parapet. On the plus side she's obviously not expecting me to rush back for the sake of the programme (just the opposite by the sound of it), so I'll have a little free time to see what I can find out, on the quiet.

If I was a detective investigating a case I guess I'd want to start by looking at the scene of the crime. In this case I suppose it would be Hassan and Amina's house since that's where the call came from and where Amina was when I rang back the next day. Assuming, of course, it was Amina who took the call. (That's a new angle, I hadn't thought of that before now.) If I'm to keep a low profile I can hardly expect to go knocking at the door but (still thinking detective) I could organize a stakeout, see what might be going on, who's coming and going. For a minute I wonder about involving Ollie in this plan since he doesn't seem to have any objection to waiting around for ages, but I quickly abandon that idea because he looks so damn conspicuous. I'll have to see what I can do on my own.

Six hours later, cold and practically brain-dead with boredom, I'm wishing I hadn't been so dismissive of Oliver. The only thing that has kept me here so long is that everything started out so well. I'd prepared properly, buying an A-Z to get a good fix on the location, a thermos flask and supermarket sandwiches to keep me going, and a miniature bottle of Macallan to give myself as a reward if I make it to midnight. It was still light when I set off in the car and I found Prince Albert Road fairly easily since I already knew how to get to Springhill.

Prince Albert Road is a long street of terraced housing running behind and parallel to Springhill Gate, or The Gate as it's locally-known, where takeaways, delicatessens and ethnic food stores compete for space with a couple of off-licences, bookies, a laundrette and a general dealer, plus a couple of premises with serious-looking grids guarding windows stacked mainly with electrical items. I take it these are some form of pawnbroker or money-lending operation. While I was still in recce mode I parked next to the shops on The Gate (single yellow line but nobody else seemed to care so I chanced it) and walked round the corner to see what I could see. There is a narrow alley running between the backs of the shops and the back yards of Prince Albert Road, but it was obvious from the comings and goings that the residents generally use the other side where little steps lead up to the front doors.

It turned out to be a good time of day to be checking my spot. Some of the people who work along The Gate must park for the duration on Prince Albert Road. Quite a few of them were leaving work and going back to their cars at the same time as I arrived, so not only was I able to walk along and find out which house was 110 without looking suspicious, I even got the chance a few minutes later to go and collect my car and repark it in a space somebody was leaving, a nice discreet spot just twenty yards or so over the road where I could get a decent view of the front of the house.

That wasn't the end of my good luck in the early part of my watch. It still hadn't turned six o' clock when I caught my first sight of Amina and her little boy. I guessed it was her as soon as she came round the corner wheeling a buggy. The little one in the pushchair looked about the right age and the mother had the same trim build as the woman I'd seen in the newspaper photograph. The only thing different, and this surprised me, was that she wasn't so wrapped up as she was in the picture, or in the way that most of the Asian women round here seem to be. No head-covering or long robes. She had a coat and scarf on, sure, but it was pretty cold; this was typical western dress for the North East weather. It was definitely Amina, though; she confirmed that by bumping the buggy backwards up the three steps and letting herself in at the front door with a key.

And that was the end of the excitement at number 110. Tell a lie; just over two hours ago a light went on in the upstairs room with the little window, I saw a woman's hand closing a curtain, and the light went dim, but not off completely. Baby being put to bed, I guess. Since then, nothing.

The whole street is very quiet now. Until about eight o' clock I'd been able to watch Amina's neighbours coming back in their cars (and a couple of vans), presumably from work, gradually filling up the spaces that had been left by the Gate workers going home, like some kind of unofficial time-share parking operation. Most of them were Asians of some description. Nobody seemed to take any notice of the TT – I guess there's always the odd itinerant vehicle in the street, so mine being there wouldn't be unusual – and they obviously didn't notice me sitting behind my tinted windows. A few (men on their own, some couples, a smattering of older children) have since come back out of their homes and either climbed into cars to drive off or walked round the corner towards the main road, but in all this activity nobody else has arrived at or left from Amina's house.

I may see some more movement in the street as people return from wherever they've been, but in the last half-hour the only humans I've set eyes on have been two teenage lads who walked past the car on my side of the road and crossed on their way to The Gate. I felt like sticking my head out of the car and asking if they'd bring me back a takeaway (I ate my sandwiches long ago for something to do) but instead I just watched them until they faded into the darkness.

I've had the car radio on low for company since the street fell quiet. Now I turn it up a notch or two as it's getting near to ten o' clock. I might as well check on my new rival while I'm sitting here. Will Ollie and his mam still be tuning in to the show? Perhaps they'll transfer their loyalties to Simon Barnes and his sidekick Marni. Barnie and Marni, the future according to mystic Meg. Agh, bollocks with waiting till midnight, I'm going to have that whisky now.

The lead story on the ten o' clock news is about the housing minister caught not only with his pants down but with his wrists chained with handcuffs around the waste water pipe in a public cubicle. These are the people who are making our laws, somehow getting our votes – all you can do is shake your head, and have a smirk, obviously. Nothing else special in the bulletin (my suicide bomb theory has died a death, to coin a phrase). I'm not sure I agree with the weatherman who says it's going to be a mild night for the time of year - he hasn't been sitting in a car with the engine off for nearly five hours. I'm professionally interested to discover there's a new ad on for a dotcom dating agency – wonder why they see my show as a good slot for it and whether they've booked up for a decent block contract or just testing the water. Then it's the sig and *here's Simon*, too quick on the mix, and attacking instead of riding in; sign of a novice.

"Good evening, good evening, Simon Barnes here again on the *Nightwatch*." (Ah, the brand queen has found her willing lackey.) "I'm just about getting used to coming to work in the dark." (Well, don't get too used to it, pal, I'm not done fighting yet. And what happened to the courtesy of *sitting in for Marc Niven*?) "Tell you the strangest thing, though, it's just how *quiet* it is around here at this time. There's me and the lovely Marni," (flutter, flutter from Marni) "sitting here all on our ownsome and the rest of the building is in complete darkness. Ooh-err. It's quite spooky, in't it, Marn?"

"It is, Simon, yes."

Well, there's a thing, he's plugged Marni's talkback into the output. He thinks he's Chris Moyles. And what's with *Marn* for Christ's sake?

"We quite like feeling spooky, though. So here's a little challenge for you all tonight. Can you get us just a little bit scared with your tales of ghostly encounters? Things that go bump in the night. We're not looking for Roald Dahl tales or, what's-he-called, Edward Allen Poe." (Edgar, dope.) "Just your own little stories of ghostly encounters you might have had yourself, or maybe you've heard from a friend or a relative. That little touch of the eerie and unexplained…"

Simon adds a touch of reverb as he says this, and a creaking door effect behind. Quite effective, if I'm honest. But I used this theme in October. Best for Halloween, not a Monday night in February.

"Tell you what, we'll get that started in about fifteen minutes, so if you want to be part of 'things that go bump in the night' give Marni a call on the usual number but of course we're open right now for anything you might want to chat about, or maybe get off your chest. Nick in Buddle is

51

going to be our first caller right after this from The Haunted. Hey, we don't just throw this programme together, you know…"

I switch off the car radio, gulp down the rest of the whisky miniature and all but throw it through my front windscreen. Instead I smack the dashboard in frustration. I shouldn't have tuned in to the show – it's just got my hackles up again. Not Simon's fault, really – he's a fairly inoffensive type, bit of a yes-man which is why Meg likes him – but everything's adding up to the realisation that I'm being eased out of my own programme. Calling it *Nightwatch* after I specifically said… Not even mentioning my name… Bringing Marni in on-air. It's so deliberately not me, that's what's so bloody irritating.

I sit in the silence for the next three-quarters of an hour, staring down the dark street, sullenly plotting revenge, until boredom gradually sets in once more, and with it a growing awareness of how uncomfortable I am. It's not just that it's cold or that my backside is numb with being so long in this car seat, the fact is I haven't been to the loo since I left the flat. Maybe it's that little tot of whisky that's brought me to the brim, who knows, but I suddenly, urgently need to pee.

I'm drumming my heels on the floor of the car even while I'm considering my options. Knocking at Amina's door and asking to use her facilities is not one of them. Nor is opening the car door and aiming into the gutter; Sod's Law tells me that, as quiet as it has been, the moment I start relieving myself in the street is the moment someone will come along and make a scene about it, blowing my cover. I'm going to have to find a public convenience somewhere, and quick.

Do I lock up the car here and walk? That leaves me open to being seen and could take too long since I don't know how far I might have to go. Best to take the car and get back as soon as possible, in time to check out what might be happening during that hour or so when people are often on their way home from one place or another as late evening turns to night.

I've been here so long that pulling away from the kerb is like ripping myself off Velcro but at the same time it's good to get some different muscles going and it does relieve the pressure on my bladder a little, like a fretful baby being soothed by the sensation of movement. That thought makes me look to the upstairs window as I pass Amina's house in the car. All still and peaceful there.

Springhill Gate is positively bustling by contrast. There's a group of Asian youths gathered at the corner, joshing and joking with each other. The takeaways seem to be doing reasonable business at this time. They are all too small to be likely to offer a public toilet so I drive past them and past the pub opposite – too close to Prince Albert Road to keep me inconspicuous. What I have in mind is the railway station, which is only a couple of minutes drive and has a Gents that I can nip into easily.

Except that when I get there I find the toilets locked. An Out of Order notice is stuck on the door with Sellotape so grubby it could have been there for months. In the bottom corner of the notice somebody has scrawled *Oh fuck* with a blue biro. My sentiments exactly.

Demanding release, my bladder starts pounding at me again. Now I'm desperate, ready to do it against a wall, anywhere I have a chance of avoiding arrest. As I waddle in real pain back to the car park I see that the road running past the side exit goes down under an old railway arch, so it must fetch up round the back of the station where there's bound to be a quiet spot, some sooty corner where I can piss long and thankfully into the darkness. I struggle into the car and head that way.

What I find when I get past the railway arch is not exactly a hidey-hole but perhaps the nearest thing – a squat, smoke-blackened public house with the filthiest windows I've ever clapped eyes on. It makes the place where Ollie and I had our bar meal seem like a trendy bistro by comparison. Even though I've been in some dives, I wouldn't normally dream of setting foot in such a five-star dump, but this is an emergency. I swing the TT hard right to park on the street a few yards away from the entrance, make sure the car is double-locked, and shoulder my way through the grimy swing doors into the saloon bar.

I'd hoped to dash straight into the bogs, urinate for England, and leg it as fast as I could get out of there, but late as it is there's not a soul in the place to screen me from the pugnacious bloke behind the bar. He stops flicking through what looks like a nude calendar lying flat on the counter, turns to see who's making the racket coming in and chucks out his chin at me, obviously expecting an order. I hesitate, distracted by my straining bladder and by the sight of the dirtiest tea-towel I've ever seen, hanging over the near set of pumps. Eventually, because I'm sure he's setting himself to swipe his great paw across the back of my head if I don't speak soon, I manage to blurt out, "Guinness, have you? Er… not draught…" (panicking about dirty lines). "Bottle. If you've got such a thing."

By way of reply he sways backwards from the bar and starts scanning the floor underneath, without actually moving from the spot.

"I'll just, while you're looking…" I say, pointing at a brown door in the opposite corner which I take to be the toilets since the only other door is where I came in. He ignores me so I interpret this as permission and make my way through to the Gents.

I spend so long there - with so much hosing out of me that I'm able to pilot some crafty smoker's cigarette-butt from one end of the urinal chute to the other - even this sloth of a barman has had time to locate a bottle of Guinness, lever the cap off (with his teeth, I imagine) and pour the black stuff into a glass that I'm hoping he hasn't just wiped out with that tea-towel. He has taken as much care with the pouring as I'd expect, so the froth is cascading over the top of the glass like Etna erupting. I pay up and lift the glass, trying to keep the suds from dripping onto my shoes as I weigh up the health risks involved in drinking from it. I have no choice, though. The barman is watching my every move as if he's waiting to be insulted so he can have a legitimate excuse to kill me. I'll just have to drink up as fast as I dare without offending him so I can skedaddle and get back to the relative safety of spying on the residents of Prince Albert Road.

I'm about halfway through what's left of the Guinness in the glass when mine host speaks to me for the first time. "You'll be round here on the tap, then?"

"Sorry?"

"Along the road. You'll have to watch your back, like. There's been fuzz poking about lately."

"Right. Thanks." I drain my Guinness, still not sure what he's driving at until I park the dirty glass on the bar and try to make my escape while he turns his attention back to his calendar. He calls after me.

"Ask for the black hooer if she's there. Nigerian. There's a lot won't touch her but she gives good head, I'll tip ya."

The idea of picking up any tart behind the railway station, not to mention one specially recommended by a greasy fat bloke in a filthy pub, makes me nauseous on top of the suspect stout lying heavy in my gut. In the car I open the window, trying to gulp in some clean air before I move off, but the air here smells as if it's laced with lead. There's a haze around the orange street lamps that line my side of the road and I can just make out some dark shapes under the fourth one, a hundred yards or so in front of where I'm parked. The ladies of the night.

I've never been with a prostitute, never looked for one. To be honest, just the thought of men that do makes me curl my nose up. It's grotesque, like the leer of the barman in the pub, and his dirty finger-ends smearing the pages of a nude calendar. Paying for sex has to be the ultimate admission of failure. It's abject, reminds me of the bloke in the Dire Straits song ogling the dancer who's pushing her arse out on the

54

telly, and despising rock stars for having everything he hasn't. *Money for nothing and your chicks for free.*

Suppose I've been lucky, really. Nothing like a rock star, obviously, but I've done OK. Alright, I've had trouble with women, relationship problems definitely, but sexually, you know... I've had my share. Till recently, anyway, and that's just a blip. If I seriously put my mind to it I could easily go out on the pull, no big deal, I wouldn't have to pay for it.

Watching the figures in the distance, my mind goes back to the slip of a girl who tried to run away from the lorry park. What was that all about? Is she here, maybe, waiting at the kerb for the next john, not because she wants to but because somebody, some pimp, is making her do it? Surely he can't be watching her all the time. Once she gets into somebody's car, can't she just ask them to drop her off somewhere she wants to go? Even if she has to do it one more time to keep them sweet.

I should be making a three-point turn right now and retracing my route to Prince Albert Road to see my shift out until midnight at least. But when I start the car I drive forward without too much conscious thought about it, just changing quietly up into second, then third and following the lights along the road back of the station. This girl has been locked in my brain since I saw her tearing off her shoes to run faster. I just want to see if she's among this group of working girls, that's all, I don't have a plan.

It's pretty gloomy even under the street lights and I have to change down into second, slowing the car and searching through the side window as I come up to where the women are standing, trying to pick out my little runaway. There seem to be about half a dozen and they break up their cluster when my headlights are on them, stringing along the pavement in front of me, a couple posing like mannequins, others parading coquettishly, one even sweeping her coat away and brazenly jutting her backside half-over the kerb, pouting at me over her shoulder. (*Look at that mama, she got it stickin' in the camera...*) I look beyond her to where there seems to be another standing back in the shadows, who could be the one. I slope across the steering wheel, peering, car slowly rolling, when the passenger door opens quickly from the outside and I have to brake hard to stop it swinging against a lamp post.

"All right, darling?" Geordie voice, smoky, strawberry blonde straggle, very short black dress under an open coat, freckles on her cleavage as she leans into the car. "After some fun?"

"I'm... I'm just looking for someone." (Why am I so scared?)

"I know that, lover. Howay, let's go for a little drive and we'll talk about it."

"Oh no, I'm…"

But she has already opened the door wider and is about to duck in beside me when she suddenly stops, stares wide-eyed into the car and pulls back with a scream that goes through me.

There's a commotion on the kerbside, girls running up ready to protect one of their own and I'm saying, "What? What?" in a daze when the crowd parts to let a bigger dark shape come through. The first I see is a thick gold ring on black knuckles round the top of the passenger door, all but ripping it off as a huge bullet head fills the space and thrusts itself at me.

"What the fuck?" he's snarling, and even as I'm pressing myself terrified against the driver's door there's a part of me registers who this is. It's the guy that threw the girl into the back of the BMW.

"I never touched her… honest," I say, the last part coming out like a frightened kid in the playground. "She just started screaming."

"What the fuck?" Bullet Head says again, only this time it's directed outside the car. Strawberry blonde is sobbing, propped up between two other women. She flinches at the question, then points past him, down to the floor-well.

"There's blood, look. Massive blood stain. He's done somebody in or summat."

Bullet Head looks down where she's pointing, and so do I, until he glares at me again and I shrink back into my seat. "It's not blood, it's wine," I say, weakly. "Red wine. A whole bottle got spilt."

The black guy stares suspiciously for several seconds, his eyes pinning me like a butterfly, before he rocks back slightly and ducks his head below the level of the passenger seat, his knees tucked between the sill of the car and the kerbside. I have an urge to smash him over the head with a spanner and drive off with his body trailing out of my doorway, except that I don't have a spanner or the guts to do it. Instead I wait while he sniffs at the mat as if it has a line of coke on it, then he licks at his fingers, rubs at the stain and licks his fingers once more. He should look ludicrous but in my eyes he's a tiger at a watering-hole, ready to spring at the intruder, being me.

The tension around him eases as a broad grin, not a snarl, breaks across his face. Something is released in me too and I'm pathetically ready to share his amusement till he straightens up and casually cuffs the sobbing woman hard across her breasts with the back of his hand. "Bitch-fool-fucker."

As one, the girls move a step away from him, giving Bullet Head room for a swaggering pace or two along the kerbside, straightening the cuffs of his Italian leather. Then he drops his shoulder and lowers himself into my passenger seat, closing the door behind him. "Emmanuel," he says affably, offering his hand in such a way that I feel bound to take it. I notice two things about him now that I missed in my panic earlier. That he has half a gold front tooth, and that his accent is some brand of African (Nigerian, maybe, remembering what the barman had said), not English.

"OK, let's drive down the road, get a little peace, mister. What's your name, sir?"

"Oh, it's… Oliver," I say, alarm starting to rise again at the thought of having this bloke next to me down a dark road, but doing his bidding anyway, since not to would very likely turn out worse.

"Oliver, good," he says, though whether he means Oliver is a good name or that I've done well to think of an alias so quickly is left hanging. He studies the floor beneath his feet and starts to chuckle. "You like red wine, Oliver. You like red wine, eh?" and he points to the floor in case I'm in danger of missing the joke.

"I do, yes."

"And what else do you like, Mr Oliver? You like girls, yes?"

"Well…"

"Of course. Everybody likes beautiful girls. Jiggle jiggle jiggle." He cavorts with his pelvis on the seat and sniggers in a surprisingly unhard manner, looking at me sideways, expecting me to join in. I offer him a placatory smile.

"Just pull up here," he says in a friendly tone as if I'm his favourite taxi driver. My heart thumps. This is the darkest part of the roadside, directly under the one lamp post that is not showing even the weak orange light the others have on offer. The bulb must have burnt out or been deliberately broken. Why here?

As we come to a stop Emmanuel turns to me, softly touching his palms together with reverent enthusiasm. "Such beautiful girls I have for you, Oliver. I can give you anything you want. Me and my associates. You like exotic girls?"

"Ermm…?"

"Beautiful black ebony girls. Chinese girls. Anything. Young girls you'd like, maybe? Tight virgin girls? Yes, Oliver?"

I can't think of anything to say. Well, let's admit it, I'm too scared to speak right now. The heels of my hands are pressing against the steering wheel and the only thing I do by way of response is push harder against them, stretching my fingers out. It's meant to suggest rejection, but it comes out as a sort of shrug that could mean anything.

Emmanuel reaches in his coat pocket and I shrink back, expecting a gun or a knife. But it's a packet of cigarettes. He flips the top and offers me one the way you do with condemned men. I shake my head and he takes one for himself, pressing the cigarette lighter button next to the gear-shift, and as he waits for it to pop says, "Nice car. What sort of car is this?"

"Audi. TT coupé."

He nods approvingly, pauses to light up with the glowing cigarette lighter, and returns it neatly into its hole. "Good cars."

We sit in silence for a while as Emmanuel enjoys his smoke, then he says, "What do you do, Oliver?"

"Sorry?"

"What is your job?"

"Oh. I'm a radio... ographer."

"What is that, radio-ographer?"

I have a moment of blind panic, absolutely unable to think, but somewhere in my brain a survival nodule flickers. "Oh, X-rays, that sort of thing. Mainly just X-rays."

"Very important job." He nods approvingly again. "In a hospital?"

"That's it, yeah."

"Hmm." Emmanuel sucks on his cigarette, then says, "Do you use drugs?"

I look at him for the first time since we stopped, genuinely confused. "Do you mean, in my work? Or... socially?"

Emmanuel laughs out loud, rolling his head back against the seat. He touches me on the shoulder, flicking cigarette ash down my sleeve.

"I can get you anything you want, Oliver. No problem. Just ask Emmanuel. I'm your happiness doctor." Another chuckle. "No prescription required. So..." He sits forward in his seat and places his hands together, consultation mode. "What can I get you today, sir?" and laughs immediately afterwards so that I'm not sure if he expects me to answer, until he raises his eyes to look at me, nodding slightly, so I guess he does.

"Nothing, thanks," I dare to say at last.

"Nothing?"

"Well no, not really."

He draws on his cigarette and slowly exhales in my general direction. I try not to cough, staying polite. "What are you doing round here, Oliver? Window shopping?"

"No, just … curious."

"Don't you like my girls?"

"No, well, yes. But I'm… just on my way home. My… wife will be wondering where I am. Maybe another night."

"Another night, yes. But what about tonight? Short time, forty pound. Very satisfying, and you'll be back to your wife in no time. I'll call Susie over here right now." He pushes at the button on the door sill and makes ready to poke his head out as the passenger window rolls down.

"No." Desperate to restrain him, I pluck at his arm (dismayed by the firmness of the muscle there) and he turns to look at me with a flicker of that earlier menace. I show him both palms, backing off, but still saying, "No, really. I mean, I do have to go now."

He settles again into his seat, narrowing his eyes, then throws what's left of his cigarette out onto the dark pavement before hitting the button to close up the window. He stares at me coldly, flaring his nostrils in a deliberately hostile, distinctively African signal, and razor-precise in his English.

"You are wasting my time, Oliver. Time is money, you know that?"

"I appreciate that. Look…" I search clumsily in my trouser pocket while he watches, and manage to locate a note. "Here's twenty. Would you mind giving that to… Susie, is it, for her trouble, and say sorry from me?"

He takes the note from my fingers and stuffs it into an inside pocket without speaking, still with his eyes on me. Not for the first time tonight I'm thinking, what the hell am I doing here? Where's it going to end up? I decide I have to play honest john.

"Listen, Emmanuel," I say. "This isn't really my thing, you know. I mean, picking up girls off the street…" His eyes narrow again. "Not that I'm saying there's anything wrong with it, don't misunderstand me, just… you know, for me."

He considers me carefully, as if weighing up whether I'm worthy of receiving his knuckles against my jawbone, then his face relaxes and I see that glint of gold tooth in the gloom.

"No problem, Oliver," he says. "You are a very respectable man, I can see that. I like that. Me too. I am not a corner boy, Oliver. You think I'm a corner boy?"

I have no idea what he's talking about, but I'm guessing the answer is no, so I shake my head.

"Right. I'm the man. For you, I have just the thing." His hand slips inside his jacket and comes out again with a white card, like a business card, which he starts to hand over, then draws back momentarily.

"This is a secret place. Can I trust you to keep a secret?"

I nod and he completes the handover with a ceremonial flourish. I can't read what the card says in the dark, but to convince him I'm treating it with respect and discretion I take out my wallet to store it carefully, though with a frisson of anxiety when I notice his eyes on my thin sheaf of credit cards. I put my wallet away quickly and Emmanuel leans towards me, confidential.

"The best. The very best girls. Not like these whores on the street." He tilts his head in a gesture behind us and sneers. "We just have to keep 'em in line you know, or they're bad for business. But this is not a place for you, Oliver, you should not be on these dark streets. No. Nice man, nice car, respectable job. You need to be safe, understand what I'm saying?"

I nod, praying for the lecture to stop so I can get out of here pronto.

"You go to that address. You ring the buzzer and wait. When they ask tell them Emmanuel sent you. Be sure to say Emmanuel sent you."

"Absolutely," nodding again, willing Emmanuel to fuck off out of my car.

Which he finally does, but not before he shows me his left hand. He flicks the interior light on above the mirror and spreads his fingers out in front of me. "What do you think, Oliver?"

"Excuse me?"

"Three months ago I broke my hand, I think I broke it."

"Aha." I can guess how.

"Do you think it has healed properly? In your professional opinion. It's still giving me pain. Especially when it's cold."

"I'm not really a doctor. If you're concerned, you should make an appointment…"

"But that's the problem, you see. When you don't have the papers. I couldn't even come to get an X-ray from your good self, Oliver. Maybe you could sneak me in some time, eh, after everyone has left?"

I'm going *Christ almighty* inside, fighting to stay calm on top. "Well, I'm not sure… Let me have a closer look." I take his hand gingerly in what I hope is a suitably medical way, and make a show of inspecting

60

closely, trying to control my own shaking fingers. "Oh, yes, it's fine. We don't really do much to treat breaks like this, they usually heal themselves eventually."

"What about the pain?"

"That's natural, in the cold. Have you thought about wearing gloves?" He glances sideways, suspecting me of winding him up. "For support as much as anything," I go on. "That's what we usually recommend... in cases like this. You'll be fine. No need to come in."

Emmanuel's face splits into a grin and he slaps me hard on the shoulder with his other hand. "Thank you, Oliver. You're a good man. A real good man. But you're not a ray... what was that you said?"

"Radiographer. No, really, I can assure you..." the panic erupting in me again.

"You don't fool me, Oliver. You are a proper doctor, I can tell. And a damn good one too, ha!" He slaps me on the shoulder again as he propels himself out of the passenger door. He pokes his bullet head back into the space he's just left and says, "Don't worry, your secret's safe with Emmanuel. Guaranteed." With that he closes the door and swaggers back along the pavement to his harem.

I sit stunned for several minutes, with nothing going on in my head but the slogan from the Premier Inn sign, *A good night guaranteed.*

I snap out of it when another car goes by, my strawberry blonde acquaintance in the front passenger seat. She waves at me briefly as they pass. I'm friends with a tart and a pimp already. I look away, embarrassed, and my eye is caught by all the numbers on the dashboard clock flipping in that moment from 11:59 to 00:00. I have to get out of here. I don't want to double back past the working girls up the road, so I carry on the way I'm facing, assuming that I'll eventually be able to turn right and find my way to the other side of the railway station.

It comes as a surprise, even for one supposedly familiar with the city, how quickly I'm back to driving under properly-illuminated street lights, with ordinary buses and people going about their business on wide pavements. I feel as if I've been a world away from it all, disconnected, but I was just around the corner from this everyday stuff. In less than two minutes I'm turning into the road leading to Springhill Gate and it's there I notice that I've forgotten to switch off the interior light that Emmanuel had flicked on to show me his hand. As I reach up to turn it off I glance in the mirror, and start when I see there's a police car following close behind.

Christ, how long has that been there? Am I being tailed, or...? Maybe they've followed me all the way from behind the station. They could be running my number through the national computer right now. Get a grip, maybe they're just in the line of traffic, nothing to do with me. What about my interior light, is it an offence to have that on when you're driving? Well, I've turned it off now, so why don't you go away and catch some real criminals? There'll be plenty of drink drivers, this time of night, go and nab one.

Now I'm calculating how many drinks *I've* had over the last few hours. I can't be over the limit. Just that dodgy Guinness in the dodgy pub. And the little bottle of Macallan – that was tiny. Mmm, the two San Miguels before I came out, but that was ages ago, and even longer since I had the beers in the pub with Ollie after we'd been to the library. How long do these things stay in the system?

I'm almost to the point where I need to be turning off to get back to Prince Albert Road. What if they keep following me? What if they wait to watch what I'm doing when I stop outside Amina's place, or they come over and question me? How can I explain why I've parked up there?

I can't take the chance of being caught out like that so I drive straight by the turn and carry on past The Gate. I glance in my mirror again and see the police car turning right towards Prince Albert Road. That's ironic. They obviously weren't following me at all, but if I had taken the turn and seen them do the same I would have had a seizure.

I'm too spooked to turn back. In any case I've been away from Amina's house for over an hour. There could have been all sorts of comings and goings that I know nothing about, so as an exercise in surveillance this evening has been more or less futile. I suppose I've learnt something tonight, mainly to stay away from street girls, but as far as solving the mystery of Hassan Malik and his widow is concerned I'm not much further forward.

V

To be honest I'd anticipated another night of bad dreams after my encounter with Emmanuel, but surprisingly I sank into a deep and untroubled sleep not long after I got back to the flat. I might have enjoyed it for a few extra hours but for the damn phone ringing first thing in the morning.

The call is from work, Neville Crawcrook's office. Not from Neville in person of course, who's too self-important to use the telephone except for ingratiating himself with Group directors. It's from his secretary (sorry, PA) Kirsten who says in her matter-of-fact way, "Marc, you need to clear your diary for a meeting in Neville's office at eleven fifteen this morning." Despite keeping as much distance between himself and his employees as possible and displaying all the mannerisms of a pompous prick, Neville, being in the media, insists on everyone calling him by his first name.

"I'm off sick."

"So I understand, but apparently your presence is required."

"What's the meeting about?"

"I don't have access to an agenda, sorry. We'll see you at eleven fifteen." With that, and as crisply as she does everything else, Kirsten terminates the call, leaving me anxiously ignorant about what might be going off.

My immediate assumption is they're going to give my slot to Simon. That's what Meg Reece seemed to be hinting at when she called, and there was a smug, proprietorial air about Simon when he opened the show last night. Most likely they'll do a straight swap for three months and make it permanent provided they don't get too many complaints, or if they've died down in the meantime. Worse still, they might switch me to the zombie zone, the shift that starts directly after mine and sleep-walks through until six in the morning, playing to nobody. For the last couple of years it's been hosted by a jumped-up hospital radio type called Alex Ray who's all easy listening and strap lines like *Take the easy way with Alex Ray* and *Relaxez Vous* which I think is supposed to be a pun on his name. For me it would be a fate worse than death. Exit through the door marked Alan Partridge.

I have less than two hours to get up, get myself sorted and down to the station for the meeting. Most importantly, two hours to marshal my arguments for hanging onto my show, with maybe fifteen minutes to make my pitch in front of Neville. I can do this.

I fire up my laptop while I make a start on washing and dressing more neatly than I otherwise would at this time in the morning, or mostly any time we're not due to have a royal visit. Luckily last night wasn't a bender and I've had my first decent sleep in a while. I don't think they can legally use my being ill to justify a move, but I want to convince them I'm one hundred percent, to use Meg's phrase. I must remember to tell Neville I was ready to come back yesterday, only Meg insisted I stay away.

Sitting at the screen to type out some bullet points for the defence, I decide to check my emails first in case somebody at work might have heard a rumour about changes and is offering any precious scraps of information. I log in as usual to the staff side of the station website.

Access denied. You may have entered an invalid username or password (case sensitive). Please check and try again.

I retype the details carefully.

Access denied. You may have entered an invalid username or password (case sensitive). Please check and try again.

That airhead Marni. First she changed the Call Log password, now she's done the same with my flaming email account. Hang on, no, she can't do that with emails, you need administrator rights… What the hell's going on here?

I try twice more to log in. Same result. I can't have forgotten my codes; I use them three or four times most days. They've locked me out. This could be even more serious than a reshuffle. Surely they're not intending to get rid of me altogether?

I'll ring and ask someone who's clued in, someone close enough to upstairs to have a handle on what's up without being part of the conspiracy. Somebody I can trust. That would be… Hmm, the truth is nobody springs to mind. That's the problem with doing a late night show, you're kind of cut off from those who are part of the daytime business. And I must admit I've not bothered much with the social side of things at work recently. Not since Sam left. I'm pretty much on my own.

Sad as it is, the next person I think of ringing is Oliver Dunn. I'm wondering if he listened to Simon last night and heard him drop any hints about taking my seat on a permanent basis. Anyway, I should let Ollie know what I discovered on my stake-out, even though that wasn't much. Of course I won't mention deserting my post or borrowing Oliver's name to help protect me from the attentions of a pimp. And I'm hoping Ollie won't mention seeing me climb out of a taxi cab while he was still on the bus.

If I'm brutally honest with myself the real reason I want to ring my loyal (only?) fan at this point is I badly need a boost to my deflated ego and to convince myself that somebody somewhere, inadequate or not, still loves me. It's come to something when I have to rely on Oliver Dunn to be my motivational guru. But there's no answer to his number when I call, so I guess he does have a life beyond anything that might revolve around Marc Niven. I'll have to go into my meeting with Neville Crawcrook without so much as a crumb of comfort from my new friend Ollie.

It turns out, however, that I'm not to meet with Neville at all. That is to say, I do meet him, but only by accident as I'm waiting for the lift in Reception and he comes out of it, apparently in a rush to get to the car park. He looks startled and irritated to see me, as if I'm trying to sell him a copy of The Big Issue. He's about to brush straight by until I say, "Er, aren't we...? Excuse me, Neville, aren't we supposed to be having a chat this morning?"

He turns reluctantly without really stopping and says, with a dismissive waggle of his fingers, "I've asked Meg to... Plane to catch. Group. Meg will see to you." And he's off through the glass doors.

His flight from the scene confirms what I suspected. Neville always uses Meg as his rottweiler and hates to be around when staff changes are made in case he has to confront misery, deal with conflict or, god forbid, exercise leadership. Meg, on the other hand, thrives on all of these things as she continually tries out for the role of Lady Macbeth.

Kirsten is on the phone in the outer office and she waves me through to the sanctum with the same slightly disgusted get-out-my-face flick of the fingers that her boss used downstairs. Even though I'm at least five minutes early for the meeting, it transpires as I poke my head through Neville's door that I'm last to turn up. I don't just mean Meg Reece, who is sitting like queen bee in Neville's black leather chair. Also facing me from the far side of the polished table are Simon Barnes and Marni. Nearer to Meg is Alice Winter from HR (a worrying sign). More surprisingly, stuck on his own in a corner of the office, next to a small table with laptop and speakers laid out, is Jim the technician. Jim is the only one who greets me as I come in, with a wry grin and a wave that could just as easily be an appeal for me to pull him out of the place where he's mired. Nobody else moves or utters a word until I say, standing in front of the big table, "What's up?"

"Sit down," the queen bee commands. I ignore the seat she's indicating directly opposite her, instead taking a chair at one corner of the table and angling it so I can see everybody in the room, persuading myself that I've shifted the balance of power. (I once interviewed a university professor on body language and have been an expert on the subject ever since.)

"What's up?" I say again.

"After last night I would have thought that was obvious," says Meg, not bothering to hide a sneer.

My confidence drains. They know about the kerb-crawling. Somebody's dobbed me in. Fuck. How can I explain? "I haven't a clue what you're on about," I say, fishing.

"Don't tell me you didn't listen to Simon's programme."

Now I really don't know what she's on about. Even while I'm trying to adjust my thinking there's a part of me bridles against her calling it *Simon's programme*. "It's not... Er, I did listen to the first few minutes actually. But I fell asleep. No offence, Simon," lifting my hand to him, point-scoring I suppose but genuinely trying to lighten things up; the mood is so brittle. They all stare back at me from the other side of the table, expressionless. "Yeah, I fell asleep. I've not being feeling the best, as you know." I shouldn't have said that, weakens my position. But I think I'm safe about the kerb-crawling thing; it's something else. Christ, it wasn't a listener rang in, was it, saw me in town maybe?

Then Meg says, "Why didn't you tell me about Hassan Malik?"

"Hassan... Malik?"

I'm floored by this. I really thought it had slipped off the radar as far as the station was concerned, had become a thing between just Ollie and me. A detective thing, our little mystery. Now Hassan's back to haunt me.

"Don't come the innocent, Marc, it doesn't suit," Meg snaps. "You know exactly who I'm talking about. Jim?"

Over in the corner Jim jerks out of his slump as if he's been electrified by his own equipment. I've been wondering since I came into the room where he fits into the scene. Now I'm about to find out.

"Play the Hassan clip." When Meg's in boss mode she dispenses with pleases and thankyous.

Jim consults a scrap of paper perched on top of his laptop. "Hassan, OK. 14 Feb." He sneaks an apologetic glance across at me as he cues up the file and clicks to play. His speakers are small but more than adequate for this room. My recorded voice sounds louder and surer of itself than the one that has been responding to Meg's questions.

'Let's talk to Hassan on line 2. Who do you want to give your heart to, Hassan?'

Heard again, Hassan's voice, though calm, seems to me now to have a hollow quality about it. A voice from the grave.

'I should like to send all my love to Amina. Amina Begum Khan.'

'Amina, is it? Nice name. Wife or girlfriend?'

'Wife, yes. My widow. Mother of our darling child.'

Meg's eyes have been settled on the speakers. As Hassan says *My widow* they flick momentarily across to me.

'Excellent, thanks for calling. Now we've just got time to squeeze in… Jed. Who's the last lucky lady tonight?'

Jim taps at the stop button and, in the silence that follows, massages his nose while he stares at the screen, ready to poke a finger up his nostril once we've turned our attention away.

"What did you think when you heard that?" says Meg. Her question is directed at me. "I mean, hearing him describe his wife as his widow?"

"I, well…" (How can I say this without sounding incompetent?) "To tell you the truth, I didn't really hear it."

"You are a talk show presenter. It's your job to listen to what people are saying to you when they call. Are you not capable of doing that job?"

"Of course I am."

"Pretty fundamental error."

"Not at all. You can't always hear every word people say to you when they call. They're not professionals, they haven't got broadcasting voices. That guy was foreign. I mean, I'm not being racist…" this for Alice Winter, who's suddenly picked up her pencil, "I'm just saying that English might not be his first language."

"He sounded clear enough to me," says Meg.

"Now he does, yes, when you're listening out for what he's saying. But did *you* hear it, sitting at home."

"I wasn't listening to the broadcast."

I can't resist the counter-attack. "Isn't it your job to listen to the station's output?"

"Not twenty-four seven, no. I hear more than enough to know who's doing well on the air and who isn't. I heard your last show, for example, but we won't dwell on that for the moment."

She turns slightly as she's saying her piece, making it clear that *we* means her people, her side of the table. Simon, resting his elbow there, presses a knuckle lightly against his bottom lip, glancing down at the polished surface. He'll have heard her saying *last show* (not *latest*) as plainly as I did. I'm not going to be done for this, though.

"What about Marni? She was there with me." I lean forward to address her directly. "You didn't notice anything odd about what he said, did you?"

"I didn't hear it. You'd sent me out to make tea, remember?"

She colours slightly as she says it and Alice Winter slides her hand along the table, grabbing Marni's to comfort her as if she's just been made to testify against a rapist.

"I never *sent* you out anywhere, that's not my style." Fighting my corner. "And unless I'm mistaken you were still in the ops room while I was talking to Hassan. But, OK, maybe you didn't have cans on just then. The point I'm making, though…" turning back to Meg, "It was just one of those remarks that slipped by. Nobody really took any notice of it at the time."

"But that's not true, is it, Marni?" says Meg, prompting her.

"No," says Marni, looking at me but responding to Meg, like she's her barrister and I'm the prisoner at the bar, "I told Marc that someone had called asking about Hassan's… mental state, but he told me to ignore it. And somebody else whose name's Oliver I think was desperate to speak to Marc. He even turned up at Reception, and I suppose it was to ask about Hassan, but Marc went out of the side door to avoid him, and he got me to do the same."

"Oh, come on…" I'm exasperated by the way Marni seems to be representing herself as some kind of victim, but before I can say anything more Meg cuts in.

"And I understand also there were emails coming in which you more or less brushed off…"

"Bollocks. On the subject of emails, why have I been blocked from accessing mine? Do you know about this, Alice? As a member of staff I've surely got a right…"

"Don't bleat to us about rights," says Meg. "What you need to think about is responsibilities. It's bad enough letting people down internally…"

"What?"

"When it comes to the public it's unforgivable."

"Do you know who you're talking to?" I'm getting irate now. "Just in case it's slipped your mind, I believe I'm the only person in this place who has been publicly acknowledged for saving somebody's life. If you want to talk responsibilities, just ask Mr…" Infuriatingly I've forgotten the guy's name again. Meg wades into the gap.

"Put another record on, Marc, we've heard that one. You can't patch up a reputation by falling back on something that happened two years ago."

"What you mean, patch up a reputation?"

"Exactly what I'm saying. I'll be blunt, Marc. You've not been on form recently. I was going to have a word with you about your… general approach anyway, but this incident, on top of everything else, has forced my hand. It's not about you alone any more, it's about the station. Last night was an embarrassment for us, frankly."

"But I wasn't working last night."

"Exactly. And it was poor Simon here who had to pick up the pieces, try and hold it together when it all kicked off. He did a very good job, in the circumstances."

Simon strokes his chin modestly and manages a smile for his boss. My confusion is evident even to Meg on her high horse, so she brings Jim into play again. "Cue Lee from last night," she instructs him.

Jim consults his scrap of paper. "Lee, Lee, Lee. 22:41."

Soon it's Simon's voice we can hear through the small speakers.

'Thanks to Meredith for her ghost hitch-hiker story. I've heard variations of that one before, but not with the local twist you gave it, Meredith. It makes it that much more real when you know you've passed the very lay-by. How about your story, Lee, on line 5, is there a local angle?'

'Mine? Well, it's not a story, like, not as such, but you've been on about ghosts, right?'

'Right.'

'Well, what about the ghost that was on here Friday night?'

'On TV?'

'On the radio. On this show I'm on about.'

Simon laughs. 'You're not referring to Marc Niven are, you, Lee?' The here-and-now Simon darts a glance at me and raises a hand slightly off the table, minimal apology. The disembodied Simon continues.

'Mind you, he was looking a little pale last time I saw him. What do you think, Marni? Did Marc look pale to you?'

'He did a bit, yeah,' from Marni, cheerful on open talk-back.

'Was that your ghost, Lee, Marc Niven?'

'No, but he talked to the real ghost, like. Seriously.'

69

In the beat before Simon replies I can detect his shift into uncertainty. He doesn't feel in control of this. I can imagine his finger poised over the dump button, just in case.

'Uh-huh,' he says. Reluctant encouragement.

'I tried to get on about this the same night but I never got a call back from yous. It was about this Hassan sending a Valentine message to his widow.'

'Hang on, Lee, you've lost me there. There's a man sending a Valentine to his widow?'

'Hassan. That was his name. He come on just before midnight saying he wanted to send all his love to his wife, which is fair enough. But then he called her his widow.'

'His *widow*?'

'Mmm. The funny thing was, Marc never said a thing about it, just thanks very much and that was it.'

'And he definitely said *widow*? Because obviously if you have a widow you've got to be… dead.'

'Exactly. So that's what I'm saying, you've had a ghost on the show.'

'Well, practical joker more like, Lee. We do get them unfortunately.'

'Not much of a joke though, eh? Didn't seem like the comedian type, like. As I say, the funniest thing was not a thing more was said about it. Either that night, or the next night. I just wondered if anybody knew who this bloke was, sort of thing. It's had me puzzled, you know.'

'That does seem a strange one. Obviously Marc's not around just now. Marni, is this something you…? No, Marni's shaking her head at me through the glass so she can't shed any light on it. There you go, Lee. Thanks very much for your call. Little poser you've set for us. Hmm. Do we have a mystery ghost, right here on this programme? Told you we were in for a spooky night, didn't I? I'll be back right after this.'

As the first commercial kicks in Jim reaches across to switch off the recording. We take a collective breath and look across the table at each other. Everybody seems to be waiting for me to speak, but for the moment I can't because I've got this intense battle going on in my head. Do I tell them everything I know about Hassan (what good would that do? what do I really know?), or do I stay schtum, go for damage limitation, shrug it off as best as I can? I make the wrong choice.

"So?" is what I say.

Meg's eyes widen and she echoes, "So?"

70

"I don't see the problem. As Simon said, just a nice little poser to conjure with. One day wonder. Quite intriguing for the listeners. Good radio. No real damage done."

"That's what you think, is it? That's your professional opinion?" says Meg.

"It's a way of looking at it."

"Tell him what happened next, Simon."

Simon shifts in his chair as he's called upon to speak and opens out his hands. "It was all hell let loose, basically. Marni'll back me on this, the board lit up like a Christmas tree. Everybody wanted to tell me about hearing that original call, thinking it was strange, OK, maybe they did nothing about it at the time but they were convinced something odd was going on. Others had got your email, thought nothing more about it, but now it's come up again... In fact, Marni had a bit of job on protecting you, to be honest. You know, people wanting to come on-air to slag you off. That's right, Marni, mm?"

Marni joins in the assassination. "Quite a few, yeah. What with those and the ones who'd got themselves convinced that Hassan was threatening to murder his wife or something. You know, wrong end of the stick, but it was chaos really, trying to sort out who we could safely let on the show. We could have been in all sorts of trouble."

"Well done you," I say, trying not to let the irony show too much.

"But then the mystery deepened," says Simon. "Meg?"

"Play the final clip, Jim."

Jim studies his list. "Is it this one marked Amina, Armina?"

The name hits me low in my gut. They have the Amina connection. Did she call the show herself? Well, this is either clear-up time or shit hits the fan. Which?

"That will be the one," from Meg.

Jim seems to take forever to locate the piece while accusation hangs heavy in the room. Meg the executioner, with her axe suspended over my head on the chopping block. The relief when the speakers come back to life is only temporary. Simon again, sounding a lot less comfortable than he did before, and his edginess feeds mine.

'Hot topic tonight, ghosts in the machine. Poor Marni is working her little white socks off next door so please be patient, there's so many wanting to have their say on this one. We'll try and get to you if we can. Right now on Line 4, is it Dave? No, Shelley...'

'Chelle. Michelle.'

'Sorry, Chelle. Go ahead.'

'Well, first of all you were asking earlier if this Hassan could get back in touch with the programme.'

'That's right, yes. You know there's such a lot of confusion about what he might have said or didn't say…'

'But he's not been in touch, no?'

'We've not heard from him yet, Chelle. But of course it may be he can't get through, the lines have been so busy tonight. Rest assured though, the minute he does…'

'He won't.'

'Well, maybe.'

'He won't, I can guarantee. For a start they don't like fuss, they'll run a mile from it in a manner of speaking. And I can tell you for certain, honey, cos he's told us he won't.'

'He's told you…? Right, you know this Hassan, do you, Shelley? Chelle.'

'I've never met him before in my life. Not in this one, anyway. But he's come through to say that.'

'Aha. When you say, come through…'

'From the other side. I've been a medium for twelve years, Marc…'

'Simon.'

'Simon, sorry. Practising medium for twelve years, but all my life really.'

'And you're telling me Hassan's spoken to you tonight?'

'Well, mental transference, yes. Not a voice like you hear on the radio, if you get my meaning.'

'And he told you he wouldn't be calling us up tonight? Did he say anything else?'

'He did. He had a message for a lady called Amina.'

'Amina, yes, his wife. Robert who came on earlier said he remembered his wife was called Amina.'

'Did he? Well, actually I wasn't listening at that time. Amina came through from Hassan. He told me to tell her he's sorry about the car.'

'Sorry about the car?'

'He was in a car crash, Simon. A few months ago. Check the details if you like, I'm just telling you what he told me. That's how he got to…'

She's cut off in the middle of her sentence, Simon hitting the dump button about forty-five seconds too late in my book.

"You handled that well," I say to him sardonically across the table, and he comes within a gnat's breath of a self-satisfied "Thanks"

72

before he catches my tone and stops his mouth. I turn my attention to Meg.

"Talk about unprofessional. You're pointing at the wrong guy over this balls-up. What the fuck else has he been letting people say?"

"There's no need for language like that," tuts Alice Winter. "You're not in the bar now."

"What's that supposed to mean?"

"Leave it, both of you," says Meg. "Listen, Marc, I want to make it quite clear that I don't hold Simon or indeed Marni responsible for any of this. The truth is you left them up shit creek without a paddle, trying to shove your mess under the carpet."

"That's a great mixed metaphor, Meg. It almost works."

"Are you trying to be funny?"

I hold my hands up in my defence, but the truth is I am just beginning to see a glimmer of the absurd in all this. Simon allowing Chelle, my resident self-styled medium, to get everybody worked up about the spirits getting in touch after she's trawled the internet for clues and wrapped them up in baloney - it has all the elements of farce. Meg, though, quickly brings me down with the next thing she says.

"What you don't seem to recognise is this has gone nuclear. Do you realise that poor woman had to call the police to stop people banging at her door in the middle of the night?"

"What poor woman? Chelle?"

"The Asian woman. Amina. She had a baby in bed. Got the fright of her life."

"Oh, Jesus." A reverse image of a police car, the one I thought was tailing me, swims into view as clearly as if I'm looking in the driving mirror. Turning off The Gate towards Prince Albert Road. The difference is that the one in my head has the siren going.

Meg piles on the pressure. "We've had calls stacking up at Reception this morning. And I'm not just talking about the public. The press have got hold of the story now. I've had to bring Sarah in from the agency to try and keep a lid on it."

"But there was no problem before," I argue. "It's your blue-eyed boy's got everybody going cos he couldn't handle it properly. If he'd followed my line and just said it was a slip of the tongue by Hassan he'd have nipped it in the bud on the first call."

"But I didn't know your line, did I?" Simon fires back. "I didn't know anything about it."

"Exactly," says Meg. "Because you went your own sweet way, Marc, like you always do. Because you think you know better than

73

anybody else, don't need me or anybody else. Well, I can assure you that's one big mistake. One big fat mistake."

Meg slams her hand on the table and juts her chin out at me, eyes blazing. She's got herself into battle mood and I guess she's expecting the next volley from me, but I don't have anything particular to say at this point so all of us just sit there for the next few seconds, some staring at this tableau of Meg as Cruella de Vil, others looking anywhere but, until she unfreezes her body and parks her bum back in the depths of Neville's leather seat. She places her wrists deliberately on the arms of the chair, looking around the assembly as if she's in a play before she speaks again. "I want everybody out of this office except Marc Niven. And you, Alice. I need you to stay."

Simon and Marni make no effort to acknowledge never mind help Jim as they leave, I notice, and he struggles to balance all his cables and speakers on top of the laptop, but he just looks grateful to be granted his release. He raises his eyebrows privately at me as he passes, part sympathy, part conspiring in my opinion of Meg and this whole affair. Once the door closes behind him, Meg draws herself erect on the edge of her big chair while Alice beside her turns to a new page in her Filofax.

Meg addresses herself directly to me, full eye contact, almost willing me to look away. "You need to understand, Marc, that I have Neville's full authority in relation to decisions that may affect your future with us here. Naturally I've discussed this situation with him…"

"What situation?"

"Don't be obtuse. I've already said I hold you entirely responsible for what is turning out to be a public relations disaster for us…"

"Oh, lighten up."

Her eyes glitter. "Are you going to let me finish or do you want me terminate this interview here and now?"

I shrug. Alice makes some cryptic note on her file. Meg continues.

"I'm also taking into account certain behaviour traits you've been exhibiting over the past few weeks which, frankly, are not only disturbing, they're completely unacceptable in our organisation."

What's this about? I lean forward in my chair and say it aloud. "What's this about?"

"Firstly, transgressing company policy on drinking alcohol."

"I wasn't even aware the company *had* a policy… and when did I *transgress* it?"

Meg turns sideways to bring in Alice, who pulls out a folded A4 sheet from the back of her file, straightens it out with one hand as she says, "From the *Code of Conduct*," then reads aloud: "*Alcohol is strictly forbidden on the premises and, while social drinking in moderation is acceptable during staff leisure time, it is unacceptable just before or during working hours or at any time in quantities that adversely affect the employee's ability to perform her/his duties."*

"Well," I say, cranking up my defence, "I can honestly say I've never been shown that rule or code of conduct or whatever you call it in nearly seven years working here. Number two, I've never brought alcohol onto the premises, but if you care to open Neville's cabinet over there you might find your biggest culprit in that department..."

"We're obviously not referring to corporate hospitality, don't be stupid," says Meg, losing her patience already, but I ignore this and press on.

"As for drinking before working hours, bearing in mind I start my shift just as everybody else is pouring into the pubs and clubs, I don't see why having the occasional half of lager with my lunch or whatever should be frowned upon, especially – and this is the important point – as it has never, ever affected my work in a negative way, and I defy you to say different."

"What did Debbie Wells mention to you earlier this week, Alice?" says Meg, prompting.

"She told me that Marc came bursting into Studio One, hours before he was due in, swearing and generally causing a disturbance, and smelling of drink. He also told her he was there for a meeting, which was a lie, and he openly criticised another employee in, well, let's say, the strongest terms."

"That employee being Marni, who has been here all of two weeks?" It's a rhetorical question from Meg, but Alice twists the knife by answering it anyway.

"Yes."

"Look, that completely misrepresents the situation. Debbie seems to have some sort of grudge..."

I'm stopped in my tracks by a magisterial hand raised by Meg and a curt "You need to listen, not speak right now. Alice has something to say about Marni. And I mean really listen, Marc. This is serious."

Alice flicks back a couple of pages to refer to some handwritten notes, gathers herself then starts up, looking at Meg, not me. "Marni came looking for me the other day, quite upset. Really upset, I would put it. It was the first day Marc was off, actually."

I close my eyes with a certain degree of resignation as she goes on. I've already got Marni well worked out, and I've second-guessed what's coming.

75

"Apparently Marc had lost his temper completely unnecessarily with Marni the night before, not once but twice, then practically ignored her for the rest of the time, even while the programme was going out,"

"No wonder it sounded so stilted," Meg puts in. I open my eyes briefly to hate her more plainly across the table.

"When I dug deeper, I found out the reason, though Marni was naturally reluctant to tell me at first." (Oh, naturally.)

"Go on," says Meg, as if she hasn't already heard this.

"The night before, Marc had insisted on driving her home, spent the entire journey telling her she was the most beautiful girl he had ever seen etcetera etcetera, and made a pass at her which Marni immediately rejected. That made Marc very angry, it seems, hence his blow-up the next time he saw her."

I open my eyes and Alice involuntarily clasps her hands together and moves back from the table as if she's expecting me to leap across it to attack her.

"That's your take on events, is it?"

"It's what Marni told me."

"And what if I tell you it's complete and utter bollocks?"

Meg butts in. "We'd believe Marni."

"Because she's a woman."

"Because you've got form."

Now I do almost leap across the table, but it's Meg I'm wanting to attack, not Alice. "What the hell do you mean by that?"

"What I say. You can't deny it. Everybody knows about your affair with Sam."

"She was my girlfriend. My partner, actually. So what?"

"So you were a married man. So you... screwed her life up as well, and we lost one of our best people because of you."

"You don't know anything about Sam and me, or why she left. You've got no right to pry into my private aff... relationships."

Meg comes back hard. "I've got every right to protect employees from inappropriate behaviour. Don't think you can just pick up poor Marni where you left off with Sam. Do you even know how old she is? And it's not just Marni. What about Kate?"

"Kate? Kate Foreman?" Now I'm absolutely at a loss. Alice fills me in.

"The same day Debbie tells us you came in drunk..."

"I wasn't drunk."

"You went into the newsroom and made advances on Kate while she was working."

"Made advances…?"

"Came up from behind and massaged her shoulders, even though she made it clear she wasn't interested. It's all documented."

"I don't believe this."

"Well, you'd better believe it, Marc," says Meg. "And you'd better believe I'm suspending you as of right now until further notice."

"What you mean, suspended?"

"I mean I want you to leave, and I don't want you back. You'll get your pay sent through until we make some more permanent arrangement. You're a walking time-bomb, Marc Niven, that's the truth, and I don't want you anywhere near the place. You can take that as an order."

I've been half-expecting something like this all morning but it still comes as a shock when it happens. Suspended. It somehow seems worse than a straight sacking. As if I was a criminal. That and all the nonsense leading up to it, making me out to be some sort of sexual predator. I'm dumbfounded. All I can muster in response at this point is, "You'll be hearing from my solicitor."

"Look forward to it," says Meg, who's walked across to the office door while I've been trying to take all this in. She opens the door ostentatiously and stands waiting, so I have to pass her to walk through it. She almost spits at me as I leave.

When I walk out of the lift on the ground floor I'm ignored by the receptionists. To be fair, they're both busy on the switchboard, but I'm convinced that on every other occasion I've passed the desk in the last seven years either one of them has smiled or nodded, even waved. I hesitate for a moment, wondering whether I should go back and clear my desk, but since the only personal possessions sitting there are my Sony award and my Newcastle United mug, and since Simon and Marni are more than likely in the office talking over what went on in the meeting, I don't bother.

I push through the glass exit door into an unexpectedly sunny February day and hesitate again, unsure whether to head for the car or the Eldon Arms, when somebody touches my arm. Oliver? But this is a tall, jaundiced-looking bloke I've never seen before.

"Marc Niven? Philip Mann, *Chronicle*. Could I have a quick word?"

VI

Well, you pay your money and you make your choice. Having just been treated like shit by Meg Reece and her cohorts, I have been handed the perfect opportunity to get my own back through the media, to dish the dirt and squeal like the proverbial pig about the injustice, my shredded rights and the real culprits in this fiasco. I could even toss in a few juicy morsels about payola disguised as sponsorship, deceit and cynical manipulation of the public that I've been witness to over the last seven years. But I don't do any of this. No beans are spilled. Don't consider for a moment that this has anything to do with loyalty, misplaced or otherwise, to my long-term employer. I don't owe them. It has everything to do with Amina Begum Khan.

Whatever is behind the mystery of Hassan's message it seems clear to me that Amina doesn't need this extra complication in her life. When I watched her struggling up the stone steps to her empty house with her child in the buggy, a carrier bag on the handle and a front door key to juggle with, it was obvious that she has a lot to deal with already, and no-one to help. Add to this the grief she must still be feeling for her dead husband and, no doubt, bills to pay.... She must be distraught with this sudden attention from the likes of Chelle and her credulous public, not to mention the press.

My technique with Philip Mann is more or less polite evasion, which is what Simon should have used with the call from Lee. (Yes, I know he was caught on the hop – I'm not trying to shirk all the blame.) Mann is persistent, though.

"So you're saying that *widow* was a slip of the tongue?"

"Of course, yes. It happens all the time. People get nervous, they say the wrong words under pressure."

"Hmm. What did he *mean* to say?"

"I...Well, I don't know. The moment was gone, you see."

"You haven't talked to him since, then?"

"No, no."

"Right." Mann clicks his pen against his teeth and scrutinises me from his position about a foot above my hairline. I feel as if I'm being questioned at the school gates by a PC trying to finger somebody for a

78

misdemeanour. He continues. "I'm just wondering, in that case, how you can be so certain it was a slip of the tongue."

"Call it professional judgement."

"And in your professional judgement, Marc, would you say that you were talking to a ghost?"

"I wouldn't, Philip, no. You see, I don't believe in ghosts. Do you?"

He doesn't answer me, says instead, "I'm just trying to find out who this guy is, or was. It's a real mystery, isn't it, Marc?"

"Actually, I'm finding it a bit of a bore. And you can quote me on that. So if you don't mind, Philip, I've got things to do."

As I walk off, he calls out to me. "Does that include preparing for your show? Will we hear you on the radio tonight?"

In lieu of reply I give him an ironic two-fingered salute on my way to the car park.

Unfortunately I wasn't aware that his photographer was in hiding, taking pictures with a long lens, probably throughout our interview. The one they use is of me walking away from the station, flashing the V-sign. Philip Mann is nowhere to be seen in the picture, so it looks as if I'm making the gesture to everybody in the building behind, which suits their headline to a tee.

DJ leaves disgracefully

The thrust of Mann's story is that I've effectively been sacked for my poor handling of the original call from Hassan Malik. The official line from the station is that I am on sick leave, but it is obvious from the unattributed information Mann uses in the article that they have been furiously spinning against me to cover their tracks. For example:

Listeners were shocked that Niven – who once famously kept a suicide caller talking on the line while a rescue operation got underway at Stephenson Bridge – failed to react to the strange and apparently disturbed message from Hassan Malik, and subsequently blocked the many who rang to express their concern over what they had heard. The award-winning presenter confirmed today that he had not tried to make further contact with Malik and described the deepening mystery surrounding the call as 'a bore'.

Simon Barnes, who has been sitting in for Niven since the incident, will again host Nightwatch tonight and is expected to do so for the foreseeable future. Radio industry sources say it is unlikely that Niven, who has presented the phone-in show for seven years, will return.

79

The one consolation I can find in this attack on me is that I have only become the centrepiece of the story for lack of any hard evidence about the real identity of the man calling himself Hassan Malik and, more importantly, any contact with Amina. The only reference to her comes near the end of the article when Mann mentions that the house in Prince Albert Road has been deserted and relatives are unable to confirm her whereabouts. Good for them.

Not so good for yours truly. The photo certainly doesn't do me any favours – three days growth of beard and, if I'm honest, a distinct lack of kempt, makes me look like shit - and Mann has even cleverly used my previous brownie points (rescue hero, award-winner) to illustrate my dramatic fall from grace, like the bishop caught *in flagrante delicto* with the actress. I'm fucked, basically.

I'm not so much angry as… well, to be honest my over-riding emotion is intense loneliness. I'm not trying to come over as some kind of bleeding heart, just telling it like it is. When things go wrong in your life you usually have somebody to turn to, don't you? In the old days it would be Linda, at least until the last year or so of our marriage, then it was Sam. Sam very much so. Now it's me and my reflection in the mirror. Cue sodding violins.

The predictable thing to do right now is to get drunk. That's exactly what Meg and Alice from HR *(You're not in the bar now)* would expect of me. There's not a drop left in the flat so I'd have to go out to the off-licence or the pub. And, yes, I do go out, risking curious stares from folk over their copies of tonight's *Chronicle*. I don't even take the car, exposing myself even more, and maybe that's because there's something in me hell-bent on alcoholic oblivion, but I don't rush to the local or the city centre watering-holes. I do something infinitely sadder. I catch the bus at what I now think of as Oliver's stop and retrace our journey all the way to the reading room of the public library.

I start thumbing through back issues of the regional newspapers, just as Ollie and I had, but I'm not here to unearth more facts about the Hassan Malik case. That would be altogether too rational. No, I'm looking for references to Marc Niven. I have some rough dates in mind - various OBs and events I've been involved in, the odd corporate do, the suicide caller story of course, the launch of my show – but I'm also skipping randomly through, happening on the odd photograph or half-remembered headline, most of which I already have in my press cuttings file at work. It was thinking about that file, regretting that I hadn't picked it up on my way out, that has brought me here.

The last couple of years are still in hard copy, but once I delve further back I have to start using one of the antiquated microfilm readers, spooling through editions of the *Chronicle* one year at a time, awkwardly at first until I develop the knack of it. The reels and the appearance of the newsprint behind the glass make even recent history seem much older. I can't understand why they haven't invested in some more up-to-date digital process, but they haven't, so I'm forced to spin through hopefully without the benefit of key-word searches and the like.

I say *forced* but of course there's no imperative for me to do any of this and it has no purpose or end to it. If I was called on to justify what I was doing I might say I'm gathering evidence for a possible tribunal, but that would be a lie since I have no notion of going down that route. Playing amateur psychologist on myself, I guess I'm trying to reconstruct my crushed ego, or maybe I'm just searching for evidence that I exist. Don't ask me what that means, I have no idea. I only know that every so often the tedium of the search is relieved when I come upon a smiling photograph or a couple of paragraphs with my name in it, and I register the tiniest blip of pleasure before I carry on.

The library closes at eight and I still have a couple of reels to look through with only quarter of an hour to go, which is why I get quite peevish when a library assistant comes across with a polite five minute warning about re-spooling the one I'm busy with, "as we'll be closing shortly."

"But I'm not finished yet. It says eight on the door."

"Just a matter of tidying up, sir. We do have to lock up by eight."

"And turn back into a pumpkin?"

"No need for that, sir. I'm just trying to do my job. We're open ten till eight tomorrow. If you'd like to finish what you're doing."

The last bit is ambiguous, but I take it as an order and grudgingly rewind the spool on the machine. I've been lost in my daft obsession for the past couple of hours, but this minor altercation is all it takes to refuel the bitterness in me. By the time I'm back on the street I'm ready to punch out a shop window. I walk along with my fists clenched in my coat pockets, scoping nameless victims for murder, until I come to the lane where Ollie and I found our drab pub, and head there to murder a drink instead.

There are two things about pubs like this that save at least a few of them from being swept away by city centre yuppification or laid waste under the weekend stampede of teenage bingers. The first is that occasionally -

81

working almost incognito, camouflaged by the surface grime and general dilapidation – there will be a landlord who actually cares about the quality and taste of the beer a whole lot more than he does about the marketing, or the customers, or the housekeeping. The second is that they can just about survive by accommodating misanthropes and misfits, low maintenance loners who compensate for not buying generous rounds for friends they don't have by staying the course, drinking steadily and repeatedly at the same three-legged table from early doors till the bell tolls. Tonight The George and Marc Niven are made for each other.

With the horse-racing long since finished the TV channel has been switched, not to Sky Sports News or MTV as in most other places, but to ITV 1, where it plays with the sound turned off over the heads of the drinkers, its tawdry images clashing with the dinge below. I watch the screen only when the adverts come on, struck by the mute sexiness of Andrex toilet paper cascading down some stairs, a girl's finger on the capstan of a roulette wheel, a dolphin in blue water. Otherwise there's plenty to divert me from sluicing down my Black Sheep too urgently as the night wears on - there's fluff to gather from the bench seat I'm sitting on, drips to soak up with a beer mat after I've separated the layers of card to make the mat more absorbent, brand names to mull over on the coasters and behind the bar, a maze of soldering to follow with my eyes from one end of the imitation stained glass feature to the other, then back again. I can even watch the levels going down in other glasses; that's a good guide when you're drinking on your own, like having company.

Three or four refills in (maybe five, who's counting? anyway, I'm kind of on holiday), when a group to my left have supped up and gone, I shuffle along to where two benches meet, and sit in the angle between, resting a shoulder blade on the back of each bench. It's a secure place, and it gives me a director's view of the pub. I may have inadvertently said "Action!" out loud as that thought occurred. Someone standing with his back to me turns and looks, as if he's just seen a flash bulb go off, then says something to his wife, or girlfriend, or mistress, who looks over at me too, just for a second. His floozy, maybe, that's what they'd call them in the 1950s when this pub had its heyday. She looks the type.

Once I've drained my glass in this new position I have a difficult dilemma. A fairly sizeable group has just wandered in from some event next door and The George is enjoying (putting up with) one of its rare busy half-hours. There are a few people standing now, in twos and threes, since there's not enough space for them to sit together. I don't want to give up this hard-won seat, but it's time to go back to the bar, and I also need a pee. I've been a bit foolish to empty my glass, because whether I

82

leave it on the table or take it with me to the bar, whichever, it could be interpreted as quitting, and one of those groups might take over my table and this whole section of bench, whereas (I say this word carefully to myself, developing my argument like a logician) *whereas* if I'd left just the right amount of beer in the glass I could have kept my claim staked while I got another. Too late for that now. I'll just have to take a chance, leaving my coat on the seat sufficiently spread out, like a German towel, and hope they take the hint.

I leave my empty glass on the table as an extra deterrent and walk very deliberately to the bar, to give everybody the right signal, but then I sneak off to the Gents before I order, not wanting to take my drink with me to the toilet or to leave it on the bar where it might get spiked or spat in, you never know

It's a cramped bog, and there's already somebody at one of the two urinal bowls. I try the lav door but that's locked, so I have no option but to stand uncomfortably close to this tallish bloke to pee. As I pull it out he turns his head just like John Cleese in that ancient 'I look down at him' sketch. He's quite shameless about it. I have a sudden urge to get back at him for this by pissing on his shoes. I've started to swivel when he suddenly zips up and steps away, leaving me to spill a splash of piss on the floor as if it was an accident instead of a protest. He gives me a look of contempt on his way out, but it's him that doesn't wash his hands.

After I've negotiated my return to the bar and ordered, and I'm turning to get my bearings for taking my fresh drink back to my seat, I see the worst has happened. Two couples that had been standing facing each other nearest my table have taken it over, one bloke squeezed between the two women in my director's place and the other one perched on a stool the other side. As I come up holding my beer I see that my coat is lying folded across another empty stool next to them.

"Saved this seat for you, pal," stool bloke says, like he's doing me a favour.

"No thanks, I'll just stand. Going in a minute," I say, nearly spilling my full pint as I reach over to grab my coat and hang it on my free arm. One consolation is that the wanker from the Gents is not with them. They do seem to be looking at me funny, though. At last the uglier one of the women says, "We were just talking about you, actually. You're that man from the radio, aren't you? The one what does the phone-ins."

Not any more, I'm thinking, but not out loud, or was it? Then I'm wondering whether they know me cos they know me or cos they've seen my picture in tonight's paper. Was it just tonight? It seems longer ago than that. Longer ago and farther away.

"Is it you, then?" says squeezed-between-two-women bloke.

"I am he as you are he as you are me, and we are all together," I say, cleverly.

"Eh?"

"I am the walrus."

Pretty woman gives a little smile. Which one does she belong to? The smile was definitely for me, either way. I sit down on the stool and push my glass onto the crowded table, slopping the beer a little. "Marc Niven," I say, to her only.

"That's the name," ugly sister pipes up. "I said it was Marc summat. You were in the paper today, weren't you?"

"Was I? Dunno. Never bother. Regular currants." My brain said *occurrence* but my voice definitely said *currants*, I heard it. I take a gobful of beer and roll it around with my tongue to get my mouth working properly.

"Drowning your sorrows. You got sacked, didn't you?" says the guy sitting in my place, who looks like a sleaze ball.

Slight burp as I swallow to answer, nothing they would notice. "No such thing. They made a cock-up. I *told* them, sort it out, not coming back till you do. Position to do it, see. Man of my..." What am I talking to him for? I turn back to smiling girl. "You listen?"

"Sorry?" Leans forward a touch. She has this cute way of raising her eyebrows.

"You listen my show?"

Sleaze ball sneaks his arm behind her, his fingers fiddling with her hair. I can tell she's embarrassed about him interfering with her like that cos she's blushing, but she keeps her attention on me.

"I'm not really a radio sort of person," she says. "What sort of music do you play?"

"What sort of music do you like?" She really is a looker, close up.

"Oh, I don't know, all sorts really. Charts stuff."

"Tell you what, tell you what, have you got a pen? Anybody pen?" I lift up my glass to bring the coaster out from underneath, taking another mouthful while the beer's handy.

"Christ, he's going to give you his autograph now," says sleaze ball, grabbing pretty girl's shoulder and pulling her towards him. Prick. Stool guy gives me a biro he finds in his jacket pocket and I hand it across the table with the beer mat.

"Just write your name down on there, and any song you'd like. Pick a song, any song. I'll play it for you, my show. Don't normally do requests, but for you. Happily."

84

"Thought you didn't have a show," says the other one, put out cos she hasn't been given the chance.

"Soon. Next time," I tell my one. "'Fact, put your number down and I'll phone you when it's coming on. Personally."

"Fuck off," says sleaze ball.

"I don't think I can write on this," says pretty girl, holding just the corner of the beer mat with her finger tips. "It's a tad wet." The others laugh at her, which hardly seems fair.

"No worries, no worries," I say. "'Nother one here." I scrabble among the cluster of drinks on the tables, feeling for a dry mat. That stupid prick opposite must have had his glass too near the edge. It gets just the slightest nudge from my knuckles and it topples off the table, dowsing his crotch with lager. He jumps up, yelling, and makes the whole thing worse by kicking his leg against the table, sending more glasses flying. Now everybody's up, backing away from the mess. It's like somebody's just vomited in the middle of a crowd. The rest of the pub turn round to stare at us.

"You rat-arsed fucker," yells sleaze ball, trying to put the blame on me as a pissed-off barman emerges from behind the counter with a mop. In the background I can see John Cleese whispering some poison to one of his gay crowd of gawkers. I've had my fill of the lot of them, so I pick my coat out of the puddle under the table and leave.

As I'm crossing the pedestrian precinct I catch a glimpse of the big clock and have to double-check with my watch to confirm it's already gone ten to eleven. I'm not sure when the last bus is, but it's odds on I've missed it. I search through my trouser pockets to see what I've got left for the taxi fare, but there's only some small change from buying the drinks. I feel around my coat for my wallet and for a few seconds the alarm bells are ringing - those bastards in the pub have nicked it while I was away to the loo. Panic over, here it is in my inside zip pocket. I open the wallet to make certain there are still some notes there, and my eyes come into focus on a corner of white sticking out of one of the credit card slots. I pull on the corner and find the business card Emmanuel gave me. Printed on the card is a simple message and one line of an address:

Please come to our party. Fun guaranteed.
29 Warkworth Street.

I don't have much time to think about it. There's a red mini-cab parked near the exit to the precinct and while I'm still yards away the

85

driver winds his window down to shout in some brand of foreign accent, "Looking for taxi, boss?"

On impulse I open his back door and say, as I stumble inside, "D'you know the way to Warkworth Street?"

VII

Eight minutes away from the city centre and ten quid lighter in the wallet I'm skulking down Warkworth Street, looking for number twenty-nine. The street is quiet, ordinary. They are large old semi-detached houses, not unlike the one I shared with half-a-dozen other students when I was at university, but these look better-kept on the whole, and quite private, with gates, little rectangles of front lawn, walls in between the adjoining houses about the same height as the gates. Some have trellis fencing and climbing plants or hedges that reach above the garden wall to give more privacy. They won't come cheap, these properties. Suburbia.

I have to work out which is twenty-nine from the numbers on the neighbouring houses because there's no indication on the gate, and the front of the house is too dark to make out anything on the door or the wall next to it. One of the reasons this house is so dark is the height and thickness of the hedge surrounding the property, especially nearest the door where it must be seven feet high. I'm surprised their neighbour hasn't complained. The hedge that runs along the side of the pathway to the front door is so thick I have to walk with one foot on the front lawn to stop the wet leaves brushing my shoulder.

The other reason number twenty-nine is so dark I don't figure out properly until I'm nearly at the front door step. Most of the other houses in this street have lights on behind one or more of their curtains, in the bay window downstairs, in the bedrooms, or both. At first I'm thinking that there must be nobody in twenty-nine, or maybe they're having an early night, party over. But when I'm closer to the window I can see that there are some little chinks of light here and there. They've obviously got really heavy curtains or blinds. In fact they look like shutters. And when I'm right up to them I can see that the windows have little vertical bars, not on the outside but on the inside of the glass, like you sometimes see in commercial premises, especially in rough areas. What am I doing here? Didn't I have enough the other night, being scared shitless by Bullet Head?

At that moment the area where I'm standing is flooded with harsh white light, shock treatment for drunkenness. I've set off the security sensor above the front door. I'm every trapped animal in that instant before the kill – the rabbit in the headlights, the fox facing the pack, the mouse under the cat's paw. Any second now the door will fling open for a guard dog to hurl itself at me. I stand transfixed. Nothing happens.

Until it does. High in the corner where the bay window returns to the front of the house a CCTV camera moves and trains on me. The speaker of an entry phone mounted to the right of the front door crackles into life.

"Who is it? What do you want?"

Flight is not an option. The guard dog or a bullet would have me long before I reached the gate. I climb to the doorstep and put my mouth next to the grille of the phone, hesitant, unsure whether you have to push the button before you speak, or as you speak, or just say something to the voice (gatekeeper) that already knows you're there. I turn to clear my throat like I'm used to in the studio but it's still a croak when I speak at the grille. "'S Oliver. 'Mmanuel asked me to come."

"Manuel? Who's Manuel?" And a laugh. Distinctly. Is there a Fawlty Towers fan in the house? I relax a smidge.

"E-mmanuel. Emmanuel. He invited me to the party. I have his card." And I show it, accidentally at first to the speaker grille, then up for the camera to see, as if I'm half-surrendering.

There's an electronic buzz at the door jamb. I wait until the voice comes back on the phone, "Come in, Oliver" and I push at the door, which opens into a tiny porch, the kind of place you'd put your wet brolly. The inner door has decorative frosted glass, and I can see a figure behind. He reaches and turns the handle before I do, opening the door a fraction at first to check me out, then wider, beckoning me in to an ordinary passage at the foot of some stairs. What's out of place is there's a CCTV monitor on top of a table where you'd normally see a house plant or a family photo.

I'd assumed the doorman would be black, like Emmanuel, but he's sallow and skinny, wearing one of those ill-fitting grey suits that suggest either Primark or East European, and loose enough to whip a gun out easy.

"Come through, welcome," he says, smiling the way if a ferret could smile that's how he'd do it. His accent confirms what I surmised from the suit. Allowing plenty of margin for error, definitely former Soviet Union. "Your first time here, yes?"

"Yeah, but really I don't..."

My new Slavic friend opens a door to his right, saying "Please" in a manner that implies changing my mind would not be acceptable at this stage. I walk through into a low-lit front room that looks as if it really has been cleared for a party, a square of carpet in the middle and all the furniture round the sides. The chairs and sofas here, like the TV monitor in the hall, betray the difference between this and your average house. They all have that second-hand office reception look. Sitting as a group on three of them, nursing drinks, are some white guys, I guess in their forties, the kind of blokes you might see manning a stand at an engineering trade show. They glance at me briefly before they carry on with their slightly forced banter as Katie Melua fills in the pauses from a couple of speakers mounted on the fireplace wall.

While I'm taking this in, another of the Russian mafia emerges from what I suppose would be the dining room if it was a family home, but here seems to be functioning as a bar, or at least the place where they keep the bottles and glasses. Drugs too, very likely. This new guy is in his shirt sleeves, and I'm relieved to see he doesn't appear to be wearing a holster.

"What can I get for you, sir, while you are waiting?" he says very politely, rubbing his hands in anticipation.

"Er, vodka martini," I say, surprising myself. I never drink vodka martini.

Still wearing my outdoor coat I perch on the edge of a chrome-framed chair as far away from the trade show group and Katie Melua as I can, almost instinctively looking around for old copies of National Geographic Magazine, when both hirelings come back into the room through opposite doors, one bringing my drink, the other to say, "Gentlemen, we have some ladies free. Would you like to meet them?"

Without pausing for an answer he pulls the door further open and makes an impatient gesture, ordering some laggard in from the hallway. Laggards plural, actually - five women in all, on absurdly high stilettos, entering the parade ring like reluctant show-horses, looking far from in party mood as he roughly lines them up near the window wall for our inspection. It's no pyjama party either, despite the fact that every one of the women is wearing a flimsy, cheap-looking dressing gown; my hunch is they're not wearing pyjamas or anything very much else on underneath. As if he could read my mind, Mr Primark Suit steps back, nods once at the girls and says, curtly, "Take off."

A jolt goes through me, rattling the ice cubes in my drink, as the dressing gowns fall to the floor more or less simultaneously, revealing the girls in their full nakedness. Another stab just under the heart as I recognise the girl on the extreme left of the line as my runaway from the lorry park. She is smaller and paler than the rest, though all but one would be categorised as racially white, none over twenty-five, and something about each of them (a cheekbone here, the curve of a bare shoulder there)

89

that tells me no-one in the line is British. I'm being very polite and English, looking and not looking, so it takes me a full minute to notice that the one black woman has shaved off her pubic hair, or has had somebody shave it on her behalf.

The barman appears from behind me to take on the role of huckster. "Please make your choice, gentlemen. More than one if you wish, but you understand that costs a little more."

Among the three blokes on the other side of the room, the ginger one with the single earring stirs and whispers to his mate, who laughs as he looks sideways at the girls. I can see freckly blotches on the hand the whisperer is using to cover his mouth.

"Sir?" says the barman, as if he's been asked a question. Ginger fires one at him, shocking me but I couldn't speak for the rest of the room.

"Which one has the tightest cunt?"

He gets an oily smile in reply, and the answer he might have been looking for. "Please. Free to test."

I don't know if I'm more astonished by the crude audacity of ginger bloke - who swaggers up to the line and starts working his way right to left, jamming one hand between each girl's legs and clamping on her buttock with the other – or the indifference (encouragement, I should say) of the brothel-keepers to this manhandling of their goods, or the lack of complaint from any of the women, who stand there mutely, just the odd twitch of a facial muscle giving any clue to how they're feeling while he carries out his examination on them.

As he reaches the second-last girl in the line, I jump up and rush towards him. It's my intention to drag the guy away and smack him in the mouth, but to be honest I get spooked by Mr Primark, who again seems to be reading my mind and moves from his place near the doorway as if to cut me off. I hold my hand up to placate the bodyguard, then drop it to brush against the hand of little miss runaway on the end of the row. It's the lightest of touches, but she shivers as if someone's walked over her grave. I try to reassure her with my eyes before I turn to the pimp and call out, a little too earnestly:

"I've made my choice. Could I... meet this young lady, please?"

It sounds such a ridiculously quaint thing to say in the context of what's just gone on, as if David Copperfield has wandered onto the set of a hardcore movie, and it provokes a rasping "Fuck me" from ginger bloke, who's at my shoulder now, but I've managed to keep his paws off my woman, first objective, and now at last I've a chance to find out who the hell she is.

90

The girl picks up her dressing gown and robes herself modestly while the Slav in the suit opens the door to the staircase. As we pass he places a hand on my chest and I freeze, expecting to be frisked or thrown out, but instead he relieves me of my coat, hanging it up alongside a row of others in the passage. He bends his head to hiss into my ear, "Fifteen minutes only. Do what you will."

At the foot of the stairs the girl pauses to peel off her stilettos (don't run away) before she leads me quietly up, carrying the shoes in one hand and holding the banister with the other as if, like a small child, she is not fully confident climbing the stairs.

We go past the first floor, where there seem to be more doors than there can possibly be rooms, and follow a narrower flight to the top of the house. The doors and frames are unpainted, and again the arrangement seems odd – two doors side by side on a wall that looks as if it fronts just one room, and both with bolts on the outside, more what you would expect to see on a storage shed than an entrance to a bedroom. My girl turns the handle of the door on the right, and solves one of these mysteries for me. Her room is tiny, just the smallest of single beds and a low wooden cabinet that doubles as a bedside table, fitting pretty much exactly between the bed and what is obviously a stud partition wall that has made the original larger bedroom into two. The same must have been done to the rooms further down, with the same end in mind – double the fucking-cells.

There's a very small high window, almost a skylight, which has been halved by the partition so that only one narrow pane is available this side of the wall, and you would have to kneel up onto the tatty furniture to see out. Like the others I've seen in the house, this window is barred, and there's no obvious way of opening it to let air in or out. I notice this because of the staleness that has me gagging slightly as I close the door behind us – a soup of male sweat, lingering alcoholic farts and whatever chemical odour is seeping from the inadequate room-freshener that's sitting on top of the cabinet.

I'm looking down on the shabby blanket thrown roughly across the bed, wondering what (whose) spots and stains might be hiding underneath, when the girl reaches into the pocket of her dressing gown, turns to hand over what she's taken out, and speaks to me for the first time. Another East European accent.

"You wear, please. Please."

The second *please* is plaintive, and she slightly squeezes my wrist as she says it. I can still feel the thrill of her touch after she has moved away to position herself demurely on the bed, her bare feet half-tucked under the top of the blanket as if she is feeling the cold. She is unknowingly, achingly seductive. It's only the clinical functionality of the condom sachet she has placed in my hand that keeps me grounded and keeps her (here's ironic) safe from my lust. That and the hollow anxiety in her eyes. I sit at the foot of the bed.

"Don't worry… Listen, I'm not going to do anything to you."

If I thought that would relax her I couldn't be more mistaken. She is immediately agitated, leaning forward, almost begging. "No, no, you must make sex with me, please. I have to do it with you."

"You don't have to do anything…"

"Yes, yes. I'm sorry you don't like me, but please, *please* I'll be good. I'm not so ugly…"

"You're lovely, beautiful, honestly…"

"Is it that thing? You don't have to wear, *jo*. No johnny is OK. Please don't tell them I said you *had* to wear. Just if you want I say. Anything is OK, please."

She opens her dressing gown and lies back on the bed, eyes closing, submissive, her buds inviting. I'm throbbing, straining against the temptation to fling myself on her. *Do what you will,* the man downstairs had said. I have permission. *She* has given me permission, she's begging me to fuck her. But her lower lip is trembling and her hands, stretching the gown open to give me access to her naked body, are gripped tight on the material.

I lean across the bed and place my hands over hers, gently drawing them together until the folds of the robe close over her again. She lies there motionless, her eyes shut as I study her face, drink it in rather. Her mouth has stopped trembling now and she looks even paler than before. If it wasn't for the slight tension at the corners of her eyelids she could be asleep, or dead. *Die young, stay pretty* Debbie Harry sang. I'm still watching, turning the words of the song over in my head, when a tear escapes from one closed eyelid and trickles over the slight mound of her cheekbone. I put a forefinger on her cheek to arrest it, and she opens her eyes to look at me.

"They'll punish me if I don't make sex with you," she says.

"Who's going to tell them? Not me."

Her pretty face crumples and she's sobbing real tears now, but quietly, afraid of the spying house, her breast bone vibrating with the effort of keeping her grief in. I move further on to the bed, lying with her, and risk terrifying her as I bring her close to me, tucking her head into my shoulder, smoothing her narrow back with my free hand. She doesn't panic though, even responds in a child-like way by nestling into my

92

embrace and letting the tears gradually subside. The waft of cheap scent around her triggers a long-buried memory of my younger sister (was she seven or eight?) experimenting with rose water, dabbing it behind her ears and on her neck.

We lie like this without speaking for several minutes until we're disturbed by noises from the other side of the partition. That red-haired bastard probably, or one of his cronies, having his way with his selection from the line. At one point they bump heavily against the stud wall and my girl winces. I find her hand and squeeze it. "Don't worry."

She opens her eyes and looks at me miserably. I stroke her hair and whisper near her ear. "Let's talk a little. Then we don't have to listen. To them, I mean," and she smiles, understanding the correction.

"My name is Marc," I say softly. "That's my real name. The men downstairs think I'm called Oliver, it doesn't matter why."

"Secret identity," she whispers in return and I can't help chuckling at that, her accent being so perfect for an old James Bond film.

"Marc," she repeats to herself, to get it right or, I'm hoping, to remember it. "I am Edona." I want to fall in love with her just for her name.

"Edona, I came here to find you."

She looks at me quizzically, and even as I say it that other me inside me is scornful. Oh, yeah? Is that the reason you asked the cabbie to bring you to Warkworth Street? Not because the girl in the pub got you feeling randy? Not for the promise on the card? Just for this girl? And why? She's special because…? What do you want from her? What do you expect to give?

"I saw you," I tell her. "Last week." (Was it only last week?) "You were climbing out of a lorry." Edona looks puzzled. "A lorry. A truck."

"Ah, *kamion*. Truck. Too many trucks. It's my story."

"You tried to run away. Emmanuel caught you."

The hand at my chest stiffens. She looks up at me, startled. "You know Emmanuel? Don't send him to me. Please don't send."

"Relax. I don't know him. I just met him one time. He's not a friend, I don't know any of them. I'm here to be *your* friend, that's all."

Her hand slackens a little, but she's still watchful. I've lost some of her trust, just by knowing Emmanuel's name. I'll have to go carefully.

"I know nothing about you, either, and I don't need to know anything that you don't want to tell me, but I promise if I'm asking questions it's only because I want to help you."

Edona tenses again. "Are you a police-man?" She pronounces the syllables separately, and with some trepidation.

93

"No. I'm… nothing. Just… I work for a radio station. Do you have radio where you come from?" (Stupid question.)

"Radio? Like Radio Tirana?"

"Where is that, Radio Tirana?"

Edona looks at me as if she doesn't comprehend, then says simply, "In Tirana." She watches my face for some sign of recognition. Not getting it, she says again, "Tirana? You don't know Tirana?"

"Well, Geography wasn't my best subject in school."

She smiles, touches my arm. Somehow my ignorance has restored her confidence in me. "Tirana in Albania," she says. "Where is my country."

"You're Albanian, right. How did you end up here?"

Edona wells up again. "I'm not meaning to be here. I'm meaning to be in Italy."

"I don't understand."

"Where is job they say, to pay back money. Good job, *restorant*."

"You owed somebody money?"

"My father owes. We can't pay so here is deal or he's dead, they say. We lend you money, take you to Italy, give you good job, and you pay back in one year. Just one year is all. As soon as you pay you can go home. Or stay in good job. It's up to you."

"So what went wrong?" Though I already know, or can guess, some of it. "Why aren't you in Italy now?"

"Because men chased our boat. Police-men, I think. *Rojë bregdetare*, is police of the sea."

"Coastguard."

"*Dakord.* They chase from Vlore in the night. We are in old engine boat, twelve, fourteen people. They are catching us. So…" Edona stops, a catch in her throat, and I can feel her body tighten against mine. I put my fingertips gently under her chin to get her to look up.

"What? What happened?"

Her face melts into tears once more. I can barely hear what she says through her sobs.

"The men in our boat…"

"What?"

"They push people into the sea." She grabs at my wrist. It's as if she's drowning and I'm her only hope. "Caterina Sopa. She's from my village, I know her. They throw in the water, in the dark. And another girl. Next to me. She's sitting next to me. He pushes her too. And he looks at me. Now he looks at me."

94

She shudders. I hold her more closely. "Ssh, you're fine. You're here now." Some consolation, but it's as much for me as Edona. We're hanging on to each other in the blackness.

"I hear girls scream in the water. I'm believing I am die. Then, uh, *prozhektor...* is, big light comes from other boat. And they are shouting *Ndalim! Gommoni, Ndalim!* But we are not stopping. We leave the girls in the water and we go sail away. Maybe *polici* save, maybe not. I watch the light searching for a long time, then, *terr.* I don't know if they found."

Edona grieves quietly, and I lie silent next to her, aware of her heart beating. When she seems more settled, I prompt her to go on with her story.

"Where did the boat go? Not to Italy?"

I can feel her in the crook of my arm, shaking her head.

"Back to Vlore?"

She seems about to answer when there's a loud banging on the bedroom door, scaring us both. I hug Edona close to me as the voice on the other side calls out, "Time is over. Please to come down."

"Not yet," I shout in return. "I'll pay."

"Of course, sir, no problem," the voice comes back. "Fifteen minutes more." He favours us with a dirty little laugh and we hear him tapping a rhythm on the banister as he retreats down the stairs.

"Where did the boat go?" I whisper again to Edona.

"North, I think, still my country maybe, but I don't know the where. The men were afraid they are caught. One man, Uri, wants to throw us all in the sea. They argue about money, who gives them money. When we land they lock us all in... what is place for keep boat?"

"Boathouse?"

"Ten of us closed in that place for two days, sleeping on the ground. The men are leaving for all of us just a little bread and water. There is not *tualet* and we have to go in the corner of the shed, like animals. Less than animals. It's coming third day when Uri is back with another man in a car. Ramiz. They come from drinking and Uri is angry with us. He calls us *bushtër.* Woman dogs. He takes out gun and he makes us all go out of boating house and down to the shore. We think he is going to shoot us there. He orders take clothes off and everybody into sea. I want to swim away but I am afraid. I am afraid of Uri and afraid of the sea."

Edona falls silent. When I look into her face she is staring past me, unseeing, still immersed in the cold waters of the Adriatic, watching Uri on the shore with his gun. I wait, and she continues.

"He is not meaning to kill us now. We are money for Uri. He is washing clean his women for Ramiz. He makes us to come out of the water. He laughs with Ramiz when we are coming out, tells him we are his *sirenë*. We are having to stand *zhveshur* in front of Ramiz. So he can look, so he can choose. Tonight also the same. Again and again, for choosing. And always I'm thinking, Edona, that first time, why did you choose to the shore and not to the sea?"

Her words reach so far into my guts I let out a whimper. It's not just that I'm feeling for Edona's pain. It's the stark and sickening recognition that I'm the latest in that long line of johns to pick her out for pleasuring ourselves on her and in her. I may not have fucked Edona, but I can't absolve myself from the guilt, because that greedy desire – the base appetite for her and other women - is in me as much as in any man that has had her since she was first raped by Ramiz.

More than rape, I discover when Edona finds the strength to go on with her story, whispering it quietly to me under the stained blanket. Ramiz was not just a trick for Uri the pimp to turn, but a pimp-master himself. He selected Edona and two others from the ten girls lined up on the beach and, after Uri had corralled the rest into the boathouse, they took all three roughly right there on the strand, like boys riding seaside donkeys, to 'break them in', they said. Then they threw the girls their clothes, forced them into the back seat of Ramiz's car and drove away.

Ramiz owned a seedy bar-cum-whorehouse at the edge of some large ex-mining town called Burrel. That's where Edona and the other two women were made to work, shuffling topless around a tiny stage except when they were being banged in a back room by whoever took a fancy to them provided they had enough cash after their drinking to pay Ramiz for the privilege.

When Edona finally plucked up the courage to ask him for wages to send to her family, Ramiz said, "I paid Uri one hundred and fifty thousand *leke* for you, child. You have to earn that money back for me, and what I spend for your keep, then we can talk about wages."

Before that day came, though (and surely even Edona couldn't be so naïve to believe it ever would) it seems that Ramiz got a better offer.

"One night," says Edona, "Ramiz drive me to a hotel in centre of town. This is not happening before. He bring me to a man in a room. Nice room, clean bed. And Ramiz leave me there. I never see him again. This man… of course, he makes sex with me. But after, he's like a doctor, making… er…?"

"Examination?"

"Yes, examine. My eyes he looks, my arms, and here, and here…" Edona touches herself delicately and approximately at the places she can't name, or won't. "He asks what drugs I take. I say, no drug. He asks am I having child or no. No. Then he dresses, looking and still looking at me on the bed. He tells me, 'I am your messiah, Edona. I am fixing you for good job in UK. For this you must pay back 2,000 Euro I am give to Ramiz.' I am shocked. 'I don't have this,' I tell him. 'You will have from your work for me in UK,' he says. 'Enough for your family also. Your father, Pjter. Your mother Anna. Your little brother Andri.' He is going out of the room, but first he pats his coat and says to me, 'Do not leave this room or I will shoot you.' He smiles as he says, but I know he is meaning this."

Edona raises herself slightly from the bed to look directly into my eyes. "How does this man know my whole family, Marc, and I don't know his name? Where his spies? You are his spy, maybe? How you are man with different names for different people? Do you know this man's name?"

"I don't, Edona, I promise you. I don't know anything about this set-up. It's… I've heard that this sort of thing goes on, but I'm just… I can't believe what you're telling me."

"It's true."

"No, I mean, of course I believe you. I *do* believe you. But it's… unimaginable."

"I'm not understanding."

"I'm not sure *I* do. I mean, how can people get away with this in… It's the twenty-first century, for Christ's sake. I mean, what about security? ID? How did he manage to bring you here? Did he just walk with you past Customs?"

"He did not come with me."

"No?"

"No. When he leave hotel room I lie down in his fine bed and I am thinking, maybe this is OK, now. I just have to be with this man. I am to be *shok shtrati*. His bed-woman. Is not so bad as with Ramiz. One man only. He will treat good. I must take care for my family. What I do? I go bathe myself for this man to come back. Is so nice. When I was little girl, before *Baba* lost all, I had such bathe, is warm up to my neck and *sapun*, is little… what is little, round…?"

"Bubbles?"

"*Dakord*. Is nice. And fat white drying-cloths. I go back to bed and wait like good *shok shtrati*. I'm made my mind to do. But he's not coming back."

"He left you?"

"Other men is come. They have key for door and they walk in. I must go with them, they say. Dress quickly. I am thinking they are *polici* maybe. Outside is *kamion*, is truck, yes? Covered like soldier truck. I am lift into back and truck goes. Out of dark I can see eyes watching – three, four people in the back of truck with me. Later I can see they are all women, young also, afraid also. The truck stops more and again a woman is lift in. I am believing we are for jail. But the truck drives on and on. It is day until we stop for little time only, then on again the same and the same. We are very tired. At night we come to a place for trees, what is?"

"Woods, forest."

"Thank you. In my language *dru*. We are waiting for long time in the dark. Then we see lights through the woods and noise of *kamion*, big one. The men shout at us *natashas, nxitoj! nxitoj!* and make us run to new truck coming. They give all girl bag for sleeping and water bottle, and show her hide places behind boxes. When man take me to place he shine light and we find girl also in place there. She is already travel miles in truck. This girl is of Romania. Another is of Moldova. I do not know how many all."

"And you came all the way to England in the back of this lorry?"

"No, two more before. We change here, we change there. Long time. For UK I am lying like now in space under floor."

"False compartments. Jesus, it's organised crime."

"Is crime, yes. I am stealed."

"It's more than a crime, it's slavery."

"*Skllavëri*. OK, is true."

I draw her in to me again. She feels so frail and light in my arms. I'm lacerated with tenderness and guilt. I have to squeeze my eyes shut because I'm losing my hold on gravity right now, and we might easily tip over the edge of the earth or float away. It's Edona that brings me back.

"So sorry, Marc."

She's saying sorry to *me*.

"What for?"

"I'm not satisfying. Please don't tell Boris."

"Who's Boris? The guy downstairs?" Edona nods.

"Listen." She waits obediently, watching my face so intently that I'm glad of the darkness, otherwise she'd see how pathetic I really am. It's only the promise that sounds strong. "I'm going to get you away from these men. Boris, Emmanuel. All of them. Trust me, I'll get you out of here."

"Thank-you, but not possible."

98

Strangely, her air of hopelessness convinces me I can do this. In fact, it's easy. How much courage does it take to call the police?

"I'll call the police."

Edona tenses up against me, just as she did when I first mentioned Emmanuel.

"Not police, no."

"Why not? That's what they're for."

"I have been give often to *polici* for favour by men. At Uri's. Also, on journey to UK…"

"But this is England. We…"

Edona's response blow-torches my instinctive racism. The words turn to ashes in my mouth as she says, "Here too, yes, in this house."

I'm speechless, haunted by the image of PC Plod getting his kit off to poke Edona. Horribly, I can see myself behind him. There to fight him off? Or joining the queue.

"There's bad apples in every barrel," I manage to say at last, listening to myself shift into phone-in mode, all external calmness and balance, then, realising she may not understand the expression, "I will find some good people to help you."

But it's me who doesn't immediately understand when Edona says, "No. They will send me back to my country."

"Well… isn't that what you want?"

"My father will be kill if I go back with no money. Maybe already, I don't know. I fear to go back."

Another wave of guilt washes over me for my complicity in Edona's plight. I'm nauseous with self-loathing, lying pressed against this half-naked young girl. I have to tear myself away, but for all the struggle inside me I try to do it with a show of gentleness. I have the sense that any sudden movement would shatter her, as if she was some fine artist's delicate creation. My hand never leaves hers. When I finally get to my feet, reluctant, she looks up at me tearfully, and I have to hug her just once more, stroking her hair like a parent trying to soothe his little girl's nightmares away.

"I will do something, but I won't put you or your family in danger. I promise." I know I'm deluding myself as well as her, but it's the only thing I can say that allows me to leave her in that narrow bedroom on her own while I steal away down the stairs.

If only I could have kept on going, past the reception room door, out through the front porch, along the path and off to make plans for Edona's escape. But of course Mr Primark Suit is at the foot of the stairs waiting for me, smiling in a way that suggests we share a secret now, him and me against the world. Which I guess we do.

I'll say this about Boris, he's good at his job. As I'm getting to the last step on the staircase he moves aside, briskly lifts the correct coat from the assortment on the pegs and hands it to me with a conspiratorial smirk. "Well, Mr Oliver. I'm thinking you are liking little Edona very much, yes? Sweet girl."

With the advantage of the step I'm perhaps an inch taller than him. I could break his face with a well-placed head butt. I hesitate, and the moment is gone. He is firmly back in control, moving between me and the door as I take my coat.

"Just the matter of the bill, sir. Our girls are please to delight for one hundred pounds. For your longer pleasure tonight is two hundred pounds. Of course, you may wish to leave a little extra, a little gift for Edona, is entirely to you. Even sweeter next time, maybe, eh?" He leers in my face. "And your drinks, sir, fifteen pounds."

I raise no objection over the outrageous price of one vodka martini, for the simple reason that I'm numbed with the sudden realisation that I have nowhere near enough cash on me to pay for anything beyond the drink. A glance inside my wallet confirms this. The ten-pound notes tucked in there look crisp and new, but there are only a couple of them.

"Mmm, do you accept credit cards?"

"No, sir. Is difficult for us."

Is difficult for me. I hook out the notes and proffer them apologetically. "Sorry, this seems to be all the cash I have at the moment."

All bonhomie discarded, the Slav takes the money with the air of a snooty head waiter, rubs them between his thumb and forefinger to confirm there really are only two notes there, then looks at me silently, inviting the next move.

"I could drop the rest in tomorrow. What time do you... open?"

He fixes me with a stare that might have lasted forever if I hadn't broken the spell by clipping my heels against the bottom step and half-stumbling backwards. That brings a contemptuous sneer out of Boris and a gesture towards the chair parked next to the CCTV monitor.

"Please to sit."

His conditioned politeness doesn't disguise the menace behind his instruction. I do as I'm told and watch him guardedly, eyes widening when he reaches to his inside pocket. He turns his back on me and walks into the space beyond the staircase, cell phone in hand. He mutters privately into the mouthpiece for a minute, then snaps the phone shut as he swivels and paces in my direction. He stops and leans on the banister, arms folded, watching me impassively without another word. Not having any options, I sit and do my best to look unconcerned, all but shitting myself on the seat.

I reckon this little tableau lasts about ten minutes. Three times it's interrupted by girls in dressing gowns leading clients from the front room upstairs to the bedrooms. Each time, the girls avert their eyes as they pass between us, Boris switches on a quick bright smile for the johns, they acknowledge him and cast a filthy glance my way. One seems very close to cuffing me as he goes by, just for the hell of it.

The muscle in my right calf develops some kind of twitch, from being too long in the same position I guess. The more I think about it the worse it gets, so I try to distract myself by working out the relative distances between the staircase, the front room and the outside door. Supposing Edona should be sent down to collect her next fuck, I'm calculating the possibility of letting her walk past me then springing up to bundle both of us out of the front door and away before the goon on watch knows what's happening.

But Edona doesn't show before the next scene in the drama, which is played out on the screen at my elbow. I recognise Emmanuel straightaway as he reaches the front entrance, even though the camera angle slightly distorts his image. The white guy behind is new to me, but he also looks a big bugger, a fact confirmed when the door opens and the two of them walk in, filling the hallway. Boris stays silent, just nods once in my direction from his place at the banister, and the two heavies make space for me to stand between them.

There's a certain inevitability about what's unfolding now and I'm experiencing something very like *déjà vu* as we file along the garden path, leaning away from the wet hedge, to the silver BMW parked outside the gate. Which is strange because I've never been anywhere near a situation like this.

The one thing that does surprise me is that Emmanuel sits next to the driver in the front of the car, leaving me on my own in the back. I'm assuming the rear doors are child-locked (family-friendly, ha), but I ain't about to test them, or to try winding a window down to haul myself out. It's not just that I'm afraid of hurting myself (I know I've got that to come anyway) or that they'll recapture me (which they surely will, big as they are). Something in me has decided I have a responsibility to sit there and take what's coming. I think I'm on a guilt trip for Edona. I still have her scent on me. It's as if she's sitting with me in the back of the car.

101

Being resigned to what's happening doesn't make me any less scared. When my eyes aren't drawn to the thick necks and shoulders of the pair who are about to demonstrate whatever form of punishment they've devised for me, I'm anxiously peering out of the window, trying to second-guess where it's going to take place. The men supply me no clues. All I learn from their desultory conversation is that the driver's name is Stefan.

The Beemer soon leaves the suburbs and seems to be following the AA signs to the new tunnel, but then Stefan turns right onto the coast road in the same direction I drove Marni just a few days ago. *Get Carter* comes to mind. Funny how the brain works; in the middle of this nightmare ride I start thinking about what made the original so much better than the remake, then I have a mini panic attack, brought on by not being able to remember what happens when Carter gets to the beach.

The car slows significantly, though we're still on the open road, and my heart leaps into my throat. Looks like they're going to do what they're going to do here on the hard shoulder. I twist in the seat, my body tucking into some sort of futile protection position. False alarm, the driver doesn't pull over – Emmanuel seems to be explaining something to him, one hand on Stefan's shoulder to talk in low tones, pointing with his other hand to where a graffiti-covered flyover crosses the motorway, as if he's describing a route – but when the driver picks up speed again we don't turn off the coast road. Not until we reach the Tesco car park.

Yes, the very place where I first set eyes on Edona. On Emmanuel for that matter, and this other guy was probably driving the car that night as well. I suppose there's a neatness to it, something appropriate about this being the spot they've chosen to knock me senseless, even if they don't appreciate the connection. I expect to be driven to the far corner, beyond where the huge lorries are parked, where we won't be seen. But we roll up to the main entrance of the store and park in a handy disabled bay, ignoring the hundreds of other spaces available nearby. The driver gets out and disappears through the big sliding doors as if he's on an ordinary shopping trip, and I'm just thinking this is a temporary reprieve when Emmanuel gets out the passenger side and opens the back door for me to step out.

"The cash machine is this way, sir," he says, politely.

"Sorry?"

"We need you to take out some cash."

"Oh, right. Yes, of course. No problem."

I follow him past the stacked trolleys to the cashpoint and he waits discreetly while I sort through my wallet to find the right card, my whole body tingling with relief. Of course, the money is much more important to them than teaching people a lesson – that's for amateur thugs. I check my current cash limit, just two hundred and fifty, but that should leave me more than enough after I've settled up to pay for a taxi to get me to the other side of town.

Or so I thought. As I turn with the wad of fresh notes Emmanuel takes one pace forward and nimbly extracts it from my fingers. He removes a leather glove and riffles through, his lips moving minimally as he counts the money.

"I think it's, er, one ninety-five I owe," I say, staking my claim. "Well, call it two hundred, cos I already paid twenty, so that leaves…"

Emmanuel flashes me his gold tooth as he pockets all my cash. "No, sir, it's exactly right. Includes travel expenses." He indicates the BMW. "Expensive motor," and he laughs, inviting me to join the joke. When I don't, he follows up with, "You have a *issue* with that, mister?"

I back off. "No, honestly. Just a slight logistical problem."

"Huh?"

"Oh, just trying to figure out how to get myself home, that's all."

Too much information. I instantly regret it as Emmanuel slips into public relations mode.

"No worries," he says expansively, like some character from *The Lion King*. "Stefan and me, we will give you a ride for sure. No extra charge," he adds, with a wink. "Where do you live, sir?"

Now that really would be too much information. I'm caught in a quandary. It's around one in the morning. Getting all the way back to my place from here with nix in my pocket is a challenge to say the least. On the other hand, do I really want to take my chance in the car with these low-lifes? (Listen to me talking.) There again, if I refuse, Emmanuel is more than likely to take offence and I could still end up flat on my back behind the lorry park. But there's no way I'm going to give them my address. Somewhere fairly close, public.

"Mmm, if you could drop me off anywhere near the Western General…"

"Western…?"

"The hospital, you know? West end of the city."

A light goes on in Emmanuel's eyes. He takes a step towards me, a finger raised, face wreathed in smiles. "I knew it. I knew I had seen your face. You are the doctor."

"Well, no, not a doctor…"

103

"Look! Look!" He lifts both arms, showing off his black leather gloves. "I got them this afternoon. You were right. My hands feel so much better already."

He smacks his right fist into his left palm, either in triumph or to demonstrate, I'm not sure which. Behind him I can see Stefan coming out of the store, keeping a newspaper in place with one elbow as he tries to light a cigarette on the move. Emmanuel follows my eyes and turns to call out to his buddy.

"Hey, Stefan, this is the doctor I was telling you of." He checks briefly with me, "Dr Oliver, isn't it? Come on, Stefan, we have to take my friend home to his hospital."

Emmanuel opens the back door for me much more elaborately than he had the first time, gracing me with the status of a minor royal, then takes his place in the front alongside Stefan. This VIP pantomime must have triggered something off in Stefan, who jams his fag in the corner of his mouth and pulls away as if we were trying to shake off the paparazzi. He takes the speed bump on the way out almost as hard as I did the other night, and my eyes flick automatically to the floor under the dash as if I expect to see a broken wine bottle there.

What I see instead gives me another jolt. Directly under Emmanuel's feet, where Stefan must have thrown it as he climbed into the car, is the newspaper he has just bought at the supermarket. Tonight's *Chronicle*. If Emmanuel takes it into his head to have a browse during the journey he can't fail to see the article and my V-flashing photo on page three. Even if they spot it later I wouldn't put it past him to come and track me down just for taking the piss. I mean, I don't know what he did to Edona after she tried to run away, but he certainly put the fear of god up her.

I lean forward into the space between the two front seats.

"Er, I don't suppose I could have a glance at your paper, could I?"

"Sure, Oliver. Why not?" says Emmanuel, reaching down for it. As he picks it up there's a slow-motion moment when his eye is caught by a teaser pic of a scantily-clad female on the front page. He angles it for Stefan to see.

"Eh?"

Full story page seven. Don't go there. He shows the picture to me, through the gap.

"Oliver, eh? Good fuck or no?"

I try a noncommittal 'Uuhh' and he follows up with, "How much you pay?" which gives me a chance.

"Dunno. Let's see." And I thrust my hand out so he's not tempted to turn to page seven on my behalf. He posts the paper between the seats and I grab it quickly. For form's sake I thumb quickly through to page seven and turn the bigger photo towards Emmanuel, putting a lads' night out ogle on for him and saying, "Not bad. I'll give it eight out of ten. You'd get two hundred for her, easy." Hating myself and apologising to Edona in my heart. But it works well enough and Emmanuel, laughing, turns to watch the road ahead as I sink back into my seat with the newspaper.

I sneak a look at Philip Mann's piece to confirm which page it's on, then grab the bottom of the sheet between my thumb and forefinger, aiming to ease it out covertly as I pretend to read the paper. It's a slow, tedious task. I'm concerned that we'll get to the end of my ride before I make it, or that they'll catch me in the act. I look up to check where we've got to, and meet Stefan's eyes in the rear-view mirror.

"There's a reading light behind you," he says through the mirror. "'S OK to switch it on."

"I can see well enough, thanks." (But I'm hoping you can't.)

Once Stefan refocuses his attention on his driving I manage to slide the double page out onto the seat beside me. Holding the rest of the paper with my left hand and making a show of studying the back page, I very quietly fold up the loose sheet with my right, anchoring it under my backside until it's small enough to stuff into my coat pocket. I deliberately mess up what's left of the *Chronicle*, pretending a close interest in the racing results as an excuse for folding it out of its normal order. Then I casually set it aside, inner pages uppermost, just as the hospital comes into view.

"Anywhere here will be fine, thanks."

"Take him right in," Emmanuel directs Stefan, gesturing towards the main gates.

"No, really…"

"Hey, no worries, doctor. At your service."

Stefan sweeps through the gates, up the hospital road and hangs a right, parking next to the ramp over the Ambulances Only markings, though to be fair there are no ambulances or people in sight. I shuffle across the back seat, crumpling the newspaper a little more, but I can't get out of the car until Emmanuel springs from the front to release me.

"Thanks. I'd give you a tip, but you've got all my money already."

Emmanuel roars with laughter and, to my great surprise, clasps me in a bear hug. "I like you, Oliver. You're my man." Thinking about it later I have to admit that, leaving aside the real Oliver, this is the friendliest anyone has been with me for weeks. His hug has put the seal on it. I'm now officially best mates with a pimp.

He eventually lets me go and, with a playful punch on the shoulder, returns to his seat, calling out just loud enough to embarrass me, "Take care for yourself, sir. Do not forget to come back and see us. Good fun, eh?"

I watch his door close and wait with my hand on the ramp rail as if to see them off, but the Beemer doesn't move immediately and I'm marooned between the road and the hospital entrance. Through the windows of the car I can see Emmanuel put his cell phone to his ear. Anxious that it may have something to do with me, I move further up the ramp towards the main doors. I have no choice, with the baddies still obstinately out there, but to walk into the building. I'll try and find a public toilet to hide in until they drive off.

The reception desk nearest the door is unmanned, but I haven't moved three yards inside the entrance before a porter or security man, one of those semi-retired types, emerges from a cubby-hole behind it. I'm rapidly working up an excuse that will persuade him not to heave me out when he speaks up quite cheerily, addressing me like a long-lost friend.

"Hello, it's Marc Niven, isn't it? How's that for a coincidence?"

"Sorry?"

"I was just reading about you in the *Chronicle*. What a load of nonsense."

"Oh, storm in a…"

"Exactly. You did right to stick your fingers up at 'em. They're not going to get rid of you over that, are they? Fools if they did. Best asset they've got."

"Kind of you to say so."

"Not at all. You pass the time nicely for me back there, mate." He crooks a thumb at his cubby-hole. "I'm your number one fan, me." He shakes my hand vigorously. "Norman Tait. Never miss a show when I'm on shift. I was here when you talked that feller down from the bridge. Watched the ambulance off in the middle of it. It was like having a part in a film and sitting in the audience all at the same time. So, what brings you this way, Marc?"

I've been so busy soaking up this unexpected praise that I half-miss his question at the end of it. He has to jog me with another.

"I say, what can we do for you?"

"Oh, erm…" I sneak a look through the glass doors. Emmanuel is still on the phone, looking abstractedly in my direction. I turn my back on him, instinctively looking for an escape route. On the wall behind Norman is a board pointing to all manner of wards and departments.

"Well, it's a kind of a scouting mission, really. There's a friend of mine, a regular listener actually, like yourself, has to come here and see about her cataracts in the morning. And I promised to be her eyes, as it were. Except I wanted to find out in advance where to go, so it's not the blind leading the blind."

I'm torn between admiring my own inventiveness and shaking my head at the absurd idea of casing the joint in the early hours of the morning, but Norman seems to buy it readily enough.

"Cataracts, eh? It's Ophthalmics you want. Here, I'll walk you along there so you'll know."

He starts down a corridor with a spring in his step, turning just once to let me catch up. I'm pleased to get out of the sight of Emmanuel and Stefan, so I follow him pretty rapidly. He continues chattering happily as we go.

"You'll know Alex Ray pretty well, I suppose?"

"Alex, yes. He's on after me. You're a fan of his as well, are you?" (Trying to tone down the disbelief.)

"Oh, yeah. In fact, he's the reason I started listening in the first place. Alex used to work here, see."

"So he did."

"Aye, you've got Alex to thank for me discovering you, Marc. Tell him I'm asking after him when you see him."

"I will."

"If they ever let you back in of course," Norman laughs.

"Quite."

We turn left down another identical corridor.

"Well, I see you're talking to the other party anyway," says Norman.

"Sorry?"

"That'll help clear things up."

"Norman, I don't know what you're talking about."

"Just those guys that dropped you off. They're to do with the Asian woman, aren't they? You know, the widow."

"What? I shouldn't think so."

"Oh, right. Must've got my wires crossed. Mind you, there was a lot of comings and goings at the time, hardly surprising."

"What *time* do you mean?" I can't keep up with this. Norman talks as fast as he walks.

107

"When your man was brought in. I mean the real one, not the joker you talked to. The one that was killed. Mr Malik. Nasty business that. Sixth degree burns, apparently."

I'm as confused by what Norman is saying as I am by the route we're taking through the hospital. I'm still trying to make sense of his ramblings when we round yet another corner and Norman announces, "Ophthalmics Department. Always busy here during the day. You book in at this reception desk, waiting room over here. Consulting rooms just down the corridor."

As I'm feigning an interest in the details I notice what looks a set of glass doors, smaller than the ones at the main entrance, leading to a car park outside.

"Is this another way out from here, Norman? Or in. I'm just thinking, this could be a bit less complicated…"

"Oh, yes, this is all part of our new Out Patients suite. All built under PFI, heard of that? It means we're in hock to some big company for the next fifty years. Smart though, eh?"

"Very impressive. Norman, do you mind if I use that exit instead of the front doors, so I can work out where it is in relation to the rest of the site? It's going to be a lot easier than finding my way along all those corridors tomorrow."

Norman contemplates the radical notion of using the entrance that has been purpose-built for the unit. "It's alarmed though, that's the thing. After hours." For a minute I think he's going to get all jobsworth on me and trail us all the way back to the main doors where Emmanuel and Stefan could still be camped out. Then he nods to show he's made up his mind to demonstrate what power he has over his domain. He unclips his walkie-talkie from his belt clip.

"Spud to Control, come in."

The speaker crackles into life. "Go ahead, Norm."

"Do me a favour will you, Rob? I'm needing the alarm on OP block disabled, just for a few seconds, yeah?"

"Got trouble out there?"

"Not really. Just we've got a celebrity visit. I'm wanting to let him out the back way, that's all."

"Celebrity?"

"Kind of, aye. Marc Niven, you know?"

"Never heard of him."

Norman raises his eyes to me, with a hint of apology.

"On the radio. The talk show guy. Comes on before Alex. Very good, actually. " Norman winks and motions me towards the exit.

"If you say so." We hear a brief electronic warble from Rob's end. "There you go. Alarm off. You know you need to fill an exception form for that, don't you, Spud?"

Norman grins. "Piss off," he says airily into his radio as he feels for the swipe card dangling around his neck. Seconds later the sliding doors are opening and I'm walking free from the building well away from the parked-up pimps, having all but genuflected to Norman Tait for his unknowing rescue act. As I dash home the only thing that stops me whooping, the way I used to when I'd foiled the ambush and galloped away from the school gates, is that my promise to Edona means I've somehow committed myself to taking on the outlaws again.

VIII

Back in my own bed I relive Edona's nightmares. A witness to cold-hearted murder, a victim of multiple rape, a sex slave perhaps not yet out of her teens – the images of her abuse tumble over each other as I pitch between wakeful anxiety and lurid dreams. Underneath the pictures I can hear Edona's hesitant voice relating her own horrors, breaking my heart as she reaches for the right words in English. I can't keep myself out of these dreams. I make my first entry as an abuser, contorting my face as I try and fail to climax, then as a coward backing away from a writhing mountain of naked bodies all fucking or being fucked, as a runaway chased along the hard shoulder by nightclub bouncers who swipe at me with knives and rolled up newspapers, finally as a hospital case, lulled into sleep or gently assisted suicide by a foreign nurse singing a haunting lament, drawing me down, already fading as I follow, leaving just a trace of where the past has been.

When I wake up what I remember immediately and most vividly is graffiti on concrete. I lie and think about this for a while. It connects. At least if the dream is to be believed. What I need now (this pun raises my spirits sufficiently to spark me into getting up) is concrete evidence. I have two places I need to visit.

Three actually, though it's just on the spur of the moment I decide to stop off at Prince Albert Road since I'm taking the car and Amina's house is more or less *en route*. I had half-expected there to be a crowd of people gawking at the door of number 110 but the street looks pretty much the same as when I first saw it, except that being mid-morning it's fully lined with cars parked by people working at The Gate. In fact I can't find a space all the way along. I do a nifty three-pointer at the end of the street and drive slowly back again, only to find that in the meantime a white van has triple-parked in the middle of the road directly outside Amina's house, blocking my way. The driver is already busy fixing a Montague & Hope For Sale sign outside the front door of 110.

Forced to wait, I sit and watch him at work, wondering whether this was something Amina had planned to do anyway, now that she has been left to cope on her own with the toddler, or whether it's the sudden unwanted attention that's made her decide to move. While I'm thinking about this, two men emerge from a car parked at the kerbside just in front of me and walk up to the house. As they engage the sign-erector in conversation I notice one of them carrying what looks suspiciously like a camera bag over his shoulder. Time to back off, literally. I reverse all the way up Prince Albert Road and make my escape before the press can find an excuse to add *stalker* to my list of endearing qualities.

Next stop is Oliver's favourite haunt (and now mine, apparently), the Central Library. I make straight for the newspaper archive section to root around in the drawers. This time I'm not looking to recapture Marc Niven glories – I'm hunting for something in the background of a picture, something that laid a track in my brain the last time I looked at the image, without my even being aware of it until it resurfaced as part of last night's stream of dreams.

Remembering roughly the date takes me to the right drawer fairly quickly, and pretty soon I'm staring once more at the burnt-out wreckage of Hassan Malik's car, snapped at the scene of the accident. In the top right corner of the photograph, partly cropped off by the frame, is a distinctive graffiti tag to the right of the bridge rampart struck by the car. It seems to be a flowing depiction of the word *toxic*, but with a number 7 in place of the *i*. The newsprint image isn't quite sharp or full enough to give me all that information – I'm filling in the rest from memory.

Getting a photocopy of the article is about as straightforward as Theseus escaping from the minotaur, only he didn't have the paperwork to fill in as well, which is why I'm waiting, hanging over the guard rail of the mezzanine floor in a state of vacant boredom when my eye is caught by a distinctive patch of yellow among the book browsers below. Oliver Dunn is in the building.

I watch him cross the aisle to return along the shelves, and as he does he glances up at random so I raise my hand, a little hesitantly given that I'd unceremoniously dumped him last time, and have since become *persona non grata* in some people's eyes. I needn't have worried. Oliver is like a labrador that's just spotted its owner on the other side of the park, and he practically runs up with a stick in his mouth when I wave him to me.

"Well met, Mr Dunn," I say, genuinely glad to have his company after the trials of the last couple of days. "Are you up for a little more detective work?"

Soon the two of us are stretching the Audi along the coast road, me driving while Oliver sits with the photocopied press cutting spread out on his knee, peering out of the passenger window. His job is to spot the tag under one of the flyovers that criss-cross the road as it pushes past the industrial estates and retail parks.

"There it is!" he yelps, much earlier than I expected.

"Are you sure?" I'm travelling too fast to stop right there on the hard shoulder so I carry on to the next exit, double back and loop the loop to let us take the same stretch more slowly.

"There, look." He points as I tuck into the side of the road just short of the bridge, turning my hazards on. Cars speed past my right shoulder and I'm conscious of how dangerously we're placed, with no proper lay-by here. I glance quickly down at the picture and up again at the bridge.

"It's not in the same position. See, this one's further into the bridge and lower down. Right tag though," I add, sensing Ollie's disappointment. "Keep looking, I'm sure it's much further along."

What I hadn't appreciated is how busy Mr Toxic 7 has been. Every mile or so along the coast road, almost wherever there is a concrete surface to spray, he has left his calling card. I'd never noticed it before – it's amazing how these things can pass you by (or you pass them by) for years maybe without ever clocking them until something stirs your attention. When I made the connection in my mind's eye with the piece of graffiti in the background of the press picture and something I'd seen on the dual carriageway I assumed that all I had to do was drive along there and make the simple match between the one and the other. I hadn't realised it would involve Ollie and me in trying to complete a jigsaw while playing a game of chicken with motorway traffic.

We have so many false dawns, back-tracking and decelerations that I'm becoming almost immune to horns blasting behind me and windows being wound down for cusses to be thrown by the time we find the genuine spot. Ironically, even before Oliver shouts "There's one!" for the umpteenth time, I just know we have finally reached the right bridge. Something about the distance we've travelled from town, the skyline, the pronounced bend in the road or just the peculiar drabness of the surroundings makes me realise that we're approaching the point where last night Emmanuel made Stefan slow down and where I sat up and took notice, expecting the worst. I've already taken my foot off the pedal and I'm pulling up to the hard shoulder under the rampart before Oliver has opened his mouth.

This time I actually get out of the car to look around, which makes me appreciate even more what a scary place a road like this can be. I'm buffeted by the slip-stream of vehicles going by. One wagon almost takes me along in its wake as I'm closing the driver's door. I move as quickly as I can to the safer side next to the rampart to examine Toxic 7's work. Oliver joins me – at least he's wearing something approximating to a high visibility jacket – and we stand close together, trying to keep the wind from blowing the press cutting away as we compare the photograph to the scene in front of us.

"This definitely looks right," I explain to Ollie as his hood flaps over his head. "The picture must have been taken from about where my car is now. If we stand this side the angle of the tag is spot on, so Hassan's car must have ended up here in the crash, unless the cops moved it before this picture was taken."

I scan the ground and along the surface of the bridge upright, looking for debris, or scars, or burns, acting just as I imagine a scene-of-crime officer would, only about three months too late. So much for my powers of observation – I'm so preoccupied that it takes a nudge from Oliver to make me glance up and notice the police traffic car that's rolled up quietly behind the Audi and is now parked next to my back bumper, blue lights strobing.

"Shit!"

The driver doesn't get out for the moment, just sits taking in the scene, and when he finally does he seems in no hurry about it. He takes a languid look behind him at the traffic, which is already slowing and bunching as if he were some river god casting a freezing spell on the flow with his eyes. His jacket might match Ollie's for colour, but only one of them looks like a melon. He's already sussed which one of us definitely doesn't own the Audi, so he addresses me over the traffic noise.

"Something wrong with your car, sir?"

"Well, ermm…" I look at it, desperately trying to think of a valid reason for stopping. "Not really, it's just, I wasn't sure if…"

A voice pipes up at my elbow. "It was me." The copper and I both turn our attention to Oliver, who rolls back under our gaze, but keeps smiling bravely for the policeman. "I get car sick, see. I asked him to stop."

"Oh, yes?" The officer stares meaningfully around Ollie's feet, looking for evidence.

"I felt better when I got out." Good old Oliver.

"Been travelling a long way, have you, to get sick an' all? Only I notice these are local plates."

113

"Just from town," I chip in. "Be something he's eaten, I expect. His diet's not the best, you know."

"Aha." Deeply unconvinced, he sizes us up for a while before he says, "So how do you two know each other, if you don't mind my asking?"

I shrug. "Just friends, is all."

"Mmm." Another look at me. I can tell he has me down for some species of pervert, preying on the vulnerable, but it's difficult for him to be direct without being able to latch onto something he could present as just cause, so he turns his attention to the car.

"You the owner of this vehicle, sir?"

"Yes. Mostly. There's some outstanding finance on it."

"Right. And do you have your driving licence with you?"

"I don't, no, sorry. I never carry it."

"You should. Can save a lot of bother in the long run."

"I've never been stopped by the police before."

"Lucky you then, eh?" As we're talking he's already examined the tax disc, checked the keys in the ignition, glanced at the tyres, opened the passenger door. He looks down at the floor-well, then inquiringly at me.

"Red wine stain. Accident with a Tesco carrier bag."

A flicker of a smile, and I release the breath I've been unconsciously holding in. He's going to let us off. So why does Oliver choose that moment to smear a snot from his nose with his sleeve? It's not the snot-smearing that's the problem – repellent though the sight is – it's the fact that he's still clutching the press cutting he had stuffed into his pocket when the police car turned up. Even that might have escaped attention if Ollie hadn't spotted it himself and done a double take worthy of the silent movies. Oliver by name… that's another fine mess you've got me into.

"What's that you have, sir?"

Ollie blinks helplessly at me as the officer plucks the paper from his hand, holding it at arm's length at first and letting the wind blow it open away from him, as if he thought it might contain anthrax spores or Oliver's mucus. Once he's sure it's foreign-body-free he brings it closer in to read. He studies the article silently, then looks at the bridge, back to the paper, finally rests his eyes on us, shaking his head. I feel like a pornographer. He jerks his thumb at his car.

"Go and sit in the back of the vehicle, both of you. Use the nearside door."

As Ollie scrambles over the back seat and I follow him in, heart thudding, the policeman opens up the spacious boot and picks out a

114

couple of red and white cones which he places carefully along the traffic side of the two parked cars before easing himself into the driving seat. He takes off his cap and places it on the seat beside him, then glances in the mirror to smooth his hair and check he has our full attention.

"I want you to take a look out of that window at those two lanes of traffic. What do you notice?"

Ollie is nearer the scene outside, but I take it on myself to answer. "They're full of cars."

"Exactly. Choc-a-bloc and getting not very far not very fast. Was it like that before?"

"No."

"So, what's changed?"

"Well, I guess we're causing an obstruction." This must be obvious to him, so why he's making us sit here for this lecture instead of travelling to the next lay-by or, better still, just letting us go, only he can answer.

"A minor obstruction is one thing," he says. "But you want to know the real reason? Rubber-necking. People slowing down to see what's going on. They see the blues, cars on the hard shoulder, and they've got their foot off the gas, looking over, hoping to see some gore. It just takes one or two and before you know there's a massive queue for no more reason than nosiness. It happens all the time here. Accident black spot. But then you two know that, don't you?"

"How do you mean?"

"Cos you're bloody train-spotters, aren't you? Or whatever the equivalent is for what you do. Seeking out accident scenes. It's sick-making."

"We wasn't," says Oliver.

"You know the bloke that died in this? Was he a relation?"

The PC picks out the press cutting from his tunic pocket and waves it at us. Ollie's opening his mouth again, so I dig hard into his side, I hope surreptitiously, and lean forward to answer, "No. Just from what we read in the papers." I'm not about to spill any beans to this patronising prick.

"I bet you bring flowers, do you? You know, just last week I caught a young lass running right across three lanes to tie some flowers onto a signpost. At least she vaguely knew the lad who'd been killed. Ex-boyfriend, apparently. Half of them, though. They've never even met the victim, 'specially when it's children knocked down. They come out in their droves. It's ever since Diana died. Got a bouquet in your boot have you? Written a poem, maybe?"

115

"No. Who do you think we are?"

"I'll tell you what you will be, if you don't give this lot up. Dead at the side of the road, like him. Hear what I'm saying?"

"Yes." I aim for as much churlishness as I can get away with.

He turns and looks through the space in the seats, sizing me up again. His eyes flick briefly to Ollie as he says to me, "Does he have a home to go to?"

"'Course, yeah."

"I suggest you get him back there, sharpish. And think yourself lucky I haven't booked you. This time. And listen…" his finger pointing like a gun as we're shuffling out of the door, "I don't want to see either of you on my patch again, is that clear? We don't do tourism."

The policeman gets out of the driver's side as we spill onto the hard shoulder, and I wait, expecting another sermon, but it's just to collect the cones that I'm sure he put out for dramatic effect. He throws them into the back of the car and returns to his place behind the wheel, where he sits watching us climb into the Audi. When I pull out cautiously into the stream of traffic he kills his blue lights and follows me, staying on my tail until I leave at the next exit, as if he's running me out of town. I cross over the dual carriageway and drive back the way we came as the police car disappears in the opposite direction.

Ollie and I say nothing to each other until we're well past the crash scene and heading back into the city centre. I feel I should apologise to him, but I'm so embarrassed - not only for myself but more especially about how the copper dismissed Ollie as some kind of retard – that I don't quite know what to say. When I've finally worked out a form of words I steal a glance across to check he's ready to receive an apology, and I'm astonished to find him sitting with a broad grin on his face.

"What's so funny?"

"Nothing, just… That was good, wannit, Marc?"

"Good?"

"Kind of, yeah. I've never been in a police car before."

"Neither have I."

"First for everything eh, Marc? First for everything. Thanks."

"Oliver, I nearly got you arrested. I don't think that would have pleased your mam much, would it?"

"She likes detectives, though. She used to like Morse. That policeman wasn't much good at detecting, was he?" Oliver chuckles in that phlegmy way he has. "I think he got the wrong end of the stick. That's a saying, innit, you're holding the wrong end of the stick. Are you going to tell them what we've found out?"

116

"Who, the police? What's to tell them?"

"Dunno. Where Hassan got killed?"

"They knew that already. I was just checking for myself. Just making a link."

Truth is, I haven't told Oliver about Emmanuel and Stefan. I've only brought him along as a kind of treat, a way of saying sorry for having ditched him last time we met, and I guess as company for me too. I've told him nothing of my growing suspicion that Hassan's death may not have been an accident, or that Emmanuel might have been somehow involved. It's not that I'm assuming he's incapable of taking it in – I swear I've stopped thinking of Oliver as a bovine – but I have no idea myself where I'm going with this. Besides, how can I tell him anything about my encounters with Emmanuel without giving him the rest of the sordid details? I'm not proud of some of the places I've been over the last couple of days. I recognise that Oliver still holds me up as some sort of hero, and if I'm honest I'm reluctant to disturb that. Anyway, he's an innocent abroad and I'm not prepared to be the one to disillusion him about the ways of the world. We'll have to proceed on a need-to-know basis. Christ, I sound just like Meg Reece.

"Where would you like dropping off?" I say to Oliver, anxious to change the subject in case he pesters me with difficult questions.

"Just wherever you're going, Marc," he says, blithely. "If you're driving back to your place I'll just get off there and walk the rest of the way. Unless the 19 bus comes along. We're only two stops from you."

"Yeah, you've said. No, don't worry, I'll take you home. Just tell me which way to go after I've passed mine." My offer has more than a tinge of self-interest - if I only take him as far as the flat I'll either have to ask him up for coffee or be made to feel guilty watching him out of my window while he stands waiting for the bus.

Ollie has the drop on me, though, because as soon as we pull into his estate – obviously still council-owned and even worse-maintained than the dross I'm surrounded by – he says, "Come in for drinking tea, Marc. Or coffee if you want, we have that, either-or."

"Well, very kind but…"

"Come on. Mam'll be chuffed to meet you, honest she will. It's no bother. Not a bit of bother. There's nothing spoilin'."

By now I've run out of excuses for standing him up, and so, if it pleases his mam… I park the car half on the stubby verge of a cul-de-sac Ollie guides me to, and follow him along the flagstones past a row of

117

wheelie bins and spilt plastic bags to his back door. He presses his face briefly at the window next to the door, shading his eyes as he peers beyond the net curtains, then shoves a plump hand into the letter-box, fishing out a length of string with a key on the end that he uses to let us in.

"Just me, Mam," he calls out as we squeeze our way through a tiny back kitchen. "Guess who's come an' see ya."

The living-room we enter is no more nor less messy than my flat these days, just different-messy. Where my clutter is mainly plastic and paper – disordered piles of DVDs, computer games, dog-eared books and thumbed-through magazines – the Dunns seem to go in for mounds of soft materials – coats, rugs and unfinished ironing strewn across the back of the furniture or stacked on the floor. Where I have empty bottles and partly-crushed cans waiting to be gathered up for a rare visit to the recycling centre, they have torn-open family size packets of crisps and chocolate biscuits, here on the coffee table, and there between the ornaments on the old-fashioned sideboard, available for grazing.

In the midst of this comfortable chaos is a creased old woman sitting deep in a faded armchair, the sort that belongs next to a roaring fire, though there's no sign of a fireplace in the room, just a glimpse of radiator pipe sticking out from behind a sofa littered with jumble by the back wall. I say old, but when I get a closer look she's not as ancient as her knitted cardi and thick tights make her out to be – probably late sixties in reality, though it's hard to be certain because of the prescription dark glasses she's wearing.

"Hey, Mam," Ollie calls her attention again. "Can you see who this is?"

She leans forward with her hands on the arms of the chair as if she's about to lever herself up to greet us, then decides against and sinks back into her seat. "You know I can't make faces out in this light," she says, surprisingly truculent.

"You'll recognise the voice."

Ollie whispers to me. "Say summat out loud. Bet you she can guess."

"What you want me to say?"

"Anything."

Nothing original comes to mind as I clear my throat so I offer Ollie's mam a few platitudes, smiling and trying to make eye contact past her shades so that she'll warm to me. "Good afternoon, Mrs Dunn. I'm really pleased to meet you. Ollie... Oliver's told me so much about you. I

118

understand you like listening to the radio." Giving her a bit of a hint, since Ollie's so keen for her to find me out.

"Telly's a waste o' time for me these days," she says, dismissing the set in the corner with a flick of her hand. "Not that the wireless is much to crack on."

I pull a face at Oliver, letting him know how I rate his description of her as a super-fan like himself. He seems a little hurt by my expression and I immediately regret it, realising he's mistaken my gurning for disrespect to his mam. I'm frantically thinking of something nice to say to compensate when she continues, "Your show's all right, though. It's Marc Niven, isn't it?"

Ollie lets out a quiet whoop like he's just won a line on the bingo and nudges me, inviting me to marvel at the wonder that is his mother. I move nearer to her.

"That's right, Mrs Dunn. Thanks for listening."

"Hmmph." She twists her face and turns her head away with a grunt that puts me in mind of a camel. Wherever Oliver gets his sunny disposition from it's not from these genes. She straightens up in her chair and I fancy I can detect milkiness in her eyes behind the dark glasses as she speaks again.

"Are they going to let you back on now they're supposed to have cleared things up?" There's an edge of disbelief in her voice that I imagine is connected with doubts she has about me.

"How do you mean, cleared things up?"

"With what they said on the news about the cousin, the babysitter."

I turn to Ollie for an interpretation, but he is looking as clueless as I am.

"What you on about, Mam?" he says, but in a deferential tone as if he needs to convince her he's not being cheeky. Nevertheless she clicks her tongue with impatience and sighs to let us know what a chore it is to explain.

"On the one o' clock news. They said a cousin of that girl, the coloured girl, was the one that phoned your programme. They had him on the news. Did it for a bit of fun, he says, cos he was bored with the babysitting. That's it."

"Babysitting?" I say it more to Oliver, not just because I can't make a connection with his mam but because she's got me half-afraid to press her any further. Mrs Dunn sighs again.

"He was in the house babysitting for her. That's what gave him the idea."

119

Things are beginning to click into place for me. That would, after all, explain why the call was made from Amina's number. Then Mrs Dunn throws everything up in the air again. She seems to shrug off her torpor at last and jabs a finger purposefully into the arm-rest as she says, "Tell you summat for nowt, Oliver. That wasn't the same one that phoned in on Valentine's Day."

"How do you know, Mam?"

"Voice was different. He might have the same accent, lingo sort of thing, but this one on the news was a younger feller, not so deep down."

"Are you sure?" How could she be, comparing a voice she's heard once today with one she heard once a week ago?

"Sure as eggs."

Well, she recognised me without any real prompting, but... a reliable witness? Dunno. Clear-up or cover-up, I've got to listen to this item for myself. "What time is it now?" I say out loud, too full of a sudden sense of urgency to look at the watch on my wrist.

"Nearly ten to two," says Oliver, consulting his.

"Is there a radio?" I start to say then, retreating from the foolishness of the question, "Any chance we could have the radio on for the two o' clock news?"

Ollie relishes the new excitement. Without even asking his mother for permission he rushes across to the radio on the sideboard and tunes in to the afternoon show, Kelly Coyle back in her usual slot. I'm momentarily distracted - trying to read the runes of the current political thinking from their presenter arrangements - while Oliver is seeking my attention for the matter uppermost on his agenda.

"Tea or coffee, Marc? We have both. Or hot chocolate."

Appropriately it's one of our own station mugs – a souvenir from one of Ollie's many visits to my road-show – that I'm draining of not-so-terrible instant coffee when the two o' clock news ends without a repeat of the item featuring Amina's babysitting cousin. That's hardly surprising; the shorter mid-afternoon bulletins tend to focus on the top news of the day, regional and national, and the little mystery surrounding my phone-in guests hardly compares to more bondage sex revelations from the minister's ex-wife or the royal opening of the road tunnel, whatever the ghost-hunters want to make of it. That means I'll have to tread water until the drive-time news programme, assuming they bother to repeat the clip at all. Too worked up to wait, I decide to take matters into my own hands. I ring in to Reception on my mobile, wandering into the Dunns' kitchen while I wait for an answer.

"Hi, it's Marc. Can you put me through to Jim Swinton, please?"

Talk about a pregnant pause. I can feel consternation vibrating down the line before Carol the receptionist says, uncertainly, "Oh, hi Marc. You know, I'm not sure if Jim is available to talk to you."

"What do you mean, not available? He's in, right?"

"Mmm, should be."

"Well, try ringing his extension and if he's there he'll pick it up."

"Well, it's not that, to be honest. Just… only I think the position is that you're not allowed access to members of staff, as it stands. That's what we've been told."

"But that's ridiculous. Jim's a personal friend. You can't stop me from talking to him."

"Just what we've been told, sorry. Mmm, you'll have to take it up with HR."

"You bet I will. Put me through to Alice Winter."

There's another pause, with Carol in an obvious dilemma, probably asking Julie sitting next to her what to do, then she comes back with, "Sorry, Marc, I'm not allowed. Best thing would be for you to send Alice an email. O-kay?" This last in a sing-song tone that means, 'Sorry, I'm about to cut you off', but before she gets the chance I stab my thumb in frustration at the red button on my phone.

"Fuck!"

I wheel round to see Ollie, halfway through a chocolate biscuit, glancing anxiously at his mam, though she seems completely unmoved by my cursing.

"All right, Marc?" he says as I walk back into the living-room.

"Not all right. They won't even let me talk to Jim."

His features cloud over to reflect mine, but he can't restrain his instinctive optimism for more than a moment. "Should I have a go?" he says, his round face lighting up with the idea like a clip-art symbol.

I contemplate the radiant, guileless, shambolic Oliver while I weigh opportunity against my prejudices and my legitimate objections; I've had personal experience of his tendency to abandon English as spoken by the rest of us. Ollie positively glows under my inspection.

"Better use your phone," I tell him, thinking about the caller display on the switchboard. "You want to speak to ops room support. If anybody asks, say you're a BT engineer."

Ollie nods enthusiastically, and scampers across to the sideboard for the telephone. It's modern enough to be cordless, but has one of

121

those expandable aerials emerging from the ear-piece like a field telephone or a transistor radio in disguise. He has the main number in his memory store, naturally, and soon enough he's speaking to either Carol or Julie.

"BT engineering," I hear him say, which must satisfy them because next thing he's winking at me and handing over the receiver.

"Is that Jim?"

"It is. Oh, Marc, is it? Thought they'd sent you to Siberia, pal."

"More or less, yeah. Your phone's not bugged, I hope?"

"Well, if it is, I'd just like to say for the record, Meg Reece is an arse-licking cunt, Neville Crawcrook is a cunt-licking arse, and vicey-versey. Exclusively available to demonstrate position sixty-nine for twats."

"I take it you're on your own there, Jim."

"I am."

"Good. Listen, you didn't happen to catch the lunchtime news, did you?"

"About your hoax caller? Yeah, I heard it."

"What do you think?"

"Well, at least they can't blame you now for ignoring a suicide call. And no ghosts involved, after all. Just an annoying little prick."

"There's a school of thought my end that reckons the babysitter's voice is different from the one on the night."

"Really? I suppose I wasn't taking that much notice. Well, anyway… do you care? I mean, the babysitter story works out better for you, dunnit? You know, nine day wonder, mystery solved apparently, forget it, get back to where you once belonged."

Jim's offering me a nugget of common sense here; why don't I take his advice? The lid's back on the can of worms.

"It's not as easy as that, Jim. There's other things involved, other people… I've no idea what I'm even talking about, but I just know there's something not right. I want to pursue it a bit further, anyway. No need for anybody else to know. Better if they didn't."

"Fair enough. What do you want me to do?"

"Do you think you could check the ROT of the lunchtime bulletin for me, when you've got a minute, on the quiet? Maybe have a listen to the Hassan clip again as well, to remind yourself. See what you think. Could you do that and ring me back?"

"I can do a bit better than that. How are you placed around four o' clock?"

"Hanging loose."

"Could you meet me at Bells and Whistles?"

"What's that, a pub?"

"Post-production place, back of The Quadrant. We use it sometimes for final mixes, they've got a much better desk than ours. I'm going to be there shortly, tarting some ads up. I'll take both files along and we can have a listen, yeah?"

"Sounds good. Thanks, Jim. You're a star."

"I'll leave the star business to you, matey. I'm happy under the radar. Just an oik, suits me. See you there."

I put the receiver down with a smile on my lips for Jim, and look up to see it magnified on Oliver, who is watching me, eyes shining. He leaves it a beat before he chirps, "Where we off to now, Marc?"

Just after four o' clock me and my shadow poke our heads round the door of Edit Suite C at Bells and Whistles, where Jim is already ensconced, cans dangling round his neck.

"Come on in, Marc, I've got these set up." If he's curious where Ollie fits into the picture he doesn't show it, just nods at him pleasantly and indicates a stool behind the two chairs ranged along the desk. "So, you want to remind yourself of what Hassan sounds like first, or go straight onto today's clip?"

"I've not heard the babysitter yet, so let's have a listen to that."

A button lights up green under Jim's outstretched finger and two waveforms appear in a pair of small windows above it, matching Kate Foreman's speech patterns as she introduces the item.

'Now, you may know we've been in the news ourselves over the last few days, following a strange incident when a man calling himself Hassan Malik rang our late night phone-in programme to send a Valentine message to a lady he described as his widow. That call sparked off a bit of a ghost hunt, and plenty of interest from our colleagues in the press. But now I can exclusively reveal that the mystery is solved. Earlier today I spoke on the phone to Anwar Malik, a cousin of the family involved, who admitted that it was him, not the late Hassan Malik, who made the Valentine's Day call.'

The insert Kate cues seems to be from a call on a mobile. Male voice, definitely British Asian.

'Yeah, it was meant to be a joke, but it kind of backfired.'

'What made you do it?' (Kate, professional empathy.)

'I was just bored. I was babysitting for my cousin and I had the radio on, so I thought I'd just do it. Just to see if anybody'd notice, really.'

'Did you not consider it would be hurtful to your family?'

123

'Never thought about it, really. Just a spur of the moment thing. I'm truly sorry about it now, though.'

'Do you have anything to say to your cousin?'

'Sorry. Astagfuralah.'

Jim hits the button and the waveforms fade from the display. "That's about it. Just a sign-off from Kate to finish."

"What's that he said at the end?"

"Dunno. Some Arab stuff. It had Allah in it. Something for Allah."

"Same guy, you reckon?"

Jim strokes his chin. "Well, I've had a listen to the other. Make your own mind up, then I'll let you know what I think."

I reflect on what I've heard so far. "First impressions, the voice is similar, but to me he sounds more casual." Ollie's heavy breathing behind reminds me he's there, so I turn to bring him into the discussion. "What do you think, Ollie?"

He shrugs. "Mam said younger."

"That figures. More informal, maybe."

Jim flexes his finger. "Ready to hear the original?"

"Sure."

He presses a button to the right of the first set, illuminating another pair of waveform windows. They spring to life as my radio voice fills the studio. I press down on my eyelids, focusing fiercely on Hassan (Anwar?) as he says, 'I should like to send all my love to Amina. Amina Begum Khan.'

I open my eyes. "He's more rounded. Richer."

Jim nods at this, and we both watch the waveforms dancing as we listen to the rest of the clip in silence. As soon as it finishes, Jim says, "Here's something interesting." He grabs the mouse on the desk and highlights two file names showing on the computer screen in the corner. One file is labelled ALLHASSAN, the other ALLANWAR. "I was playing about with these before you came. I've put all Hassan's lines – if it is Hassan – together in one file. Here, I'll drop him into Channels 1 and 2." He drags the file and deposits it, then comes back for the other as he continues. "Anwar's lines are all in this package, so let's give him Channels 3 and 4. I'll kill the audio, just watch the screens."

Some dextrous knob twiddling and button punching, and the desk lights up with two pairs of waveforms bobbing up and down either side of the desk, soundlessly.

"See the diff?" says Jim. "'Course you've got to allow for one being a landline and the other a mobile, but the levels on the recordings

124

were practically identical. The different spectrums – spectra, is it? – show you two different voice types. That's plain enough."

"If you say so, Jim." I study the pulsating graphs carefully. I don't have Jim's eye for it, but with concentration, yes, even I can see that the waves on the screens to my left are peaking more in the lower frequencies than those on the right. "So how conclusive is that?" I ask him.

"Does it for me. By the way, I noticed something else while I was working on this. I missed it before." Jim kills the two running playbacks and drags HASSAN 14FEB from his on-screen folder into the edit mode window. He lifts one earpiece over his left ear for a moment while he marks an in and an out point, then opens a channel saying, "Listen hard," and double-clicks.

I'm surprised that it's only my voice on Jim's edit, and just one line.

'Amina, is it? Nice name. Wife or girlfriend?'

"Play it again."

'Amina, is it? Nice name. Wife or girlfriend?'

I shake my head at Jim, unsure what's he's expecting me to hear. In the spirit of inclusion I look round at Oliver, and catch him in the act of freeing a pink marshmallow from an open bag in his coat pocket. "Sorry," he says, as he pops it into his mouth.

"Listen to what's *behind* your voice," says Jim. "Hang on, I'll try and boost it with the EQ." He puts his earphones on and adjusts knobs minutely with the main feed closed so that all I can hear for a while is the sound of Oliver masticating marshmallow.

"Try it now," Jim says at last, handing over the cans. He double-clicks on the file.

'Amina, is it? Nice name. Wife or girlfriend?'

There *is* something there, like the mewing of a cat, in the pause between *name* and *Wife*, and once more as the question ends.

"Again."

I blank out my voice and listen only to the background. It's there, not in the studio with me, but behind Hassan.

"There's somebody crying in the house," I say to Jim.

"There is," agrees Jim. "Sounds like a baby. Not so near to notice straightaway. Upstairs, I guess."

"That *is* interesting."

But what am I to make of it? A man claiming to be Hassan Malik – who has been dead three months - calls me, unquestionably from his home number. There's no knowing whether Amina is there... Could it be *her* crying in the background? It sounds more like a young child (obvious candidate, her little boy), but can we be sure, when it's so indistinct? The significant thing is it's a *real* sound, I mean one that grounds Hassan, makes *him* real, not some voice from beyond the grave. Then this other guy Anwar, supposedly a cousin, insists that *he* made the call from the house, even though it's clear to us now that he didn't. Is he just trying to protect Amina from media harassment? Maybe, but who knows? Certainly not me. I'm more confused than ever. And that's before I plug in the Emmanuel connection, if there really is one.

"You're very quiet, Marc," says Jim. "Not like you."

He and Ollie are both looking at me as if they're waiting for a Hercule Poirot exposition.

"Just trying to get my head round it, guys. I can't help thinking of that old joke. What did the farmer say when the motorist stopped to ask for directions? 'Well, If I were you, zur, I wouldn't start from 'ere.' That about sums it up for me."

Unexpectedly it's Jim who nudges me onto the way forward. He says, with such a flourish it surprises me as much as if Oliver had said it, *"Cherchez la femme. "*

Which is just the prompt I need to go house-hunting.

IX

The estate agent seems initially reluctant to arrange a viewing of 110
Prince Albert Road at just twenty-four hours' notice. I'm informed the
owner is in the process of vacating the place, with the removals people
there as we speak, and he (*he?*) has plans to finish decorating before
prospective buyers are allowed in. I blag my appointment by claiming I'm
on a whistle-stop tour of possibilities, looking to make a quick decision
before my new job starts up here in a month. The chance of an easy sale
with no chain wins the day and I'm told a lady called Samantha will meet
me for a quick trot round the house tomorrow at three-thirty. My heart
misses a beat when I hear who my contact will be, but whether that's
through fear of discovery or emotional associations with the name I don't
stop to analyse. I suppose it's possible that my ex-lover might have landed
a job with a property company, but unlikely I would say, knowing Sam.
I'm a mite disappointed that Amina won't be around at this stage, but at
least I've got my foot in the door, or will have soon.

I feel strangely let down, I have to confess, when I turn up at the
doorstep of 110 to find that the woman waiting for me with the keys is
not in fact my Sam, or anything like her. Relieved as well, of course, since
that would have completely blown the gaff but, hell, I might have traded
that for the chance of seeing her again…

As it is, this Samantha shows no sign of recognising me other
than as the potential buyer Tom Etherington, a designer currently based
in Liverpool. I have my ex-brother-in-law to thank for the alias this time,
though he's no more aware of it than Oliver was the other night.
Samantha is a bustling type of woman, mid-forties I guess, who just about
succeeds in shaking my hand, unlocking the front door and holding onto
her file at the same time. It's clear as we walk through, our steps echoing
in the front passageway, that the removal van has been and gone.

I'm not at all sure what I'm looking for here, just trying to get a
general sense of the place to help me build a picture of what may have
been the scene on the night of Hassan's telephone call, but it is hard to
find many clues in rooms that have been stripped of furniture and effects.
At least they've left the light bulbs in, which is just as well since we're
already losing daylight and Samantha has to locate a switch each time we
move to a new room. I try to keep my senses sharp as we walk through

the downstairs area, tuning out the agent's sales prattle while I stay focused on assimilating anything of possible relevance. One thing I can see easily in the bare rooms is where there are fittings and sockets which suggest telephone or internet connections. I've already noticed a single telephone point in the hall. There is a fairly large living-room at the front of the house, and an archway through the back wall of this room into a smaller dining area. The front window wall has a television aerial point in the corner and a double electric socket. The outside wall of the dining room also has two electric sockets and two telephone-type connections, the most likely spot for an internet source downstairs.

So far, so ordinary. As I walk through into the kitchen I can smell fresh paint - the decorating must have started. All the signs are that Amina had been planning this move anyway, though the media exposure might have forced her hand. Through the kitchen window I can see a tiny back yard.

"Can I take a look out here?"

Samantha finds the right key and lets me out, keeping vigil inside as if she expects squatters to invade should the house be left unguarded for a second. There's not much to see outside - three worn steps down to the damp concrete area where there's just enough room for a short clothes line, and the regulation green and black wheelie bins behind the yard gate. I trip the sensor light above the back door as I step out into a light drizzle. The gate is unlocked, so I wander through into the back lane to see what the access is like from this side of the property. There are double yellow lines painted both sides of the narrow lane, presumably to leave it free for the odd delivery van to squeeze through to the rear of shops in Springhill Gate, and for the council to collect the bins.

The neighbour's yard door is wide open. From my viewpoint in the middle of the lane I watch an old Asian woman, traditionally dressed and with her head covered, struggling down next door's back steps carrying a tied bin bag in one hand and pressing the other against the wall for support. She slowly brings the bag to the back gate where her bin is already so filled with rubbish that the lid can't shut properly. The woman seems only to notice me in the lane when she has finally reached her bin. She fixes me with a look of extraordinary contempt that she continues to hold as she crams her bag ineffectually into the other rubbish before swinging back the lid to let it rest on top of the pile. We stay staring at each other, saying nothing, until she puts her bony hand on the edge of the yard door and shuts it with more force than I'd expect from a frail old lady. I'm guessing she's not too keen on young white guys nosing about her neighbourhood.

Out of curiosity, I lift each of Amina's bin lids on my way back in. They are both completely empty and seem (I can smell the disinfectant) to have been recently scrubbed and sanitised. Amina is nothing if not house-proud.

"I've met the neighbours," I tell Samantha as I step in over the threshold.

"Aha. Asian?"

"Yes."

Subtly *sotto voce* Samantha says, "Just to reassure, there are lots of white people in this area too, Mr Etherington."

"I don't have a problem with it."

"Jolly good." Samantha switches back into bright mode. "Can I take you upstairs?" No innuendo intended, nor do I react as if there had been, which I might have done a week ago. We take a slight diversion at the foot of the staircase so she can show me a downstairs loo conversion, hardly more than a cupboard, with a miniscule sink. The floor has a dark patch below the basin, as if there has been a minor flood, but neither of us remarks upon it. What's much more interesting is what I find at the top of the stairs. A door. It's set in a plaster wall, clearly not part of the original design, separating the small landing at the top of the stairway from the bedrooms beyond.

"This is odd," I say, tapping the door frame as we pass through.

"Mmm, it is a bit unusual," Samantha agrees. "Good safety feature, though. Do you have little ones, Mr Etherington?"

"No, but if I had I think I'd be perfectly happy with one of those gates from Mothercare."

"Possibly, but this way you wouldn't have to worry so much about the noise from the TV waking them up."

"Or hear them crying," I say more or less to myself as we walk into the smaller of the two bedrooms at the front. My mind is on the Hassan recording, trying to place where he might have been when his little boy woke up. I look along the street from the bedroom window, confirming it's the one where I saw the woman's arm closing a curtain. The dimmer switch on the wall is another sign – this is probably where the child slept. There's nothing else remarkable about this room, nor the one next to it, nor the bedroom at the back, all completely stripped. No separate telephone line. One little detail I pick up, hardly significant, is that all the sockets upstairs have those flat plastic plugs covering the holes, presumably to protect the sockets from inquisitive fingers, though I hadn't seen any downstairs – maybe they've just forgotten to take these ones away.

The only other room upstairs is the combined bathroom and toilet and an airing cupboard, all empty. The ceiling outside the bathroom has a trapdoor, but I don't feel I can ask Samantha to let me look in the loft, even if we had a stepladder to do it, though I do notice the slight smudge of dust along the edge of the hatch that suggests it has been recently moved, so I guess anything that might have been stored up there has been taken along with everything else in the house.

"So, are you going to be working in the city centre, Mr Etherington?" Samantha asks as we're making our way downstairs. "Very convenient from this part of town."

"No, I'm… I work from home mainly."

"Well, you won't be disturbed here. You couldn't pick a quieter street. What do you think?"

"It is quiet, yes."

"I mean what do you think about making an offer?"

"Oh, I'm interested, certainly. Thing is… I'm wondering if I could meet the owner, before I make my mind up."

"There's no need, really. We have full responsibility for the sale. If you're looking to negotiate on price…"

"It's not that, honestly. I'm not trying to go behind your back. I'm just keen to know a little more about what it's like living here, you know, in this house, in the neighbourhood… From the horse's mouth, as it were," I add to save me from Samantha unloading her local knowledge.

"I can see where you're coming from," she says. "I can't promise. We were asked to handle all the details ourselves, but if you give me your contact number I'll see what I can do. I'll also be able to let you know if another bid comes in, give you a chance to top it. We do expect this property to go very quickly, Mr Etherington, so I'd recommend you don't take too long to make up your mind."

"That's good advice, Samantha, thanks." To keep up the pretence of not having a local base I give her my mobile number and even double-check with her which way I need to go for the city centre. I leave her trying to rub bird muck off the For Sale sign with a paper hankie, and as soon as I'm round the corner I drive off in the opposite direction.

Back at the flat I stretch out on my bed and stare at the ceiling, trying to fit what I've just seen to what I know about Amina and her dead husband, which isn't much more than jack shit. I'm certain now that Amina's move had been planned – the evidence of decorating suggests she'd already been tarting the house up for sale, and who leaving a place

130

in a hurry would take the time and trouble to clean out the dustbins? Besides, a move makes perfect sense with her and the kid left on her own – the house is too big for just the two of them. I've learnt nothing beyond the mundane, but that door at the top of the staircase bothers me. Why? Samantha's take on it was perfectly reasonable; it's there to stop the child falling down those dangerous stairs. But there's one detail about the door that still niggles. The fact that it has a keyhole.

Bizarre as it seems, I'm starting to relate some of what I've come across at Prince Albert Road to my eye-opening experience at Warkworth Street, the unobtrusive whore-house. Those added partitions and doors. The upstairs rooms that can be locked from the outside. The arrangement is slightly different in the Springhill property, and there are fewer bedrooms, but it could serve the same function. I'm even thinking that the below-stairs conversion into a toilet might have been for the convenience of clients gathering downstairs, drinking, waiting their turn. Was Hassan Malik another one involved in running a brothel? Were punters told to turn up at the back door, away from prying eyes, where they'd be checked out under the light and maybe a camera as I was in Warkworth Street? Was that behind the old woman's look of contempt, seeing me in the back lane, another of those strange men she has witnessed sneaking in and out of the house next door? And Amina...? Did she know about it? Was she even living in the house at the time? What about the baby?

I shift across to my desk. Before I left the edit suite yesterday Jim gave me a memory stick containing the two voice files we'd compared. I've had a couple more listens already, and now I want to hear the Hassan piece again through my cans so I can really concentrate on that background sound. I've trained my ears to virtually block out my voice at the point where the cry can be heard in the distance. Each time it has sounded like an infant voice, not so much crying as faintly protesting, bleating even. But suppose I ask myself a different question. Timid as it is, could this be the cry of a young girl – Edona's age, or less – startled by some painful abuse? lacerated? almost unheard behind firmly closed doors? It's possible.

Possible but not probable. Amina's house as a knocking-shop? Possible but not probable. Until I bring the other unlikely association into the equation. Until I remind myself of the two firm clues I have already collected, linking the fate of Hassan Malik with the movements of one person I know to be steeped in the sex trade cesspool. My bullet-headed friend Emmanuel.

131

Judging by the activity at its main entrance, where there's a couple of ambulances with their double doors open and people moving up and down the steps, the Western General Hospital gets a good deal busier around eleven on a Friday night than when I was here earlier in the week. It might have been more sensible for me to turn up at normal visiting time, but as I had no idea when Norman Tait would be starting his shift and since it's him I've come to see I thought I'd leave it until an hour when I was pretty sure the night porter would be on duty. Norman told me he always listens to my show, so I'm guessing he'll be here by now.

He's nowhere to be seen around his cubby-hole. There's a younger porter helping paramedics transfer a patient onto a trolley, so maybe I've been unlucky and come in on Norman's night off. I'm not inclined to ask this guy if Norman's working tonight as I don't want to draw attention to myself, so I sit down in the waiting area and basically skulk for a while. This is easier than I expected - nobody takes a blind bit of notice of me. The time is punctuated by flurries of activity around the main entrance and noises off of people and equipment moving about in corridors and bays, followed by periods of silence.

I've waited and watched for over twenty minutes with no sign of Norman, and have just resolved to leave at the half-hour mark when I hear someone whistling as if he owns the place, enjoying the echo as it bounces off the long bare walls. I stand to investigate and there is Norman, pushing an empty wheelchair along the corridor in my direction. He recognises me from thirty yards away and calls out cheerfully, "Aye-aye, back again? Not looking for a job, are you?" He pulls up alongside. "I see they haven't given you your old one back yet."

"Not yet, no."

"'Bout time they did, yon other lad's crap."

"There's some complications."

"You sound like one of our doctors. See, I was right about that being a hoax call. One of the family, wannit?"

"Apparently."

"Well, they've got no reason to keep you off your programme now. Do you want me to start a petition?"

"No, thanks for the offer. Actually, I'm on a sort of secondment. I'm doing a TV documentary. Investigative programme. That's what I've come to talk to you about." I've rehearsed this opener in my head and it must sound fairly convincing the way Norman reacts.

"It's not hospital hygiene, is it? There's things I've seen, I could tell you, but no names, no pack-drill, hear what I'm saying?"

"No, it's not that. Nothing to do with the health service. It's about... Listen, is there somewhere more private? Your office?"

Norman laughs. "My *office*, I like that. Howay, I'm due a break anyway. I'll make you a brew."

Despite Norman's self-deprecation, his hideout is quite comfortable in a posh broom-cupboard kind of way, fitted out with surplus hospital furniture. He sits me down at a square table that has an ancient cribbage board set up between the two facing chairs. There's a couple of lockers along the wall and one of those wooden bedside cabinets where Norman keeps his tea-making stuff and his portable radio. He fills the kettle from a low sink that has cleaning buckets stacked next to it while I fiddle with the game, randomly sticking pegs in holes, trying to recall the rules my grandad taught me. I wait until Norman has finished his domestic duties, and brought two steaming mugs across, before I continue with the tale I've concocted to explain why I'm pumping him for information instead of taking my suspicions to the police.

"Thing is, Norman, I'm working as an undercover reporter on a story that could fly or not, depending on how it stacks up."

"Fly?"

"I mean, we're at the research stage. We think there's something there, some very dodgy business going on, but we can't be certain yet. And I have to tell you this is potentially dangerous ground. Which is why it's so hush-hush. Can I trust you to keep the lid on? I mean, treat everything we talk about as completely confidential?"

"Son, you're looking at an ex-TA man here." Norman straightens his back for a moment, somehow seems to spruce up his senses as if he's readying himself for guard duty, then leans over his mug, fixing me with a firm stare. "I'm the sort of feller you can trust with your life, hear what I'm saying?"

"That's more than enough for me, Norman, thanks. I want to ask you about those two guys you saw me with the other night."

"The blokes in the BMW? I *knew* it would be them," he says, congratulating himself like he did about the hoax caller. "I knew there was something off. It's had me puzzled what you were doing with that pair."

"Gaining their confidence. Working on the inside, sort of thing."

"Miked up, were you?"

"No. As I said, we're still at the research stage. There might be nothing in it. But I was intrigued by you saying you'd seen them before. And in connection with Amina Begum Khan."

"Amina...?"

133

"The widow of the dead driver. Didn't you say you'd seen them with her?"

"Well, no, not *with* her. But they came in as well, looking for Mr Malik, or rather the baldy black one did, I never saw the other feller. He was first, as it happens. Baldy, I mean. She came after, with the police, time I saw her." Norman takes a sip of his tea.

"Could you give me as much detail as you can remember? This is really useful."

"Not much to tell, really," says Norman. "First I heard about the accident was when the ambulance came in with a DOA, sometime after two in the morning."

"DOA, Dead on Arrival?"

"Sorry, yeah. That was Mr Malik. According to the ambulance guys, there'd been no way of saving him. The fire must have caught hold once the car hit the bridge. It was well alight before somebody come across it and called 999. They thought it had been torched by twockers, that's what they call the thieving little bastards, innit? Happens all the time. In fact it wasn't till the fire engine got there they even realised anybody was left inside. Whether he'd had a seat belt on or what I don't know. They found him slumped under the dashboard."

"How much later did Amina... did his wife turn up?"

"Oh, a good bit later. Must have been getting on for six cos it wasn't that long before I went off shift. Her and this bloke came in the back of a police car."

"The guy with her... That wasn't our man, the bald-headed one?"

"No, no. This was an Asian type. Indian, Pakistani, same difference. Like I say, your man was earlier. I found him, well, what I thought was snooping around. Tell you the truth, I thought he was sniffing about looking for drugs to nick. We do get them. I followed him down the corridor and he's poking his head round half the doors, so I challenged him."

"What did he have to say?"

"He was quite apologetic, actually. Nearly too much, know what I mean? He said he was looking for his friend. Heard he'd been in a bad car crash and he was desperate to find out if he was going to be OK. Well, it figured, what he was saying, but I told him he couldn't just go wandering about like that. He asked me straight out if the guy was dead, said he needed to know before he contacted the family. I told him it wasn't my place to say. See, Marc, I could have told him, but I didn't. Not professional. I showed him the way to Admissions."

134

Norman stops to consider something, eyes in his brain, and I wait, hoping that he's dredging more from his memory bank. He looks up at me and clicks his fingers. "I bet it's drugs, innit? He's heard some talk on the way in, that's how he's got his story to trot out if he's copped snooping about. It *will* have been drugs he was after, am I right?"

"We think there's a drug link, yes." I feel a bit guilty, allowing Norm to jump to the wrong conclusion, but I'm still hacking my way to the truth myself and I feel I can't divulge the direction I'm moving in until I'm on surer ground. And definitely not until I can somehow get Edona safely away from all this. There are too many risks involved, and the more I'm learning about Emmanuel and his cronies the more evident the risks are becoming.

"He's a drug pusher, got it written all over him," Norman continues, quite animated now. "I hate those bastards. It's our lot has to pick up the pieces, hear what I'm saying? Overdoses, collapses. You wouldn't believe how young some of them are what gets rushed in here. You don't know whether to pity them or smack their faces. The dealers, though, they're just despicable. If I can help get some of them put away, well, count me in, son."

"I can't tell you how helpful you've been, Norman," I say, reaching across the table with a gesture that ends up being a cross between a handshake and a high five. And I mean it too. He rescued me last time I was here. Now, without his being aware of it, Norman Tait has provided me with a genuine Eureka moment.

X

The second time a mini-cab drops me at the corner of Warkworth Street I stand a minute or more gazing at the row of houses in the darkness, trying to work out what has changed here, wondering even whether the cab-driver has made a mistake and brought me to the wrong address. It takes that long to realise the difference is in me. For one thing I'm sober to my nerve ends, not having touched a drop over the two days I've researched and prepared for this. The other more significant shift started when I came here before and heard Edona's story. What hasn't changed is my trepidation as I walk up to the gate. Except that it's magnified tenfold, knowing what I have to try and do.

My first concern is over my Slavic acquaintance at the door. Perhaps he'll throw me out, if he remembers the trouble I put him to last time, or at least demand cash up front since I've shown myself to be an unreliable customer. But I pass the camera scrutiny and intercom challenge without the fuss I anticipated, and as Boris opens the door he greets me with a nod of familiarity that implies he already has me down as a regular client. He motions towards the reception lounge, where I can hear voices, but I touch his arm and incline my head to draw him to the space at the foot of the stairs. I'm privately thrilled when he responds to the gesture and follows quietly - the only way my plan can work is if I am the one in control.

"I'm here only for Edona," I tell him in an undertone. "She's the one I must have."

"Of course, sir, no problem," he says, matching his voice to mine. He glances up the stairs. "At this moment she is occupied. Come, have one drink, then you can go to her."

So much for control. As soon as he mentions that Edona is *occupied* I can feel prickles behind my eyes and a flush spreading from my neck. To cover up I massage my temples between thumb and ring finger saying, "Sorry, bloody migraine."

"Is there anything I can get for you, sir?" It's some posh household's loss that this guy didn't take a regular career path. Take away the ferret features and the ill-fitting suit, he could have made a serviceable butler in the new European style.

"No, I'm... Well, just a glass of water." Wondering how much they'll stick on the bill for that. "Do you have a Gents around here?"

The ever-helpful Boris points along the hallway. "On the left, please," he says, and withdraws discreetly to the lounge, synchronising his movements with mine so that we open the doors simultaneously and I half-expect to meet up with him on the other side of the wall.

Instead I find myself in a conventional downstairs lavatory, so domestic I might have been at a dinner party in a relative's home, except that the towels would have been fluffier, and not many of my lot would be likely to hang above their cistern that print of a naked woman with her finger on her clit. I check my face in the mirror to see if the word *impostor* is printed clearly on my forehead the way I feel it is. I'm relieved to see a fairly normal-looking reflection staring back at me, albeit a degree too intently. I wash my mouth out under the tap and blow into my cupped palm, testing for bad breath. I'm hoping Edona will be moved to give me one chaste kiss when she sees me again.

Once I step back into the hallway, to find that the doorman hasn't returned to his place, I have to deal with the temptation of exercising a spontaneous Plan B – simply dashing up the stairs, grabbing Edona and running like hell. The fact that I even contemplate this (how do I deal with the john, probably seven feet tall, who's with her right now? what are the chances of the hallway still being empty after I've run up and down two flights of stairs? what do we do if we make it to the roadside, hijack a passing car?), the fact that I consider it betrays my level of confidence in Plan A, now that I'm here to execute it in the timid flesh, not running the heroic reel in my mind for the thousandth time. But I'm going to have to stick with the original idea, fragile as it is, or leave without Edona. I need to keep the odds on my side (or less stacked against) by behaving like a normal punter at this stage. Lurking in the hallway is suspicious behaviour. I turn the handle on the lounge door.

Frankly, it's hard to appear unfazed by the scene I walk into. The furniture arrangement is slightly different from last time. A smoked-glass coffee table occupies part of the centre space. Two men with their backs to me have their seats tucked up to the table and they're bending over it as if they're trying to get closer to the female who is kneeling on the floor at the other side. She's the black girl from last week's line-up, and she's topless.

As I move to what's apparently my seat at the far wall, where Boris has set down a crystal tumbler of water, I see that the reason the men are bending over the table is they are each snorting up a line of white powder with a rolled-up banknote. The topless girl has a credit card in her

137

hand. Not, I'm surmising, for financial reasons, but because her job has been to cut the lines of coke. Almost simultaneously, the two men lean back and wipe a knuckle over their nose. One of them – young, trendily dressed – unfolds the twenty he's been using to sniff up the coke, and presents it to the girl, laughing. His friend follows his example. The black girl smiles and tucks both notes into the elastic of her knickers, being the only item she has on. I play nonchalant, sipping at my water, regretting I didn't ask for a scotch at least. I couldn't look more out of place if I was wearing a dog collar. A vicar's one, that is – the other sort would have raised no eyebrows here, just someone up for a little bondage and ritual humiliation.

What these guys seem to be up for is a little three-in-a-bed action. Soon enough they go out together with the black tart, one holding her wrist, the other slipping a hand in to massage her bum-cheek before they're even out of the room. Some roasting in store, I imagine. What makes her a tart in my mind, and not Edona? Because she looks like she's enjoying it? Maybe she's just a better actor, learning to survive here.

I'm left on my own for a while, trying to distract myself by guessing which country might be to blame for the faux-exotic instrumental wafting out of the speakers over my head, when Boris appears at the open door. His face reminds me of one of those kids' games where you mix up the features of different characters – his hospitality smile doesn't go with his assassin's eyes.

"Your favourite is waiting for you, sir. Please to go up."

As I pass through to the hall he makes to relieve me of my coat, like last time, but I'm ready for that.

"No." I give him what I hope is a knowing look. "I like to do it with it on." Boris plays his part with a wink in return, but he can't quite conceal the sneer or the venom welling in his throat as he watches me climb the stairs.

The way to Edona's room is imprinted as if I've been up to it a thousand times, which I have in my mind. I hesitate at the closed door, gripped by doubt. When that voice in my head is saying *this could turn out so badly* I hope it's addressing an anxiety for Edona, not just the cowardice in me. I rest my forehead on the door. She might be better off if I walk away now, let her find her own way of coping, like the black girl. I look down at the bolt fixed crudely onto the wood panel. That's what settles it for me.

I turn the handle and find Edona sitting at the head of the bed, facing the door, naked under the sheet clutched to her breast. If anything, she seems even frailer than last time – otherwise everything is as it was when I left her, just as if I'd returned moments later to collect something I'd left behind. Which I have.

"You come back to see me," says Edona with a smile, tired but genuine.

"I came back to get you. I mean, to take you away."

She curls her legs, making way for me on the bed, and looks seriously into my eyes as I sit down. "Are you buying me from the men, Marc? Am I for being your *shok shtrati?*"

"No. I wouldn't do that."

"I'm not minding."

She's caught me off guard. I hadn't even remotely considered that possibility. How much easier it could be, just hand over a sack of cash and take her away. I'd have to raise a loan – how much would they want? I haven't a clue – but, man, no hassle. No risk of being shot, thrown off some bridge… Just play them at their own game. Their rules. I reach out and Edona lets me take her hand. So trusting.

"Edona, we don't have much time. I need you to do something very dangerous."

Her eyes widen and her thin fingers turn cold in my hand. She searches my face for clues, must find some solace there while she bites her lip in anxiety because the next thing she says is, "All is danger now. So OK, I can do."

Letting loose of Edona's hand, I move back a little to create some space on the bed. I touch my lips briefly with a forefinger, warning her not to react as I bring out the props I've secreted inside various coat pockets and place them on the blanket between us – a disposable lighter, tin foil, a single shoelace, a table-spoon already blackened underneath, a couple of tubes of stage make-up, some cotton balls. Thus far Edona has watched transfixed, like a child at a magic show, as one item after another is added to the weird array on the bed. It's only when I peel off the bubble-wrap protecting a needle and syringe, doctored to appear used, that she has a quiver of alarm. I rush to pacify her, whispering, "It's OK, it's OK," willing her not to scream.

My scenario setting had envisaged a rapt and submissive Edona listening intently to my plan for her escape, entranced by its brilliance, obedient to the letter of my instructions. In reality explanation proves a much harder currency to exchange than emotion. I stumble through the detail of the plan, trying to hurry but only wasting time by having to repeat and rework my words several times before she has a clear enough understanding of what I need her to do. Worse, we're touching off nervousness in each other until I seriously doubt that either of us can find

139

the poise we need to carry it off. There are unexpected practical problems too. I'd assumed that, as a woman, she would naturally be able to apply the subtle touches of make-up required for the part she has to play, but I've over-estimated her experience with cosmetics and, without the benefit of a mirror, she struggles to apply the stuff properly, so I have to take on the job of make-up artist. Fortunately I had experimented on myself a bit while I was searching for just the right shades and colours. The results on Edona don't look too bad in the weak light of her room, but whether they'll pass under harsher inspection I can't really tell.

I'm still rushing to get everything laid out when a knock comes at the door. My hand goes out instinctively towards it and I screw my eyes tight as if the power of thought could prevent the door opening. I guess I look very much like a man in flinch mode, expecting a bullet in the head, but the handle doesn't turn. From outside, the voice of Boris. "Time is over. Please to come down," and he slopes off without disturbing us further. Thank Christ this time for his nauseating customer sensitivity.

"Be right with you!" I call after him, my voice cracking slightly. I'm trying to suppress the rising panic, busying myself with the final arrangements in Edona's room. She's already lying mutely in place, following me with her eyes as I set out the things beside her and hide the debris of our preparations under the bed. She's calmer than I am now, putting all her faith in me it seems, or maybe just composing herself for the drama to come. I have to meet her eyes at last, locking us in to that moment when we choose to do or not to do.

"Are you ready for this?"

She nods her head, says nothing. Her eyes are already closed by the time I'm at the door, and I creep out softly as from a child's bedroom, releasing the door handle slowly so she doesn't stir. Whether I'll be first to go back into that room or someone else, I don't know yet – the gambit rests on the next few minutes – but however it plays we're now in a game of convince and control. Starting now.

Boris is waiting at the foot of the stairs, hungry for his money on a slow night. This, I'm telling myself, is one of the clever parts of my plan. He will say something ingratiating, stroke my ego, tot up the bill, add on the number he first thought of, and ask for the cash. And so the first act begins.

"Truly, you are a man of the finest tastes, Mr Oliver," he says, on cue. "Edona I'll have for you always. She is the most delicate flower, eh?" And he kisses the tips of his fingers like a stage Italian while a new Plan C flashes through my brain, one I'd put into action instantly if only I'd had the foresight to bring a samurai sword in under my coat.

140

Boris, still smiling sweetly in his pantomime of appreciation for Edona but not so warmly as to unfreeze his eyes, rolls back his loose sleeve to study his wrist watch. "Well," he see-saws his right hand, "Perhaps we charge one hundred fifty pounds for your pleasant time this evening but, sir, please to know drinks is on our house tonight."

I make a show of going through my pockets, both coat and trousers, before I say, "Ah, I think I must have left my wallet upstairs."

A shadow of annoyance falls across the Slav's brow, but he remains polite, inviting me with a gesture to return to Edona's room. He looks to follow me up, which could work out just fine when the time is right, but there's another piece of the jigsaw I need to fit in first. I pause at the bottom stair, tap my hand on the knob of the banister as if something has just come to me, and turn to face Boris, saying, as lightly as I can, "Oh, you know, I've just realised... You're gonna hate me for this. I've forgotten about needing cash. Can't believe I've done it again. Sorry."

The blueprint in my head has Boris tutting, reaching for his mobile phone, calling Emmanuel to come and make the cashpoint run. He doesn't do any of those things. The shadow on his face turns to storm. Surprising me with his strength, he bodily lifts me off the step by my coat, pulls me into him, then flings me along the passage. My hand smacks against the banister, jarring my little finger as I try to keep from falling. Christ, that stings.

"Hey, back off. Cool it, will ya?"

Backing off is not on his mind. His rage, too long repressed by false courtesy, has erupted. He takes two paces forward, aims to knee me in the chin as I'm getting to my feet and hits me in the breastbone instead. I snap back and he jumps on me full-length. My knees come up in a reflex action and catch him in the groin as he drops on me. He squirms and I wriggle out from under him. What I could do now is stamp down hard on his nads and run like fuck out the front door, but I can't for Edona. Everything's gone pear-shaped.

"Listen, stop. Can we not just talk about this?" I sound like a Sunday School teacher. "I mean, genuine mistake, you know?"

I offer my hand to help him up, show willing, and the bastard grabs my leg, digs his teeth into my calf. So I *do* stamp on him, or try to — my foot seems to scrape off his pelvic bone and I end up on the floor with Boris. I get half a punch into his face as he's trying to roll over onto me, but that doesn't stop him. Seconds later he's got both my shoulders pinned down with his legs and I'm sniffing his crotch.

"How about I give you a blow job and we'll call it quits, eh?"

141

Maybe humour doesn't translate so well. He swings a back-hander with the force of a cricket bat. I have the excruciating sensation of my head swelling in all directions while being nailed firmly to the floor. My eyes, squeezed tight, seem to be leaking blood. When the trickle reaches the corner of my mouth I taste only salt. The relief that allows me to blink open my eyes lasts just until I focus on the wicked blade held inches above my face. Shit, this guy is serious. He's going to cut my fucking ears off.

A door opens directly behind my head. I'm torn between not daring to take my eyes from the knife, and needing to know who else I have to worry about, but the newcomer seems to be gunning for Boris. He gets a blast of hard consonants and I get the spray in a tirade of what I suppose to be Russian swear-words. Boris throws a few back, working himself up and waving his blade in the general direction of the new guy, giving me a chance to twist my head enough to discover that it's the barman, leaning in to have his say from the kitchen doorway. I can't understand a syllable but it's not hard to deduce the barman is suggesting that blood spilt on the hall carpet would be bad for business, while Boris is making the not unreasonable point that his partner in crime hasn't had to suffer the arrogance of this bilking little prick who deserves to have his brains skewered.

Fortunately for me the drinks man wins the argument and Boris reluctantly climbs off my chest, still eyeing me with a menacing glare as he tucks away his knife and replaces it with his cell phone. As he calls (I hope) Emmanuel I get back on my feet, my head still reeling. I want to ask the barman if he stocks aspirin among his drugs of choice, but I've already sailed too close to the wind with Boris so I go and sit quietly on the chair next to the TV monitor, trying to reassemble my plan while Boris huffily straightens out some of the creases in his suit and goes about his duties.

As well as my thumping headache courtesy of Boris I'm getting serious gyp from the little finger I banged against the banister rail. Possibly broken. Nursing the hand makes me think of Emmanuel in his new leather gloves. I have the feeling that if *he* chooses to whack me across the head my brain damage might be permanent. I'm really not looking forward to this next bit.

At least I've manoeuvred myself into a reasonable location. From here I can watch for Emmanuel and Stefan coming to the front door. Once they arrive I can remind Boris that my wallet is still up in Edona's room, so I have a valid excuse for going back up there at just the right time. Convince and control. I'm rehearsing the moves in my head when

142

Boris comes out of the reception room with a punter. This guy has a time-served civil servant look about him, and I imagine him handing over a battered briefcase along with his coat at the peg. He also seems very wary, looking around the hall and sideways at me, while Boris is in maximum reassurance mode, almost massaging his shoulders. I reckon this john has heard the commotion earlier and wonders what he's let himself in for. Boris guides him past my seat as if protecting him from a tethered dangerous dog, and points up the flight of stairs, whispering instructions in his ear.

I watch this bloke's progress up the stairs. I have a notion, because he seems so unsure of himself compared to most of the punters I have seen here, that Boris will have put him with the girl who is likely to appear least threatening. As I suspected, he doesn't turn at the top of the first flight, just pauses slightly before he tackles the second short flight, up to where there are only two bedrooms, one of them Edona's. If he goes into her room I've lost the initiative, will just have to go with the flow. I turn to study the CCTV screen; no sign of Emmanuel yet at the front door. Come on.

Even before I turn back to check the staircase I know that something has happened. Next to me I see Boris stiffen, then move forward. Now he's obscuring my view of the stairs. I stand and peer past his shoulder. Our nervous punter is back at the first landing, holding on to the banister like death. He looks as if he could have a heart attack and plunge headfirst any second. He tries to call to Boris, can't get his words out at first, then says with a croak, "The girl upstairs, I think she's... Needs help."

With that he sinks onto his backside on the top stair, thoroughly shaken. Boris dashes up two steps at a time and I follow him. Boris stops to check out the punter and I try to squeeze past him to get to Edona. He grabs a piece of my coat.

"*Nyet!*"

"He says she needs help. I'm a doctor."

"Is not your business. Go down."

The punter's eyes swivel from one to the other of us as we struggle on the stairs above him. He plucks Boris timidly by the sleeve. "She needs medical attention. If he's a doctor..."

Boris, utterly exasperated, finally lets go of my coat and yells through the banister rail, "Lev! Lev! *Nxitoj!*" while I take my chance and rush up the second flight of stairs. The door to Edona's room is half-open. I push it further to reveal her lying apparently comatose on the bed. A shoelace is tied around her thin left arm, just above the elbow, with a

143

blue-red bruise showing at the vein below. Next to her on the bed where it may have dropped from the vein is a used syringe, with blood visible in the chamber and the needle stained. In a mess on the bedside table the discarded paraphernalia of the heroin addict. Most shocking of all to the onlooker, Edona's closed face is deathly pale but for a blue tinge to her lips. Her fingers, too, spread helpless on the bare mattress, show nails faintly discoloured, unhealthy. As I move towards the bed I can just about detect the smell of vinegar. I kneel at the bedside and lean across the motionless girl, trying to catch her shallow breathing. My lips grazing her ear, I whisper softly, "You're doing fine. Not long now. Stay calm."

I'm glad Edona has the nous not to respond or move because the very next moment Boris appears at the doorway. I'm encouraged when I see shock register on his ferret face, as that tells me a couple of things instantly – he's fooled, at least for the moment, by our simulation, and he knows he has a big problem to deal with.

"What is... skag? How she get?"

"She got it from me. I was just trying to make her happy. God, look..." I pick up the plastic bag that I'd placed on the cabinet earlier, and show it to Boris, empty but for a few brown traces. "She must have mainlined the lot. We've got to get her to hospital – urgent."

"Not possible. If you are doctor, treat her right here."

"Sure. Do you have Nalaxone? A stomach pump? Oxygen?"

"No, of course..."

"That's what she needs - and quick - or she'll die."

He looks at me stony-faced and says very deliberately, "So, let her die." The heartless shit. My fingers find Edona's exposed arm, the nearest I dare get to holding her hand.

"Great. So then you'll have a body to get rid of. Maybe that's easy in your country but not here, you brainless goon." Boris moves towards me, but I'm in too deep now. "And what about the guy who found her? How do you know he'll stay quiet? Eh? What about me? You gonna kill me as well? Cos I'm not walking away." I can feel Edona's pulse quicken under my fingers. Boris is close to me now, ready to strike out, and I'm tensing myself. His eyes dart across to Edona. Did he see that little shiver of movement? Is he suspicious, or uncertain what to do? His hand is reaching inside his coat.

"What the fuck is going on here?" The voice, African-rich and deep, is at the bedroom door. Emmanuel.

"Massive heroin overdose," I say quickly, trying to grab back the initiative. "I've got to get her to the hospital right now."

"We can't leave her go," Boris argues. "Questions. Examine. Is like bomb. Everything blows."

"I can handle it," I say, exclusively to Emmanuel. "My neck's on the block as well. Look, I can keep it all hushed up. Just get me to my hospital. We're losing valuable time."

Emmanuel takes charge. "I know this doctor, he's with us," he says to Boris. "Get out there, clear the way. We want no eyeballing, no johns. Fix it."

Whether Boris is outranked by Emmanuel in the scheme of things I don't know, but he's certainly out-muscled and he has no choice but to do his bidding, pushing ungraciously past him at the bedroom door. I hear him calling for Lev as he makes his way downstairs, trying to reassert his authority around the house. Emmanuel stays in the doorway while I lean over to examine Edona. This close I can see her make-up is starting to run, probably with all the heat generated by people crowding into the tiny bedroom. I take off my coat and wrap it round her, obscuring as much of her face as I can without exciting suspicion, then put my arms under her slight frame to lift her easily from the bed.

"Is she going to make it, doc?" says Emmanuel, as if he were auditioning for a minor role in *Casualty*. I try my internet-learned smattering of knowledge on him, as I had with Boris.

"She needs a shot of Narcan, the sooner the better, and oxygen. If I can get her breathing controlled I'll be able to start gastric lavage (I remembered it!), stomach pump to get the toxin flushed out."

"I'll carry her for you."

"No, I have to stay close to monitor her condition. She may need resuscitation at any time. Best for you to keep well clear – it's vital we give her as much air as possible."

Emmanuel nods sagely and turns to go downstairs, ducking away from the sloping ceiling, keeping a respectful distance in front of us. Lev is on guard at the first landing. In the hallway Stefan is standing side by side with Boris. There is the atmosphere of a funeral, with these guys waiting to act as pallbearers. I bring Edona closer in to my shoulder as we pass a silently seething Boris on our way to the front door and out.

As soon as we're installed in the Beemer, we switch into emergency mode. Emmanuel gets Stefan to push down all the window buttons to give Edona plenty of air. Once we've hit the dual carriageway and Stefan puts his foot down it's like riding in a wind tunnel, which adds to the sense of urgency. I can feel Edona's bare legs getting colder and I try to stroke some circulation into them with my free hand, feeling some pain in my little finger, while she subtly snuggles into my armpit searching

145

for warmth. After a while I notice some of the theatrical make-up is rubbing off onto my shirt, leaving a tell-tale patch. I move my hand from her calf to the back of her head, aiming to hide the stain as Emmanuel turns to speak with me over the wind noise.

"How she doing, doc?"

"Hanging on in. As long as we get there soon."

"How you want to do this? You have a private entrance? Side door?"

"Er no, they'll all be locked. Just drop me where you did last time. I'll blag it, don't worry. In hospital, the doctor is god."

Emmanuel laughs, revealing his gold tooth. "Doctor is god, I like it."

We pass the rest of the short trip in silence except for the noise rushing past the car windows. When we get to the Western General, Stefan nearly takes a wing-mirror off as he negotiates the IN gate without changing down, and he screeches to a halt in the Ambulances Only bay. So much for a discreet entrance. Emmanuel rushes to open the back door and I shuffle across, bending well over Edona in my arms, not so much to avoid hitting my head as to keep us protected from too-close inspection as we get out. Emmanuel starts to follow as I carry Edona to the main doors. I have to risk yelling at him.

"No, stay outside! It's easier if I do this on my own."

Emmanuel raises a glove in acknowledgement. "Doctor is god," he jokes, and retreats to the car as the automatic doors open for us. To the right of Norman's cubby-hole is a row of parked wheelchairs. I grab the first one and empty Edona into it just as a porter, not Norman, emerges from behind the desk.

"Hey, it's not self-service, you know," he bawls. "What do you think you're doing?"

"It's OK, Norman Tait said I could use it."

"Norman Tait's not on tonight."

"Thought not. He wouldn't be letting that BMW park in the ambulance space."

"What BMW?" He hurries to the main entrance to investigate. As soon as his back is turned I wheel Edona round and sprint along the corridor under the sign marked Out-Patients Department.

What is it about hospitals? Twice we take a wrong turning and have to track back. Fortunately the duty porter hasn't caught up with us by the time I find my way to the out-patients' entrance. I stand waving my arms at the sensor above the glass doors, but they remain firmly shut. At one side of the doors is a red square box housing a fire alarm. I lift my

146

elbow and jab it through the Perspex cover. Edona jumps at the sound of the alarm, shockingly loud in the quiet of the empty corridor. I wave my hand at the sensor – halleluiah, the doors slide open.

In the outpatients' car park – almost full when I came a few hours ago – my Audi TT is now the only vehicle to be seen. A worrying thought occurs as I push Edona's wheelchair along the path towards it. I paid for my ticket up to the stated closing time at six o' clock, but suppose there's no parking allowed after that? How come mine is the only car there? What if I've been clamped?

There's a tingle of relief when we roll up to the car. A quick check around confirms there is no clamp, not even a penalty notice on the windscreen. Nor have I lost my keys in the fight with Boris or our mad dash through the hospital. I open up and gently lift Edona into the passenger seat, leaving her my coat to cover herself.

"Sorry, Norman, I know I should be returning this," I say aloud as I abandon the wheelchair by the ticket machine and climb into the car next to Edona. She turns as I settle in the seat next to her and squeezes my arm gently with both hands, smiling.

"Told you I'd get you out," I say, with just a touch of self-congratulation. I lean across to fasten her seat belt securely before I do mine. The plan hasn't yet developed to the point where I've worked out how I'm going to help Edona get some independence in this country, but first things first. We're safe and home free.

I switch on my headlights and drive along the narrow drag by the side of the main hospital building. Now the excitement is over I've suddenly realised that I've been so absorbed in creating the escape plan I've forgotten to buy groceries this weekend. There's barely a crust in the flat between the two of us. The *two* of us. Distracted by these thoughts, I fail to notice the give way markings and drive straight across the path of a car coming down the main hospital road. I see it peripherally and we both jam on our brakes, missing a prang by inches. My fault. I acknowledge that, pointing two fingers to my temple and pulling an imaginary trigger as I turn to show the other driver apologetic eyebrows and a wry grin. The grin freezes on me. I find myself staring through the windscreen of a silver BMW. I don't need to see through the tinted glass to know who's behind the wheel.

The Audi exhaust roars as I launch from a standing start, my back wheel mounting the kerb as I swing hard left to squeeze past the front end of the Beemer. Stefan is right up my arse as I speed down to the OUT gate. I'm about to ignore another give way sign, but deliberately this time – I just can't afford to stop. I cringe, fully expecting a side-on

147

collision as the car leaps out blindly into the main road. But I'm lucky, nothing coming. Not so lucky. Stefan gets away with it too, bar a blast on the horn from a taxi driver forced into an emergency stop.

I'm travelling in exactly the opposite direction to the flat, but right now that's the least of my worries. I step on the pedal, heading towards the city centre, but suddenly swing a right, hoping that Stefan will be forced to stop for the car that's coming the other way. He does momentarily, but it's only seconds before I'm seeing his headlights again in my rear-view mirror.

I throttle through the next crossroads, still riding my luck, and continue along the street that I now recognise is descending towards the river. If we keep going this way I'll soon be running out of options. At the next junction I pull a right so hard that Edona is thrown sideways into the door panel.

"Sorry."

Edona briefly puts her hand over mine on the gear-stick – to bond with me or to steady herself – and as my eyes flick in response I catch her tracing the sign of the cross on her chest with her other hand.

We're on Drummond Road, boy racer territory. Chicanes have been added at regular intervals to break up the tempting long straight line of tarmac. My first reaction is to curse until I realise my compact TT is better-built for nipping around the obstacles than the Beemer. I start wriggling through as fast as I dare, bumping shoulders with Edona as we lurch from side to side. Another glance in the mirror reassures that I'm putting some distance between us and Stefan on this stretch. Big mistake. Distracted, I clip the next chicane hard and my front wheel lifts, slewing the car to the right.

"Shit!"

I fight with the steering wheel, trying to manage the skid as we're swiped into the far gutter. Both tyres scrape the kerb helping to keep us on the road, and by the next chicane I have just enough control to negotiate the gap. I don't look in my mirror again until I'm safely through the last of the obstacles.

At the end of the straight the road curves round and up. For a moment I have lost the headlights behind. I notice a narrow lane to my left and on instinct hit the brake and make a hard left into the cut, hopefully out of vision from the chasing car. I soon discover that this short lane leads only to a warehouse with a loading bay and turning circle in front of it. If Stefan has spotted my tail-light disappearing he can block us off easy and we're finished.

I do a three-sixty in front of the warehouse, killing my lights before I complete the turn, and we sit facing the exit but out of sight from Drummond Road. It comes to me too late that I should have cut my engine as well to give me a better chance of hearing the Beemer go by. As it is I can't hear a thing, nor can I see any lights from the road.

We wait in silence for what seems like several minutes, though I suspect anxiety is playing havoc with my sense of time. If my tactic has worked they could be miles away by now, maybe given up the chase and gone back to Boris. On the other hand, once they realise we're not in front of them they might double back, and we could be unlucky enough to bump into them when we set off again. Worst case scenario, they might have seen us cut up this narrow lane and they're waiting to pounce, like a stoat watching quietly for a rabbit to pop out of its hole.

I'm tempted to get out of the car and sneak down to Drummond Road in the shadows to check the lie of the land, but that would mean leaving Edona alone and vulnerable, quite apart from leaving me without the protection of metal over my head if they do happen to be waiting at the end of the lane. No, the only practical thing to do is to take our chance in the Audi. I turn to look at Edona, still pale with the make-up so I'm not sure if her degree of stress matches mine.

"You might want to try that cross thing again."

"Pardon me?"

I hold up my left hand and show her my crossed fingers. She smiles, reaches across to take my hand and uses it to touch her forehead, the space between her breasts, her left and right shoulder. Finally, she kisses the back of my hand and returns it gently to me. I could die happy.

I leave the headlights off while I taxi slowly through the cut, guided by the street lamps at the opening to the lane. A yard or two from the exit I stop and roll down my window, straining to hear anything from the road beyond, but the only sound I pick up is my own engine noise vibrating off the walls. I raise the window again, for protection, place both hands on the steering wheel and roar out of the cut onto Drummond Road. I just miss clipping my front wheels on the opposite kerb as I pull the car round left in an arc and accelerate to sixty on the straight before I switch on the headlights. Nobody in front. Nobody, thankfully, behind.

From Drummond Road to my place is less than ten minutes even travelling at thirty, so I guess we make it in much less time, but it feels far longer with every nerve tingling and attention at snapping-point, on the lookout for a silver BMW. In fact we only see a couple of innocent vehicles, as you would expect at this time of a Monday night, and I reach

149

my spot outside the flat with no more drama. I hesitate to leave the car in such a visible position on the road, but I really don't have an alternative. I park up and come round to open the passenger door for Edona. I offer to carry her, saving her bare feet, but she declines sweetly.

"OK to walk, is fine. Thank you, Marc, from my heart. I'm meaning for all."

"Well, not quite to plan, but we're here."

Adjusting my coat round Edona's shoulders, I leave my hands there as I guide her gently through the main door and up the stairs to the flat. I really wish I had remembered about the groceries. She tries to hide a shiver as she waits on the cold landing while I search for my key, and shakes her head with a smile when she sees me noticing. I turn the key and push open the door. In the interval between the door opening and my reaching for the light switch I sense a movement in the darkness of the room. I suddenly feel defenceless, my arm stretched out, a target. The light goes on. I blink once, adjusting to the brightness, peering into the room. Edona, half-naked, exposed by the pool of light, moves in to me, seeking cover. A figure rises from my bed at the far wall, and faces the two of us framed in the doorway. For a moment I'm speechless, then, vacuously, "Oh, hello, Sam. You've come back."

XI

There's something I need to say about why Sam left me last month. A confession, I'd have to call it, from the guilty party. It's been easy so far, since I'm the one telling this story, to paint myself as pretty much the good guy. Even, like just now, the hero. I haven't done this deliberately, I mean, I didn't set out with that intention. Quite the opposite – I've tried to be frank and open, and if you look back at these notes you'll see there's quite a few occasions where I've held my hands up to being a bastard or a schmuck, such as the way I've treated Oliver at times, or where my motivation has been a bit iffy or, let's be honest, where carnal desire has raised its ugly prick. Yes, well, it's that last item I'm going to have to come back to now. There's a thread I've left lying, a piece of information I haven't supplied yet. Just because, quite frankly, I'm ashamed of it and I'd rather not talk about it. I deeply wish it hadn't happened.

It was New Year's Eve. Or, strictly speaking in terms of the act, the early hours of New Year's Day. It's the one time in the year when people in the entertainment business can charge just about anything for their services because all the local impresarios are desperate to put on some sort of do for the revellers, but nobody wants to work. The station was on festive schedule which meant I was off for the week, and so was Sam. We'd been invited to see the New Year in and stay over at her big sister's house. They were having quite a get-together, with their daughter home from university and various expat relatives back in the region for a couple of days. But somebody made me an offer I couldn't refuse. It was the same guy that had arranged the Christmas show at the Arena who asked me to host the New Year party there, only at four times the normal fee, cash in hand. As I said to Sam, if we want to save up for a house we can't afford to turn down that kind of opportunity. She wasn't too chuffed though, even after I promised to join her at her sister's as soon as my stint was over.

This was one of very few gigs I'd ever done without Oliver hanging around my deck all night – thinking about it now, I guess he felt he ought to be at home with his mam to see the New Year in. There were plenty of others to take his place though, including a fair smattering of fit-looking girls, some with boyfriends but plenty without. To be candid, I found myself wondering whether Oliver's presence had put some females off in the past; he looks so nerdish, even creepy in certain lights, if you don't know how harmless he really is.

Naturally, being New Year, the booze was flowing free (well, quite expensive actually, but another perk for me was not having to pay for a drink all night), plus uppers, 'E' etc which have never been my bag but the younger crowd seem to munch them like sweets even though a Marc Niven gig could hardly be classed as a rave. I was drinking fairly steadily, but not so I couldn't do a professional job. I'm not normally one for those raunchy games on stage, but the occasion seemed to demand it so there were various smutty things done with balloons and squirty cream as we warmed up for midnight.

One dark-haired beauty, Anji, who was wearing the skimpiest red-and-black spangly number, seemed to be up for everything, and when she wasn't joining in one of the games she stuck very close to me at the side of the stage. She'd started out with a couple of girlfriends, but I saw less and less of them as the night wore on. Picked off, I suppose, by some of the guys looking for action. Anji had her share of offers – alluring would be a good word for her – but she didn't seem interested other than taking part in the silliness on stage. In fact the only person she danced with all night was me. Every so often when I played a tune that got me moving she'd come up and briefly make it a twosome, not so much dancing as fluttering in and out as if I was a lamp attracting her. She kept getting me to sign things too – her ticket, at least two of my publicity shots and, towards the end of the night, her own bare shoulder. Quite an ego-booster, I'll tell you, made me put a swagger on. After a while I started ordering a vodka and Coke for Anji every time a fresh lager was on its way for me.

Time came for the countdown to midnight, and the guy with the follow spot homed right in. I could see nothing beyond the glare, but I remember Anji being so close as I marked off the seconds that the hard edge of the spot was broken by a band of glitter on her wrist. The crowd joined in on the final count.

"Four, three, two, one… Happy New Year!"

The follow spot left me and started to move over the heads of dancers belting out *Auld Lang Syne* and crushing towards each other in the middle of the floor. Out of the sudden darkness on stage came perfume, shimmer and the soft touch of fingers around the nape of my neck. Anji slunk into me with the litheness of a cat.

"Happy New Year, Marc."

152

She kissed me, surprised me with her tongue reaching inside my mouth. I responded, tasting a lick of lipstick as I eased myself in. Anji pushed her body further into mine, playing her fingers down my back to nestle under the waistband of my jeans. Again I followed her lead, as if we were playing an adult version of Simon Says. Moving my hands down to rest on her bum-cheeks, feeling her panty-line under my fingers. As we kissed, she made a slow belly-dancer movement against my arousal, and when we stopped she ran a palm all the way down my front, lingering on the bump, shielding her hand between our bodies. She lifted her eyes to mine.

"I'll wait for you after then, eh?" she said, then undid a button of my shirt, kissed my chest once, and slipped away to the Ladies to fix her make-up while I moved strategically behind the desk, burying myself in the serious work of cueing the next track.

Two hours later the crowd was reluctantly moving off, coaxed to the exits by the ever-subtle Arena Security, while Dave the roadie and I were winding cables and packing flight cases on stage. Anji was being Girl Friday, carefully tidying what was left of the publicity photos, removing dirty glasses from the tops of speakers and placing them on the floor for the cleaners to take away. Dave caught my eye as we both bent down, going for the same cable, and he lifted his eyebrows to me, with the slightest inclination of his chin towards Anji. I just said "Me Tarzan," quietly, making Dave grin and shake his head.

After we'd loaded Dave's van at the back of the complex - Anji chafing her elbows against the cold as she propped open the emergency exit with her pert little backside - Dave touched my arm and said, "I'm away for a smoke, be about ten minutes or so, right?" and disappeared round the corner of the building. His expectation, as well as hers, was what tore away the last strip of my resistance against the temptation. It was almost as if I would be letting him down if I *didn't* do it. I didn't want him to see me retreating from my earlier bravado – it would be as bad as walking away from a fight. Even so I hesitated for a beat, nerves and conscience knocking, before I opened the passenger door of the van.

"It's a bit warmer in here," I said to Anji, and she left her post smartly, letting the emergency door swing shut as she clipped across to me in her short stilettos. I helped her into the cabin with a hand under her bottom and she shuffled along the bench seat to make room for me.

"Sorry, but we've not got long," I said, unhooking her doll-size shoulder bag and placing it gently on the floor. She dropped the same shoulder, swivelled her hips and prised off her shoes so that by the time I turned back to her she was ready, supine, chin raised, for our second deep kiss of the night, and more.

I know people do it all the time, have done all over the world since the invention of the internal combustion engine, but I'd never actually made love in a vehicle before. Whether Anji had, until that night, I've no idea, but she was responsive to every touch and turn, every shift in position we seemed to need to make it work in that cramped space. Our love-making was lustful and clumsy, clothes half-on, half-off, bodies turning in, around, behind, upside-down, kneeling on the floor, sprawling on the seat, half-jammed against the dashboard, randomly bumping against the gear-stick or the handbrake. It was awkward, chaotic, exciting. I didn't use a condom – never carried one in hope as this sort of thing didn't happen – and if Anji had one in her bag she never offered it to me or made any move to stop me as I entered her here and there and, finally, shaftingly, shaggingly, climaxed with protracted moans from both of us, Anji smearing lipstick on the seat, me stretching and straining my torso in ecstasy.

The quiet afterwards was almost eerie by contrast. I don't mean the peaceful afterglow quiet, the satiation. I mean the getting-it-back-together quiet – wiping down mess, buttoning up clothes, concentrating on the functional to excuse not talking, avoiding eye contact. When Dave reappeared, with apparently expert timing, the three of us drove without speaking to the taxi rank at the railway station. I asked Dave to wait for me while I climbed out of the cabin with Anji.

"Look, I don't know how far away you live, but will this cover your taxi fare? It'll be dearer than usual, being New Year." I handed her two twenties which she took a little shame-faced – embarrassed, I'd say, about accepting money from me – but she held onto my hand as I offered it. We stood a little awkwardly like this, not looking at each other, then she kissed my hand, her eyes, soft and liquid, searching for mine like a close-up from some Jane Austen drama.

"Are you sorry you did it?" she asks, unexpectedly.

"No. No, why should I be? It was... amazing."

"Thanks, Marc. Have a nice New Year."

"All the best." I sounded as if I was passing her in the corridor at work.

She stepped across to the only taxi waiting at the rank and, after a brief conversation with the driver through the window, opened a back door and slipped in, holding her dress down modestly. I lifted a hand as she rode away, then climbed back into the van beside Dave. "Would you mind dropping me at Welbeck Grange?" I asked him.

154

The party was in full swing at Sam's sister's and it took three rings for them to hear me at the door. Nothing wild, you understand, just the music was pretty loud and there were plenty of guests, including some of the neighbours who had wandered in, all competing to share their tales of house prices, holidays and appalling customer service. Sam was in the kitchen warming some corned beef pie in the microwave (for me, as it happens) so our New Year kiss was a bit perfunctory, but enough for her to jerk her head back to look at me strangely and say, "What have you been doing? You smell of baby wipes."

"Oh, I found them in Dave's van. I was sweating like the proverbial from the gig, and having to load up after."

"You're not supposed to use them on your face."

"Just to cool down, was all. Do you think Chrissie would mind if I went up and used her shower?"

"What, now? I've just put this on a plate for you. Anyway, you can't wander round having showers in the middle of a do, not with all these people here."

"I'm honking, though," I said through a mouthful of corned beef, trying to act normal but at the same time taking my plate of pie to the far kitchen bench so Sam wouldn't catch the whiff of Anji on me.

"Our toilet bag's up in the spare room. Go and splash some stuff on, you'll be fine. And don't be long – I'm sick of people asking where you are."

I had to wait for someone using the bathroom loo, exchanging a brief 'All the best' as we passed on the landing, but when I finally got the bathroom door locked behind me I went into overdrive, tearing all my clothes off as if I'd had a last-minute invitation to an orgy. I felt permeated with the smell of Anji and illicit sex, even more so with my genitals released to the air. I washed them thoroughly, using Chrissie's soap, and lathered all parts of the body that Anji could have touched, which was just about everywhere. Then I dried off, talced and sprayed man perfume all over myself from the toilet bag before I put my clothes back on. I wished I dared make a complete change into tomorrow's stuff, but I knew that would just make Sam suspicious.

I felt I'd done enough to get through the rest of the party without somebody exposing me as a rabid adulterer, but when we were on our way to bed around four o' clock in the morning I went through the same process in the bathroom as well as cleaning my teeth thoroughly, gargling mouthwash and dipping under the tap, pouring cold water over my lips for an obsessive amount of time, so that Sam asked, "Have you been making your will in there?" when I eventually joined her in the spare bed. I knew exactly how Lady Macbeth felt, trying to wash away that damn'd spot.

I lay apart from Sam in the bed, not turning my back because we would only do that if we were in the huff with each other, but avoiding physical contact, still feeling contaminated. She snuggled up to me though, giving me little nibbles on my mouth and neck, then my shoulder, rubbing the inside of her ankle against my leg. When I didn't respond she stroked her fingers over my nipples, then down my front, as Anji had done, and felt for my cock, cradling it in her hand. I could feel it lying there, damp and limp.

"Mmm, call that a New Year present?" she said quietly in the dark. "Wham bam, thank you Sam. Not."

"I'm tired, that's all. Been a long night."

She wanked my sorry cock rhythmically three or four times then gave up and let it go, dropping her hand to the space between us. I kept my eyes closed, but I could sense hers on me, watching my face. After a minute she turned her back on me and lay silently on her side and I lay watching her until I was sure she was asleep.

The strange thing is, it's not as if I hadn't been there before, with Linda. Only that time the lover was Sam. Why did I not feel that overwhelming sense of guilt then - I mean about Sam - the many times we did it in her bed-sit while I was still in my relationship with… that is, still living with, Linda? If anything, it was the opposite. Towards the end I felt guilty when I'd had sex with my wife, and seen Sam later, as if I was letting *her* down, as if I wasn't taking our relationship seriously, as if I was being unfaithful to Sam way back then. I suppose in a sense I was. Maybe because with Sam it was a slow-burning affair. I didn't just take her right there and then, as I'd done with Anji because she was easy and available. With us, it grew into something. Slowly. Naturally. Inevitably. I guess the difference, when you come down to it, was love.

Our coolness with each other lasted all the next day, and I was waiting for it to build up to a row, but it didn't, even after we'd said our goodbyes to Chrissie and the clan, and gone back to the flat. We sat and watched TV most of the evening with a bottle of red between us, picking at some leftovers from the party that Chrissie had insisted on us taking when we left. We hardly talked at all. That night, even though Sam came to bed with her nightie on, I showed willing, tried to give her what she'd

156

wanted at her sister's, but Sam was having none of it, told me to stop pestering, lay facing away from me, with her nightie pulled firmly down over her bum.

I suppose she was giving me the signal for the row to start, but I wasn't going to be drawn into it, not knowing where it was going to end, so I avoided doing what I would normally do, asking her what's up to release the valve, knowing that after the blow-up and the tears we'd generally be all right again. Because this one wasn't over some trivial annoyance, and I didn't know how to negotiate my way round it, so I pretended not to notice her mood. Did that for the rest of the holiday, actually, and by the end of it we were more or less talking to each other normally, getting on with things without ever getting close, just kind of existing side by side in an indifferent sort of way. It wasn't unlike living with Linda again. Part of me was aching to get back to work, just to break the cycle, except of course Sam would be with me there as well.

We arrived at the radio station an hour or so earlier than normal, knowing there would be a backlog of stuff to wade through before we could prepare properly for the programme, plus I had a boxful of CDs and tracks I'd borrowed for the two Arena shows that I had to book back in to the music library. While Sam sorted out coffee I logged onto the computer so she could get on with checking through the emails. A sudden thought occurred, one that sent alarm bells ringing. What if Anji had sent me an email, using my contact details from the station website? She wasn't to know that anybody but me read my messages, much less my partner. She might be saying *anything* about the other night. I sat at Sam's chair and started to work through the clutter in the inbox. Sam pushed through the ops room door with the coffees.

"I'm on a roll with these," I said, my eyes on the screen. "Why don't you take that lot upstairs, book 'em back in? I'll have everything cleared by the time you've done."

"Fair enough," Sam said. She set down one coffee mug next to me and did a balancing act with the other on top of the DJ box as she negotiated her way out again. I know I should have held the door open for her, but I didn't - I was too desperate to track down any incriminating evidence and get rid of it while she was gone.

I needn't have been so paranoid. There wasn't a squeak from Anji among the emails – a huge relief, as I'd been having nightmares about her wanting to carry on the relationship in some way. Thank god, it looked as if she was happy to treat what we'd done together as a one-night fling.

That was it for me. I'd had my scare and I was never going to put myself into that position again. The last thing I wanted to do was hurt Sam. I'd make it up to her somehow, put the smile back on her face. If I needed reminding how much I loved her, this little escapade, in an odd way, had done it.

When Sam came back to prepare for the show I was deliberately upbeat, chatting to her about getting into the groove again, full of ideas about things we could do with the programme for the new year, but I have to admit it was hard work. She still hadn't got over my huff with me, and I knew I'd made a basic error letting her struggle with that box in the doorway when all I had to do was stand up to lend a hand – little things like that can sometimes just turn it for Sam. Still, by the time I was on-air and we really were into the swing of things I could see her through the glass chatting cheerfully with the callers, smiling down the phone, seemingly back to normal.

Which lasted precisely until two in the morning when we handed over to Alex Ray and were on our way home. We were back to square one. She said nothing to me in the car, went straight to bed without our usual nightcap, and carried on with the cold shoulder treatment. Next morning she was up earlier than usual, got dressed, and said, "I'm going out for a while. There's bacon in the fridge," and was down the stairs and away before I even had my head off the pillow.

It must have been nearly six hours later when the key turned in the door and she marched in with what I guessed was clothes shopping from the New Year sales in one hand, and something in an oversize carrier bag in the other. I'd just been idling the afternoon away really, playing a computer game when she got back.

"Retail therapy?" I said, looking at the bags. She ignored the comment, just placed the smaller bags down on the bed, and shook out the contents of the larger bag onto the floor. It was one of those massive sports holdalls, the kind of bag you could put cricket pads and stumps in as well as kit for a whole team. Only Sam wasn't intending to use it for sports. She laid it out on the bed, unzipped the flap all the way round, transferred all her shopping into the holdall, then started packing it with her stuff from our drawers and cupboards.

"What are you doing?" I said, leaving my desk to come and stand behind her. The question was redundant - what I really meant was *why*, except by now that was obviously a no-brainer as well, so I guess the real questions were *what* do you know and *how* did you find out? But I couldn't ask those questions at this stage. Didn't need to. Sam was about to answer them anyway.

158

She straightened her back, half-turned to glare at me coldly, and reached into the pocket of her leather coat. She handed over what looked like a note – I thought it must be her Dear John letter to me – but when I opened it out I found myself gazing at my own grinning face, creased across the nose where the picture had been folded and put in Sam's pocket. It was one of my publicity shots. I stared at it blankly until Sam lost patience.

"Other side," she said. I turned the photo over, and there on the bottom half of the white card, written probably with the same black permanent marker I always used for autographs, was a mobile telephone number and a short message. *Call me! Anji xx*

"Where did you get this?" I said, my eyes still on the card. I have to admit that, even with the blood chilling in me, my brain was already at work on innocent explanations.

"If you hadn't been too lazy to do your own library filing, I wouldn't have found it at all," said Sam. "Not that it was any big surprise."

Shit! My mind leapt back to the Arena, Anji tidying up my stuff while I helped Dave with the get-out. But it's circumstantial evidence.

"I've no idea who this is. You know what it's like at the gigs, there's loads of people come round looking for photos and freebies. Some girl must have written this while she was in the queue or whatever. Having a laugh with her mates, probably. Or maybe she fancies me, I can't help that, can I? I don't even know what she looks like."

"She wouldn't be a brunette with a shimmery little red and black dress, then? Showing her knickers up on stage with you half the night."

"Doesn't ring…"

"Don't, Marc. Don't even go there, cos I'm there already. If you're going to carry on behind my back you shouldn't start the first round in full view of fifteen hundred people. Including some that know me as well as you."

I was floundering. Outright denial now out of the question, I had to go for damage limitation. "Look, it was just a New Year kiss…"

"I've said, don't start with the excuses. I know about her staying behind at the end of the gig. In fact I probably know more about this girl than you do."

"What do you mean?"

Sam paused, making sure she had my full attention. "Because I rang the number on that card this morning."

I was tipping over the edge. "Right. And… what did she have to say?"

159

"She didn't answer it. Her mother did."

"Her mother?"

"It was ringing in her bedroom, and her mam picked it up. You see, as her mother told me when I said I was a friend trying to get in touch with Anji, they're not allowed to take their mobiles into school."

"School?" The image of Anji and me at it furiously in the van came, stark and lurid, into my mind. I hadn't even worn a condom. How old *is* she? What if she's pregnant? What if she accuses me of rape? *Are you sorry you did it?* she'd said.

"She looked at least…"

"Whatever." Sam turned her back on me and continued her packing. I couldn't think of anything else to say, just stood stupidly watching her. As she reached out to take another top from the drawer, head bent, I saw a tear splash onto her wrist. Instinctively I put a hand onto her shoulder, comforting, and she twisted away violently.

"Don't touch me! Get out, get out!"

I really had no choice, backed away to the door and opened it to leave, then realised I didn't have any shoes on. I came back to fish them out from under the bed, took my coat as well, while Sam was still sobbing at the drawer. I thought about trying again to go to her, but her rejection, her repulsion, had been too strong to be anything but final. I closed the door quietly behind me as I went, levering into my shoes at the top of the stairs before I walked out, head bowed, as if I was escaping through a crowd that had witnessed everything and was standing ready to spit at me.

I don't know what it is about the pull of water in situations like this, but I ended up down at the riverside, staring across at the far bank without really seeing it, letting my hands go cold on the top of the safety rail. By the time I came away there were lights reflecting on the surface of the water, and it was fully dark before I finished the long walk back to the flat. Sam was gone, of course, with her stuff. No note. When I caught myself thinking about her struggling with that heavy holdall I swore aloud and punched a door-post in frustration, deliberately hurting myself for having the gall to worry about her too fucking late.

Naturally Sam didn't come in to work, and when Debbie turned up instead, giving me the evil eye, I knew exactly where Sam had got the gen on what Anji looked like and what we got up to on stage. I'd forgotten about Debbie bumming the comps that the organiser had sent in case I wanted to bring a friend. I tried to find out from Debbie where Sam had gone off to, but she claimed not to know. That was the start of the Marc Niven freeze-out as far as the whereabouts of Sam was concerned. Everybody in the station closed ranks. All I got to find out was that Sam had first taken some sick leave, then handed in her notice with immediate effect. And I was stuck with Debbie until Marni came along.

Marni. Oh, I can't get away with this, can I? Here's me on the one hand talking about how guilty I feel and how I'd never hurt Sam again after the Anji affair, how I'm so in love with her... and barely a month after she'd gone I was trying to hit on her replacement. Not to mention the girl in the pub when I was drunk. And who was it exactly who got involved in kerb-crawling behind the railway station? Turned up at a brothel? And other offences to be taken into consideration, in the mind's eye at least.

Well, your honour, I'd like to bring in a key witness for the defence. Name of Edona. I *am* a changed man, and it's not being caught out over Anji that's done it. It's meeting Edona and hearing her sad, sad story. Yes, I confess I was tempted by Edona as well, ached to enter her as she lay there so sweet and vulnerable. But surely that's a count on my side, a tick in the plus column, that I was so tempted and resisted anyway, not once but twice. And helped her escape. You know what? I'll be honest. The real reason I risked my neck to get Edona away... It wasn't just a Good Samaritan act, helping somebody in dire need; it wasn't even entirely driven by guilt, though that was a factor. No, the real reason was that I thought somewhere along the line I might get some recognition for it, get in the papers maybe like the time I talked the suicide down from the bridge, and maybe Sam would see it, and realise I wasn't such a bastard after all. Maybe even come back to me.

So here's the bitter irony. Sam *has* come back to me on her own account, for her own reasons, and she's no sooner settled into our bed than I make my grand entrance with Edona all but nude under my coat, snuggled up close. Sam is staring at both of us from the bed, and the roof is falling in.

The two women mirror each other in a silent reflex action, both trying to hide their nakedness, like Eve after she's eaten the apple. My inane *Oh, hello, Sam. You've come back* dies on my lips as the tableau in the doorway, or her interpretation of it, dawns on Sam, drawing her expression. In the eternity before anyone speaks again I have time to notice the holdall, unzipped but still largely unpacked, on the floor by the bed. That signals limbo, but hell is gaping.

I know I can't talk any more right now. I'm waiting, racked up, for Sam to let loose. I'm braced for a howl of rage or pain. But the sound,

161

when it comes, is tiny, hardly more than a whisper, and it comes, not from Sam, but from Edona.

"Please. I am Edona. Your man has save my life. He is *guximtar*, brave person. Believe. I am being prisoner no more. Men have hurt… *përdhunoj*, understand, hurt to woman… here…" Edona moves a hand to her womb and, as she does so, seems to lose all strength. She sinks to the floor, my coat parting to reveal her pale nakedness as I try to catch her arm. She clutches at my hand and holds it to her face, streaming now as she breaks into tears. I crouch down beside her, wrapping my coat around her again while she weeps and Sam looks on, saying nothing. Edona so close and upset, I can't be worrying about Sam's interpretation, I just have to hold the poor girl, drawing her head under my chin and soothing her with my hand stroking her hair. I even kiss her on the forehead and whisper some comfort to her, closing my eyes, rocking her.

We stay like this on the floor until I sense a shadow moving between me and the light, and I open my eyes. Sam, beautiful unclothed, is there with a glass of water, offering it to Edona. She says, "Thank you," meek as a lamb, and almost spills the water as she accepts the glass, so that Sam has to keep a steady hand on it until it is secure in Edona's grasp. She crouches with us and studies the girl's face discreetly while she drinks. We must look a strange trio, hunkered down on the floor between the bed and the doorway. I want to include Sam along with Edona in my arms, but don't dare reach out to her, not knowing how she'll react. At last Sam says the first words I've heard from her since she screamed at me to get out of here six weeks ago. She is speaking quietly to Edona.

"How old are you, love?"

The question I'd never asked hangs in the air for a moment. Edona blinks through tears at Sam. "*Pesëmbëdhjetë.* Fifteen years," she says.

It's like a punch in my gut; I let out an involuntary gasp. Sam's eyes move across me, then back to Edona. She holds out her hand. "Come, come with me," she says. As Edona softly breaks from my embrace to follow her I have the guilty sensation that Sam is rescuing the girl I saved, from me. My hands feel suddenly dirty. Sam turns back the covers on the bed, inviting her, and takes my coat from her shoulders as Edona slips under the duvet. Sam tucks her in gently. She pauses, holding the coat to herself, looking down on the girl in our bed, before she turns her attention to me. All I want is to curl into the foetus position at her feet, but I feel called upon to do the opposite. I stand unsteadily, formally, a soldier wounded in reckless dereliction of his duty, returned and confronted by his superior officer roused from bed in the middle of the night. I'm expecting to be sentenced.

162

Sam offers me my coat. When she speaks she is still very hushed, as if Edona is asleep and she doesn't want to disturb her.

"Can you find somewhere else to stay? I mean, just for now?" If this is banishment, it's gently done.

"Of course, yeah. No problem."

The coat passes between us slowly, neither of us sure what we're meant to do next. Sam is trying hard to stay composed, quietly efficient, and succeeding outwardly, but I can detect her agitation and incomprehension underneath, and she's finding it difficult to look directly at me. This isn't the reconciliation scene she'd envisaged.

"Got some money on you? Credit cards?"

"Fully solvent, don't worry." Putting on a light manner, almost patting my pocket.

"If you get your stuff out the bathroom I'll... I'll pack an overnight bag for you."

"Don't worry about it, we'll sort something out tomorrow."

"Yes." I'd meant clothes and toiletries, but Sam's long, slightly distracted *yes* implies much more. "Do you have your mobile with you?" she adds.

This time I do pat my pocket. "Got it, yeah. Same number." As if she'd been away for years.

"Call you tomorrow."

I take a look past Sam's shoulder at Edona in the bed, eyes closed, and whisper a goodbye aimed at both of them as I turn to go. Sam watches my exit, arms forming an *X* across her breasts, fingers caressing her bare shoulders. She's wearing the eternity ring I bought her last Christmas.

XII

A good night guaranteed. Well, I've stayed in better billets, but the hotel is clean and what Meg Reece would no doubt deem fit for purpose, ie somewhere she personally wouldn't be seen dead in, but ideal for the likes of me. As a place used to white van man arriving at all hours, there was no problem checking in at that time of night, and the receptionist didn't turn a hair at the fact I didn't even have a change of clothes, while the machine in the Gents (the other one) dispensed a useful overnight travel kit that allowed me to clean my teeth, and even supplied a disposable razor, though I ultimately decide to stick with the beard I seem to have grown by default over the last few weeks. I've rinsed my socks and boxers in the sink and they're more or less satisfactorily dry on the radiator (still slightly damp on the skin) by the check-out deadline at eleven.

Sam hasn't called my mobile yet, so I gamble on leaving the Audi in the hotel car park while I walk the short distance into town. I resist the pull of the Eldon Arms and, after a short pretence of window shopping, end up once again in the reading room of the Central Library. There I flick through the pages of this morning's local, just to check there's no *Disgraced DJ in stolen wheelchair drug chase* story, then start thumbing through last week's back numbers, killing time until Sam rings.

Funnily enough I do find a reference to me, and a cheering one at that, on the letters page of Saturday's *Chronicle*. Under the heading *Bring back Marc*, it's from a reader asking why I haven't been restored to my *rightful place* as host of the phone-in show now that I've been *totally exonerated from blame* over the hoax call affair. The letter doesn't exactly rip into Simon as a presenter, though it does finger him as *bland* (true) whereas I'm a *loyal servant of the station and, indeed, the local community.* Name and Address Supplied. Hmm. Can't be Oliver because, aside from some excusable tautology, the letter is more than passably literate. Norman Tait, maybe? Or another of my vast army of fans.

The quiet of the library is shattered by the opening bars of Van Morrison's *Brown-Eyed Girl.* By the time I've fished my mobile out of my pocket I've suffered daggers from several pairs of brown, blue and possibly psychotic red eyes around the room and Van is already skippin and a-jumpin loudly and Irishly. I smile my apology in all directions as I press the button to answer.

164

"Hello, Sam?" I whisper to save any more disturbance. I must sound furtive – the voice at the other end is nonplussed.

"Well... yes. Mr Etherington?"

It's my turn for a double take. "Who? Is that you, Sam?"

"Samantha, yes. Is that Mr Tom Etherington?"

The penny drops. It's Samantha from the estate agent. She'd promised to get back to me about meeting the client.

"Oh, Samantha, sorry. Wires crossed for a moment there. How are you?"

Having suddenly gone from conspiratorial to hail-fellow-well-met in tone and volume, I'm attracting more eye venom from the desks around me. I raise a hand in acknowledgement of their right to despise, then stick up one finger umpire-style as a promise this will only take a minute.

"Fine, thanks" says Samantha. "I'm wondering if you are going to be in town anytime this week. Just, if you're still interested in the property at Prince Albert Road I've persuaded the client to come and meet with you. Actually, between you and me..." she drops her voice as if she really is sharing a secret, "They're quite keen on a quick sale, so when I told them you're looking to get fixed up soonest they were prepared to put themselves out a bit."

Other things have pushed Amina to the back of my mind since the viewing, so my reactions to her offer are a bit slow. "Oh, well, I'm not really..."

"You *are* still interested? Believe me, there's not a better house in the market at this price range."

"Oh, I'm sure you're right. Just... what day did you say?"

"To suit yourself, sir, you're the one has to travel, but I was hoping before the weekend?"

"OK." I'm trying to factor Sam and Edona into my possible movements, but I haven't the first idea how that's going to pan out, whether I'm even going to see either of them again. I'll just have to take a punt – I can't miss my chance to peel another layer off the Hassan mystery. "Well, how about Thursday? I'm... I'm in the area on Thursday. Around two o' clock, say?"

"Perfect. I'll only ring back if that doesn't work for the other party. Otherwise we'll see you there."

"Thanks, Samantha. Bye."

Most of my fellow library-squatters have gone back to their reading by the time I terminate the call, but there's still one or two smouldering in my direction. I nod at them agreeably and am about to pocket my mobile when that famous guitar lick strikes up again. Shit! I answer a mite too brusquely.

"Yes?"

"Marc? Sorry, have I called at a bad time?"

"Oh, Sam." (Sam-Sam) "No, it's cool. Just…" I grab my coat off the chair and continue in a stage whisper as I escape from the furies, phone clapped to my ear, "I'm in the library. Just leaving the library, actually, hotly pursued by members of the Noise Abatement Society, militant wing." Is that a little giggle on the other end of the line? Could that be much-missed vivacious Sam enjoying one of my jokes again? "I love you, by the way," I add, chancing it. "Meant to say that last night."

"Yes, well." (Noncommittal.) "Do you want to meet for lunch?" (Oh, committal. Surely committal.) "Not the Eldon, somewhere else."

"How about Paolo's? You used to love Paolo's." I'm doing it again. She's only been gone six weeks.

"I'll be about half an hour, OK?"

"Fine, I'll get along there now, grab us a place."

I quicken my step as I hit the high street. Table for two, or three? I didn't ask. Didn't have the nerve to mention Edona.

It's just the two of us. As she approaches the table I've composed myself enough to risk asking, "Where's…?"

"Taken her to Chrissie's. She's fine to stay there a few days. Well, till we work out what to do with her." It sounded veterinarian but, trust me, when it comes to TLC there's no-one better to turn to than Sam and her big sister. Chrissie trained as a social worker, and both of them deserve sainthoods for the way they looked after their mam when her cancer took hold.

We talk no more about it while we concentrate on what pizzas to order, but in the lull before they arrive I say, "What *are* we going to do with her, do you think? Edona, I mean. I don't know how much she's told you, but she's seriously scared for her family back home. And her faith in the police is like zilch, for good reason, possibly."

"Yes, she told me. This isn't London though, is it? I doubt if those pimps are so well-organised they can keep tabs on all the girls that come through their hands." (I can't help shivering at that expression.) "From what Edona says, it sounds like she's been sold on, two, maybe three times. Can't imagine they keep records. Probably nobody here has any idea who her folks are, and vice versa. Hope not, anyway."

"I'm not so sure. The guy who sent her to England knew all their names. Used them like a threat over her, you know, if she didn't do exactly what he wanted."

Sam drops her eyes at this. She's quiet for a while, lightly brushing her edge of the tablecloth with her fingers as if there are tiny crumbs there, and I'm thinking, OK, we're going to get into the difficult territory of how I got involved in all this seaminess. But when she looks up she says in a matter-of-fact tone, "Anyway, I was talking to Chrissie about it this morning. She's heard of something... the Poppy Project, I think it's called. Volunteers, or charity, whatever. They work with the victims of trafficking - well, the sex slaves not the cockle-pickers and such... They try to get the girls sorted, help them get back home if they want to, that type of thing. Before, if there was a raid, the women would be arrested and deported along with the slavers, end of story, but they've stopped a lot of that, the Poppy people – kind of step in between the women and the police."

"Sounds good."

"But Chrissie doesn't know whether they even operate up here. She's going to ring around some people she knows, just on the quiet. She won't mention Edona until we find out what the score is."

She breaks off as the young waitress brings pizzas to our table, and we give her our undivided attention while she does the business with the grated cheese and the big pepper-pot. As she leaves us to our meal, I speak closely to Sam, "You notice? She's..."

"East European, yeah. Polish, probably."

"In an Italian restaurant. That's where Edona thought she was going - to serve tables in Italy."

"Mmm, Chrissie and me were thinking. I'm sure we'd be able to help her get fixed up with something if she really wanted to stay for a while, earn some money. Maybe she could go to school, even, apply for college. We'd have to find what she needs as far as papers..."

"You know, you're amazing, you two. Listen..." I put my knife down and stretch my hand out on the table, on the off chance Sam might feel like covering it with hers at some point. "Thanks for doing this. You couldn't have expected... I mean, last night must have come as a shock... I'm amazed you've taken it all in your stride like you have. Well, I'm not really in a way..." (I'm babbling) "Cos that's what you do, that's Sam." (I nearly said *my* Sam. Maybe that would have been all right – she has come back.) "You're an incredible woman. You *are* an incredible, wonderful woman."

Sam stopped eating at *Listen*, still holding her fork above her plate as I struggle to organise my drivel into something meaningful before my emotion takes over. She watches my hand on the table, but she doesn't take it. In fact, she looks as if she's resisting the temptation to stab it with her fork. When I've finished speaking, eyes a touch damp, she looks at me, takes a breath.

"I haven't *taken it in my stride*, far from it. It's just that things need to be done, so I'm getting on with doing them. Don't jump to conclusions. Don't dare think, oh Sam's back, everything's sorted, everything's going to be all right now."

"I wasn't thinking that," I lie.

"Because that's not the way it works. You're not a kid – not officially, anyway – and I'm not your mother."

"I know that." I look at her sheepishly. "I don't expect you to be my mother."

I suppose I sound ridiculous. Something softens in Sam's expression. Despite herself, a little smile breaks out, which she tries to hide with a touch of her nose. She's trying to stick with the programme, keeping me at bay, but her eyes disclose some private joke that's popped into her head.

"What?"

"Nothing. Just... I *have* done something a wee bit motherish this morning."

"Which is...?"

"Made you an appointment at the hairdresser. We're going right after this."

"Is it that bad?"

"I thought the picture in the paper was bad enough, but you're even worse close up."

"Thanks. Oh, you saw the *Chronicle* story, did you?"

"Not at the time, no. Just this weekend I did. Christine had kept it, in case I was interested."

"Were you?" Sam looks down, intent on cutting up her pizza, so I try a different tack. "You've been away?"

"Been down to Devon for a while. Carl's been pestering me to come and stay ever since he moved, so I decided to go and wish him Happy New Year."

Carl was long before my time, though I knew they still exchanged cards, the occasional phone call. Sam knew him at uni in Nottingham. A friend is how she described him, that's all. I'd never met Carl, but I hated him.

168

"Right. So, what, you stayed there, did you? At Carl's."

"Mmm."

"Right."

Sam glances up from her plate, watching my face, which might look a touch sullen. Eventually she says, "His partner was there."

"Right. What's she like?"

"He. Philip. Carl's gay. I must have mentioned that a hundred times."

"Not to me, you haven't."

"A hundred times, at least. It's not my fault you don't listen. Bad habit for a phone-in host. Carl, by the way, is a great listener. That's partly why I went there, I suppose, though I never thought it through to that extent. Did you have the idea I'd gone down to make mad passionate love to him? On the rebound? Act of revenge?"

"Wouldn't have blamed you if you had."

"You would, actually, but let it be."

I'm like one of Pavlov's dogs whenever I hear a song title or a lyric. By reflex I start singing, under my breath at first. "*Let it be, let it be, let it be, yeah, let it be…*"

Dropping her guard again, Sam joins in, softly, "*Speaking words of wisdom, let it be.*" Like she used to. Then, strangely, we both get embarrassed about it and start taking unusual interest in what's on our plates, as if we were on our first date, not practised in our relationship. I guess it's because we're both experiencing such a confusion of emotions. I'm so pleased to have Sam here with me again, but at the same time I'm ashamed of what I've done and I'm still waiting for her to start in on me – almost willing it. Sam is being unpredictable – so unlike herself – one minute edgy, the next smiling, even singing. It's as if she wants us to be the way we were, but isn't quite convinced we can be, or won't allow it, as if some part of her feels she has a responsibility to stay mad at me. I'm wondering what made her decide to come back, so I force the issue and ask her.

"Was it your friend Carl? Did he put a good word in?"

"Carl's not the type to give advice. Like I said, he's a good listener. He's not like most men – most people, actually – who can't wait for you to shut up so they can tell you what's good for you. He just listened to me rabbiting on, mostly about you. Starting off with what a lousy bastard you've been."

"Thanks. I mean, sorry."

Sam frowns, twists her mouth, maybe at the memory of my lousiness or at the understated apology, or both. She goes on.

"One nice habit Carl has…" (I'm still hating this bloke; he's making me look so bad by comparison.) "One thing he does is always ask about the good things. You know, he'll say, tell me how you got together with Marc, what attracted the two of you to each other?"

I'm thinking, nosy sod, but a minute later I'm mentally hugging old Carl because Sam is telling me how their talks reminded her of why she fell in love with me in the first place, and how she got from that to realising how much she was missing me. "There you are, she says, "That's the plain truth of it. I came back because I was missing you. Feeling a bit sorry for you as well, actually. And you can take that silly grin off your face cos I can tell you now you don't deserve it."

"I know."

"And last night I thought I'd made the second biggest mistake of my life."

"What was the first?"

"I suppose, running away, and letting you get yourself into all sorts of mess. I couldn't believe it when Chrissie phoned and she told me about the trouble at work and you getting suspended."

"A lot of that was about me missing you as well. I think I went downhill a bit."

"You can say that again. I was quite shocked when I came back and saw your picture in the paper."

"Wait till I've been to the hairdresser's. You'll see a new man."

"Getting the old one back will be a start for me," says Sam. "If you expect…" She looks at me directly for the first time since we'd started talking about our month apart, apparently winding herself up to deliver a lecture, but she stops suddenly in mid-stream, shakes her head and says, in what I could only describe as a tone of resigned amusement, "You know, you really are a sight."

Yes, when I take a candid look at myself in the see-all-evil mirror at Devine's, I have to agree. A month adrift from Sam's tender loving care, plus the ravages of a poor diet, steady drinking, stress, fatigue and downright self-loathing have left their mark on Marc. My unkempt chestnut locks, uncut since before Christmas, unwashed for days, and whiskers unshaved since- not that I'd admit it to Sam - Marni's first night in the studio, have left me an uneasy mix of tramp, pro-wrestling villain and Glastonbury veteran in the looks department. No wonder Meg Reece wanted rid of me - even by the casual standards of the creative industry I'm a deadbeat.

"OK," says Tristan from behind, touching me lightly on both shoulders and speaking to my reflection. "So it's a wash, shave, trim and dye."

"Dye? Oh, dry. I thought for a second you said *dye*."

In the mirror I watch Tristan turn to Sam sitting in the corner of the salon. His body language is all question.

"Yes," she assures him. "We want it dyed. Could you do some sort of subtle blond? He'll need his eyebrows tinted as well, won't he?"

"Definitely for the best," Tristan agrees.

"Hey, don't I get a say in this?" I crane my neck around to look at Sam. What's she playing at?

"It's for the best, trust me," says Sam.

"Do you mean the eyebrow tint, or the whole dye thing?"

"The whole thing." And she gives me one of her meaningful expressions, so meaningful that I spend the rest of my time in the chair trying to work out what it means, while Tristan merrily carries on with his mini-makeover.

To be fair, he does quite a decent job. The unfamiliar face that stares back at me from the mirror when he's finished might seem a bit anaemic, but it's a definite improvement on the wino look. Pale and interesting. Sam must think so. As Tristan is waiting to help me on with my coat, she comes up close to smell my fragrance. "Mmm, nice, I could fancy you myself," she says, and reaches up slightly to peck my newly-shaven cheek, thrilling me beyond reason with the merest brush of a breast against my shirt. The tingle goes to my scalp, adding emphasis to the strangeness there.

As we're walking from the hairdresser to retrieve the Audi from the hotel car park Sam allows me to hold her hand inside my coat pocket in our old way, which she hadn't on the way there, still slightly edgy then.

"Not ashamed to be with me now, eh?"

"That's it." She squeezes my hand and walks close enough to breathe me in. "Well, now you'll look nice and smart for your meeting on Thursday."

This throws me. "How do you know about my meeting on Thursday?"

"How do *you* know about your meeting on Thursday? I was just going to tell you about it. Meg Reece called the flat. She wants you to go in and discuss coming back to work."

"Really? Left it a bit late, hasn't she? I bet she got a surprise to hear *your* voice on the phone."

"Not really. She knew I was back."

171

"How come?"

"Cos I called in on Friday to chat with Debbie. Bumped into a few others on the way, including Meg, as it happens."

"Hmm, well, far as I'm concerned Meg Reece can go and..." I kill the *fuck herself* on my lips. Trying to clean my act up around Sam. "Bottom line, I'm not meeting her, and I'm not going back."

Sam looks at me sideways. "And what would you intend to do instead?"

"Get another job, obviously."

"In radio?"

"That's what I do."

"And how often do those jobs come up?"

"Well..."

"Could you see yourself doing something else?"

"Not really."

"So why are you being so stubborn? Nobody asking you to crawl to Meg. All you have to do is go along and see what she's got to say. You never know, if they're keen enough to have you back you might be able to negotiate a better deal. You'd like to get the drop on them in that way, wouldn't you?"

I reach across to rub Sam's sleeve with my free hand. "You know, for a well brought-up girl you have a touch of Miss Devious in you." She looks ahead with a 'who-me?' innocence on her face. "What time is the meeting?" I ask.

"Twelve. Anyway, I thought you said you knew about it."

"No. I was thinking about something else. I've arranged to see the mysterious Amina on Thursday afternoon."

"The Valentine woman?"

"The same. Oh, did you get mine?"

"Your what?"

"Valentine card. Well, email, actually."

The Premier Inn sign is glowing with promise on the other side of the road as we cross at the lights. I'm praying my car hasn't been clamped to spoil a perfect day.

"Oh, that was from you, was it?" says Sam. "I thought I had a secret admirer." (I love it that she's joshing me like this – she's bringing me back in to her.) "No, well, I only started checking my emails again last week, so I read it a bit late I'm afraid. I was glad to get it, though, thanks. It made a difference. Sorry I didn't send you one, I'll make it up to you." (Will you? Oh, please, please do.)

172

The TT has escaped clamping over the four hours or more I've been an ex-guest of the hotel. Sam, though, is starting to look anxious again as we climb into our seats. I wonder if she's making the assumption that the car is where I did it with Anji. Then I'm thinking, is she concerned about going back to the flat with me? About making a definite commitment to restarting the relationship, maybe only to be let down again later?

"They'll know the car, won't they?" she says, out of the blue.

"Who?"

"The guys who chased you and Edona. She told me they're really dangerous."

"*Everything is danger now.*"

"Sorry?"

"Nothing. Just what Edona said when I asked her if she was ready to try escaping. She's been through much more than I've risked for her. I can live with that."

"Yeah, but you've done your bit," says Sam. "I'm petrified one of those thugs is going to recognise you on the street, come up and shoot you in the back of the head."

It finally clicks why Sam had been so keen for me to get my hair dyed. And why she seemed so nervous on our way to the salon. Her concern makes me fall in love with her for about the third time today. I reach across to touch her, run the back of my fingers over her cheek and down under her taut chin to the soft yielding under her throat.

"Don't worry, they're like vampires, they only come out at night. I'll stay well away from their hiding-places, promise." Even as I say it I have the image of Stefan going in to Tesco for a paper, like any ordinary Joe. Emmanuel buying leather gloves. I *will* have to be careful, for a few days at least. Sam, facing forward, lifts her hand to close over mine. I'm finding it really hard to interpret her movements since she came back – is this affection? anxiety? or is she saying, don't touch me like this? Her eyes are ambiguous. To be on the safe side I slip my hand out of hers and concentrate on reversing out of the parking space.

While I'm waiting to join the traffic at the main road Sam's mobile rings (*La Valse D'Amélie*) and she fishes it out of her handbag to answer. I hear her cooing, "Well done you," and "Twenty minutes, yeah?" before she puts the phone back in her bag and says to me, "OK if we go round to Chrissie's? She's been putting some feelers out. Seems the Poppy Project only deals with women over eighteen. But one of her old contacts in Children's Services is coming round this afternoon."

Children's Services. I feel my face go hot. "Is that wise at this stage?"

"Nothing official. Off the record, sort of thing. Just to give us some advice, tell us the options."

Quite apart from my discomfort over Edona being a suitable client for Children's Services, I'm really not sure about this development – the cack-handed meddlings of Social Services have been a regular topic on the Marc Niven phone-in over the years, as Sam knows only too well – but I'm certainly not going to put up any significant objections now, not after the way she and her sister have taken Edona under their wing. I take the next left and aim for Welbeck Grange.

Embarrassment is piled on embarrassment by the time we're sitting having tea with Chrissie. Even before she lets us in I'm reliving the furtive guilt of waiting on her doorstep New Year's morning with the musk of Anji hanging on me. It's the first time I've seen Chrissie since Sam walked out, and I've no idea how much she knows about why, but she can't disguise a flicker of disdain in my direction even while she's welcoming us both in. Fern, the social worker, has arrived and is already closeted with Edona in another room, no doubt pumping her for information. I find it difficult to contribute much to the conversation while we're waiting for Fern to come and give us the lowdown on what to do – at the moment I feel more like a suspect than a Good Samaritan.

I'm simultaneously lifted and disturbed by the sight of Edona peeping through from the dining room before she walks shyly in to join us. She's wearing light blue jeans and (a further embarrassment to me in my confused mental state) an outmoded pink *fcuk* top that I reckon must have belonged to Chrissie's daughter Lois circa 2005. With her slave-girl tart's makeup cleaned off (replaced by a modest enhancement around the eyes) and a refreshed optimism in her demeanour, Edona, despite the suggestive message on her tee-shirt, does indeed look your typical attractive, artless, adolescent girl. I want to weep.

Fern follows her through. She stops at the edge of the group, her eyes moving quickly from one to the other of us as if she's constructing a sociogram before she touches Edona lightly on the elbow and draws her back, whispering in her ear. She's a big woman - more trunk-like than fern-like - though, with her playground clothes and the incongruous bunches in her hair, she could be an am dram trouper aiming to convince in the role of Edona's over-sized schoolfriend. Her off-stage whispering done, Fern releases Edona's arm and negotiates around the back of the

174

sofa towards the one empty armchair while Edona, with a gentle smile for us, leaves the lounge at the door nearest the stairs, presumably to go to the room Chrissie has prepared for her. Fern settles into the wide-bottomed seat and reveals herself as unmistakably Lancastrian when she says, "Any more brew on the go, love?"

While Chrissie disappears to top up the teapot Fern introduces herself and addresses Sam with, "Not hard to spot who you are. You look right like her, 'cept for fairer hair."

"Everybody says that. I can't see it myself," says Sam, smiling.

"So you two are...?" Fern continues, waving a finger between us, still drawing her sociogram.

"Partners," I fill in. "We live together." I glance at Sam and fancy she blushes a touch as I say it. "We used to work together as well," I add, more to cover up any awkwardness than to arm Fern with more information than she needs.

"Yeah, you're on the radio, aren't you? I think I was on your programme once, good while ago. Respect agenda."

"OK. Rings a bell." (My usual response when mists-of-time callers and guests ask if I remember their fifteen seconds.)

"Marc, isn't it? I hear you're the one that, let's say, *found* Edona." She's getting down to business, inquisitorial.

"He *rescued* her as well," Sam puts in. Her turn to cover for me.

"Tell me about it, Marc," says Fern as Chrissie comes back with the teapot and a spare mug.

I'm not sure I'm ready for this interrogation in front of all three women, but I'll play her game for now. "Do you mean tell you about the rescue, or the whole thing?"

"I've already heard the saving part of it from Edona. Dangerous and stupid, but very well done. No, I'm curious to know how you got involved in the first place. Thanks, Chris," as she receives the mug and watches the weak tea pouring into it while she waits for me to compose an answer to the sixty four thousand dollar question. Sam is waiting as well. And her sister. What are my options here? I don't have to answer her questions – I'm not on trial, even if it feels like it. On the other hand, what is Sam going to think of me if I make it obvious I'm not going to cooperate when her sister's gone to all this trouble? And at the end of the day it's all for Edona's benefit, supposedly. Anyway, I'm not under oath. I don't have to tell the whole truth and nothing but the truth.

"Mmm, I first saw her coming out of a lorry one night at Tesco's car park. I think she was being used to return a favour, if you know what I mean, probably somebody involved in the trafficking business. The

175

reason I noticed her is she tried to run away, only she got caught by the guys who ended up chasing us the other night. Anyway, I followed them...." So far I've been honest, but now a little economy with the truth won't harm anybody. "Yeah, they took her to this house in Warkworth Street. I guessed it was some kind of brothel, and I realised she was there against her will, so that's when I decided I was going to try and help her out somehow."

"Which you did by becoming a john?" says Fern, then adds a glossary for Sam and Chrissie. "That's a client."

"Well, posing as a client, to see the lie of the land, so to speak."

"Edona told me you'd said you'd come to find her."

"Exactly."

"Why didn't you just go to the police in the first place?"

"Because I was afraid she'd get arrested and be treated as a criminal along with everyone else."

"Well, actually," Fern pauses to take a sip of her tea, then looks around at the group, enjoying her role as the expert. "That does happen a lot. All the agencies are supposed to work in partnership now... Supposed to. Not everybody follows the protocols. Funny thing though, *we* always end up getting stick for it. Always Social Services' fault, 'twas ever thus."

"That's one of the reasons I got out," says Chrissie.

"Believe me, love, it's worse than ever now."

"So, anyway, that's why I came up with the pretend overdose idea," I say, eager to finish before this pair get sidetracked with internal politics.

"Oh, what happened?" says Chrissie, who clearly hasn't heard the details of the escape. I'm about to answer when Fern takes charge of the story.

"Quite clever, actually. He smuggled bits and pieces in and made Edona up to look like she'd OD'ed on heroin, then he conned the pimps into driving them to the hospital. What a cheek, eh? Soon as they got there the two of them did a runner!" She explodes with laughter. After a second Sam and Chrissie join in, a bit less boisterously. This isn't going too bad for me after all. I would like to have impressed them with all the specifics of my careful planning, not to mention bravery under fire (almost), but I can't complain about this result. I'm sure I can feel Sam moving closer in to me on the sofa. Even Chrissie's looking at me with a certain warmth now.

While Fern subsides, composing herself with another draught from the mug, Sam takes the chance to ask her, "What can we do to help Edona? She told me she wants to stay in this country, at least for a while, so she can make some money to help her family. I mean, legally make money, not... you know."

Fern puts her mug back and stays leaning forward, placing outstretched fingers on the coffee table as if she's about to get up and leave (which she isn't) or start laying the law down (which she is.)

"Edona is a minor and, technically speaking, an illegal immigrant. To be honest, I should be taking her away with me right now, except there's no safe accommodation set up, no specialist foster care... or I should be handing her over for the police to deal with." I turn to Sam, expecting some reaction. This isn't what we're wanting to hear – we've invited in the child-snatchers. But Sam stays calm, listening carefully as Fern continues. "That's why this conversation is strictly off the record. I'm not here, if you get my drift, and I've never heard of anybody called Edona."

"Naturally, we respect that completely," Chrissie says. "So what's the score, suppose we go down the official route?"

"Number one, she gets arrested and deported back to her own country."

Stung by the stark way Fern says it, I'm up in arms for Edona. "Come on, that can't happen. That way she's going to walk straight back into trouble, not to mention what the Albanian mafia or whatever's going to do to her family."

"Well, the family now, that's another kettle of fish," says Fern, raising a forefinger.

"How do you mean?"

"I'm not convinced they really expected her to be going to a restaurant job in Italy. You know, a huge percentage of women trafficked from Albania are under eighteen, and you'd be surprised how many of them are actually sold by their families."

"You're joking."

"Wish I was. That's what poverty does to people." Fern pauses, seeming to reflect on this herself for a moment, then resumes. "Even if the family weren't involved in her abduction, there's another possible problem."

She's a real joy-bringer this woman. "What's that?"

"It's to do with the culture. The Canon, I think it's called, something like that, sort of the traditional law. Not great for the female of the species. If Edona goes home and lets on what's happened to her there's a fair chance she'll be banished from the family, maybe even handed over to the traffickers. Once a woman has been dishonoured there's no going back for her, even if it's no fault of her own. That's the way it is."

Chrissie chips in, "But doesn't all this strengthen the case for Edona to stay here? Apply for asylum? Surely it's all about what's best for the child, isn't it? That was the mantra when I was working."

"Still is, supposedly." says Fern "The UN Convention on the Rights of the Child, all that. Trouble is, our caring government signed a Reservation on the charter in relation to children under immigration control, so there's no protection for them."

I've stopped being angry with Fern now – there's too many other buggers to be mad about. "That's scandalous!"

"Tell me about it. Better still, tell your listeners. Get a campaign up. Although frankly..." says Fern, world-weary, "I suspect most of them couldn't give a toss. They'll be quite happy seeing another illegal immigrant sent back where they came from."

Sam has been quiet for a while. Now she leans forward to get Fern's attention. "You know you were saying before about there not being any specialist foster care for dealing with somebody like Edona? I know this might sound stupid, but, well... could we not step in? You know, volunteer to foster her until she's old enough to deal with things herself."

Fern straightens up, glances at me as she says to Sam, "We being...?"

"Me and Marc, yeah."

I have no time to assimilate this idea because Fern immediately pulls a sour face, looks from me to Sam and says, "Frankly, I think that's a non-starter. To be brutally honest..." (Frank and brutally honest, I sense there's no holding back here) "I suspect your application would fall at the first hurdle. The assessment criteria they use are very strict. One big no-no would be Marc's... well, on the face of it, fairly compromising position over where and how he met Edona."

I'm back on the defensive. "Look, I explained how it happened..."

"Absolutely, you don't have to persuade me. I'm just telling it like it is, that's all. Anything that seems however faintly... I'm not saying *dodgy*, but just the whiff of the thing..."

Even Fern can't carry on in face of the withering look I'm giving her, and there's an embarrassed silence around the room until Chrissie breaks it by saying, "Well, what *are* we supposed to do with the poor lass? Seems to me you're saying she's going to have to go straight back home and probably get, I don't know, *recycled* as a prostitute."

178

Fern shows her open palms and calms the class while she rediscovers her speaking voice. "You asked me for the options, I'm giving you them as far as I can without looking further into it. Listen, I'm on the case and I'm on your side, believe me. I know where you're coming from. There's a few things I've got to get up to speed on. If memory serves, Save the Children might have something going in Albania. There's the NSPCC to check out, ECPAT..."

"What's ECPAT?" Sam asks.

"Stands for... it's... *End Child Prostitution And Trafficking.* There's a bit on the end. *End Child Prostitution and Trafficking for Sexual Purposes.* I think that's right."

"You mean there's a whole organisation devoted to that one issue?"

"There's a whole network. International."

"Christ, it must be one hell of a problem," Sam glances at me as she says it, and I'm struggling to know whether she's including me in the conversation or the problem.

"Trust me, there's a lot of Edonas," says Fern, reassuring us of the world's depravity. I'm still in discussion with myself about Sam's looks and glances. She can't mean me, can she, not after she's just volunteered my services as a foster parent. Our services.

Fern studies her watch, big chunky strap. I catch myself wondering if she's a lesbian and colour up as if I've said it out loud.

"Sorry, I'm going to have to run," she announces, a mite too importantly. "I'll do a bit of digging and come back to you soonest, Chris."

"Is Edona OK with me just now?"

"Edona who? Don't know, don't want to know. We'll just see what comes out in the wash, eh?"

"I'll take that as a yes, then," says Chrissie, still a bit confused. So am I. On balance I'm giving Fern the benefit of the doubt, but part of me wants to smuggle Edona away again.

"Did you mean what you said to Fern?" I ask Sam, almost as soon as we get into the car. (She's coming home with me, which is a huge relief. For a while back there I had the feeling she was going to ask her sister to take her in as well as Edona.)

"About what?"

"About us offering to be Edona's foster parents?"

"If it means keeping her safe, yes."

179

Safe. Fern might have me down as a potential sexual predator but Sam, who holds the damning evidence, has chosen to trust me. Halleluiah.

"What are you smiling at?" she says.

"Mmm, just at the thought, I suppose. The idea of being a parent at all, never mind to someone nearly sixteen. You'd have had to be a child bride yourself. Under-age, actually."

"It was to try and help her out, that's all. Just an idea."

"A nice idea. Mam and Dad, eh? I kinda like it."

"Hmmm." I guess she doesn't want me to pursue the subject. I steal a glimpse at her as I'm stopped at the lights, but she's pretty closed off. I'm going to have to start getting used to this new inscrutable Sam.

"Oh," she says as I signal left. "We need to get some shopping in. There's nothing in the fridge."

"Yeah, sorry about that. I've been a bit busy."

"Go the coast road way. Tesco is nearest from here."

"Are you sure? We'll be going back on ourselves." Alarm bells ringing immediately.

"Still be quickest, though."

"OK, no sweat." Which is a lie. I can already feel a slight prickle of perspiration as I switch lanes and head towards the coast road. Part of me recognises it's an irrational fear, brought on by association. There's no logical reason why I should bump into Emmanuel or Stefan at this particular Tesco at six o' clock in the evening. They'd be just as likely, if they shop at all, to be in their local branch of Sainsbury or Asda. Netto, maybe. But the road to the store and the car park in front of it are so linked in my mind with these guys that I'm expecting the silver Beemer to cut across my bows any moment.

Naturally I don't admit this to Sam, not wanting to feed her fears, and after we get to the supermarket unscathed I make every effort to resist moving like a British soldier in Baghdad while she browses the shelves for provisions. Nothing happens, but the adrenaline has my brain racing on the journey back to the flat and I start stressing about my appointment at Prince Albert Road on Thursday afternoon. Emmanuel seems to be connected with the house in some way; suppose he's set a trap to catch me? It's another illogical fear - neither he nor anybody else I've come across in my extra-curricular activities has any clue that would make the link between my three separate personae of DJ Marc Niven, doctor/radiologist Oliver Dunn and designer Tom Etherington – or have they? I've learned a lot through behind-the-scenes detective work; what's to say they haven't too?

I'm still restless when we return to the flat, and to be honest it's obvious that both Sam and I are feeling strange and uncomfortable with each other here, just the two of us now back in the place that was at the heart of our post-Linda, pre-Anji relationship, but also where we had the row that split us up, and the bizarre scene with a half-naked runaway girl. Sam finds distraction in cooking supper. Once I've set the table I'm at a loose end, hovering around aimlessly in an unreconstructed male sort of way, until I decide on something I need to do and, as a cover, say to Sam, "Do I have time for a run before we eat?"

"A run? You haven't done that for a long time."

"Trying to get back in shape, that's all. You said I was a sight."

"'Course, not a problem. The meal will be half-an-hour yet."

My guess is she's glad of the chance to ease the awkwardness between us and settle down into her space before we eat. It's a release for me as well, but I have another ulterior motive for leaving the flat. I have a destination.

I'm usually pretty good at remembering places I've been to just once, so even in the dark and on foot I find my way to Oliver's estate in just ten minutes. I do have some anxiety passing a couple of hoodies slouched at an unlit corner, worried they might take umbrage at this middle-class ponce daring to jog across their patch, and I'm relieved not to hear chasing footsteps as I slow down to pick out Ollie's house near the end of the cul-de-sac. Not surprisingly, the door isn't exactly opened with alacrity after I knock. In fact, I can hear signs of consternation from inside, Oliver and his mam debating whether to believe the evidence of their ears and agree that somebody has come calling on them at this time of night, and whether to risk opening up.

"Who is it?" I hear eventually from Mrs Dunn on the other side of the door.

"It's Marc, Mrs Dunn. Marc Niven. Could I have a quick word with Oliver?"

A bolt is drawn back and there is Ollie, faith in humanity immediately restored, beaming a welcome, his mother at his elbow looking decidedly more circumspect. "Come in, Marc," he says, bubbling. "I can make you a cup of tea or a cup of coffee." It occurs to me that these are lines he must practise at some Independent Living course.

"Thanks, Ollie, no, I've only got a minute. I've come to ask if you'll do me a favour."

He pulls the door open wider to let me in. His mother is like a limpet at his side, inadvertently blocking my way to the living-room, so we all stand immobile until she pokes at him, saying, "Shut that door,

181

you're freezing the house out." Then she turns her back on us and shuffles into the warmth inside, probably expecting us to follow her. Instead I grab Ollie's elbow as he closes the door and draw him near to me, the two of us crowding the tiny kitchen space next to the sink.

"I don't want your mam to hear this," I whisper. "Ollie, do you know what a lookout is?"

"Like looking out the window?"

"No, I mean looking out for a person. You know, I look out for you, you look out for me."

"Like looking after somebody?"

"Sort of, yeah. But a bit like guarding them as well, in case people are after them."

"Yeah, like a bodyguard. Like Madonna has."

"I suppose." I wonder if Madonna is another of Ollie's celebrity obsessions. "Anyway, I've come to ask if you could maybe do a lookout job for me, Thursday afternoon."

Ollie looks perplexed at first, then grins. "Are we going back to where the car crash was? I can look out for the policeman."

"No, but it's like that. You remember Amina, who got the Valentine message?"

"Yeah, who Hassan said."

"That's it. Well, I'm going to her house on Thursday. There's some people I need you to look out for, just in case. I need you to watch the house while I'm in there, but secretly. We don't want to let anybody know you're watching."

"I can do my leaflets," says Oliver, brightly.

"What?"

"Show you." He sidles past to get to a cupboard built into the wall next to the living-room door, calling "All right, Mam?" on the way. There's no answer. I take a quick peek into the room while Ollie is on his knees in the cupboard. Mrs Dunn, ensconced in her chair with her head on one side, is dozing. Oliver crawls out with what looks like a green plastic pouch. He puts it over his shoulder in the manner of a newspaper boy and pulls out a brightly coloured brochure which he presents to me proudly. It's an advertisement for conservatories and double glazing, with plenty of examples and quotes from satisfied (no, delighted) customers.

"I didn't know you had a job. When do you do these?"

"When the van comes. I'm my own boss, Marc." He points to the inside of the cupboard door, where a newspaper cutting is sellotaped grubbily. It reads: **Be your own boss.** *Deliver leaflets and get paid. The more you drop, the more you earn.* I'm betting you'd be ready to drop dead by the

182

time you earn anything significant, but Oliver is made-up to be a bread-winner, however few the loaves he can buy with his wages.

He's not so daft, though, my wide-bellied friend, as I keep discovering. He's had the nous to work out this could be the perfect cover for our purposes, allowing him to hang around Amina's street for quite a while without drawing undue attention to himself. We spend the next few minutes discussing the details and by the time I hit the road back to the flat I'm feeling a tad less alone in my search for the secret behind the door of 110 Prince Albert Road. All right, I'm nagged by the doubt that in adding a little protection for myself I could be exposing Oliver, but the risk is minimal, and he's so obviously thrilled to be part of what I'm doing that I don't feel I'm exploiting his good nature. He probably hasn't had so much fun in years.

I have a vestige of guilt to do with keeping Sam out of this particular loop, but it's reduced by the notion that it's for her own security, and it doesn't add much to the weight already on my conscience, or to the slight uneasiness that neither of us can yet shake off, even while we seem to be definitively back together.

While I've been away Sam has prepared and cooked lamb cutlets, which we settle down to enjoy with a more expensive red wine than we'd normally allow ourselves, especially so early in the week, in unspoken recognition that this is a special occasion. We both know we need to let go of things, cast them off, and start a new journey, but neither of us seem able to make that explicit. It's as if we're launching a new boat but prefer to slip away quietly from the harbour, hoping the debris of the past will float off behind us, not stick around to clog up the engine.

After a month living out of tins and packets, relieved by the occasional takeaway and too many Big Macs, this meal is manna to me, served by an angel. Without specifically deciding to, we make it a genuine dining experience, sitting together at the table, not in our usual position in front of the TV balancing plates on our knees and fishing wine glasses from the floor. Candles would be too obvious – and anyway there aren't any in the flat – but I do tilt the shade on the lamp, choose the music carefully and lower the volume below quiet conversation level.

Slowly, tranquilly, the evening works into us like a sensual massage. We talk more and more gently with each other about nothing of any importance except shared experience. As we pass seasonings and wine across the table our fingers touch without design at first, later more deliberately, lingering. Afterwards, the last of the wine is drunk on the sofa, Sam relaxing against my chest, letting me caress and play lightly with her hair.

At last she turns to face me, studies me with softened eyes, then stretches to brush my lips with hers. I settle lower into the bed of the sofa, bringing her to me, breathing in her scent, kissing her under her chin, then back to her lips, which she parts to allow our first French kiss since...

I don't mean our sex to become so urgent, but it does. It's the hardness of her nipple that excites me when I find it with my hand stealing up beneath her top and under her satin cup. It presses against my palm as our tongues wrestle. My maleness gathers and hunts. Both hands move to her waist and upward, taking top and bra in one smooth movement over her head and arms. Sam giggles at the pinging of her fasteners as they fly apart, a reassurance that this is all OK, and as I tear off my own tee shirt she drops back to the sofa, her back arching slightly, her pink breasts firming and her chest muscles stretched across her ribs.

My hand goes back to fondling one breast while I take her untouched left nipple into my mouth, lapping and sucking as if I might find milk there. Her liquid, though, is further down, and soon I'm peeling off her jeans and knickers in search of it. I'm too thirsty for patient foreplay, but Sam is excited, ready. I bathe my face in her wetness and dig with my tongue for more. It finds a rhythm at her clitoris, and Sam, engorged, starts to pant with pleasure, stiffening me near to bursting point as I free myself from my pants, pushing and kicking them away from my ankles.

"Yes, now," she gasps, legs wide, and I raise myself taut to enter her. Smoothly in, oh, counting in my mind to keep the rhythm and divert me from coming too soon. My fingers stroke her wet clitoris till Sam's hand reaches down to entangle with mine, then take over so I can lever myself onto both arms and ride her fully, matching rhythms as her fingers flutter under me. I lick sweat from her breasts and suck at her nipples then up to the lobe of an ear just as her mouth stretches wider, her chin jerks back as if for air and she wails, "Yes, oh, yes, yes, yes." Her pelvis lifts as I fuck and I erupt into her, flowing thickly through her shudders. Yes, oh, yes.

The waves subside and still. My boat at anchor in her safe harbour, my body sunk into hers. I'm spent. My right hand glides down over her breast, her flat stomach, her hip bone, to hold her bum cheek gently, and feel our dampness at my finger ends.

"Wham bam, thank you, Sam," I whisper at her ear.

184

Sam says something I can't quite catch. I lift myself up to look at her face, her closed eyes. "Sorry, darl?"

She opens her eyes, looks away from me. "I said, was Anji better than this?"

"No, don't..." I sink down onto her shoulder. "Please don't." I nuzzle into her hair, and we lie for many minutes without speaking, though I can feel the slow trickle of Sam's tears on my cheek.

XIII

As we walk together into Reception I spot the significant glance that passes between Carol and Julie at the desk, and I don't imagine it's an unspoken comment on my new hairstyle. To remove any doubt from their minds I let my hand linger just for a second on Sam's tidy bum as she steps over to the visitors' chairs while I wait to tell them who we've come to see, and immediately regret the gesture, remembering how I've been badmouthed for lechery by certain of the station staff.

"Hi Julie, Meg Reece is expecting me," I say, trying to shrug off self-consciousness.

"Yeah, she said to tell you go straight up. I like your hair, Marc."

"Nice," Carol agrees from behind the switchboard. Perhaps my stock has risen in my absence.

"Thanks. We're to go straight up, Sam," catching her before she gets seated.

"Are you sure you want me to go in with you? It's you she's asked to see, not both of us."

"I want you to, please."

On this occasion Meg Reece is in her own office, so she can't play the queen bee quite as grandly as she did in Neville's big chair, waited on by his PA. No HR police with her either. The coffee she offers us is from a filter jug by her desk, where it's been standing all morning judging by its acrid taste. Meg, by contrast, is mild with the essence of smoothness.

"I must say, Marc, your little holiday seems to have done you good. Never seen you looking so fit. New hairstyle as well – we're going to have to update your mug shots."

"I'm still on the books, then?"

"Naturally. The whole idea was you should lie low while that Hassan nonsense was sorted out. It's all blown over now, so, welcome back, basically."

I raise my eyebrows at Sam, sitting quietly in the background, then turn my attention back to Meg. "It's not as simple as that, though, is it? For one thing you've handed my show to Simon Barnes. I'm not prepared to start back on some graveyard slot."

"Of course not. Obviously we want you to return to *Nightwatch*."

"It's not called *Nightwatch*."

186

"Whatever. *The Marc Niven Show.* That's exactly what it is. To be perfectly honest, the feedback we've had on Simon has not been one hundred percent. Not really his forte as it turns out, so he'll be reverting. Useful experiment, though. Thanks for being understanding about it."

It's typical of Meg to rewrite the music to suit the beat of her own drum, but I'm not prepared to fall in line so easily. "Fact is, Meg, I wasn't understanding about it. You kicked me in the nuts, threw me out effectively, not to mention questioning my professionalism and practically accusing me of sexual assault..." I catch Meg's glance at Sam and say, "Sorry, Sam, but I'm not going to be pissed on and then helped to my feet. I want an official apology."

Meg is staying uncharacteristically calm. "Marc, this is water under the bridge..."

"It might be water under your bridge, but it isn't under mine. I want an apology."

"OK. I'm sorry."

"In writing."

"I'll... write you a letter if that's what you want."

"Not to me. I want you to write a letter to the staff, making it clear that any imputations that have been circulating against me are entirely unfounded and that you take full responsibility for any misunderstanding. In other words, hold your hands up to it, your fault." I've had two days to think about my terms for coming back, so I've got them off pat, and to be truthful it's been my plan to have Sam witness my wiping the floor with Meg Reece.

Meg sits back in her chair. Her outer calm is cracking under the strain of keeping her fury suppressed, but she manages to say with an effort, "Fine, fine. I'll have that done for you." Desperate to reassert her authority, she adds, " In return I need you to be ready to hit the ground running immediately after this weekend. Agreed?"

"No."

Meg's exasperation is boiling over. She flexes her fingers across her desk as if she's considering strangulation. She dips her head, either counting to ten or preparing to hurl herself at me, and I take the opportunity for a surreptitious wink at Sam before I say, "There's one more thing."

"Is there?" Meg is curt now.

"I don't believe that, in the circumstances, I can continue to work alongside Marni. Seems to me you could shift her to another slot and..." here's where I'm to play my trump card, "Ask Sam very nicely if she'd like

187

her old job back." I sit back, and grin cheerfully at Sam. "That's why I asked you to come in with me," I say, quite the dog's bollocks.

We have a few moments of silence. Meg reflecting on my ultimatum. Sam hasn't reacted, but I guess she's playing it poker face, waiting on Meg to show. Eventually she does, addressing Sam. "I take it you haven't discussed this?"

"No."

"Should you tell him or me?"

Sam shrugs her shoulders. "Carry on." I'm baffled by this exchange. What's going on here?

Meg swivels in her chair to confront me. "First, I can tell you that Marni has already left. By mutual consent. She was on a three month probation, but quite frankly I think her shortcomings were obvious to all concerned, including herself. Nice enough girl, but... Let's say she was a bit lacking in organisational skills. As far as a replacement..." Her eyes shift past me.

I'm beginning to get the picture. I cut through Meg's speech and say directly to Sam, "So, you didn't just drop in here last week. Did they make you an offer you couldn't refuse? Is that the real reason you were back in town?"

"Not at all," Sam says, shaking her head.

Meg comes in. "It was a complete coincidence, actually. On Friday I heard Sam was downstairs with Debbie, so I asked her if she'd come up and have a chat."

"And you gave her her old job back?"

"Broached the subject, yes, but she wouldn't confirm. Not right then." Meg swivels her chair towards Sam. "The offer's still open, as discussed."

"I'll have to get back to you," says Sam, looking at me. For a moment I'm confused, thinking she's talking to me direct, then I realise she's responding to Meg. It's Sam that has her by the short and curlies, not me. She's the one that's calling the shots.

"So why didn't you mention it to me?" I'm moaning as we drink a more palatable coffee in the Eldon Arms.

"I was going to, but things got in the way. Anyway, you said you wouldn't accept working for them anymore."

"Not without certain conditions. And one of those conditions, no, *the* condition, was that they had to beg you to come and make the old team up."

"Which, by the way, you neglected to mention to me."

"I didn't *neglect* to mention it, I just wanted to surprise you. Well, impress you. Please you." I reach out my hand and I'm thrilled that she accepts it, if a shade reluctantly, holding it lightly as we continue talking. "I realise I'm still on trial with you."

"You're not on trial. There's no three month probation."

Her remark lightens the mood, recalling the meeting with Meg, which we'd come to from such different perspectives. Sam starts tracing the lines of my veins on the back of my hand as I say, "Fact is, you were the one giving Meg the ultimatum. That's why she had me in."

"No, don't be daft, she knew they'd made a balls-up over your suspension. Julie on Reception told me there's been a lot of listeners making a fuss, asking where you've got to. As far as my job is concerned, the only thing I did say to Meg was that I wouldn't consider coming back unless you were definitely committed to hosting the show."

"You said that last Friday?"

"Yes."

"So why didn't you accept it today? Have you changed your mind in the meantime?"

"No." She pulls at my hand. "Stop beating yourself up. Just, I wanted to talk it over with you first. We need to be sure this is what we both want to do."

"Start again, you mean?"

"Yep."

"In every respect?"

She hesitates. "Yes." Then, "I haven't stopped loving you, even while I've hated you – that's what's made it so much worse. I'm still not sure I like you very much at the moment. I'm working on it."

"So am I. I mean, working on me. I'm sorry."

"You don't have to keep saying that. Just show by the things you do. Including telling me if I disappoint you, or piss you off sometimes, like I do with you. It's about being honest with each other."

"'Course."

She lets go of my hand to finish her coffee. I sit back and look around, hoping there are people in who know us, who can see we're together again.

"What time are you expected at Amina's house?"

"Oh, two o' clock." Looking at my watch. "I'll have to go in a minute, actually." (I'm early but I have to factor in meeting up with Ollie.) "Should I drop you off at the flat?"

"Well, I thought I might go with you if that's all right."

This I hadn't allowed for. "Oh, well, I don't know..."

"I was thinking, if the idea of meeting this woman is to find out more about her, maybe that's something another woman would find it easier to do."

"I suppose..."

"I could be your partner, couldn't I, come up from Liverpool to look at this place we're thinking of buying?"

"Yeah... that makes sense. Only..."

"What? Are you frightened I blow it?"

"'Course not."

"What's the problem, then?" She screws up her face. "There's something you're not telling me about this. What have I just said about being honest with each other?"

"Straight up guv, you've got me bang to rights." The mockney impression is my poor attempt to deflect her, but Sam's not to be budged. She watches me seriously, waiting for an explanation. "The thing is, the truth is, I think there's a slight risk involved. That's why I'm not so keen for you to come along."

"What do you mean, what sort of risk?"

I present Sam with a version of my suspicions of the link between Hassan and Emmanuel, hiding the truth about my run-ins with Emmanuel before the escape attempt, pretending instead that I'd met Norman Tait while I was casing the hospital layout and he'd told me about the comings and goings on the night of Hassan's accident. (At least that last bit was true.) I go over with Sam the clues that have led me to believe that 110 Prince Albert Road might have been another base for the sex traffickers, maybe right up to the time that my gaffe and Simon's stupidity had brought unwanted attention to the address.

"So you're intending to go round to this place, knowing full well that the man who's been chasing you could be waiting?"

"I think the chances of him being there are so remote that it's worth the risk. Besides, there's no reason for Emmanuel to make the connection between the guy who ran away with Edona and the guy who's interested in buying Amina's house. Plus, I'll have somebody watching the place, just as a bit of extra insurance."

"Who?"

"Oliver Dunn."

Sam looks at me incredulously. "Oliver Dunn? *The* Oliver Dunn? He's going to be your lookout? You're joking, right?"

"No, honestly, don't judge the book by the cover. Ollie's a lot more switched on than you'd think. He's just there to watch my back, that's all."

"In that case I'm *definitely* coming with you."

Sam's decision to tag along creates one immediate practical problem, and some discomfort for her. I'd arranged to pick up Oliver outside his house, which was a perfectly reasonable arrangement at the time I thought there'd only be two of us in my car, but with an extra passenger the TT's ludicrous rear seats – normally folded away – have to be pressed into service. There's no way that Ollie's corpulent frame can be squeezed into the tiny space available, so poor Sam has to contort her shapely legs and duck down behind us.

Ollie is beside himself with glee, not just at the prospect of a secret spying mission, but at discovering Sam is back on the scene. All the way to Springhill Gate he plies her with inappropriate questions about why she left the show and whether she'd be coming back, all of which Sam bats back with tact and charm. By the end of the journey I'm convinced that, while Oliver may have a couple of my signed pictures in his drawer, he probably keeps photos of Sam under his pillow.

I've already staked out a quiet parking place a few streets away from Prince Albert Road and there, having levered Sam out of the back seat, we regroup for a final briefing before sending Ollie ahead of us to commence his lookout duties. He proudly shows us his delivery bag, where he has meticulously stocked enough leaflets for the whole neighbourhood.

"You *have* remembered to check my number's in your phone?" Oliver stares at me blankly. "Your phone?" I say again. When we talked on Tuesday night he'd assured me they had a pay-as-you-go mobile phone in the house that he used occasionally. I'd left him a slip of paper with my mobile number on so he could add it into the memory. Unfortunately he'd obviously forgotten to add our conversation into *his* memory. At my prompting Oliver checks through all the pockets of his waterproof and his trousers. He brings out his digital camera, a relatively clean handkerchief and an opened packet of Polo mints, but no telephone. Bugger.

"Give him yours," Sam suggests. "He can always ring me if he needs to tell us anything."

I fish out my cell phone and bring up Sam's number so that Oliver doesn't have to search for it. "OK, touch nothing else on this and you'll be able to get straight through to Sam's mobile if you press that green button. Anything suspicious, anybody you see coming up to the house and you give us a call, OK?"

"What if we hit trouble inside?" asks Sam. I hadn't thought that one through. She's quicker on the uptake. "Listen, Oliver," she says. "If Marc's phone rings don't answer it, but check the screen. If my name comes up on the screen, still don't answer it, but ring 999 straightaway. Ask for police and tell them there's big trouble at 110 Prince Albert Road. Is that OK?"

"If you call, it's big trouble. I have to ring the police."

"Exactly." Sam checks her own mobile, cues up my number and puts the phone back in her pocket. "I'll keep it right here in my hand," she says to me. "Just in case."

"The 999 thing's a bit over the top, isn't it? Nothing's going to happen."

"Just in case."

Thus far Sam has trumped me on the ideas front, but I have one of my own as Oliver is sorting out what goes where in his coat. "Can I borrow your camera, mate?"

Ollie is uncharacteristically reluctant, the merest trace of petulance starting on his mouth at the idea of giving over his prized possession, even to me. Sam joins in to coax him.

"Don't worry, you'll get it straight back later."

The cloud disappears. "'Course, Marc, here y'are." He's happy to have an opportunity to please Sam and, once the camera is handed over, relieved to have one less thing to think about. Suitably prepared, he sets off towards Prince Albert Road, and a minute or so later Sam and I head in the same direction, one hand linking us together, the other nursing metal in our pockets as if we might be packing heat.

Samantha from the agency answers our ring at the front door with a welcoming smile that segues into confusion as she tries to recognise this couple on the doorstep. I help out. "Tom Etherington, we met last week."

"Of course, Mr Etherington, sorry, I wasn't quite sure... And this is...?"

"My partner, Chrissie."

"Fantastic, so pleased you could make it as well. Come in, come in."

As she ushers us into the bare front room I can't help a reflex jolt at the presence there. Not, thank god, the bullet-headed Emmanuel, but two figures hardly less alarming at first sight. In the centre of the room, watching our entry without stepping forward to greet us, a well-built Pakistani or Afghani male, perhaps fifty, impressively bearded under headgear that's halfway between a skull cap and a turban, and dressed in a loose-fitting white tunic that would look casual except for a stiff band collar that seems designed to dignify, and for the fact that he's standing so erect. Behind him and scarier still (am I xenophobic?), a smaller figure, female (I guess) draped from head to foot in black, wearing one of those veils that covers all but the eyes – the kind of clothing I've always associated with Arabs rather than further east - but surely this can't be Amina Begum Khan, who I've seen, if only from a distance, in ordinary western dress. True, she was well covered up in her press photo after Hassan's death, but not to this extreme.

Samantha addresses the man rather than the woman, respectfully. "Here are our clients, sir. Excuse me, interested party." The amendment is for my benefit and she adds brightly, "Clients soon, I hope."

The man nods solemnly and breaks his silence without introducing himself. "I believe you have already inspected the property?"

"*I* have, yes, but not my... Sorry, Tom Etherington, this is my partner, Christine. And...??"

He ignores my cue to make good on the introductions, turning instead to Samantha and, at the edge of brusqueness, announces, "The lady wishes to look over the house."

"I'll come with you, one sec," I say, holding up a hand to Samantha as she makes a move towards Sam, then extending it in an informal offer of a handshake to the woman in black. "Sorry, don't mean to be rude. I'm Tom."

Behind her veil the eyes flick once to the right before a hand emerges from the darkness of her robes to shake mine briefly (timorously), and I sense that she's concentrating hard as she says, like someone practising her vowels, "I am Amina."

The man seems primed to intervene, almost interposing his body between us as he says, "My niece has lived in this house for several years. I understand you have some questions about the area."

"Sure." I stay focused on Amina, saying to her as casually as politeness allows, "Should we talk as we walk?"

Again the party-pooper butts in. "We will wait for you here. Please go on with your tour."

193

Opening gambit repelled, we have no choice now but to leave Amina chaperoned while we tag along with Samantha as she whisks us through the rooms. At least it gives Sam a chance to see in reality what I've been describing, with me nudging her secretly every now and again to draw her attention to certain details like the outside light and the downstairs loo conversion. The one time her eyes meet mine is after I deliberately trail my fingers over the keyhole as we pass through the doorway at the top of the stairs, though I can't tell if this means she agrees it's significant or is warning me not to be so obvious.

In what I've been calling the child's room I take a look through the window at the scene outside. It's currently deserted, with one exception. On the other side of the street I spot Oliver walking slowly back from dropping a leaflet through a letter-box. He's gazing in the general direction of the house, and I notice he has his hand jammed firmly in his pocket where he must be holding my phone. That reminds me I have his camera in my pocket. I take it out and start snapping here and there as Samantha bustles through the rest of the upstairs rooms.

Downstairs Amina and the man who claims to be her uncle don't seem to have moved an inch from where we left them. Sam walks up to try her luck with Amina.

"The house is bigger than it looks from the outside. Have you lived here long?"

Uncle takes closer order as Amina starts her reply. "Nearly three years now. Since just before our baby was born."

"Right. So are you moving out of the area now? New job or something, like us?"

The woman hesitates. Through the veil I can see her looking at her chaperone. He answers for her. "Unfortunately, there has been some sadness. Her husband recently died, and my niece is moving to be closer to her family."

Sam's acting is sublime, or more likely she's feeling real concern and sympathy for Amina, but still probing as she says, "Oh, I'm so sorry to hear that. Poor thing. Had he been ill a long time?"

Uncle intervenes again. "It is best not to speak about this, it is too upsetting for us all. Do you have any more questions about the property?" He turns to me. "Do you wish to make an offer?" I shrug, redirecting him to Sam, who is still hanging in.

"Sorry, I didn't mean to upset anyone," she says. "Can I just ask, Amina, is there a good playgroup nearby?"

The woman answers quietly, with both Sam and her uncle bending their heads to listen, while I free the camera from my pocket and step back a few yards, intending to take a picture of the group under the pretext of photographing the room. As soon as the flash goes off the man turns, startled, in my direction, and bears down on me.

"No photographs. Put your camera away." He looks as though he'd rather seize it. "This is great rudeness."

"No, sorry, I wasn't taking pictures of you, just to remind us what the rooms look like."

"I cannot allow." He brings himself up to his full height as if to offer violence. I make a big display of stuffing the camera back in my pocket and presenting a baffled face to Samantha, who smiles blandly. Uncle moves back to his position next to the two women saying, "We must go. I have business to attend to."

"That's OK, we're done for now," says Sam, which disappoints me since I'm sure we could have kept this going for a while longer and maybe got some more information from Amina. Sam does have one more trick up her sleeve when she says, "I have to say we're really keen on the house. Could I just take a number from you, Amina, in case there's something I've forgotten to ask?" A brave try, but there's no getting round uncle.

"Please direct all your enquiries to this lady here," he says, pointing, not very politely, to Samantha, who nods at us eagerly. There's seems not much more we can do, so, with promises to call Samantha before the weekend, we take our leave. Samantha sees us to the door, while the other two stay in the positions they were in when we arrived.

"Pity about the uncle," I'm muttering to Sam as we walk to the gate. "Kind of a missed opportunity there."

"We've got to catch up with Oliver quick," says Sam, mysteriously. "In case he hits that phone."

"It doesn't matter now."

"It matters. I gave mine to Amina. Didn't get the chance to switch it off."

"What?"

Without answering, she's away on a sort of stuttering run down the road, interrupted every time she passes a garden hedge to check if Ollie's behind it delivering another leaflet. We soon bump into him crossing the road to work his way up our side of the street, and Sam recovers my mobile before she says another word.

"What's going on?" from me.

"Tell you when we get back to the car. Quick, I want away from here."

But even when we reach the car she can't speak freely. There's a young guy showing off his motor-bike to his mates right next to where the TT is parked. We climb into the car, and Sam's cramped position in the back makes it virtually impossible to have any sort of serious conversation. "We'll talk at the flat," she says.

Sam has transmitted an undefined sense of urgency to me. I over-rev out of the parking space, causing the trio of youths to look up from admiring the bike as we pass. I pick up acceleration on the side street and take the left into Springhill Gate with little consideration for the give way sign.

"Hey, I don't want to get there dead!" Sam yells from the back as I speed past traffic and open out on the clearway. She's hardly finished her sentence when there's a bang like a pistol shot. I duck instinctively, the car shudders and slews to the left. I grip the wheel hard, but there's nothing in the steering. Some sort of debris thuds under the car. I slam down on the brake and cause a skid. Sam, thrown across the back seat, lets out a screech. My back end's at forty-five degrees to the road, out of control. An oncoming car dives for cover at the verge. A horn blasts from behind. Desperate to stop, I wrench at the handbrake. The car whips further round and finally stops, pointing the way we came, and I'm staring through my windscreen through another windscreen at a face that must reflect mine in its look of shock.

Fortunately the driver has managed to stop in time and there's only pride injured as I step out of my door in front of a queue of traffic that's already starting to build and will soon stretch all the way back to The Gate. I can see shreds of rubber strewn along the side of the road for several yards, so I've diagnosed the problem before I walk around the front of the car and find the evidence of a blowout on my front passenger wheel.

Ollie and Sam clamber out of the TT and pretty soon, with the help of the relieved driver behind, we've shoved the car out of the way and the traffic can get moving again, though it's slow enough past us while the people inside the vehicles enjoy a good view of our predicament.

"We could've been killed there, eh, Marc?" Oliver burbles happily, his cheeks red with excitement and the effort of pushing.

"I thought somebody was shooting at us," says Sam. She wasn't alone with that thought, but I say nothing about the image of Emmanuel and Stefan that sprang immediately to mind.

196

In fact I discover that those two may well have been indirectly to blame for what happened. Once I've got over the difficulty of fitting the spare wheel I drop off Sam and Ollie at the flat, restraining my curiosity about Sam's strange dealings with Amina while I hunt out a tyre services place to get the car sorted – I am a degree-level incompetent with anything mechanical so the odds of the spare wheel spinning off are short and I don't fancy my chances of cheating death that way a second time. The guy who fixes me up with a new tyre takes a good look at the remnants of the old one.

"Have you had a bump on this wheel?" he says. "I mean, before. Or a scrape?"

"Mmm, not sure. Why?"

"See here?" He rubs his finger at the edges of a hole in the rubber. "This has been distended, kind of blebby – looks like the blowout's happened here, where the bleb has weakened the tyre. It's the kind of thing that can happen if you mount a kerb too hard, or scrape against it maybe."

The memory of my race through the barriers on Drummond Road is still fresh. Banging the front wheel off the edge of the chicane as I looked for Stefan in the mirror. I nearly lost it then, and I've been fortunate to get away without injury again. I don't believe in you, God, but thanks for everything. "Make sure you put those nuts on tight," I tell the mechanic later while he's fitting the new tyre. Whether it's luck or divine intervention I don't want to push it too far.

I can see Sam watching from the window of the flat, anxiety personified, as I park the TT down below. Ollie, by contrast, is the picture of contentment indoors, his coat off, slurping a cup of tea Sam's made him, clocking the details of the room so he can describe it to his mam later. He'd be taking pictures if it wasn't for the fact that his camera is still in my pocket. My mobile phone is on the table.

"What's the story?" I ask Sam as soon as I get in. "Why did you give your phone to Amina? If it was Amina."

"So she can contact us."

"Well, I'm sure she'll have a phone of her own. Besides, the interfering uncle says Samantha has to handle everything, so I don't think she'll be rushing to give us any more gen about the house."

"It's not about the house. Listen, Amina's not free to talk for some reason..."

"That's obvious."

197

"But she's desperate to warn you about something."

"Warn me?"

"Yes. As soon as that feller got distracted, trying to stop you using the camera, she came up close and whispered *I have to warn Marc*. There was no chance to say anything else, so all I could think to do was give her my phone. She hid it in her whadyacallit. *Burqa*. That's why I wanted us to get away quick after that, just in case Oliver rang."

Ollie smiles at the mention of his name. "I kept the lookout, Marc. I kept the lookout, but there was nobody came."

"Thanks Ollie," I say perfunctorily, my mind on Amina's words. "She definitely said *warn Marc*?"

"*I have to warn Marc*. That's exactly what she said. Her eyes close up... They were intense. Frightened, really. I got the shivers."

"But how does she know my name is Marc? As far as she's aware I'm Tom Etherington. And Emmanuel thinks I'm called Oliver. Presuming that's who she's warning me about."

"I don't know. Maybe she recognised you from your photo in the paper. She's bound to have seen the piece, don't you think, or somebody's shown her, with it mentioning Hassan."

I rescue the *Chronicle* press cutting from where I've kept it folded under a corner of my laptop. I open it out on the table and stare at my infamous V sign picture, Sam studying it as well from behind my shoulder. "You look completely different there," she says. "I'd be surprised if she made the connection just from that shot. Unless she knew it was you coming to the house today. That estate agent woman saw you before you got your hair done, didn't she?"

"Yeah, but she didn't know me from Adam. I'm Tom Etherington as far as she's concerned. That bloke today the same, the way he was asking if we were going to make an offer. It's all he was interested in."

"That's how it seemed," says Sam, taking the press cutting from the table to examine it more closely. "Anyway, however she found out, Amina knows who you really are."

"Which probably means Emmanuel does as well. A wee bit disconcerting."

Sam replaces the cutting under the computer, stands tracing her finger aimlessly over the mouse in a state of quiet abstraction, then turns with a worried expression to say, "Do you think Amina could be in the same situation Edona was? A prisoner, basically?"

"Dunno."

"It's a possibility, isn't it, if like you say that house is fitted up in a similar way to the other one, and this Emmanuel's in the background somewhere?"

"But she's a local woman, and married. Or was. With a baby. It hardly fits the profile of a sex slave, does it? Plus, don't Muslims stone prostitutes and adulterers?" I'm suddenly highly conscious of Oliver sitting there on the sofa, listening to all this, and I feel like a parent who's dropped his guard and talked dirty when his kids are in earshot. I slap him on the shoulder. "Hey, Ollie, I'd better take you home, your mam'll be wondering where you are."

"Give me your car keys, I'll do it," says Sam, fetching Ollie's coat. "I need you to stay here in case the phone rings."

"I'll just take it with me."

"She might ring the landline. Your name's under both numbers in my phone. I've got a feeling she's not going to have many chances to call – don't want you to miss it, cos I'm pretty sure you won't be able to ring her back."

"Fair enough." I hand Sam the keys to the Audi and thank Ollie again for his help as they're going out of the door. It's not until I'm watching them from the window that I remember I've still got his camera. I rattle at the window pane, but they're already seated in the car, so I dash across to get the camera from my coat pocket and hare down the stairs to the street, only to see the car disappearing along the road. Without thinking, I run back up the stairs and bring up Sam's number so I can ring her mobile and get her to come back for the camera. I've already pressed the dial button when I realise what I've done.

"Oh, shit a brick!"

I hit the red button to stop the call, sweat breaking out on me. I hold the phone to my ear, praying that I don't hear a ring tone or, worse, the uncle's voice. Or Emmanuel's. Or Boris's. Nothing. Does a mobile phone automatically ring as soon as someone's pressed that green button? I don't know. As an experiment I ring my own mobile from the house phone, but directly after I push to dial I hang up. I'm staring at my phone on the table, willing it not to ring. It doesn't. Have I stopped the other call in time, or have I compromised Amina? I flop onto the sofa, worrying about this. Then I find something else to worry about. I've just let Sam go off in the Audi without considering that she might be spotted by the bad guys. What if they chase her, like they did me the other night? That's infinitely worse than the Amina gaffe.

199

"Don't panic," I say aloud to myself. *Hitchhiker's Guide to the Galaxy.* DON'T PANIC. I'm panicking. I stand up again to stare through the window, as if I could haul Sam back home with the power of thought.

All this time I've been holding on tight to Ollie's camera, squeezing it in my grip like a stress ball. I don't even notice until I accidentally switch on the power button and the zoom lens nudges through my hand. Glad to have anything to stop me feeling helpless and sick, I sit back on the sofa fiddling with the controls on the back of the camera until I've worked out how to bring the images onto the little screen there. The first one that comes up is the group of three clustered together in the living room of Prince Albert Road. I've caught it just as Sam seems to be asking Amina a question while the uncle, oblivious of the camera at that moment, is bending his head over the pair to listen. Sam has both hands in her coat pockets, more natural-looking than Ollie out in the street with his determined hold on the phone. The other woman is slightly smaller than Sam and of a similar build, as far I can tell, which marries with my memory of Amina that day she was pushing the buggy. The uncle, now I have a chance to study him without inhibition, could well be the guy next to Amina in that press photo I saw in the library – something I'll have to check.

I use the back button to flick through the pictures I took upstairs. Nothing special there, just reminders of the layout. One with Samantha in it, smiling in that exaggerated way people do sometimes when they catch sight of a lens pointing at them. Further back again and I'm into snaps Oliver must have taken on his travels. A dog on a leash for some reason. An anonymous couple posing for the camera in what could be a city park. A couple of indeterminate images of the street, possibly shot through the bus window. The front of a pub – actually the pub where Ollie and I had lunch after our library visit. I can't remember him taking that one; I wonder if he came back on another day to add it to his collection. Maybe I just missed it - the next one back is me on the bus, my face in shadow because of the light behind. And the one before that is outside my flat, just the building with the Audi parked in front. I'd guess from the angle that Ollie was standing at the bus stop over the road.

I keep on flicking idly back, but with less and less interest as by now the random images have nothing to do with anyone or anything I know, except for a medium close-up of his mam in her dark glasses and outdoor coat, apparently on a trip to somewhere – the shops, maybe. The pictures go on and on – Ollie doesn't seem to have acquainted himself with the delete function – and I've almost given up hope of getting to the end when... I'm gazing at the proffered rump of a naked female, arsehole

200

protruding, pink labia below. The vagina is so generously inviting in the close-up that I can only assume some unseen fingers are stretching the outer lips apart. I'm at once dumbstruck, revolted and aroused. How can this filth have found its way into Oliver's camera?

I stare until decency overcomes lasciviousness and the moral thumb presses down to click away from the image. It's as if I've pulled back the camera lens, for I'm now watching the same (I suppose) female rear from a distance where I can see her jeans and knickers pulled down, a blouse flipped over her back. On this shot the woman's hands are prising at her own backside to separate the cheeks. Another click and she's front end to camera at pelvis range, showing off her snatch in the same way. Next it's a mid-range shot of a bare torso, blouse open and bra held up to allow plump naked breasts to poke out below, jeans and knickers down to reveal dark pubic hair. I can see enough of a brick wall in the background to deduce that the photos have been taken outdoors, maybe in a back street somewhere. The reverse sequence of naughty poses ends (or begins) with a head-and-shoulders-plus shot of the girl getting her tits out and pouting amateurishly at the camera. I can say *girl* with confidence now because this is the first time I've seen her face, street-pretty with two-tone hair in need of attention, and a couple of teenage spots not quite covered by orange make-up. Then it's back to the bland, indiscriminate shots that are more typical of the Oliver Dunn *oeuvre*.

I shut off the camera and try to bring myself back to the reality of the room, but my mind is racing with the thought of Oliver, in his bright yellow waterproof, snapping away as this young tart performs her low-grade striptease for him in a back alley. Starters before the main course? Or is he content with the voyeurism of the camera, perving to be recollected in tranquillity? My preconceptions about Oliver Dunn have just taken a flip-flop. I can't get my head round this. I just can't imagine... But why not? Perhaps Oliver has more need than most of us to find relief in this kind of interactive pornography, or actual sex, what could be more natural? I'm assuming he's paid for it, saved up cash from his delivery job and... And what? Where has he come across this girl? Presumably she's local. Did he just bump into her on a street corner? Did he proposition her? She him? Of course, it happens all the time, doesn't it? Why shouldn't it happen to Oliver? Well, it never happened to me, not until I specifically went out in search of Edona. It's a subterranean world that belongs to the street-wise and the low-lifes, not.... But what about that old civil servant type who Boris sent to Edona's room, the night of the escape? He was quite plainly neither street-wise nor low-life. How did he

201

get to be in that place at that time, consorting with pimps and criminals and prostitutes?

I recall an especially lively phone-in night after I'd talked to a studio guest from an organisation called Outsiders. Whether they're still going I don't know, but this charity specialised in helping disabled people with their sexual problems, including helping them to find sexual partners. The phones went hot directly after my guest told me about their Sex Angels scheme that had volunteers or sometimes people who were paid to have sex with their members. It caused something of an outcry on the show, and for a while in the local press, with some listeners deploring the whole idea, others applauding it, some even wanting to get involved. My guest told me there was a strict vetting procedure for these angels. Judging by some of the people I talked to that night I guess there'd have to be. It was amazing how the whole subject of sex and the disabled got people going, in every sense of the phrase.

I wonder whether Ollie was tuned in that night. Not that he's disabled as such, but... Maybe it gave him an idea, a contact. Maybe this girl in the pictures is a sex angel herself, who knows? What do we really know about how people live their private lives? I've had my eyes opened so much over these past two or three weeks.

All the time I'm having this discussion in my head, and deluding myself about my liberal credentials, there's another part of me getting the creeps from what I've learned about Ollie in the last few minutes, even to the extent that my concern for Sam is switching from the threat of Emmanuel to the threat of... I once called Ollie my stalker. Does he have somebody else in his sights? Why does he always carry that camera around? Why, come to think of it, is *he* always around? What are his motives?

That's absurd, ridiculous. Now it's the other part of me rightly slapping me across the face about my feelings. What makes me superior to Ollie? What's the difference? Who am I to be disgusted by what he might choose to do? Where's the crime?

But the strongest voice is the one that says, *Come on, Sam. Walk through that door right now. Come home to me.*

Half an hour later (it seems like two hours) she does, apparently unmolested.

"What took you so long?"

"Been on the phone to Mrs Dunn's GP. You know, she's been on the waiting list nearly six months for her cataract operation. Apparently

202

she's got so many health complications she'll have to go as an in-patient, so it's a question of bed availability. He promised to chase it up, so it was worth ringing."

"Why d'you have to get so involved? I was worried. Didn't see any silver BMWs on your tail, did you?" I don't mention my new concerns about Ollie, but I've put his camera away in a drawer in case she starts trawling through it like I did. Sam has a bit of a soft spot for Oliver, and I don't want to shatter any illusions.

"No," she says. "What about you – any phone calls?"

"Not yet."

Nor do we hear from Amina for the rest of the evening, though we spend plenty of time talking about her, and about what we're going to do with Edona. Our conversation is still going on when we're lying side by side in bed. Something troubling Sam is the fact that, while we procrastinate, not only are dangerous characters like Emmanuel roaming round, they're still in business in Warkworth Street and maybe other places too. At least Edona is in a safe place for the moment, but what about the other women in the house, still being abused on a daily basis? Sam is all for going to the police, but I'm more cautious, telling her what Edona said about possible police involvement in the sex rings. I prefer to see what Fern comes back with, though we've heard nothing from her since she promised to check out what the various agencies might be able to offer.

Sam responds to my argument with another idea. "What if we went in at the highest level with the police?"

"I don't think you can just walk into a police station and demand a private meeting with the Chief Constable. It doesn't work like that."

"I know one person who could get to him," says Sam.

"Who?"

"Neville Crawcrook. He's best pals with all the higher-ups. Probably all masons together. He's our best route in, get him to invite the top guy for lunch or whatever, and get ourselves invited as well. Or you, anyroad. Then you can work on him."

"Not likely."

"Why not?"

"Listen, there's no way I'm going to involve Neville Crawcrook in this business. The guy's a prick and a fake. Bad combination."

"You're just being pig-headed. If it's going to help Edona, or protect..."

"No way. Arse-licking to Crawcrook so he'll do us a favour then take the credit... I don't even want to talk about it." Being careful to kiss

Sam first to demonstrate she hasn't put me in a huff, I turn on my side and make it clear that I'm going to sleep. But, just as they say eating cheese before bedtime gives you nightmares, so this unsatisfactory end to our discussion weighs heavily on me and, what with all the other disturbing episodes of the day, I have a deeply troubled night.

Emmanuel and Stefan are the bogeymen of my dreams, crashing into the apartment and dragging Sam naked out of our bed. I try to run after them, but I just slither onto the floor. I've lost the use of my legs. Now I'm dressed in a Bruce Willis vest, rolling myself along mean unlit streets in a wheelchair, my calls for Sam hampered by having to bite my lip against the awful debilitating ache in my arms from the strain of pumping the wheels. Sinister, tantalising things are happening just beyond my view in dark corners and alleyways. A man that might be Lev the barman (but in the way of dreams looks like the shopkeeper from *Mr Benn*) steps out of the shadows and asks if I want *cheap steroids very dear.* Without waiting for an answer he brings out a huge hypodermic syringe from under his fez and stabs the needle into my nearest arm. It's agony. I'm lifted out of the wheelchair with the pain. I'm aware he's given me a lethal dose of Toxic 7 and now I'm on a stretcher in an ambulance. Next to my head, stuck up in the ambulance, I can see dozens of pornographic pictures, unknown women offering up their backsides for medical inspection. I feel a hand on my prick and think it's mine, but when I turn the other way there's Fern the social worker at the side of the stretcher, her hand under my blanket, smirking, and saying *Care in the community.* Behind her is Ollie, dressed in a high vis jacket, eating an Orange Maid. I try to get off the stretcher and find I'm lying on a marble slab, unable to lift my shoulders. Somebody's saying *Warn Marc.* I can only move my head, and when I do I see Sam on her marble slab on one side of me and Edona on hers on the other. The three of us are naked and exposed. We're in a huge church, all marbled stone, with *Warn Marc* echoing around the roof like a whispering gallery. When I strain my head to look between my feet I can see a sloped aisle with big doors at the far end and a congregation of nuns on either side, hands to their lips in prayer or to hide their whispering. They are all facing me, but they can't keep their sly eyes away from the aisle. Sam says something. I turn to her and she says again, *Awaiting entry,* but she's looking past me, talking to Edona. The doors open with a flourish and in walks Amina's uncle, splendid in white ecclesiastical robes, with a trio of men behind him, all wearing loose white cambric shirts, open at the chest, and pirate breeches, carrying knives across their hearts as if they are about to cut off their own left breast. The three are Neville Crawcrook, the old civil servant, and a man I recognise as the Chief Constable but who has the face of the traffic cop. As they process up the aisle all the nuns open their hymn books and start singing together.

Hey, where did we go? Days that the rains came.
Down in the hollow, playing a new game.

"There's a synch problem," I say to Sam, who's stretching her arm from her slab to mine. "Don't worry about it, I'll fix it." She keeps tapping me, agitated. "No, it's interference," I explain. "Another signal leaking in."

"Marc! The phone!"

"Yeah, got it."

"Marc!"

I open my eyes. Van Morrison is filling the bedroom. The mobile on the table is glowing in the dark. "Christ!" I leap across Sam and grab the phone, hitting receive just before my recorded message is due to kick in. "Yes, hello, this is..." I stop myself. Who am I? Marc? Tom? Oliver?

"I am Amina Begum Khan." The voice is an urgent whisper.

"Yes. Yes, I know."

"I only have a few seconds while they let me use the toilet."

"Who's they? Is it Emmanuel? Boris?"

"I don't know these names. Please don't talk, listen. I am being held against my will. I am not trusted. Something is planned for the *Jihad bis Saif*. I don't know what." Sam turns on the lamp and I make a rapid writing sign. She scrabbles about looking for pen and paper while Amina continues. "It must be local – the plan is to call you, I heard them say."

I can't stop myself interrupting. "Call me?"

"Your show. For publicity. When it's too late to stop it. Hassan will call."

"Hassan? Your Hassan? Is he still alive?"

"Dead to me now." There's a noise in the background, another woman's voice. A pause, then it's Amina again, briefly. "I have to go."

"What's it called, that thing you said?" I have the pen ready, but we're cut off. I write *Jeehad bus? Jihad? + ...?* on the paper. Sam crawls over the bed to me, watches what I'm writing.

"Has she gone? Did she say where she was?"

"In a toilet. That's as much as I know. There was another woman, other side of the door maybe. You were right, she is being held prisoner."

"Is it the same? The ones who had Edona?"

"I don't think so, she didn't know the names. No, I think this is a different thing altogether. Have you heard of this?"

Sam looks at the words on the paper. "I've heard of *jihad*. Is that what it is?"

"I think that's what she said. *Jihad*, something else. That's an *Al Qaeda* thing, yeah?"

"Something of the sort. I don't really know much about it."

"Nor me, but I guess we're about to find out. I'm being sucked into some kind of terrorist plot."

"Oh my god, Marc."

Sam moves in to hold me, and we embrace on the edge of the bed, both naked and shivering, though the room is warm enough. I stroke Sam's hair and kiss her once gently before I say, "No more argument from me. This is way too serious. Forget lunch, but I think we'd better get Neville to call his friend."

XIV

Once Neville Crawcrook has calculated what's it in for him, and worked out how to position himself so he can gain maximum advantage from a successful outcome, or disown anything that might go tits up, he makes the call and fixes a meeting. Which causes the first of several rows I'm destined to have with him over his handling of the affair.

"In his office? Have you not explained to him that I've got people on my case? I can't afford to be seen wandering into police headquarters – they'll know we're onto them, and Amina could be in even more danger."

"Philip Finch is a busy man. If it's more convenient for him..."

"Bugger that. Call him back, you're going to have to change it. Meet him here, or better still somewhere neutral. Find a hotel suite."

Neville looked obdurate behind his big desk until I mentioned the hotel suite, which must have been sufficiently swanky-sounding to get him to change his mind, though I notice this time he gets his PA to ring to change the arrangements, the better to save face and bolster his own importance, and underline the fact that he too is a remarkably busy man.

Chief Constable Philip Finch, I find, is either a wise man or a fool. Soberly suited like the others in his retinue at the meeting, he sits and listens carefully to my story, then leans forward and says with forensic calm, "Have you considered the possibility that this could be another hoax?"

"Another hoax?"

He sits back, ensures he has everyone's attention before he continues. "Well, assuming we have no spiritualists here, I take it we are all agreed that the original call to your radio programme was a hoax. Indeed it was admitted as such, even though your engineer's test revealed that the person making the original call and the person making the confession were not necessarily the same. That does not negate the obvious conclusion that someone was, as they say, having you on, though the family suffered rather too much media attention as a result. I think you also mentioned that on your first visit to the house there were clear signs that this lady had been planning to leave before you got involved, so there's no particular mystery around the empty house or the encounter you had with Amina and her uncle. I think you'll agree, Sayeed..." he turns to an Asian man on his side of the table, "The protective, maybe over-protective, attitude shown by the uncle to the niece as described by Mr Niven is not untypical in traditional Islamic culture?"

"Quite right, sir. Particularly when the lady has experienced some recent trauma, as is the case here."

"Exactly." Finch looks at me across the table. "Let me suggest the hypothesis that Amina Begum Khan did indeed recognise you for who you really are when you came in posing as Mr...?"

"Etherington."

"Etherington, thank you. That imposture might have been quite provoking, don't you think, to a lady who has had her fair share of trouble from the media when all she wants to do is sell her house and get on with her life? Perhaps her dramatic turn was nothing more than her way of getting her own back. Reasonable theory, or not?"

"Not," pipes up Sam, sitting next to me. "Excuse me, but I was inches away from Amina when she gave me her warning. I can assure you, she wasn't acting."

"And you could see that clearly through a full-face veil?" The policeman smiles thinly at Sam.

At the head of the table Neville begins to shuffle uncomfortably. "You know, Marc," he starts, tapping his forefinger on the polished surface, "I did caution this could be much ado about nothing, but you would insist..." He's interrupted by a cough from the bottom end of the table. One of Finch's men – I'm guessing a senior detective, though he's quite a young man – has been looking through the printouts I've supplied of the shots taken at the house, together with the press cuttings I've culled from the library.

"If I might put in a word, sir." He's addressing his boss, not mine. Mr Finch nods at him to continue. "I might be one hundred percent mistaken here, but I have a strong hunch that the face I'm looking at in this picture could be Imam Zaid bin Ali."

Sayeed immediately takes an interest, reaching for his glasses and putting his other hand out for the paper, which the guy at the end passes up the table.

"Remind me...?" says Finch.

"Security Service have been watching him on and off for a while now, since his days in Birmingham. Suspected of preaching militant *jihad*, radicalising the young men at the mosque. They had started gathering evidence through infiltration when he moved up here maybe a year ago.

That's when they touched base with us, though there's been precious little to write home about since, to be honest."

"I know of him," says Sayeed, looking at the picture. "He's connected with the Springhill mosque now. It's a moderate community, however, perfectly respectable."

"On the surface, maybe," mutters the detective.

"I've heard nothing to suggest otherwise," Sayeed shoots back, obviously peeved by a comment that presumes to doubt his professionalism. In the silence that follows Finch appropriates the printout from under Sayeed's nose and studies it before he speaks again.

"We don't expect you to be the fount of all our Asian intelligence, Sayeed, so forgive me if my question is naive, but are you aware of any blood relationship between this man and the family Khan?"

"I'm not familiar... I would say it's unlikely."

"Mmm." Finch looks up from the image to take in Sam and me opposite. "Tell me again about the room arrangements you noticed in the house."

I recount what little I'd gleaned from my visits to the unfurnished property, even down to the location of telephone points and the fact that the upstairs sockets had plastic guards on though the downstairs ones didn't, as well as the more obvious features such as the toilet conversion and the partition at the top of the stairs. I keep it factual, as I've done from the start of this meeting, making no mention of my original supposition that the house had been used as a brothel, because I'm now thinking I must have been mistaken about that, but also because I have made no mention at this stage of Edona or Emmanuel. The fear of a terrorist plot has relegated all of my other concerns, and I don't want to further complicate matters that seem complex enough already. Nor, frankly, do I want to give my employer the impression that I've been consorting with prostitutes.

"What's your take on all this, Liam?" Philip Finch asks his colleague at the other end of the room after I've gone through my account a second time, with some extra contributions from Sam. "Have we come across a cell on our patch?" I thought he meant *prison cell* until I work out from the response that he means *terrorist cell*.

"Sounds like it might have been used as a safe house," says Liam. "The thorough cleaning of the dustbins suggests they were trying to remove all possible traces when they vacated. The whole Hassan thing is a mystery at the moment. I remember when that little media storm blew up a couple of weeks ago we doubled-checked the records on his accident and we have a positive DNA match to the body as well as other evidence,

209

so mistaken identity is not an issue. Amina also intrigues me. She told Marc on the phone that she was being held against her will, and obviously her behaviour corroborates that. That could perhaps explain the lockable door upstairs, except for one thing that niggles." He directs himself at me. "Marc, you told us that when you first went to watch the house you saw Amina walking freely out in the street, dressed in western style, with her little boy in the pushchair. That doesn't seem to fit with the rest of it. How sure are you that it was the same person you saw in the *burqa*, and in this press picture?" He points out the cutting on his pile of paper.

"Can't say I'm entirely sure except for the height and build. To be perfectly honest, I can't say I'm sure of anything very much at this stage. One thing I am certain of, and Sam was making the same point earlier, this woman is not party to any hoax. She's genuinely frightened, definitely in some sort of danger."

Neville interrupts. "I think we'd better let the police be the judge of that, Marc."

"Actually, Neville," says Finch, "I think Mr Niven is probably right. Despite my earlier reservations I do now think we have a genuine case for investigation here. Directly after this meeting I'm going to be asking for the full involvement of the Security Service. MI5, if you will. Obviously I'm going to have to ask everyone here for the utmost discretion and cooperation."

Sam stirs. "What about Amina? Shouldn't your first priority be to find her?"

"Absolutely."

"Well, this man here knows where that *imam* person preaches." Sam indicates Sayeed, who acknowledges her silently. "And there's the estate agent. They must have a contact."

Finch's smile is a touch patronising. "Yes, but we also have to look at the bigger picture. Safety and security are paramount, but sometimes it can be more effective to gather and wait until the right moment before you pounce, otherwise the whole flock gets away and you end up grasping at thin air."

I guess Liam can see from Sam's expression that she is not satisfied with his chief's answer, so he steps in to reassure her. "Don't worry, we'll be making every effort to locate Amina, even if we don't charge in as soon as we find out where she is. Actually, the fact that you had the presence of mind to give her your mobile could be a godsend."

"Not if she doesn't get the chance to use it again."

"Even if she doesn't we should be able to get a rough fix on her last location from the call she made to Marc. The telephone company may still have the information stored. Better still if she does make another call, or even if she just keeps the phone switched on. Electronically speaking, the phone will be looking for the nearest cell tower. There's a system called triangulation that looks at the signals to the different base stations and from those can work out where the phone is. Well, within about fifty yards or so, anyway. Once we've tracked her down we can start getting people into position so we can secure her safety at the critical time."

"What about Marc's safety?" Sam asks. I wish she'd stop being so fearful, but I could kiss her for her concern.

The detective seems about to answer until Finch raises a finger and commandeers the response. "We appreciate your anxieties, but let's assess this situation calmly. If a plot is going to unfold as envisaged it is the phone-in programme, not the particular presenter, that is of interest to the conspirators. On the other hand, of course we see Marc as absolutely key on our side because that is where the connection is being made with the lady we might think of as our mole in the camp. We'll be looking after him, but round-the-clock police protection carries the risk of being detected by the other party, causing them to change their plans, which could be more dangerous still. Currently we have a chink of light, no more, on what these people are intending to do. If we lose that we're all in the dark." Finch is obviously fond of his metaphors. He pauses for us to appreciate his latest, then carries on. "In these situations it is very important to view things through the mind of the criminal. No purpose will be served by their causing Marc harm. They want to use him as a conduit for their message. Oh, and Neville..." he turns to his friend, "I imagine our intelligence people will want to talk to you about fixing some extra lines into your studios."

Neville is expansive. "Just say the word – anything you need from us you can have, of course, it goes without saying. You know..." He chuckles as if he is about to share an anecdote. "I should feel flattered that our little station is regarded as such an important channel of communication, even by these..." he struggles for the word and amazingly comes up with *blackguards*. "By these blackguards. But you wonder why they don't tackle the national boys. I mean, I'm very proud of our reach, but for impact beyond the region..."

This is a man masquerading as a media professional. Time to help him out. "Well, number one, they're statistically far less likely to get through to somewhere like Five Live on any given night. Number two, they're already guaranteed national, probably worldwide, coverage if what they're planning is big enough."

"Why bother with us, then?"

"Because the bomb, or whatever, is the act but not the message. Not an articulated message anyway, one they can control and transmit directly. This group wants the chance to justify what they're doing in terms of their mission, and to take credit for it. They might only reach a local audience at the time they call, but they know full well, once it's done, it will be replayed on every station that carries news, plus YouTube... everywhere. You will be ruing you can't sell ads on the back of it, Neville – you'd kill for an audience that size."

Talk about my boss's choice of words, that last phrase was a lead balloon moment from Marc Niven. All the eyes that were on me are lowered at once, and I feel a prickle at the nape of my neck. Finch comes to my rescue with a speech of his own, alerting us to it by tapping a pen twice on his glass of water, and squaring his shoulders in the military style that Neville tries on sometimes when he's addressing a group of staff. Finch is more successful at commanding the meeting than Neville ever manages. "Gentlemen, and lady, I'm conscious that time is pressing, and we all have a lot of urgent work to do. Can I just say to everyone, I'm grateful for the information you have given me today, and for your continued cooperation. This may yet prove to be a mere squib of a thing – and in many ways I hope it does – but if not, *if* it is the turn of our city to be the target of terrorism, I'm confident we can beat it by working together." It's easy to see how Finch got to be where he is today (says the residual cynic in me) but I can't help feeling just a smidge inspired.

Sam remains to be convinced about Finch, though she is impressed with the young detective Liam Guthrie. "Why didn't you tell him about Edona and the other house?" she says later. "I think he'd handle it well."

"Because Edona is relatively safe with us just now – I want them to focus on finding Amina. Besides, I'm less confident about the connection than I was. Don't worry, I'll talk to Guthrie about Edona before long – I've got his direct line."

I'm pre-empted on that front by Fern, who finally has some news to give us when we meet up with her in the evening at Chrissie's house. Edona stays downstairs this time, and it's so nice to see her curled on the settee in comfortable clothes, drinking coffee with us and keeping half an eye on the TV that's murmuring in the background, as ordinary teenagers do.

"OK," says Fern, "So what I've discovered is there's an IOM shelter in Tirana which could be ideal for repatriating Edona safely."

212

"What's IOM?" asks Sam.

"International Organisation for Migration. Sorry, love, acronyms abound. Like somebody once said, the trouble with bureaucracy is too many TLAs."

"TLAs?"

"Three Letter Abbreviations. Anyway, point is this is a damn good place. It's secure, so the pimps and criminals won't get to her. They've got counsellors, also people who can check out the family position, maybe even help them out financially. It's part-funded by the Catholic Church - make what you will of that, but Edona tells me her family is of the faith so it's a plus point in my book. And there's a properly controlled migration programme that organises real jobs in Italy. On the downside most of these tend to go to the Albanian men in the programme, but 'twas ever thus. It's still an excellent scheme."

"What do you think of that, Edona?" I ask her.

"Sound good. I like to see my family again when is possible. Maybe jobs in England too, from this place?"

"Don't know, love," says Fern. "That might be more difficult."

"We'll keep working at it this end," Chrissie promises. "So when you're old enough you can maybe come back. Very least you can come for a nice long holiday, stay with us, if you'd like to."

"I like, of course. Thank you."

"You're welcome, any time."

Fern lifts both hands. "Whoa there. Remember, we're just at first base. Edona's existence isn't even officially acknowledged yet, not by me nor anyone else. My understanding is there are very few places in the Tirana shelter, so we've got to make sure that Edona is seen as a priority. What I'd like to do is go through Save the Children – they have a close association with the IOM projects and they could provide us with the route we need."

"Great," says Chrissie. "Can we call them tomorrow?"

"It's not as simple as that. I mean, how do they know Edona isn't just any illegal immigrant? First, we have to provide some evidence that she's been trafficked and prostituted. We also have to work with the police and other partners on getting that brothel closed down and the rest of the girls away safely. We're going to need your help with this, Marc, otherwise Edona doesn't have a witness."

I glance at Sam before I reply, and she gives a sort of internal shrug. How complicated can our lives get? "I'll do anything to help, of course." (I sound like Neville.) "But could we hold off a couple of days? There's so much going on around me at the moment."

213

All my recent Brownie points with Chrissie suddenly count for nothing. "Yes, well, I know you've got to get your career back on track and all that, Marc," she says snidely, "But I would have thought that Edona deserves... She's been through a lot, poor girl."

Sam weighs in on my side. "It's not all about Marc's career, sis. There are things going on – confidential, important things – that could have major, major consequences. Sorry, we can't say any more at this stage."

Chrissie's disbelief is caustic. "Oh, yeah, well sorry if I'm not out saving the world, or whatever, only I'm the one with the house guest to look after, in case you haven't noticed."

"I thought you said she was welcome anytime," Sam shoots back, riled now.

"Of course she is, that's not the point. Marc standing up to his responsibilities, that's the point." The air is heavy with implication. It's up to me, I feel, to smooth things over.

"Look, I'm fine with whatever you want to do. Just push the button, Fern, and let me know where you want me to be and who you want me to talk to, whenever. Chrissie's right, Sam. We've can't neglect Edona while we deal with... everything else."

Well, I may have manoeuvred her sister back on my side with that little soft-shoe shuffle, but I can see by the expression on Sam's face she's now got *her* nose out of joint since I seem to have put her in the wrong. And, as she's the first to remind me when we get back in the car, it was my idea to leave the Edona story out of the account I gave to the police. If I do ever quit broadcasting, perhaps the diplomatic corps would not be my best alternative.

My kind of diplomacy these days involves avoiding full-on confrontation with Sam, so when we get back I decide another spell of solitary exercise might be a good idea, prompted by seeing Oliver's camera still attached to my laptop from the morning's printing session.

"I think I'll take a run across and give Ollie his camera back."

"What if Amina rings again?"

"Don't worry, I'll take my phone – she called the mobile last time, so that's the number she'll use."

The run gives me the chance to think through the developments of the past few days, and I suppose it's the quickening of my pulse rate as I pound the streets that starts me off mentally plotting the changes in graph form, with Sam's leaving as the origin. There's the life-line, which is my physical well-being, or rather the danger to it. At the start the only threat was self-neglect and the abuse I was giving my body through drinking too much and getting generally run down and unfit. The graph in my head registers the blip of shock on Valentine's night when I realised that I might have missed a suicide's cry for help, but the first jag of real danger coincides with meeting Emmanuel, the line rising from there and reaching a peak on the night I carried out my plan to rescue Edona. It dips slightly after the car chase, (with another sharp point marking the blowout later) but the line gets thicker with Amina's warning, and it's maintaining a consistently high level – at what I'd call the fear-mark – right now, despite any reassuring noises the police are making.

There's the heart-line of emotions, passions – love, if you will. This is intricate, the one that shows most annotations and variations, starting in a trough when Sam left me and digging down deeper as my failure to cope became more and more apparent. My attempts at lifting myself out of the despond, hitting on Marni and flirting with other assorted females, ultimately had the opposite effect and sapped my vitality. Ironically it was my meeting Edona – for all the sordid circumstances and the details of her distressing story – that stopped the slide, rebuilt me emotionally. I'd go so far as to say that little lost Albanian girl restored my capacity to love. (Note for the chart: *libido suppressed, heart expanded.*) The line goes seismic at the point where Sam suddenly re-appeared, face to face with the semi-naked Edona. Emerging from the shockwave, the graph has started to log the slow progress of a recovering patient, on an upward trend but not without its swoops and dips.

The soul-line almost exactly matches the heart-line, dangerously low from the date of Sam's departure and descending to critical. The graph clinically records the damage to my pride and ego caused by the various rebuffs I've had along the way and especially my fall from grace at work. Again the change to an upward curve is marked from my first encounter with Edona, and it's still generally rising, if a bit wobbly. I'm beginning to believe in myself again, worries and fears notwithstanding. Part of me is nourishing the idea that if this dangerous affair should turn out well I might even regain my local hero status. Or better.

A larger bunch of no-hopers than I came across last time is camped near the cut that leads into the area of the estate where Ollie lives. I can make out the glow of cigarettes and the shapes of family-sized pop bottles passed between them, with god-knows-what inside. There's not the space to give the group a wide berth, so I pick up speed before I reach them –

215

last time, my acceleration was late enough to look suspiciously like running away. As I gallop past, one voice yells out, *Fuck me!* and another follows up with, *Cost you, like!* which could be the best joke of the year, judging by the cackle of laughter it sets off. What strikes me is that the first voice, raucous as a football rattle, is unquestionably female.

Ollie is prompt in unlocking the door on this occasion, as if he's expecting me. Which I find he is, having just come off the phone to Sam. He rang to tell her his mam finally got a date for her operation. "She asked me to let her know, Marc, that's why I done it," he says. Once again Oliver is showing more tact than people give him credit for, reading my expression and feeling he needs to excuse himself for being so presumptuous. His interpretation is spot on – I'm unreasonably pissed off that he'd called Sam on our unlisted number - though of course I pretend otherwise.

"No sweat, Oliver, thanks for keeping us up to speed. When's the big day?"

"On Tuesday. Would you like to see the letter what came, Marc?" He starts to make his way into the living-room, but I stop him with a touch on the arm.

"No need for that, Ollie, don't want to disturb your mother. I'm sure Sam's got all the details." I take his camera from the pocket of my training top, "Here, I brought this back for you," and Ollie accepts it like a kid being given a new toy.

"Thanks, Marc."

"Thanks for lending me it, I know what it means to you." Now I'm watching *him* for give-away expressions, but Ollie doesn't react, just opens the cupboard door to stuff the camera into the pocket of the coat that's hanging there with his delivery bag. "Keep it in a safe place, eh?" I say, but still nothing. He moves into his hospitality ritual once he's closed the cupboard door.

"Would you like a cup of tea or a cup of coffee, Marc?"

"No thanks, I'll have to get back." A day or two ago I would have been happier to spend time with Ollie than I am now. Like it or not, he's gone down in my estimation.

"Has Amina called you up yet?" I'm wrong-footed by the question, simply not anticipating it, even though of course Ollie was party to what went on at Prince Albert Road. I'm not sure how to answer. It was me who asked for his help, he has every right to know what's going on. But I have visions of his mother, sitting in a hospital ward, spilling the beans to all and sundry.

216

"Er, I hope she'll be calling soon," I tell him, not convincingly, though it's not an outright lie.

"Let me know when you hear anything." Almost certainly what Sam would have said about the hospital appointment, now rote-learned and absorbed into Oliver's stilted social vocabulary.

"I will. Give my regards to your mam." There's another stock phrase for him try out some time.

The group that was squatting at the far end of the estate seems to have disbanded, a relief to me since there's no other obvious way out. The street, though, is not quite deserted. As I walk past a gable end, there's a flick of a lighter. Someone leaning against the wall. My attention is caught by the face of the smoker illuminated briefly as she draws at the flame. Almost-attractive urchin looks, marred by acne; straggly, two-tone hair. She lets the flame burn longer than she needs for lighting the cigarette while she watches me looking at her then, metallically, "What you staring at, you fucking perv?"

"No, I'm not, sorry. Thought you were someone I knew."

"Yeah, right."

Curiosity gets the better of me. "You know Oliver Dunn, don't you?"

"Oh, yeah, he's my favourite spakker." She gives me a gratuitous snort of contempt. "Dickhead. What you been doing in there, tossing him off?"

"Funny you should say that. I was wondering..."

"Oh, want a wank, do ya?"

"No, don't be stupid. That's not what I..."

"Hey, lads," She flattens her cheek against the brick wall, calling out. "Got a right wanker here!"

Before I can move away, three youths appear round the corner of the house that the girl is leaning against, cutting off my exit. Somewhere between sixteen and nineteen years old, they're an alarming sight, with one in particular, bottle in hand, towering over my head as he steps between me and the girl. He prods me once on the shoulder with his free hand. "Who the fuck are you?"

"Nobody, I'm just..."

"Nobody, right. You trying to tap up my lass?"

"'Course not. Don't be silly."

"Ooh, don't be silly," another whines in my ear, mimicking.

The big one persists with the questions. "What you doing round here? You're not from round here."

"He's a friend o' the retard," the girl supplies. "Ollie."

217

"Oh, Ollie, we like Ollie, don't we? He's a good lad."

"Quality," says somebody behind me. I don't know whether he's being ironic, but I'm faintly reassured. Which lasts about a second.

"So what are you fucking him about for?" says the big lad, pushing me again.

"Get off. I'm not fucking him about."

"'Course y'are, s'obvious. Getting him to suck your dick. You know what he is, Ollie? He's a vulnerable person. Ever heard that word, vulnerable?"

"Yes," though I think he's addressing his group as much as me. Showing off his cleverness.

"Wanna get reported?"

"Eh?"

"Don't answer me back." He flicks at my cheek with the back of his fingers. "I'm sick of you answering me back. Gi' me fifty quid or I'll report you for doing Ollie."

"I've done nothing to Ollie."

"I said, gi' me fifty quid!"

"I haven't got fifty quid. I haven't got any money at all." Which is true. Standing exposed in my running gear, I'm bitterly regretting that. I'd happily buy off their attentions.

"Look in his pockets." The other two lads grab me from behind by both arms, while the girl dives into the pockets of my training top, emerging with the mobile phone.

"Nice." She studies it for a moment, then points it at my face. A flash lights up the dark street. The girls looks at the result on screen before she pockets the phone in the back of her jeans.

"Give us that back," I hiss at her, straining to get loose. "Seriously, I've got to have it back. I'll pay you for it."

"What with, your knob end?" she says, and flashes a V sign, then grabs her boyfriend by the arm for protection as they walk off up the street, leaving me hanging in the grip of their two mates.

"Police! Thief!" I yell at top of my voice. The big guy turns, takes a run up, and buries a foot into my crotch. I slump with the pain. The other two lads let me drop into the gutter, winded, and run to catch up with the couple sprinting away in the darkness. One lets out a loud *yee-hah* as he goes.

I lie fighting for breath, my mouth working like a baby searching for the teat, trying to suck in air. When it comes at last my relief gives in to the ache in my pit. I struggle onto my knees, head down, holding in the pain, clutching at my balls. I must be crouched like this on the pavement, heaving, for five minutes or more, with no-one coming near. When the deeper breaths come my brain starts working again, or rather panicking. My mobile, Amina's lifeline, is gone. She could be ringing right now. Christ, they might call her back, laughing down the phone while Amina, caught in the act, is staring at the wild eyes of her gaolers.

Oh, surely they wouldn't answer a phone they've stolen? They'll leave it to ring, or switch it off. Amina, not able to get through, will try the landline. I'll have to warn Sam. I force myself to my feet and make my way back to Oliver's, breathing a little less laboured by the time I get there. Ollie and his mam, not expecting more visitors, have reverted to fortress mode, and more minutes have passed by the time the bolt is drawn back and I hear Ollie's cheerful, surprised, "Oh, hiya Marc."

"Could I please use your phone?"

"'Course you can. Would you like a cup of tea, or cup of coffee, Marc?"

I can't match the Dunns' politeness, brushing past the pair of them on my way to the telephone. Our line is engaged. Is it Amina? More likely Sam making her peace with her sister while she waits for my return. All the while she's talking Amina could be desperate to get through, but I can't alert Sam on her mobile because Amina has it. Nor can I ring DI Guthrie's direct line - his number's stored in the memory of my mobile. Communication stalemate. Should I ring 999? How long would they take to get here and what could they do? What sort of unwanted fuss will it kick up, when we're all trying to be so discreet? Shit. Why did I let my eyes meet that girl's as I passed? Why did I stop and talk to her?

"Ollie, that girl in your camera, the local girl? Who is she? What's her address?"

"Who, Marc?"

"You know, those pictures you've got of..." I glance sideways at Mrs Dunn, back in her usual armchair. "Here, I'll show you." I gesture for Ollie to follow as I dash into the kitchen and display more bad manners, opening their cupboard without asking, to bring out the camera. I turn it on and as I'm flicking through the random gallery I say to Ollie, "The gang that hangs about at the end of your street, you know them?"

"Yes." His eyes are following the images scrolling back.

"They've just nicked my phone."

He looks up. "Nicked your phone? That's pinching, innit, Marc?"

"That's right."

"Don't worry," he says. "One time, they pinched my camera."

"What? This one, or another one?"

"That one, yeah. They was just funning, though. They give it back. Did they pinch it out your pocket? Did they run up the alley?"

"They ran away."

"Prob'ly be back soon. Same as me."

My rapid thumb-flicking stops at the picture of an approaching Number 19 bus. The image in my mind is of Ollie standing stoically not, as so often, at a bus stop, but in his own street, patient if a bit bewildered, while the council estate gang are out of sight planting dirty pictures in his camera, postcards of affection for the lovable retard. He probably hasn't even noticed they're there. If he has, good luck. I turn off the power and hand the camera back to him. Ollie's brow creases, unable to fathom what I've been doing.

"Do you know where they live exactly?"

"No. Mam might." He wanders back into the living-room. "Mam, you know that girl what used to come for the Christmas Club money?" (Christmas Club? They barricade the place up every night, but they let that toe-rag in and trust her with their money?) "Do you know where she lives? Marc needs to get his phone back."

Mrs Dunn stops staring at the floor in front of her feet and she looks up at me (I think) through her dark glasses. "Has that stupid girl pinched your phone?"

"Her and her boyfriend, yeah, 'fraid so." I'm feeling almost apologetic about it now, given the Christmas Club connection.

The old woman's lips purse. "He's a Hedley. She's a stupid little bitch, and it's not often I swear," pointing a crooked forefinger up to include me in the blame. "They're just not biddable, not now. What wi' all this binge drinking and drugs and such nowadays. Makes you weep." She stares down at the floor, saying half to herself, "I went to school wi' Bella." Adding, for my benefit, "That's her nan."

"Would you know where the girl lives?" I prompt her, conscious of time passing.

"No point going there." She looks beyond me. "Oliver!" she commands her son. "Take him round to the man with the dogs." Oliver promptly goes to the cupboard for his coat as Mrs Dunn hoists herself from the armchair. I'm already through the door and waiting impatiently outside by the time he's zipped up and ready to go. His mother is fussing with him in the doorway, muttering instructions and stuffing something, a hankie probably, into his pocket before she lets him out of her sight.

"I don't post any leaflets there," Ollie says cheerfully as he leads me through short cuts to the north end of the estate.

"Where?"

220

"The dog man's house. He hasn't got a letterbox. Anyway, I'm scared o' them animals."

When we get to the property I can see why Oliver wouldn't want to venture up the path with his bag of circulars. Situated in a cul-de-sac more sullen than Oliver's place, the house is grimmer still than the others around it, shadowed by the addition of a sturdy and heavily-padlocked outhouse inside the metal fence. The gate has a *Beware of the dog!* sign displayed prominently. The house door, as Ollie mentioned, has no letter-box for the simple reason that it is reinforced with sheet steel.

"What are we doing here?"

"Mam says he might have your phone."

"Does one of the gang live here?"

"No, just the man with the dogs." I notice that Ollie hangs back as I find the latch on the gate and start walking up the path, setting off ferocious barking and growling from inside long before I reach the door. No surprise that the owner doesn't bother with a bell or knocker. What he does have, though, is a CCTV camera, more primitive than the version installed at Warkworth Street, protected from any dullard tempted to steal it by a nest of vicious-looking barbed wire. I can hear a man's gruff voice on the other side of the door yelling to quieten the dogs, followed by the slamming of an inside door and a fumbling with lock and chain. I can't control a sharp intake of breath, bracing myself for the dogs, but the door opens only to the limit of the security chain and it's a man's nose that pokes out.

"Huh?"

"Er, sorry to disturb," (ridiculous opener) "Only, I was told you might have my phone. Mobile phone? Silver Nokia?"

"Says who?"

"A Mrs Dunn. Kielder Close."

There's movement behind me. Oliver shuffles to where the man can see him through the gap in the door. I watch the guy look at him, then at me, trying to compute. "Wait," he says at last, and closes the door on us. We wait. Two minutes later the door rattles a little way open again and the man is back, showing a silver Nokia mobile, switched off but otherwise exactly as I last saw it, through the gap. "This the kind o' thing?"

"That's the very one, thanks."

"Two hundred."

"Eh?"

"Two hundred. I can only take cash."

221

I'm back at square one. The reason I got into this bother in the first place is I haven't a bean on me. I'm not even absolutely certain this is my phone.

"I can't... I haven't got any money."

"Fuck off then," the guy says evenly, and makes to shut the door.

"Mister!" It's not me shouting, it's Oliver. The chain pulls taut again. Oliver has his purse in hand, and he's pulling a wad of notes out. The door closes and opens, free of its chain. I can now see another chain, a thick gold one, round the neck of the man standing at the door. His skin is unseasonably red under his white tee-shirt, plainly a sun-bed enthusiast as well as a dog-lover. Gym fanatic as well, I'd hazard, with the muscles on him. He takes the notes that Ollie is offering, and places my mobile on the floor to free his hands for counting.

"There's only a hundred and forty here," he says.

"A hundred and forty," Oliver repeats.

"I said two hundred."

I'm gazing down at my phone on the threshold, dangerously near his Doc Martens. Don't even think about it. I try draining all adulthood out of my expression as I lift my face to him. "A hundred and forty is all we have."

"A hundred and forty," Oliver agrees, equably. Laurel and Hardy.

The man stares, daring us to escalate this into an argument. I place my hands behind my back, naive, non-confrontational. If he was to swing a Doc Marten now he'd probably kill me.

Instead he stuffs the money into a pocket of his combats and bends down to pick up the phone. "Found this in the street when I was walking the dogs," he says. "Hope it's the one you're looking for, I like to do a good turn." He passes it over, careful not to touch my fingers – that would be gay -and retreats into his fortress. The dogs start up again indoors as we make our way along the path.

"I'll pay you back tomorrow, Ollie, you're a top bloke, thanks."

"Mam gave us the money."

"She's a star." I mean it too, about both of them. Expectations confounded once again.

I wait till we reach the first unbroken street lamp before I stop to examine the phone. For a horrible moment, as I press down the power switch and hold my breath for its revival, I have a doubt that this lifeless piece of metal has anything at all to do with me. Then the screen lights up and the warm tones reassure. No missed calls registered. A couple of seconds later the message alert beeps. Sam's mobile. Amina. Nerves at my wrist quiver as my thumb searches for the button, and I have to grab at

222

the phone to stop it spilling out of my hand. Staring at the screen, jaws set. The black band flows across the screen and the text appears.

Sending me away wthout tarik pls pls help

XV

I'm in the back of an unmarked police car alongside Detective Inspector Liam Guthrie. I haven't been introduced to the driver who's taking us to Manchester, or to his colleague in the front passenger seat. Not exactly James Bond types, these two - anyway, he's MI6, not MI5 – but I've been impressed by their efficiency. They sussed out what was happening to Amina pretty quickly, though Liam assures me it wasn't rocket science.

While she probably didn't know where she was being packed off to, Amina's phrase *sending me away* gave them a start. It could have been anywhere in the world, but logic suggested either somewhere in the UK or in Pakistan. Difficult to keep an uncooperative legal under wraps for a long period in this country, so the Pakistan option seemed more likely. From there it was a matter of checking reservations for upcoming flights, and it didn't take that much digging to come across the name of Amina Begum Khan booked, along with someone called Fatima Bhat, on a flight to Lahore from Manchester Airport via Abu Dhabi. The secret service guys, according to Liam, were encouraged by the fact that the bookings were made in real names onto a cheap flight – they inferred that this is neither a well-funded nor a particularly sophisticated set-up (what they called a typical *Al Qaeda* franchise) and that the conspirators have no notion anyone is looking out for Amina.

The plan is to apprehend the women after they've passed through security on their way to boarding, just in case their departure is being monitored. Two female decoys will take their places on the flight and will travel as far as the stop-over in Abu Dhabi. It will be at least twenty-four hours before anyone waiting to meet them in Lahore will be aware that they've gone missing. That's a vital window, the chance for us to find out what's really going on and try to stop it. I say *us* – my role at the airport is to confirm Amina's identity and be the friendly face she sees when they bring her through for questioning. Someone she can trust. After that, I go back to being the man waiting for the call in the studio, just as I've done for the last couple of nights.

It's been nerve-wracking for Sam and me, even though we were told it was very unlikely the plotters would play their hand before they'd spirited Amina out of the country. First there was the pre-recording, with agents acting as callers, which we'll turn to in case of an emergency. Then the shows themselves, me trying to act naturally on-air while there's half a dozen extra bods in the ops room and god knows how many unseen others on surveillance duty, all of us on tenterhooks for that call from Hassan. So far, nothing.

"Any idea where Amina is travelling from?" I ask Liam in the car.

"Only roughly. Unfortunately the location of her first call to you had already been deleted by the time we contacted the company. Sam's cell phone must have been switched off after that, no signals were being picked up. The only information we have is from the time of Amina's text message, which was very brief. Just one tower picked up the signal, in a fairly remote spot, so we know the phone was being used in a 26-mile radius between the borders of Northumberland and Cumbria. So, surprise surprise, she's not being kept anywhere near the home of Mr Ali. If she'd been in town we'd have had a good chance that two or three towers would be in range of the signal. That's what the engineers need to get a close fix through triangulation."

"Pity. I was thinking you might be able to track her journey, find who was bringing her to the airport, that kind of thing."

Liam smiles. "You'll make a detective yet, Marc." He nods in the direction of the two in front. "These people will have spotters in and around the terminal, but it's quite likely they'll make the last part of the journey by themselves using public transport. We'll be trying to cover all the bases, that's all we can do."

"What about this other woman, Fatima something?"

"Fatima Bhat. Interesting. Not that we really know much about her, but she lives in the Birmingham area, so there's another possible connection with Mr Ali. The worrying thing is the likelihood of some networking going on between cells. These guys'll tell you, it's a lot easier to deal with when things are done purely on a local basis. That's right, isn't it, guys?" he says louder.

The passenger immediately in front of him doesn't respond. The driver makes languid eye contact with Liam through his rear view mirror and says, in a tone of Oxbridge urbanity, "I'd recommend another topic of conversation, Inspector Guthrie. Football, perhaps?"

I can see Liam's ear colouring slightly as he turns away to look out of the window. We spend the rest of the journey in silence.

While I'm waiting for one police operation to get properly underway I can reflect on another that seems to have gone off half-cock. The strategy that we agreed at Chrissie's the other night, whereby we would officially

225

report Edona's existence to Children's Services through Fern and let her use that as a springboard for a multi-agency exercise aimed at closing down the brothel, rescuing the other girls and getting Edona (as the whistle-blower) on a privileged path to properly-managed repatriation, has been pre-empted by a police raid on 29 Warkworth Street, acting on information from another source. What Fern predicted has happened – all of the women in the house have been arrested along with Boris and Lev, though it appears that others, including Emmanuel and Stefan, have slipped the net. Fern has been effectively shut out of any involvement with the other females as none of them are as young as Edona. They all face deportation, and Edona could even now be swept up with the rest, though for the moment they've left her with Chrissie, if only because they have nowhere else to accommodate her but a cell. Fern is frantically working behind the scenes to prevent her being transferred to a deportation centre. The police, though, are very much in charge of the investigation. They've been in touch, very keen to interview me as a witness, but internal politics has prevailed and the guys that have got me working with them on the Hassan case have quietly told their colleagues to back off. So much for mutuality and partnership.

I feel as if I'm leaving Edona in limbo. Of course I can argue there is nothing I can do for her right now – chance has chosen me to be a major player in a drama that could have far greater consequences, and potentially cause far more suffering, than Edona's individual plight, however pitiful that is – but I have to question whether my head is being turned by... well, let's say the glamour implicit in this situation. What with all these secret service types, Home Office engineers tapping into the show, experts coaching and attending to my every word, fancy equipment, sleek cars – it has a Hollywood aspect to it. Does that make it any more important, any more worthy of all this attention (mine, theirs) than the abduction and rape of a fifteen-year-old girl from a poor village in rural Albania?

I feel guilty - somehow personally responsible - for the contrast between the meticulous planning, energies, resources expended on this project and the botched up-and-at-'em raid on the whore-house in Warkworth Street, the indifference reported by Fern to the prospects of the victims there. I only hope that at least the investment in this operation will produce a better result. What I hold on to most – what I use to assuage my guilt over Edona – is the idea that I can maybe help rescue one more innocent woman from a desperate situation, reunite a mother with her child. The fate of Amina Begum Khan is the thought that steadies.

I've never been in a security control centre before, but this one looks pretty impressive to me. I know Manchester Airport has had its lapses, but maybe the problems of the past have helped them raise the bar. Liam and I sit facing a huge video wall, focusing on monitors showing the key areas of Terminal 1, the main entrances from the car parks and the Skylink walkway that connects to the railway station. If we miss something or want to see it again we can ask for it to be retrieved from the CDR units that capture the images, or we can ask Barry, the operator sitting with us, to pan across or zoom in on anything that catches our eye on one of the screens showing the live action. It's still more than two hours before the flight, so we have plenty of opportunity to spot Amina and her travelling companion. Our hope is that we can pick them up on arrival so they can be put under constant surveillance and any contacts they make there can be tailed by one of the spotters.

I have to admit the fascination of watching a multi-screen display of people going about their humdrum business in the airport pales pretty quickly. Liam is still in taciturn mood from that subtle reprimand in the car, so there's little relief in conversation, and I have to invent games to stop myself drifting off. I say games - truth be told they are more variations of voyeurism, based on a points system I've developed in my head to rate the attractiveness of the women I'm observing. I've even got a broad-based international league table going, with the oriental types currently ahead, largely based on my sighting of one stunningly beautiful member of the cabin crew from, I think, Singapore Airlines. These games are shamelessly sexist, but at least they're only in my head, and it does keep me focused on the females in view, which I persuade myself makes me more likely to spot our targets.

It works, in a weird counterintuitive double-take sort of way. I've become so focused on the game that at first my eyes skip over the two women coming into range of the camera trained on the Skylink, as their long, loose-fitting coats and headscarves give me no clues for assessing them. My brain catches up, registering vague disappointment, and a fraction of a second later clicks into why. It's the Muslim *hijab*, protecting the women from the lustful gaze of men.

"Barry! On the walkway. The two pulling the cases along, dark clothes." Liam perks up and watches the monitor as Barry guides a lever with the heel of his hand, squaring onto and closing in on the two women. The camera moves to the face on the left – a stern-looking woman in her late forties, searching out information boards, then across

227

right to a younger woman, chewing her lip, eyes lowered except for momentary glances at people passing by on the other side.

"That's Amina," says Liam, beating me to it.

"Agreed – she looks a lot like she did in the press photo. I was half-expecting them to be wearing the full veil."

"They'd have to lift them anyway, going through clearance. Probably reckoned it would bring undue attention."

Now that we have a fix on the pair we can follow them from camera to camera around Terminal 1 as they check in, hand over their luggage and wait for their flight to be called. I know that the spotters will be tracking them too, but I don't see either of the women making contact with anyone other than airport and catering staff. I'm taking a close interest in Amina's body language whenever she shows up on a monitor. She certainly looks anxious, but at no point does she make any move away from her chaperone, or try to speak to other people in the terminal except when asked questions by the check-in staff. She has several opportunities to simply get up and walk away, for example when Fatima is queuing at the café counter, but she doesn't. Uppermost in her mind, I imagine, is what they might do to her little boy if she manages to escape. She must be relying on some miracle to happen as a result of her messages to me. I can feel that responsibility weighing me down. How on earth are the police going to find little Tarik and get him to safety in that narrow window of time before the gang realises Amina has eluded them?

Shortly before the flight is due to be called, Liam and I are moved to one of the interview rooms in the customs area where we will be able to talk to Amina. It's not the most comfortable place – just a bare room with a table in the middle and a few chairs – but it will have to serve the purpose. Liam has recovered enough poise to tell me that the other woman, Fatima, will be detained under the Prevention of Terrorism Act and interviewed separately by the men from MI5. Amina, we hope, will gain confidence from seeing me when she's brought in here. We want to try and keep things as informal and supportive for Amina as we can, but it's vital that she helps us fill in the blanks as quickly as possible to give the police the best possible chance of a result.

We learn that the flight has departed more or less on time, but we're kept waiting in that room for almost an hour, already on our second cup of coffee, before the door opens and a female member of the airport security staff ushers in Amina, then stations herself discreetly on a seat in the corner. The first thing I notice is that Amina has changed her clothes.

She's now wearing a sort of hooded kaftan, slate-grey, still conforming I suppose to the *hijab* dress code, but far more fashionable than the cloak thing she had on earlier. It doesn't click at first that both women will have been strip-searched and their clothes borrowed by the decoys while they have been provided with replacements from their own bags, which never made it to the hold. I don't have time to think that through right now, because as Amina sits down in front of us, freeing her black hair from her hood, she immediately gives me something else to think about.

"I have hidden Sam's mobile in the lining of Tarik's cot."

"Eh?"

Impatient at my blankness, she turns to Liam, the obvious policeman in the room. "You can trace phones, can't you? Like they tried with those Soham children? I've left it switched on. Will you be able to find him?"

"We'll try," says Liam. He stands away from the table and draws out his own cell phone. Amina's eyes follow him while he retreats to a corner to make his call to base, and I have to touch her shoulder lightly to bring her attention back to me.

"How do you know her name is Sam? How did you recognise me?" It's true Liam and I had agreed to avoid interrogation, but I'm bamboozled by this.

Amina turns reluctantly from watching the progress of the call and settles her dark eyes on me, her brain adjusting to the questions I asked. "Oh, I wouldn't have known you. Not when you came to the house, I wasn't expecting... And you've changed your hair. No, it was Sam I recognised straightaway. Then I realised it was you. *Tabarakallah.*"

"You know Sam?"

"I have met her. I've met you both, briefly. Eighteen months ago, maybe, less. I know it was the first time I left Tarik with a babysitter." She pauses, turning this over. "You were compèring an awards evening at the Park Hotel. Young Enterprise. Sam was with you as well, she had a lovely blue dress on."

"I remember the occasion, yes. Sorry, I don't..."

"No, well, I went along with Hassan. He'd designed the website for one of the businesses that was nominated, so they invited us onto their table. They did not win, actually, but we were having a chat with you afterwards. Hassan introduced me, you introduced Sam, you know, the way you do."

"That's amazing." But of course it isn't. It's perfectly ordinary, logical, the kind of thing that happens all the time. Meet once, pass the time of day... The way you do. There must be hundreds of people Sam and I have come across in the normal course of events. But I'm irrationally astonished by it. To think that I'd met Hassan before...

Amina goes on. "That is what started me listening to you, as a matter of fact. Never bothered in the past, not on the radar, really. But there's a bit of curiosity, isn't there, when you have met the person? Like you feel part of it. I've seen Sam around the shops a couple of times since, not that I have said hello or anything. It's not as if we really know each other." Amina's just vamping, not paying particular attention to what she's saying, but she refocuses immediately as Liam comes back to the table. "What is happening?"

"They're onto it. I promise you, if that phone and the cot and the baby are still together we'll be able to find out just where he is."

A tear starts in the corner of Amina's left eye, and she uses the fabric of her hood to dab it away. I wonder if, like me, she's thinking of the opposite condition – if the phone and the cot and the baby are separated, what that implies. I also know that Liam is not being altogether candid. Even if the mobile stays switched on and the battery lasts, there is no guarantee that the engineers will be able to get a precise enough fix on it.

"Can I get you a drink of something?" Liam asks Amina as she composes herself.

"No, I'm fine, thanks."

"OK. Listen, I want you to know that you're not under arrest or anything, not in any kind of trouble as far as we're concerned. In fact, you've been a very brave woman."

"Thank you. I don't feel brave, I feel frightened. I don't mean of you. I just want my son back. I do not want him hurt." There's a flash in her eyes as she says it, a warning to us that she won't be responsible for her actions if we fail to take the utmost care.

"We all want the same thing, I promise." Liam looks at me, and I nod, but I'm thinking, we all *want* the same thing; can we *deliver*?

"You can help us," says Liam, "By maybe providing us with some of the information we don't have yet."

"I'll try."

"Good girl." (Fern would pull a face at that.) "Let's start with this woman you were with today."

"Fatima Bhat."

"You know her?"

"I heard her name for the first time at the check-in desk. I had never seen the woman until a few days ago, and she has never really

230

spoken to me, just given me orders. She is not from our community, I'm sure."

"Is she the woman who was outside the toilet, the night you phoned me?" I ask.

Amina turns a little bashful. "Yes."

"Where was that?"

"I don't know. Sorry..." She sighs, loses focus. "I'm not being much help. Since I was taken from my home I haven't really known where I've been. Some of the time I have been made to wear a blindfold."

"By whom?" says Liam, trying to bring her back in.

"Different people. That woman. A couple of the men who used to live downstairs."

"Downstairs?"

"In my house."

Liam and I glance at each other. He permits himself a sly smile for the first time since his put-down by the secret service agent. He has a right to it. Looks like his theory about Prince Albert Road as a terrorist cell is spot-on.

"OK, we'll come back to that," he says. "What about Imam Zaid bin Ali? Where does he fit into this? I'm assuming he's not your uncle."

"No, he is not my uncle," says Amina, back in the zone, and we can see her bitterness rising with the volume as she speaks. "He's my gaoler. He's a kidnapper, baby-snatcher. And a husband-killer!"

In the silence following Amina's outburst I see the woman security guard stand up and take up a position next to the door, as if she expected Amina to try escaping from the room any second. Liam gives the guard a nod of reassurance, then mimes a cup to his mouth as he indicates Amina, who's hiding her weeping, head down. The woman goes quietly out through the door. Liam reaches out to place a hand on Amina's arm, tensed on the table. "It's OK, it's OK."

We wait while the security woman comes back into the room with a plastic beaker of water that she places at Amina's elbow. "Thank you," Amina says, straightening up to show the woman some courtesy, then, to us, "Sorry."

"No problem," says Liam. "You're doing well, you're doing great." In the softness of his voice I detect for the first time the hint of an Irish lilt – I'd assumed an educated Northern upbringing like my own. "Can we talk about your husband for a minute, Amina? Is that OK?" She nods. "How long were you two married?"

"Coming up, four years." I notice how she establishes the date in terms of the future.

231

"Right," says Liam. "And, do you mind me asking, was that an arranged marriage?"

There's a sad, reflective smile on Amina's face as she says, wiping her eyes. "Oh, no, not at all. We did not do the traditional Muslim thing. We weren't..." She pauses, sips at the water, then continues her story with a simple list. "We met at university, fell in love, simple as that. Got jobs, eventually got married, had a baby, bought a house. Same as most people. Normal, normal. Until last year."

"When, unfortunately, Hassan had his car accident and died," Liam fills in as gently as he can, knowing she might not want to conclude the story herself.

Amina looks at him for a long moment, her fingers absently squeezing the top of the plastic cup near to breaking point before she releases it. A little water slops over onto the table as the cup springs back into shape. Amina looks down at the spill. "Sorry," she murmurs as she tries to smooth the water away with her hand, then, almost matter of fact, "Hassan Malik did not die in a car crash. As far as I'm aware, at this moment, my husband is still very much alive." She catches my eye across the table. "I told you he was dead to me, but he's not dead to the world. Not yet."

"Mystery solved," I say, my mind on Valentine's Day, 11:59.

Liam demurs. "Not quite. Amina, there were remnants of Hassan's documents in the car. We also have a DNA match. You provided it yourself from..."

"From the disgusting toothbrush," says Amina, "Of a horrible Afghani man called Rasoul." The bitterness rising again.

"I'm losing the plot here," I say.

Liam leans back on his chair, lacing his fingers together to support his neck. He is quiet for a while, ruminating, then he says, "OK, I think I've got it. Rasoul – that his name? - was an illegal, housed with you, presumably one of the cell members. Hassan basically loaned him his identity, his papers, as well as his car. Big problem was, Rasoul smashed the car into a motorway bridge, and wrote himself off along with the vehicle. Hassan panicked, thinking everything was going to fall apart. He persuaded you to provide a false identification while he went into hiding, effectively became a non-person. Is that about right?"

"Except it wasn't Hassan who did that," Amina replies. "Hassan wasn't even there at the time. It was the *imam*. He was controlling everything. Him and Ahmed between them, they ruined our lives."

"Ahmed?"

"Ahmed Aziz. Hassan's friend." There's a degree of venom in her pronunciation of the word. Amina turns to me. "Actually, you met him, too, Marc, at the awards night."

"Really?"

"Ahmed runs the business Hassan did the website for. An Islamic bookshop - Hassan helped him bring it online."

Liam stands up and takes a few steps around the room, stretching his long frame. He comes back to us, hands on the back of his chair. "There's a lot to take in. Amina, would it be all right with you if I brought a colleague in to hear what you have to say? I can't tell you how helpful this is. I think the more we learn from you now the more chance we have to stop what's happening, help you get your little boy back."

"I don't mind."

Liam walks over to speak with the woman at the door and they go out together. Amina and I are left sitting opposite one another, silent at first as I'm not sure I should continue the questions with no-one else about. It's Amina who breaks the silence. "Was it you who rang the night after Hassan left? You asked to speak to him."

"I rang the night after he called me, is that when you mean?"

"Yes. Sorry, I was so rude to you then. I was just... I was left on my own. Just Tarik and me. I did not realise who it was until I thought about it later."

"You don't have to apologise to me. If I hadn't been so slow on the uptake...Well, you might not be sitting here now. I could have done something."

Amina purses her lips, dabbling a finger in the puddle of water on the table. There's another pause before she says, "Maybe, maybe not. I don't know quite what Hassan was thinking – it was a strange... In some ways very romantic, but..." She looks up and there are tears welling in both eyes now. "But he was leaving us, Marc. That very moment. Even when he was struck with love and wanting to stay, he was leaving. How could he do that? How could *jihad* be so powerful in him that he could leave his wife and child forever? Can you tell me how?"

I reach out for her hand, as much for my comfort as hers. Amina's fingers feel slightly wet in my palm from the spilt water. I'm not sure what to say. If she can't understand, as his wife, as his lover, as a person brought up in the Muslim faith... what chance have I got? My response, when it comes, struggles for any coherence. "I... I don't know, Amina. He must have been so close to changing his mind. I think now that his call to me wasn't just a goodbye to you, it was a cry for help, you know, like a suicide reaching out for someone to rescue him from

233

himself, without even knowing that's what he's doing. I've had some experience..."

Her hand tenses in mine. She leans forward. "Hassan was... he *is* a suicide. He would be dead now if he had not made that stupid mistake. I mean in Ahmed's eyes. Calling you."

"Tell me what happened."

Before she can say any more the door opens and Liam returns with the agent that drove us to the airport. He stands and looks at us for a while without saying anything, but a glance from me to the doorway provides the clue to what's on his mind – he thinks it's time for me to leave. I start to rise from my chair. Amina notices the movement and immediately puts her hand out, nervously. "Please." I make eye contact with the agent. Your call. The slightest inclination of his head allows me to settle back again, at the same time sealing my silence. Amina dries her tears on her hood and prepares herself for a more formal explanation.

Hassan had not been attracted to any kind of activism, even after 9/11 when they were still students. 7/7 was different, only because they did seem to encounter a degree of prejudice for a while after that but ironically, in Amina's opinion, it made them more determined than ever to show they were no different from any young British couple. They worked hard enough to be able to afford a mortgage in time for the baby coming. They enjoyed themselves socially, liked music, drank in moderation with the occasional binge, as neither of them were particularly observant Muslims except as a courtesy around their elders or when they travelled home to visit either set of parents. Similarly with dress. Amina would follow *hijab* rules when it was seemly - attending weddings, say - but generally adopted a simple western style. The change in Hassan sprang from his involvement with Ahmed, and it was surprisingly rapid.

"Hassan looked up to Ahmed," says Amina. "I could see why. Ahmed is clever, successful, good-looking too, actually. He was a sort of role model for my husband – in fact Ahmed was the inspiration for Hassan to start up on his own as a website designer instead of working for others. I think that accelerated things, once he was away from a corporate environment. More and more of the contracts he got came from Islam-related organisations. To be fair, it was actually Ahmed that found him a lot of that work. And they spent more and more time together."

Amina found herself increasingly on the edges of Hassan's friendship with Ahmed. In fact the awards evening was one of the last occasions they went out socially. Hassan gave up alcohol, stopped listening to western music, started attending the mosque regularly, which he hadn't done since he was a child. The rest of his spare time he'd spend with Ahmed, either in the bookshop or at home, discussing politics for hours.

"Ahmed was always asking Hassan what he stood for, what he thought his purpose was on earth. For a long while that bothered Hassan – it bugged him that he didn't seem to have an answer except to say us, his family. That didn't satisfy Ahmed. He kept pushing and pushing. Ahmed's big thing was the supposed western conspiracy against Islam. 'They want to keep us down, keep us poor', he'd say. 'They call us terrorists when they are the greatest terrorists, the western governments, attacking our people, invading our lands, taking our resources for themselves.' I was so tired of his rantings, I would go upstairs and lie next to Tarik in his cot, listening quietly to the radio while those two kept on talking half the night."

"Was Mr Ali involved in these discussions?" our man from MI5 asks.

"Not at first, no. Hassan met him at the Springhill mosque. I didn't know who he was until Hassan told me one day he'd invited some people round for a religious discussion. Ahmed was there, of course, and Hassan's cousin Anwar, who is a student here. About half a dozen more, all young men, parked like great bears in our front room, and this *imam* turned up. He looked at me as if I shouldn't be there, in my own house. And stupidly, he got to me. I took Tarik out in his buggy. We walked around for hours, even after it started raining. When I got back, fortunately Mr Ali had gone, but a lot of the men were still there. I had to ask Hassan to get them to leave eventually – I could not get Tarik to sleep with their noise downstairs. It became a regular thing, this discussion group."

"Is that why you had the door added on the landing?" Liam asks. Amina's smile is so cynical it spoils her good looks for a moment.

"I did not get my own prison made, no. Just as it was not my idea to have that poky lavatory put in where the cupboard used to be. That was when they had taken over – after Rasoul arrived."

"The illegal immigrant," says Liam, partly as a reminder to his colleague. "How did he come onto the scene?"

"They called him the fundraiser." She sneers at the description. "Pity he did not raise any funds for us to live on. By now Hassan was doing very little paid work. He was spending most of his time on the project."

"What was the project?"

"Oh, the *thing*, the *cause*, that's how they would refer to it. Actually, that was the first time Hassan lied to me. He told me they were raising money for an Islamic centre in the neighbourhood. Devoted to all things Islamic. Culture, the arts... and these religious discussions. He said I would be able to claim back my front room once it was built. Of course, that was the same day he told me this man Rasoul would be living there. Temporarily, he said. A friend of the *imam*. He had come specially to help raise money for the project. I hated Rasoul from the moment I set eyes on him. He was a weasel, and his breath was bad. I can't tell you my private nickname for him. This man was living in my house, in a sleeping bag in our front room. Soon he was even driving our car. Hassan told me he needed to drive for the work he was doing."

"Which was?"

"I had no idea at first. One day I came in from shopping and for once I used the back door, to unload all my groceries in the kitchen. I found Rasoul there, making up bags and bags of brown powder, there on my own kitchen table. He just grinned when he looked up and saw me, as if I'd discovered him baking bread."

"Drugs?" says Liam, redundantly.

"The worst. Heroin." Amina looks directly at me, her fellow-citizen, wanting to share her disgust and frustration as so many callers do night after night on my programme. "This man had been brought to our community, to our home, by someone who set himself up as a religious leader - to raise money by selling drugs on the street. What kind of hypocrisy is that? How can that be justified under Sharia law?"

If Amina is looking for an answer from me I'm in no position to provide one. My brain is overheating with suddenly-plugged-in connections. Rasoul. Emmanuel. Hassan's car. The crash on the coast road. Finally, the link is made. Meanwhile, the man from the Security Service is making his own. "*Al Qaeda* regularly funds its operations through the sale of illegal drugs," he says. "There's a ready supply in Afghanistan. As for justifying it, anything that further corrupts and weakens the kuffs is OK by their logic. All part of the jolly *jihad.*"

I'm only half-listening as Amina talks about the row she had with Hassan over Rasoul, about retreating for a week to visit her parents with Tarik and coming back to find the alterations done to the house, and more strangers living at her address. My brain is still reconfiguring the scene between Rasoul and Emmanuel. A drug deal turned sour? Or, more likely, Emmanuel trying to run a rival out of town. A high-speed chase late at night, leading to the accident? Or the crash engineered – a nudge, a

236

bullet in a tyre? The thought of my own tyre-burst reverberates like a gunshot. When Emmanuel visited the hospital it wasn't, as I'd supposed, on Amina's behalf, it was to double-check that Rasoul was good and dead.

"Shut away in my own home," Amina is saying. "In *purdah*. Hassan tried to persuade me of the moral obligation, but I believe my incarceration with Tarik in the bedrooms was to stop me learning more of what was going on downstairs. There was a small group of men living there now, as well as Rasoul. They ate together, prayed together, but also there were computers around the walls, a fax machine, papers lying about... Hassan was working all the time down there on this project, whatever it was. When he came to me at night he would say nothing about what he was doing. Then for one whole week he and Ahmed and another man went off on a trip, he didn't say where. Worse, Zaid bin Ali came to our house and stayed. He kept me under lock and key all day and night. When I asked him where Hassan and the others were he just laughed, said they had gone to find their souls. On another occasion he told me I should be proud that my husband was fighting for the return of the Caliphate. I believed then that Hassan must have travelled abroad, to Afghanistan perhaps – but later a man who brought a meal up to our door told me Hassan and the others were simply camping in the Lake District. I did not know what to believe, I was frightened. Then, while my husband was away, this thing happened with Rasoul..."

"The car crash, you mean?" says Liam. I'm listening fully now.

"The police came in the middle of the night, pounding at the door. Everyone was in a panic, hiding. The *imam* told me to stay in my room, and he͏ opened the door himself. That was when he first claimed to be my uncle. When the police asked for me he told them I was not yet decent and wheedled the story out of them, then left them on the doorstep while he came up to tell me – better coming from a member of the family, he said. Pghwah!" Amina mimes a spitting gesture and scowls at the memory. "He warned me not to say a word out of turn, if I valued my baby's life. That's how the lie about Hassan's death began. It was so simple, actually. The checks were...Well, they had no reason to disbelieve."

I glance across at Liam, who looks suitably embarrassed. The interview room door opens and the second MI5 man slips in. He makes as if to join us, then recognises the tension in the room and retreats to the wall, watching proceedings with his arms folded as his colleague asks Amina, "How did Hassan take the news that he'd been *disappeared*?"

"Strangely. Tell me Marc, what is the word for a person who feels many different things at once?"

She's asked me directly, I have to answer. "Mmm, ambivalent? Schizoid? Conflicted?"

"Conflicted, yes, that's a good description of Hassan. Sometimes around people it was like he was really a ghost. Of course, now he could hardly ever go out of the house except the rare times he slipped out at night, but around our home too he would sometimes walk around aimlessly, vacantly, as if he wasn't really seeing people. Or he would kneel and pray or sit in a corner reading the *Qur'an* for hours. Other times – especially around Ahmed – he would laugh and tease, as if it was the world's biggest joke that he was meant to be dead. He said then it suited the purpose, it was meant to be. But then, upstairs, with just the three of us, he would wrap his arms around Tarik and me like a condemned man, as if he was afraid of losing us. Then one night he quietly kissed our little boy in his cot, embraced me, and he left us for good."

"The night of February 14th?" Fuck their protocols, this is where I come in.

Amina nods. I hold myself back, out of respect for her feelings, but now our *agente incognito* presses on, wanting more. "Was the cell still active at that time?"

"Everything changed that week," Amina replies. "For two days they mounted a huge clear-up operation downstairs. All the computers were taken away, the furniture, the fax... They were rubbing down the doors and walls, painting over marks. Even the rubbish was cleared away. Then everybody left without another word – I have no idea where they'd gone off to, but I was so happy, because the one person who didn't go was Hassan. He stayed with us all evening, and I really thought, this is it, we can get our life together now. We didn't bother moving back downstairs - there wasn't a stick of furniture left down there – so we sat upstairs as usual, getting Tarik to bed, listening to the radio. I'd even started making plans for buying furniture, designing a new layout for the front room. But it was like being at the ball with Cinderella because, just before midnight, Hassan told me he had to go. Just like that – he had to go."

I feel so much for Amina as she lifts her arms from the table, palms up, demonstrating that look of pain and surprise she must have shown at that moment when Hassan said his final goodbye. I feel part of the moment too, as I was there, or my voice was, filling the background of his leaving from the upstairs radio.

"He must have called me from the phone in the hall," I'm saying, almost to myself, reconstructing the scene in sound.

"Yes. He asked me to stay with Tarik, and closed the door behind him. I was looking out of the window to watch him down the steps – there was a dark blue van waiting at the kerb, and I was just wondering if it was waiting for Hassan when I suddenly heard you say the name *Hassan* on the radio, and then his voice. It was the strangest thing. I rushed over and turned the volume up so loud I woke the baby. By the time I'd shushed him and got him back again it was all over. Hassan had gone. The van had gone. That was it."

Amina stops again, looks as if she might spill over into tears. The agent shifts forward in his seat – either to comfort her or question her – but he is distracted by the sudden, insistent ringing of a mobile phone. Next to him, Liam reaches into an inside pocket. "Sorry," he mumbles to the room in general, and seems about to switch off the phone when a peek at the screen changes his mind. "Sorry, I'll just have to take this," and he swings his long legs away from the table. "Yeah?" he's saying, the phone already at his ear as he leaves the room. The agent standing against the wall takes the chance offered by this break in proceedings to join the group. He parks himself on Liam's seat and immediately leans sideways, whispering into the ear of his colleague for several seconds, while Amina and I, excluded, exchange an awkward glance across the table. I give her an encouraging smile and she returns an anxious one. I know her mind is on Liam's telephone call. The two MI5 men finish their tête-à-tête and settle back in their chairs simultaneously. The first agent addresses Amina.

"So at this point you were on your own in the house? You and your son." She nods. "But somebody came back, didn't they? Was it bin Ali, or somebody he sent for you?"

"Nobody came near at first. I think they expected me just to get on with my life without Hassan. Muslim women, they know, are passive and stoical. Sadly, that is indeed what I was going to do. From what the *imam* had said to me I truly believed that Hassan had gone to fight alongside the Taliban, and that he knew he would be killed, which is why he left me that last message. As far as my neighbours were concerned he had died weeks ago. He was dead to me, except in my heart. I realise now that this was just what the *imam* and the others wanted, it suited their plans. But everything changed when I started to receive these strange telephone calls, then people started coming round to my door, ringing and knocking, waking Tarik. Eventually I called the police."

"Why didn't you take the chance then to tell them what was happening?"

"Tell them what? I had no idea what was happening. Besides, by the time they got there Mr Ali was back – I believe Hassan's cousin Anwar had told him about the fuss on the radio. He was furious, but very charming with the police. He told them he would see that I was safe." Amina pauses, then repeats, in a hollow tone. "Safe. Tarik and I were taken away that night."

"Taken where?"

"I really don't know. Somewhere not far, that first night, judging from the length of the journey, somewhere in the city. I think it may have been some kind of store-room, I could feel cardboard boxes at my back. They separated me from Tarik and I was straining all night to hear if he was crying, but all I could hear was the sound of men talking and arguing. One voice was Ahmed's, I think."

"What were they arguing about?" I ask, caught up in this. Amina shakes her head.

"I really couldn't follow much." (Again that use of the word *really*, as if she sensed that someone in the room was doubting her story, or believed she knew more than she was letting on.) "I heard Hassan's name mentioned a couple of times. Something had gone wrong, that was certain. And I think they were quarrelling about what to do with me and the baby."

"You must have obtained some hard information, however," says the Oxbridge man. (Amina, like me, must notice the slight narrowing of his eyes. That's her doubting thomas. But what would she have to gain by lying?) "Enough to know of their intention to pull something off, and to use Marc, or at least his programme, to advertise themselves."

"I found that out later," says Amina, "When they moved us." She turns away from her interrogator's cool stare, finding more empathy in mine as she continues. "They seemed a lot more organised by then. Eventually they gave Tarik back to me. He'd been changed and fed, and there was a big bag of clothes for us both in the back of the van. When we got to the place where Fatima was waiting the baby's cot was there, and a few other little things from our home."

"Was it out of town?" I ask her.

"Pretty sure, yes. We travelled a few miles. There were no windows in the back of the van, so I couldn't see where we were going, but the driver answered his phone on the way and I listened to his end of the conversation as much as I could, especially after I heard your name, Marc. He talked about my husband as well, he said he didn't know what Hassan was playing at, but it was fine, it would turn out for the best. It will be just as big, he said, bigger with the new plan. I heard him ask *whose*

240

idea was it for Hassan to call Marc Niven? then he laughed and shouted out *Genius.* I thought he meant the other call, the one from the house, but then the driver said, *Tell him from me, that call will make up for it. Tell him - Hassan, when Allah hears your voice praising him, he'll have those virgins lined up ready.* He was laughing just as if he'd told a dirty joke. What a horrible thing that is."

"Virgins?" I'm confused.

The secret service man has the pleasure of enlightening me. "According to Islamic tradition, the reward for male martyrdom is the enjoyment of 72 virgins in paradise." What immediately springs to my mind, unbidden, is a snapshot from my nightmare - the image of Edona, strapped down on a marble plinth, naked and frightened.

Liam steps back into the room, looking pleased with himself. Finding his seat taken, he remains standing behind Amina. He places his hands lightly on her shoulders, cocking his head on one side to attract her attention. "I've got some good news," he says. "The signal from Sam's phone is still strong, and the engineers have fixed a location, right in the middle of town. I think we'll be able to protect Tarik. There's officers moving into position as I speak."

The Home Office man stands up, uncharacteristically urgent. "Call back, right now!" he orders Liam. "I want them well away from there."

"Obviously they're not going to wade in..."

"I mean, right back. And tell them to make plans for a possible evacuation of the area. We're on our way now." As Liam, bemused, steps away to make the call, the agent turns his attention to me. "I think you'll find you are needed tonight, Marc."

"How do you know?"

His colleague, still seated, speaks for the first time. "I've been talking to our people in Birmingham about Mrs Bhat, but actually the most interesting information they gave me concerns Mr Ali. Apparently he's making a guest appearance at his old mosque this evening. Special event. We believe that's more than a coincidence."

"I don't get it."

"We think that's his alibi," says his partner. "Lots of people to confirm he was many miles from the scene of the crime, whatever the crime might be." He places his palms together as if to suggest we wrap things up here, then, almost as if it's an after-thought, he speaks directly to Amina. "You did tell us earlier, didn't you, that you were not acquainted with Fatima Bhat?"

"Not until she became my prison guard, no."

"Hmm, curious. We liberated Mrs Bhat's mobile telephone from her a short while ago, and we've been having a little look at her call history. A series of calls in the last week or so have been made to a cell phone registered in the name of Amina Begum Khan."

Amina looks stunned. "I don't know what to say. I... My phone must have been stolen."

The agent smiles. "I don't think so." With the air of a conjuror he fishes out from his pocket a neat little light-blue flip-top. "We found this buried in your luggage." He releases the cover with the holding hand and shows the face of the cell phone to everyone in the room. The screen display lights up to reveal in close-up a cute Asian child, about two years old, with a broad grin on his face.

XVI

The agent's name is Peter. That much I found out on the return journey from Manchester as he and I travelled together in a hire car while his colleague drove Amina and Liam back in the other vehicle. Perhaps we're friends now; he's just winked at me through the glass - encouragement I guess, as I slide up the fader to open the show. There's more encouragement on the screen at eye level to my right – a simple *good luck* tapped in by Sam. I save my wink for her.

"Evening all. Marc Niven here for your nightly fix of chat and choons till two. No special theme tonight, just whatever you want to get off your hairy chest – yes, you, madam – give us a ring. Sam's flexing her fingers at the switchboard next door cos I'm going to squeeze as many calls in as I can tonight. Yeah, Squeeze, remember them?" I fade in *Labelled with Love* and push away from the desk, swivelling slightly, urging myself to relax. I'm glad I managed to knock back Neville's arse-covering proposal to have our company lawyer in the studio – I already feel like somebody flying by the seat of his pants under scrutiny from the Health & Safety Executive. Too many suits, too much tension in the air. Relax. Relax.

Peter and I have competing theories. Mine is simply this – I believe Amina is telling the truth. All right, she may have been a tad disingenuous about how long it took her to realise her husband was planning for engagement in some sort of terrorist activity, but whenever she twigged I'm sure she genuinely thought his intention was to go abroad as a *jihadi*, not start waging war in his own country. Maybe she should have blown the whistle earlier than she did, but Hassan is her loving partner after all, and Afghanistan, where she thought he'd gone, is a long way from here. It's a bit different when the bombs are aimed at people you actually know. The most important factor, though – what for me determined her willingness to act or not to act – was the threat to her own child.

Peter suspects that I've been set up, which is why he wanted me to ride with him on the journey back home. Reluctant as he might be to share his conclusions with anyone who hasn't signed the Official Secrets

Act or been thoroughly vetted and pronounced *one of us*, Peter appreciated he could no longer keep the innocent conduit of the action in the dark.

"In a nutshell," he said after a preamble that took us past Preston, "I think that Hassan and Amina are in this together."

"Despite all the evidence to the contrary?"

"Do you mean the evidence, or your interpretation of the evidence?" he asked, with that air he adopts of being one step ahead of everybody else in these matters. "Or indeed Amina's representation of the evidence."

"Such as what?"

"Well, to take a simple example, the famous lockable door at the top of the stairs. Your interpretation, and Amina's representation, has it acting effectively as a prison door, with Amina as the victim." (Actually my original interpretation of the door's purpose was something altogether different, but I was not about to undermine my pretensions to be a detective by admitting that to Peter.) "Whereas, if you accept the alternative reading that both Hassan and Amina are born-again radical Islamists, there is nothing more likely than that they would want to protect Amina's modesty and create a tangible barrier against the community of males living downstairs. That does not preclude her from taking an active part in the conspiracy."

"You seem to be neglecting the fact that Amina has come to us off her own bat. How many conspirators do you know that give themselves up to the enemy before they even start to execute their plan?"

Peter smirked at the windscreen in front of him and started reciting in his best public school Latin:

equo ne credite, Teucri.

quidquid id est, timeo Danaos et dona ferentes.

"What the hell is that?"

"Virgil's *Aeneid*, Book II."

Do not trust the horse, Trojans! Whatever it is, I fear the Greeks, even when they bring gifts.

Peter consciously shifted his view off the road for a second so I could get a good look at his ironic eyebrow.

Sam's voice seems steady enough as she comes through on talkback, surfing over the music in my cans. "Colleen from Wynburn, wants to have a moan about school homework. Line 1."

I nod at Sam through the glass, and a few seconds later get Liam in my sights as I do the cross-fade. "Let's talk to Colleen on line 1. Now,

244

that's an Irish name you'd be having there, Colleen, is it? Is it?" Liam shakes his head in grim amusement at my dreadful attempt at the accent.

"No, well it is, Marc, yes, but I'm not, if you see what I mean."

"Well, there's Irish for you."

"It is, isn't it? No, well, anyway, I'm just on about homework."

Normal voice. "Colleen, if you don't mind me saying so, you sound a wee bit mature to be doing homework. Housework possibly, unless your husband does that..."

"I wish."

"But homework, no."

"Exactly the point I want to make. Only I've just finished mine about twenty minutes ago. My son's, I should say. I've been on half the night with it, Marc, seen no telly or nothing. It's hardly fair, is it?"

Sam's too busy on the phones to see me trying to catch her eye. Pity - I wanted to try a little telepathy with her, find out what she'd think about helping our boy out with his homework. A few years down the line, that is. When we have one.

"Now, Colleen, talk about fair. What about all the other kids in... What's your son's name?"

"Harry."

"What about these kids in Harry's class that have to compete with you, Colleen?"

"But they're not competing with me, are they, Marc? It's their dads that are, or their mams, like me. That's what I'm on about. We're all at it."

She's a star, this Colleen. Even Peter's having a little smile there to himself. This could be a runner tonight. Hassan might struggle to get on.

"So you're saying Amina deliberately targeted me so she could get in on this side of the fence?"

By now Peter had found cruise control and was driving with both feet planted squarely on the floor. "They originally targeted you through Hassan. I'm suggesting Amina took her chance when it presented itself."

"At the house? But they had no way of knowing I was going to fetch up there."

"They invited you."

I shook my head, pleased to score a point. "They invited Tom Etherington. That's a situation I was in control of. Remember, it was *my* decision to make the original visit. They weren't even around then. Are you claiming the estate agent is part of the conspiracy as well?"

Peter's right toe stroked the accelerator to sweep past a dawdler in the middle lane, then came back to the floor mat. "We've already checked the estate agent. No problems there. But the fact is that Prince Albert Road is in the middle of an Asian community. Agreed your face is not as well-known as, say, a local TV weather-man," (subtle put-down) "But your photo had recently been in the paper in connection with the family, and no doubt that's just how you looked on that first visit. It takes no stretch to imagine you were spotted going in or out, by a neighbour, perhaps." The furious expression of the woman next door popped out of a folder in my memory, but I didn't offer it to Peter as corroborating evidence. "From that moment on you were offering yourself for the hook, and on the second visit you took it – or to be more precise your partner did. The rest is them playing the line. It was very convenient for us, wasn't it, that Amina was booked onto the Lahore flight in her own name? So much easier to ensure that we caught up with her at precisely the right time."

"Or simply that they had absolutely no idea Amina was in touch with us, or that we were looking for her," I countered. "Liam told me these local cells aren't particularly sophisticated."

"Sophisticated enough to import drugs for sale, however, and a man to do it for them."

"But not wise enough to protect him, or well enough organised to supply him or anybody else with a fake passport." I was enjoying our version of head tennis. "Besides, who has given us the best possible information about the folk involved in this cell? Amina, right?"

"None of which information is worth a bean if she proves to be an unreliable witness." Peter counted on his fingers to make the point. "Every one of these people – Ali, Aziz, even Fatima Bhat – can portray themselves as innocent dupes, fitted up by Amina and her partner. Assuming she still has a partner. What evidence do we have that Hassan Malik is still alive? Only the testimony of Amina Begum Khan. Suppose this character Rasoul is another invention. Suppose we have been persuaded that the chief protagonist of this plot is a man who actually died accidentally more than three months ago. At the very least we end up with egg on our faces. Worst case, we fail to prevent a major act of terrorism and end up with no suspects on whom we can pin a charge more serious than wasting police time. Amina could retract her evidence anyway, once it's over. If everything goes according to their plan, they won't even have to kill themselves for a result. Which could be quite a double whammy."

Amazingly, the atmosphere is good tonight. Despite the presence of police and Home Office types in the ops room, not to mention bomb disposal and armed response teams waiting for the word in strategic parts of the city, the on-air banter is relaxed and friendly. Does the condemned man appreciate his last meal? I'm pleasing myself, I'm relating to my audience; they are being quirky and funny, without that undertow of misery we get some nights. Sam has a smile on her face – that's always a good sign, and tonight especially, when she has such a huge responsibility on her shoulders. The only worry I've got in the back of my mind is how obvious the change of tone might be when (if) we have to switch to the dummy tape. The agents were great, and we tried our best to produce what would pass as a typical unstructured phone-in – a rich variety of topics and we even had a few laughs along the way – but in real time, will it play as a seamless continuation of what went before? I mustn't let this thought distract me too much. Does it matter, anyway, once the shit hits the fan?

I'm chatting to Fletch from Spinney Vale about his idea for organising an online gurning contest when Sam pops a message on the screen: *Oliver on line 2.* 'Oliver Dunn?' I mouth to her through the glass and she nods. Unusual. This will make it possibly the third time that Ollie has asked for a speaking part in all his hours of listening, and the previous two were fairly inglorious. It bothers me slightly. Ollie might be disadvantaged in some ways, but he is alert to every nuance in the show, and I'm concerned he might have noticed some discrepancy he wants to point out that will make it apparent we're not acting in the normal manner. Worse, he might be picking up on some point of reference from our recent time together, and accidentally blurt out something compromising, something that reveals to the plotters we know things they don't think we know. For safety's sake I shouldn't take the call. On the other hand, I can't give him the bum's rush again – especially after all he did to help rescue my stolen mobile.

"Thanks, Fletch, I genuinely think that's a great idea and a lot of fun. So, if anybody wants to have a go at becoming the world's first-ever online gurning champion, get in touch with us and we'll pass on the details. Now here's a great friend of the programme on line 2, it's Oliver Dunn. Ollie, how you doing, mate?"

The question stumps him for a couple of seconds and he hesitates, snuffling, wondering whether to answer or get straight into what he's doubtless been rehearsing. Eventually he says, "Hi Marc, this is Oliver Dunn speaking, very well thank you, how are you?"

"I'm absolutely fine. This is a rare treat, having you on-air. I should explain to listeners that Oliver here knows more about this show than anybody else in the world, certainly including Sam and me put together. Isn't that right?" I wait, expecting an answer, but nothing comes. "So, what brings you on tonight?"

"Hi Marc," Ollie starts again, then checks. "It's for my mam," he says, after a pause.

"Uh-huh?" I'm trying to prompt him as subtly as I can.

"In hospital."

"Oh, right." I get it at last. "When did she go in, Marc?"

"Tonight. Just tonight." Ollie suddenly sounds lost. "She's having her operation tomorrow, Marc. Her op." (An expression he'll have picked up from the nurses.)

"Of course, yes. Well, I'm sure it will go really well. Is she is in the Western General?"

"It's the same stop but one past yours, Marc." (Thanks, Ollie. You could have picked a better time to announce that to the world.) "I just wondered if you'd say hello." At first I think he's inviting me to pop into the hospital on my way home, but the message Sam has just put up on screen keeps me right. It says, *She's called Vera.*

"Oh, right, I'll be pleased to. She's called Vera, isn't she, your mam?"

"Vera Dunn. Mrs Vera Dunn."

"Well, Vera. I hope you've settled in well, and the nurses are looking after you properly." (Does Patientline even carry our station?) "If you come across a porter called Norman, tell him hi from me. And Vera, the best of luck for your operation tomorrow."

"Thanks, Marc."

"Don't mention it, all part of the service."

"And Marc?"

"Yes, Ollie." (Please don't ask me to drop by for a cup-of-tea-or-a-cup-of-coffee-we-have-both.)

"Just to say it's really nice that you and Sam are back together..." he swallows noisily, "On the programme. It's not been the same without you."

Sam's eyes meet mine through the glass. "Thanks, Oliver," I say. Heart-rending. I mean it.

For Peter it was the two mobile phones – one hidden, one found – that convinced him of Amina's complicity in the plot. "Let's track the journey of your partner's phone," he said. "Obviously Amina was fortunate to get it – Sam's impulsive decision to hand it over couldn't have been anticipated – but having been given that gift she made the best possible use of it to achieve their aims. Note that it was switched off except on the two very brief occasions she used it – once to call you, once to send you the text message – and both times in situations where they knew it would be difficult to track down the location. Both calls were calculated to give us the opportunity to find her at the place and time of her choosing."

He was about to continue, but I couldn't hold back my objections. "Naturally she switched it off when she wasn't using it," I said. "How about if somebody, Sam's sister, say, had tried to call her? That's Amina's lifeline gone. I almost did it by accident myself." I was reluctant to admit that stupidity to Peter, but it helped support my case. "She only used the phone on the two occasions when she was able to snatch the chance. We know she was being held well away from the city – that's why there weren't enough cell towers, not because she chose the spot to keep her location secret. By the way, if they were so keen to make sure we found them, don't you think she would have given us a bit more information?"

Peter, watching the road, couldn't suppress a smile. "Little enough to establish credibility, sufficient to test our intelligence without confounding it. We're pretty good at this, they know that. So are they, but they make mistakes. Didn't Amina say Fatima was outside the toilet when she called you?"

"Yeah, so?"

"Don't you think she would have heard Amina's voice, through the thickness of a door? After all, you could hear hers at the other end of the phone."

"Well... Only because she was calling out to Amina, hurrying her up..." But Peter had the bit between his teeth now.

"And then we come across Amina's phone, which turns out to have been in use throughout the time of her supposed abduction, and who has she been talking to? Fatima Bhat. Meanwhile she abandons Sam's phone –her lifeline, you called it – when they supposedly took her away from her child, even though she'd surely be desperate to call you again as her last chance for rescue."

"She didn't abandon Sam's phone. She had the nous to hide it in Tarik's cot so at least there was some chance the police would be able to track his whereabouts."

Peter inclined his head. "Or that is what she wanted us to think. Suppose, instead, that the phone is sitting right now in the middle of an empty, booby-trapped room, waiting for us to come crashing in to rescue the little boy. Ka-boom. Nobody hurt but the law enforcers and whichever unlucky sods are in the vicinity to count as collateral damage. Significant, isn't it, that the engineers have picked up the signal right in the middle of the city. Why bring the baby back into town at this juncture?"

I sat quiet for a minute, my eyes on hills that seemed pushed back to let the motorway through, thinking things over. Peter's arguments were beginning to sound persuasive, or at least planting doubts in my head. Could she have talked to me without Fatima overhearing? Who packed her bag? What was her own phone doing there? What about these calls from Fatima's mobile? Was the baby brought back into town, and if so why? So many questions – too many possible answers. By then I was finding it nigh on impossible to separate what I knew to be true and what I accepted as true because Amina had told me so.

I turned my head to observe Peter, eyes forward, ears alert to my next objection. He looked so fucking smug. "Do you have any idea how fucking smug you look?" I said. His mouth twitched slightly at the corner, hurt or amused, I couldn't tell which.

"So let me ask you this," I said. "If it was all part of their plan for us to catch up with the two women at the airport, how come Amina left such incriminating evidence in her suitcase?"

"I guess, because she didn't expect us to treat her like a criminal, going through her things."

"Bollocks." Peter's 'I guess' betrayed his uncertainty and restored my self-confidence. "Simple truth is," I said, "The person who put that phone there was expecting it to go all the way to Lahore, because they had no reason to suspect the women would be stopped. Whoever picked it up when they cleared Amina's house – maybe bin Ali or somebody else in the cell – thought it was a bright idea to use it for contact with Fatima in case they had their own mobile records checked out later, when the police started rounding up known activists after the big event. And what would be a nice easy way to get rid of the phone once it has served its purpose? Put it in the bag that's going to Pakistan. Bye-bye."

Peter didn't respond. I had him on the run. "Tell you what, as well," I carried on. "If you're so damn smart how come you didn't check for a cell phone registered in Amina's name long before you took it out of her bag at the airport?"

Peter addressed himself in the mirror, smiling as he said, "Oh, but we did. That's why I've been rather more reserved in my trust for Amina than you have, Marc. Her call history over the last month does not entirely support her depiction of herself as the isolated and imprisoned wife. Maybe it even casts doubts on the lady's fidelity to her husband."

"What do you mean?"

"It's interesting. For several days before Hassan famously popped up on your radio show we have found records of calls between Amina and Hassan's friend, Ahmed Aziz. This is the man she told us she hated for taking her husband away from her. At the very least these calls suggests that Amina is an active part of the conspiracy. It could, of course, be even more significant. Suppose the lady protests too much, that instead of despising her husband's friend she has the opposite feeling for this man. Didn't Amina herself describe him as attractive and successful? What if the reason Hassan was chosen to be the martyr in this plot was not only that it advances the cause but very conveniently removes an obstacle between two lovers?"

Peter looked across his shoulder as he formed the question, somehow making it seem more like an accusation, before he faced the road again and continued. "The plan was all going very smoothly. Hassan was down to play the part of the suicide bomber, blowing himself to pieces in the vicinity of whatever target they'd identified - with the added advantage that he had already officially become a non-person. The others involved had already covered their tracks and there was every chance that Amina and Ahmed, with little Tarik, would be able to start up a new life together without the inconvenience of a prison sentence. Until, ironically, Hassan made his impulse call to declare his love for the wife he believed to be true. So abandon Plan A, bring on Plan B, which is a variation of Plan A with extra propaganda value. Then you show up on the doorstep, Marc, and a new Plan C is called for. Meanwhile Hassan probably thinks they're still working on Plan B."

"And what is Plan C?" I closed my eyes and sagged slightly in my seat. My head was throbbing, and I wasn't sure whether it was caused by all these ifs, buts and maybes scuttling through my brain like so many laboratory rats, or by Peter's offhand slights on Amina's morality, which somehow diminished me as well as her.

"That we don't know, but my huge concern is that we are allowing ourselves to be sucked up in it. Hassan may have been the patsy at the start of this operation. My fear is that now it might be you, Marc."

We drove without speaking for a while. When I opened my eyes again Peter was concentrating on the road, and yet still seemed to have a mental camera trained on me. Did this guy ever have unguarded moments? I wondered if he had someone in his life who could stop him

251

working so hard on his show of effortless superiority. Someone to say, Darling, take a chill pill, relax.

"You married, Peter?" I said, and couldn't help smiling as I watched him processing the question as if it was a chess move. He chose to counter with a simple pawn.

"Possibly."

"Only, I was wondering, do you ever borrow your wife's mobile phone?"

He hesitated, then nodded minimally. Not a *yes* to my question, I realised, but as an acknowledgement of the motive for it.

"Suppose you didn't have one of your own," I continued. "Suppose you couldn't use your old one because... well, say the phone company had been told you were dead. Only you wanted to speak to your best friend. Maybe you were planning something together. In those circumstances, do you think it's possible you might borrow your wife's phone? To contact that friend?"

"It's possible," said Peter, evenly. I sat back again and waited for him to develop his next line of argument. We sat in silence for a good while. Eventually it was broken, not by Peter but by me, as I peered out of the passenger window. "I think we might have missed our turn," I said.

Of course Peter could be right. In which case, as he warned me when my argument prevailed over bringing Amina into the studio, I am acting exactly like the Trojans. My sense is she may prove to be our secret weapon. Now the plate glass separates our two opposing male egos. My domain is in here and on the air waves. Amina is sitting opposite and to the left of my board in the studio guest position where she has been throughout the show, hood down to accommodate headphones fed by the studio output, listening sombrely even through the most light-hearted exchanges. She can't hear Sam on talkback or see the messages I'm getting on the screen – I'm in control here – and she had to suffer another body search at Peter's insistence before she stepped through the door.

Otherwise Peter's domain is out there, specifically coordinating the teams waiting to close in on any action. One of these is already outside the address pinpointed as the current location of Sam's phone, and has quietly evacuated the surrounding properties - not too difficult a job as it's almost exclusively a commercial area, deserted at this time of night. The team is primed to move in, using sniffer dogs and robot detectors, as soon as Hassan has contacted me and the game is on.

Which will be when? It's past eleven-thirty now, and the only caller out of the ordinary has been Oliver. Peter's theory is they won't leave it until the small hours because there will be less movement around the city then, easier for them to be spotted. Maybe this is not going to be the night after all, maybe Mr Ali's trip to Birmingham has put us on a false alert. As I go to another commercial break, suddenly I feel weary – the adrenaline that has helped me lift the show (are you listening, Meg?) is beginning to drain now, leaving me sapped. Sam looks tired too. I've just realised that we haven't had a coffee since we started.

"Like a coffee, Amina?"

"No thank you."

Suit yourself. I move to the talkback button – I'll get Sam to send one of the coppers out to make it, give them something to do – but I have to wait; she's chatting to another caller. As I watch she straightens up and raises one hand in the air as though she's asking to leave the room. Every pair of eyes behind the glass turns to her, then switches to me as she brings her hand down on to the desk and leans into her talkback mike.

"Hassan on line 1. Cell phone – I think he's on the move."

She points at Peter, the agreed signal when she's closed her voice channel, so he can safely speak. He's immediately on his line, face taut, giving instructions to the teams on the streets. They'll move in on Scrivener's Row now, towards Sam's cell phone location, leaving the technical guys to try to get a fix on Hassan. Now it's me, dexterity called for. While I'm opening the channel to line 1 I deliberately cut the last commercial short as I switch the station to the dummy output – that will help make sense of the pratfall intro...

'Oops, what happened there?' my recorded voice is saying. 'Came off in me hand, mister. Never mind, let's see who's waiting on....' Switch monitor and, while the region listens to the one we made earlier, I can hear myself live on the closed circuit, saying, "Line 1, we have Hassan. Good evening, Hassan, how's tricks?" Out of the corner of my eye I can see Amina, startled, come to attention on the edge of her seat.

"You know me, I think." Same steady voice.

"Sorry Hassan, interference, can't hear a thing. If you've a radio there could you switch it off, please?" Not getting howl-round in reality, so we're probably safe, but no harm in belt and braces. We don't want him cottoning on.

I've managed to confuse Hassan, throw him off his stride a bit. He comes back almost apologetic. "No radio, no. Can you hear me now? I'm travelling. Is that better?"

"Driving, pal? Can't talk to you while you're driving – you'll have to stop."

He chuckles, a little embarrassed, having to deal with this jobsworth. Elements of farce, not what he expected on his mission of death. "Don't worry, my friend is driving."

"Still dangerous, though. It's a distraction. You'll need to pull over, or we can't carry on. Seriously." This is a high risk strategy. I hadn't planned this, just riding my luck.

"Slow down," he says to somebody. My eyes seek out Liam's and I give him the thumbs through the glass. Two Asian men (I assume the driver is a man) in a vehicle. Moving slowly, passenger on the phone. Something to go on. "We're fine now, Marc," Hassan assures. I consider pushing it further, but it's not in our interests to lose him now.

"OK, Hassan. What's your point tonight?"

"Don't you know me, Marc?" he says, recovering some composure. "I caused you trouble before."

"You're not a swearer, are you, mate?" Playing daft laddie. "I don't want to have to dump you now."

"Not swearing, no. You remember Valentine's Day? Some of your listeners thought I was dead."

Amina's fingers are steepled at her lips, concentrating, looking past me. I let Hassan know I've caught on. "Right, *that* Hassan. You caused quite a stir there. What was that all about?"

"I'm going to die, Marc. I want to tell you that. I need your help."

OK. He's playing suicide caller, like the man on the bridge, so I'll keep him talking, give him a platform. Suits us, pal, just don't push any fucking buttons. "I'm here for you, Hassan, I'm with you. We all are, all the listeners."

There's a pause. I can hear road noise in the background, no obvious traffic. Hassan speaks again. "It's an evil world, Marc."

"It's not perfect, of course not. But there are so many good people, we have to remember that, don't we, hold on to that. You're a good person, aren't you, Hassan?"

I look across at Amina as I wait for his answer, intending to encourage her with a smile, but her eyes are closed, palms still together, fingers poised. She could be praying.

"I live simply, Marc," Hassan replies, "By the word of Allah, and by the grace of Allah. I try to live without greed. *Hasbi Allah*. Greed is our enemy, Marc. Greed and corruption, and sin."

There's a stationery pot at the far end of the shelf that curves round with the contour of Amina's desk. Maybe it always sits there - I've

254

never noticed it before. Maybe Simon or Marni brought it in for some reason while they were occupying my space. What has caught my eye is the red handle of a large pair of office scissors sticking out from the pot.

"To live simply is to live without greed, Marc. But this part of the world has not learnt that lesson. Greed is good in the west."

I look through the glass at the team. Most are listening intently to Hassan, eyes shaded. One is staring at a computer screen. Liam is talking on his mobile. If Amina chose to lunge at me across the desk with those scissors... but why would she do that?

Hassan is warming to his subject. "Who stokes the fires of greed, Marc? Big business, the firms that buy ads on your station and on TV to paint fools' paradises for the gullible. And big governments, who feast on greed, and get drunk on power. These are the forces of international evil, chief among these the Americans and the British."

"But are you not British yourself, Hassan?"

Amina's attack on me would be her statement, her act of accord with her husband, her personal bid for salvation through violence. Or maybe she's there in case I'm too successful in talking down Hassan. Maybe she's the reserve force. The second wave. For Hassan? For Ahmed? An image of my blood-soaked body, slumped across the console, leaps across synapses.

"I am a Muslim," says Hassan. "At one with my people, who are being wiped out for the offence of being Muslims." The VU meter in front of me bobs with the rise and fall of his voice as he becomes more animated. Next to it another meter tracks the levels of the dummy programme, innocently transmitting. I take Hassan's voice down a touch, then move my left hand to the channel offering monitor audio for the pre-recorded programme, should I need it. I slide the monitor volume to maximum. If Amina makes a move my plan is to switch her headphones to that feed – she'll be tazered by sound.

"Hassan, I know there is prejudice, and there's no excuse for it, but surely most..."

Hassan cuts in. "This is not merely about prejudice. I am not speaking only about the humiliation that is our daily experience. I am speaking about real blood spilt, lives lost in their thousands by my brothers and sisters internationally. I'm speaking about the crimes committed by the forces of evil in Iraq, Afghanistan, Chechnya..."

A message flashes up on my screen through Hassan's tirade. Sam returns a tense smile as I glance at her momentarily before reading it. *Baby's cot found with phone in lining. Store-room. No Tarik. No people.* And no booby-trap. Through the glass Sam has her head turned towards Peter, taking some instruction. She nods and leans forward to speak to me on talkback, over-riding Hassan for my ears only. "We can use Amina," is what she says. She releases the button and I tune back in to Hassan's speech.

"...Women raped and violated by the kuffar oppression. Families torn apart. Entire states of the Muslim faithful kept poor and desperate by the terrorism of the west. Our people do not own aeroplanes and tanks, but we have one glorious combat technique, our heroic stratagem for fighting enemy occupation and tyranny. Do you know what I am talking about, Marc Niven?"

"I'm listening, Hassan." Damp sweat is collecting under my headphone band. Amina has her eyes fixed on me now. At the very moment Peter has chosen to trust her, my faith is slipping. I'm afraid to let her speak. Sam has turned once again to Peter. Look at me, Sam. I need to see what you're thinking.

"Human bombs, do you hear?"

"We hear you, Hassan."

"I am a blazing torch for Allah. Yes." Someone in the background, male, says something – a prayer. Hassan repeats it. "*La Wajhillah.*"

Sam seems about to open the talkback channel again, changes her mind, taps at her keyboard instead. I come in at the beat after Hassan's invocation. "This isn't a war zone, Hassan. Lots of people in this country want out of Afghanistan, Iraq, you know that." Sam's message is on the screen. *East of city. Keep going.* "There's sympathy here for your cause, but not the means. I've heard that many times sitting in this chair, from non-Muslims and Muslims..."

"To be Muslim is to challenge the enemy of Islam," says Hassan. "That is our obligation. That is our finest act of worship."

Amina is still focused intently on me. I raise my eyebrows, enquiring, and she nods. I push the guest mike a little closer to her and get ready to open her line, more nervous than before, fearful of an endgame I can't control.

"Hassan." I have to clear my throat and try again. "Hassan, I have someone here with me. Please listen to what she has to say." Hassan seems to make some reply I can't catch, then I realise he's speaking away from the phone, probably to the driver. "Please listen, Hassan," I say again, and nod at Amina as I bring up her mike.

"Hassan, it's me," she says, simply, and waits. I can hear some traffic noise behind the silence, a heavy gear shift, then the other man's voice, more clearly than before, speaking sharply to Hassan, 'No more time - who is it?'

"Amina? What's going on?" says Hassan down the line at last. Amina withdraws a hand from the desk to rest where her heart must be beating. Behind her, through the glass, I can see Peter standing next to Sam's chair, both arms ramrod tense at his sides.

"You can't do this, Hassan. The *imam* is wrong. Ahmed Aziz is wrong. Listen to me, Hassan. You cannot kill innocent people."

"Amina, you know. I have told you. *Jihad* is my obligation. It is *Fardh-e-Ain* for me and every man."

"Your obligation is to your family, Hassan. To me and especially to your son. Did you not tell me you loved me, the night you left?"

"Yes."

"And Tarik?"

"Yes. The glory is his also." There is a long pause before Hassan speaks again. "Allah demands my love, Amina. You must know that. My love and my duty are owing to him."

Amina's eyes are stone. "You owe him nothing," she says. "Your prayers, if you must."

"The *imam* told me that one day of *jihad* is better than eighty days of praying."

"I say the *imam* is a liar. Much more than a liar. Bin Ali is an evil man. He imprisoned me. Hassan..." She hesitates, presses her fingers to her temples and moves so near to the mike she almost pushes it aside. "Hassan..." Close, confessional. She shuts her eyes. "He raped me."

Behind the glass is a tableau of shocked faces. I'm paralysed in my seat, unable even to breathe. Amina is expended, limp. The only sense of motion comes from the road noise at the other end of the line as Hassan's vehicle accelerates through the darkness. Hassan himself makes no sound. Twenty, thirty seconds passes before anything happens. Amina lifts her head painfully, eyes shadowed, and speaks into the microphone. "He has Tarik." Still nothing from Hassan. Amina waits, then tries again, enunciating every word. "The *imam* has stolen our son."

Hassan's voice is like the moan of an injured animal. "No," he says. "Tarik is here with me."

I watch, dumbstruck, as the fever surges, licks fatigue from Amina's face and ignites the terror in her eyes. The VU meter leaps to red as she screams "Hassan, please, no!" into the microphone. Sam lifts from her seat and I can see her striking her desk with her fist. Peter is animated, and Liam springs towards the glass, helplessly ready for action.

Hassan reacts to his wife's cry. He shouts, "Stop!" then again, "Stop! We'll lose the signal."

Lose the signal. Lose the signal. East of the city. First plan aborted. The royal opening, two weeks ago. They're trying for the same target. Close enough to lose the signal. I wipe out both mikes and jab at the talkback switch, frantically yelling, "The tunnel! They're heading for the tunnel!"

There's movement next door. Amina is wailing into her dead microphone. The sound of a furious row in my cans. A child cries, shaken out of sleep. A horn blares in the distance. A thud. The line goes down.

XVII

I can hear the music playing from downstairs. If I concentrated I'd probably be able to work out exactly what it is, but Chrissie's collection doesn't interest me enough to bother, so I just lie there, vaguely following the bass line as it pulses through the floorboards. Besides, I have all sorts of stuff in my head already. Like remembering that tonight will be the first time we've slept in this bed since New Year, and thinking, really, that was the start of it all, rather than Valentine's Day. Well, that's seeing it from my usual egocentric point of view. It started months earlier for Hassan and Amina. And Edona? How long it is since she left her home I'm not absolutely sure – I wonder whether she knows herself.

When I was a kid, getting into one kind of scrape or another, my dad always used to warn me that actions have consequences. If it wasn't for my fling with Anji, Sam wouldn't have left me, and I wouldn't have ended up in Tesco's car park at three o' clock in the morning on my way back from my unsuccessful hit on Marni. Consequently I wouldn't have seen Edona trying to run away and would never have become involved in her predicament. In fact, the incident with Anji subtly influenced my behaviour towards Edona, though I didn't recognise it at the time. Where might Edona be now, but for the original action?

Where was the original action that locked me into the destiny of Hassan and Amina? Not, come to think of it, from taking the call on Valentine's Day, but before that – accepting the job of hosting the awards evening where Sam and I met the two of them for the first time. The consequences of that action were the events of February 14th and the exchange of cell phone between Sam and Amina, which ultimately saved her.

Which ultimately saved a disaster. How else could Hassan, in thrall as he was to Ahmed Aziz and Zaid bin Ali, have been prevented from carrying out his act of destruction in the tunnel? The truck itself seemed innocent enough, and could easily have passed an inspection since it contained no explosive material at all – it was simply packed with flour and butter. Add a full tank of petrol and a spare can to set the blaze off, and all the ingredients were there for a massive tunnel fire. The plotters could be sure of it; they were replicating the 1999 accident at Mont Blanc. Forty lives were lost then. The fire took nearly three days to put out, and kept the tunnel out of action for the best part of three years with two hundred million Euros' worth of damage. A deliberately engineered British version would have left quite a monument for our little local cell. Of course there would have been no chance of survival for Hassan or Imran Khalid, the driver, or little Tarik – all three would have been burnt or asphyxiated long before they were able to escape the tunnel. For the glory of Allah. Instead, by the grace of whoever, they all got away with a bruise or two from the collision at the entrance.

Actions lead to consequences. Would Amina's pleas, on their own, have been enough to break Hassan's resolve, trigger his fight for the wheel? He had ignored them before. Was it the revelation of the rape that lifted the spell bin Ali had over him? I doubt the trial will throw any light in that direction – I gather on the QT from Liam that Amina has refused point blank to add rape to the charges the *imam* is facing. The code of dishonour is as strong in Pakistani culture as it is in Albania, it seems. Still, there's enough on bin Ali to keep him in prison a long time. Ahmed as well - the evidence from his store-room means he'll be charged with abduction and dissemination as well as conspiracy. My view is they both deserve a longer sentence than Hassan, whatever that turns out to be.

The music seems suddenly louder, but only because someone's opened the bedroom door. Sam, in her sleek crimson dress, slips through, closing the door behind her before she comes to sit on the bed next to where I'm lying.

"I wondered where you'd disappeared to. Got a headache?"

"No, no. Just chilling. Thinking."

"About what?"

"About everything. Everybody."

Sam glances a tad ironically at the near-empty glass on the bedside table. "I see you've started on the malt. That always makes you... whatsit."

"Introspective. See, I can say it, so I've not had that much."

"Budge up." Sam eases out of her heels and slithers across the duvet to lie with me, smoothing down the satin of her dress before she snuggles in. She kisses me lightly under the chin, nibbles at my ear, and whispers, "Who you thinking about now?"

"Amina."

Sam digs me playfully under the ribs. I catch her hand and bring it up to kiss, then lay it on my breast while I stroke the back of her arm. "No, I don't mean like that. I *was* thinking about her though, just then. Being without Hassan. Wondering what she's going to do."

"Leave the area, I should imagine. If I was her I'd want to get well away from here. Change my name. There might be people after her, you know, for what she did."

"What about Hassan? Will she stick with him, d'you think, after all this? Wait for him?"

I can feel Sam's warm breath on my neck as she contemplates. "I don't really know," she says at last. "I would have said yes, but... look what he was prepared to do to their own little boy. And the fact that he had Tarik with him means he must have known what was happening with Amina, and he let that go. Until she told him about the rape. Supposing there was a rape..."

"What you mean, *supposing?*"

Sam props herself up on her elbow. "I mean, if I was desperate to save my child there's nothing I wouldn't say if I thought it would... And this is me, not even a mother yet."

"Yet." My hand moves instinctively to her flat stomach. Hers follows and holds me there, as much to stop me roving while she finishes what she has to say.

"I might be wrong. I mean, quite possibly she was raped – Ali's an evil... But the point is Hassan believed her. And it was only then that he stopped what he was doing. If you ask me, that was more about him, about his own pride, or warped sense of honour, whatever you'd call it, not about her. Otherwise he wouldn't have abandoned her in the first place, would he?"

"Guess not. So you think she'll leave him, then?"

"Who's to say? Probably not. She loves him, that's obvious. Women are stupid like that." She pecks me on the cheek. "As you know."

I'm a wee bit hurt by the link Sam's making. "Hey, it hardly compares..."

"I know, I know." She rests her head on my shoulder. "You're a paragon of virtue, relatively speaking."

"And a hero. Don't forget that bit."

"And a hero, of course." She pulls back a little on the pillow. I can feel her watching me, and I'm reminded of the last time we lay together in this bed. Last time I kept my eyes firmly closed. This time I open them and turn to watch her studying my face. Sam meets my eyes, and smiles. "I *have* forgiven you," she says.

"Completely?"

"Completely."

"Why?"

261

"Because you made a mistake. You were offered the chance of free and easy sex with a good-looking girl, and, because you had quite a lot to drink, you couldn't resist the temptation. I hated you for it. Even when I came back, I wasn't ready to forgive you, not fully – there was always going to be that resentment. Then I had to get my head around the thing with Edona."

"I didn't go there to..."

"Don't, Marc..." She brings her cool fingers up to my lips and rests them there. "Don't start again with the excuses. We've moved on. I've moved on. What I say to myself is, however you ended up in that place, you faced the same temptation that you had with Anji. But this time you made the right decision. More than the right decision. I'm not going to spend the rest of my life calling you a hero, bighead, but it'll do for tonight. You done good."

"Thank you. Can we make love now?"

"No. Later."

"You might be too drunk later."

"Excuse me," she says, pretending affront. "I haven't had one drink tonight. I told Oliver I would take him home."

I let my head roll back on the pillow. "Hell, I forgot about Ollie. Why don't we just put him in a taxi?"

"No, I promised his mam. Anyway, I want to pop in and see how she's managing, if it's not too late. I don't mind, honestly. Come on." She springs up off the bed, straightening her dress. "You've got a speech to make before you're incapable."

"Speech?"

"Yeah. We're all going to give Edona our presents, and you're going to do a speech, make her feel special." Sam stretches both hands to me. "And if you do a good job..." She leans over to haul me from the bed, allowing me a good view of her cleavage. "I'll let you make babies with me later. Deal?"

"Deal."

For a party it's quite a modest gathering. Edona has not been here long enough to make many friends, so we've had to pretty much make up the numbers. Nobody from work – Debbie would be the only likely candidate, but she's standing in for Sam while we're on R&R, as my new best buddy Neville called it. Fern is here, of course, upsetting my assumptions by bringing along her husband, Dominic. She introduces him to me for possibly the third time this evening – memory loss induced by an inordinate number of margaritas – and says, patting my backside, "This man, friends in high places."

"Only temporarily, I expect," I say, grinning at Dom, because our conversation opener about half an hour ago went along similar lines.

"No, on the up," Fern says enigmatically then, clutching my shoulder, "You're not one of those frigging masons, are ya?"

"Definitely not, no." At which Fern places her finger at the side of her nose, and winks conspiratorially. "Actually, Fern," I say, spotting another guest on his way through the hall from the kitchen, "This is the man you really need to thank. Come and take a bow, Liam."

"What's the crack?"

"Fern here has been going around giving me credit for the police changing tack on the Warkworth Street girls. But I think that one's down to you."

"No, not really," says Liam. He speaks pleasantly to Fern as she tries to keep her eyes focused on him. "Word came down that one of our colleagues had got the wrong end of the stick, that's all. Mr Finch asked me if I would help sort it out, so that's what I did. I'm glad it's all worked out well for little Edona, eh?"

"Do you know this man?" says Fern to Liam, as she grabs at my arm again. "This is a man with friends in high places."

"I'm off to have some of what's she's having," I say to the guys, on the move to the kitchen. I find Oliver in there, perched on a stool by the bench, scooping out a tub of Ben & Jerry's. It's the first time I've seen him with a tee-shirt that doesn't have our station logo on it. Whether lilac is his colour is debatable, but it's new and clean, or was before he dripped strawberry ice cream on it. I give Fern's cocktail selection a miss once I notice that there's still nearly half a bottle of Laphroaig on offer.

"Can I get you a drink, Ollie?"

"Yes thank you, Marc," he says, surprising me. "Can I drink what's the same in your bottle?"

"You sure?"

"What is it?"

"Malt whisky. It's called Laphroaig. Only it's quite strong."

"That's OK. I'll have that, then."

"Fair enough." I find a spare crystal glass in Chrissie's top cupboard and rinse it out before pouring as short a nip as I dare without insulting Ollie. "Would you like water with this?"

"Are you having water in yours, Marc?"

"No."

"I don't like water in mine neither."

263

I bring both glasses across to Ollie's stool and hand one to him ceremonially. "Here's looking at you, kid," I say, saluting him with mine.

"He's looking at you, kid," Ollie says, twinkling, and we drink off together. I let the whisky linger on my tongue, a smoke signal of peatiness rising to my palate as I watch Oliver. The effect on him is extraordinary. It's as if the whisky is playing on the inside of his face like a flame-thrower. His eyes redden and prick. When he opens his mouth with a gasp I fully expect to see dragon fire. "Pgghwah!" is what comes out instead.

"What do you think?" I say, not quite keeping a straight face. His is contorted, his cheeks tweaking at the sides of his mouth, preventing him from saying anything at all for several seconds. When the effect wears off he stares at me through watery eyes, blinks twice.

"It's quite strong, isn't it, Marc, that. What frog's it called?"

"Laphroaig. Would you like some more?"

"I think inside me mouth's burnt off. I done that one time with extra strong mints. Have you ever sucked extra strong mints, Marc? It's like them, except it's a drink." He hesitates, thinking about this, then adds, "And not really minty, more mediciny."

Sam pops her head round the kitchen door. "It's present time. Everybody's in the front room." Oliver follows her through and I do too, after a sneaky refill. The music has been turned down low. Edona is sitting in pride of place, looking happy but a little bashful as the centre of attention for guests standing, cradling their glasses, waiting for something to happen. She's wearing a long but very simple white cotton dress, tied at the waist with a gold cord to match her sandals, like a handmaiden for the Ancient Greeks. A touch more make-up than she's been used to wearing around Chrissie's house helps her look just about old enough to be up so late at an adult party. She smiles when she sees me coming through the crowd, and I can't resist bending for a soft kiss and a squeeze of her hand before I start my speech.

"Friends, I feel a bit presumptuous standing here when it's Chrissie who's the hostess with the mostest," (cries of 'get off, then' 'better-looking than you' and 'well done, Chrissie' from the guests, smattering of applause) "But I've been asked to say a few words before we all say goodbye to Edona who, I have to say, looks absolutely gorgeous tonight." ('Hear hear' and more applause as Edona's cheeks pinken around her smile.) So far, so predictable, but I'm gaining confidence from the whisky. "As some of you know, Edona has had to endure some hard times, as young as she is, especially over the last few months, and now is not the time to dwell on the past, except to say this."

The guests detect the change of tone and quieten down for me. "From the moment I first saw her, as frail and delicate as she was and is, I could sense a spirit there, a greatness of heart, that would keep Edona going, help her survive." The room is hushed, reflective. "After all, the first time I saw her she was pelting across a car park in bare feet, trying her damnedest to out-run a BMW." There's laughter, but of a different quality than before, enriched with the admiration I want them to feel for Edona, and tinged with British middle-class collective guilt.

"I'm so grateful to have made a friend of Edona – I trust and believe she's made me a better person – and I know she's grateful for the help of the friends she's made here. Sam and especially Chrissie, who have done so much to make her stay here a pleasant one. Of course, Fern," (she raises her glass in acknowledgement at the name check) "who's been tireless in investigating the best possible route for Edona's secure return home. A couple of people from Save the Children who I know are here tonight – apologies, I have forgotten your names," (some of the crowd turn to thank the pair standing at the back of the room) "And lately, Liam, the friendliest copper I've ever met, who helped us out with a little local difficulty even though he has rather a lot on his plate at the moment." ('Top man, Liam.') "I'm pleased to tell you that, as a result of all your efforts, Edona will be repatriated initially to a shelter in Tirana – I'm assured it's a lot more comfortable than it sounds – and from there we have every expectation she will be going back as soon as possible to her own village and her own family, in safety. So, on behalf of Edona, thank you all for your help." Everyone applauds noisily while Edona, radiant, mouths her thankyous. Sam moves towards her, carrying a small parcel, which she holds up to me as a reminder. I raise my hands to try and get a bit of hush before I speak again.

"Even better news, folks, is that Edona has not only promised to come back and see us as soon as she can, but she also plans to come back and study here, and eventually hopes to find work in this country. With that in mind, and to keep Edona to her word, Sam and I have chosen our gift carefully."

Sam places the parcel on Edona's lap and encourages her to open it. Inside she finds a silver charm bracelet, with a few charms already hanging there, and plenty of space on the chain. Sam has spent days searching out one contemporary and stylish enough to please, and Edona seems genuinely delighted by it. I explain to her. "The bracelet and the charms we've chosen for it are for you to remember us, Edona, after you go home. But our promise to you is that every time you visit us we'll be adding one more charm to your bracelet. We hope you'll come and see us so often that the chain will be full before very long."

"Thank-you," says Edona simply. "I will." She smiles affectionately at me, then up at Sam as she bends to give her a kiss. Soon there's a crowd of people around Edona's chair and the discarded gift wrappings begin to mount.

"I still preferred the adoption idea," I'm saying, sitting at Sam's feet a little dopily, while guests are starting to drift off from the party.

"We would never have got approval. Anyway, you're not allowed to have a crush on your own daughter," says Sam. "Just kidding," she adds as I squint up at her, and she leans over to plant a kiss on my forehead. "Besides, we've already got another adoptee, practically."

"Who do you mean?"

Sam nods towards the chair Edona was sitting in earlier. It's occupied now by Oliver, head on one side, eyes closed, his bottom lip quivering slightly with the suggestion of a snore. "Poor lamb," she says. "I'm going to have to wake him up for his lift."

"I'll take him."

"Oh, yeah, 'course you will." Sardonic Sam. "You know, I'm sure you've drunk that whole bottle of whisky on your own."

"Not at all. Ollie had some. Well, I'll come along for the ride."

"There's no room."

"'Course there is, I'll squeeze in the back."

"Oh, best of luck, mate. You're welcome to it."

If there's one time, and one time only, to be in the back seat of a TT coupé, it's when you're drunk enough to find it hilarious, and too drunk to mind the discomfort. I may as well be on a rear window-shelf for all the space I have, lying diagonally with an overspill, my feet dangling dangerously close to Sam's head as she drives us to Oliver's place. Keen to get back before Chrissie goes to bed, Sam makes no concessions to my precarious position, nipping along pretty smartly even on the tight bends. It's alarmingly like the solo ride I took on the waltzer at the fairground as a ten-year-old; having nobody on the ride to prop myself up against, I ended up lying full length on the curved seat, hurtled between exhilaration and panic, praying not to lose my grip on the safety rail as the car jerked one way then another. Just as I did then, I feel now as if I'm in

266

some Buster Keaton movie, but unlike The Great Stone Face at least I can laugh out loud about it, courtesy of Laphroaig.

The trouble comes at the other end, once Sam pulls up at Kielder Close. Maybe it's the twisting and turning I have to go through to extricate myself from the back of the car, maybe it's the strangeness of *terra firma* under my feet after all that swishing round, like a sailor just back from a long voyage – whatever, as soon as I try and stand up straight at the kerb, I feel distinctly woozy.

"'Scuse me, I'll just be... just be one second," I say to the pair of them, spastically waving them away as I wander up the road in search of a hidey-hole to vomit in. A misguided neighbour on the corner has tried to relieve the sameness of brick and concrete by planting a thick evergreen shrub in a tiny square of garden, bordered by a low wall. I'll hate myself for this tomorrow – tonight, necessity trumps decorum. I bend over the wall, pressing the bush back with my arm. The stench tells me I'm not the first to find this spot convenient, and it's enough to prompt my heaving into it.

When I've done, my eyes are watering like Ollie's were earlier, and I'm dabbing at spittle with my hankie when I see a group of dark shapes further up the cut. Sober, I would have cleared off sharpish, away from trouble; drunk, I stand there foolishly, trying to pick out who's who. It's the estate mob. There are five, maybe six of them, congregating like vagabonds for a hand-out around one thick-set guy, obviously better-groomed. Just as I've come to the conclusion this must be the muscular sun-bed fan who sold me back my mobile, the guy makes with a few high fives around the group and breaks away, ambling in my general direction, unthreatening.

I turn and start making my way back to Oliver and Sam, still waiting for me at the end of the cul-de-sac, next to the car. Hang on, no, the car's just here, on the other side of the road. Sam must have... No, they *are* with ours – this is another TT coupé, not NIV. Hmm, same colour and... What a coincidence, you wouldn't have thought anybody round here... Fuck. I look over my shoulder and peer at the guy walking in the same direction as me. No through road for pedestrians. He's coming back to his car. Not a silver BMW, the police might be looking for that. He's changed it. *Nice car. What sort of car is this?* I'm bending down, looking to see if Stefan's in the driver's seat. Not there.

"Hey!"

Christ, he's seen me inspecting his car, thinks I'm going to nick it. He's starting to run. Light from the lamp post reflecting off his shiny black bullet head. Can't run, he'll chase me for a thief. Nowhere to go.

"It's all right, mate, just looking." Backing off. "It's cool, really." Maybe he won't know me. He stops. He's staring. He knows me. He's running.

"Call the police!" I'm shouting at Sam. Fuck, her phone is *with* the police – evidence. I'm searching through my pockets, can't find mine. Sam's running to the house. Ollie's still standing there, like a dummy. "Go with her, let her in!" He's still standing there. "Oliver!"

"Oliver!"

That shout comes from Emmanuel. Him to me.

"Oliver!" he yells again, a thunderclap of menace booming down the street. I'm turning at his call. I'm in the middle of the road. He's in the middle of the road. Who is the fugitive here? He stands like a gunslinger, but it's a knife he has in his hand. I can't go back. People in danger. I stand my ground.

"What good will it do?" I'm howling at him. "What good will it do? Get in your car, why don't ya? Fuck off out of here. The cops are coming."

He's looking at his car. He realises I'm right. He's the fugitive, hold on to that. Pile the pressure on.

"They know you caused the crash on the coast road. They know it was deliberate. It's murder they'll do you for. Get out now, while you can."

Still hesitating. He's *got* to go. Go on, get out, you bastard, bastard, leave us alone. "Get away!" I scream at the top of my voice. But he doesn't. He takes a pace away from his car. Another pace towards me. I can't back off. He's lifting the knife. My life doesn't flash in front of me: people do, all coming at me with the knife – Norman Bates, Jack Torrance, James Watson, Emmanuel, Boris, Hassan, Amina, Anji, Sam.

Something flies past, smacks into a bullet head, and smashes onto the ground. Emmanuel staggers two steps away from me, his free hand up, too late to protect him. I move forward, but he steadies, thrusting out the blade to ward me off. For a second we both stand transfixed, staring at Ollie's broken camera on the ground between us. Emmanuel dabs at the cut above his eyebrow, and studies the blood on his fingers. I glance quickly over my shoulder. Oliver is standing there, rocking on his heels. "Back off!" I'm shouting to Ollie. He's squeezing the space behind me. Back off, you stupid fucker.

Emmanuel gathers himself, then summons up a huge roar like Kong and hurls himself at me. I duck, cowering under my arms as he lunges. A shadow passes, takes the impact of the knife.

"Oliver! Christ!"

Oliver stumbles between us, falls sideways as Emmanuel bodily wrenches the knife out. I can see red on the blade as it flashes in front of my eyes again.

"Bastard!" I yell, and swing with my right as wild and violently as I can, eyes closed, missing completely, my momentum making me trip over the outstretched Oliver. My knees bounce, my cheek scrapes on the road, my shirt rips. Numbness spreads. I'm struggling to get up. My back's exposed, I'm tensed for the blade.

There's a scuffle above, and a black figure drops heavily down to my level. I'm still trying to lift myself when boots and trainers come thudding in from all directions onto Emmanuel as he's sprawled on the ground– his back, his arms, his groin, his face, his bullet head. A Doc Marten stamps down on the hand with the weapon and I grab the knife quickly. I scramble to my feet, holding it out, expecting more trouble. But the youths from the street are working only on Emmanuel, kicking him viciously, none with more venom than the big lad whose girlfriend is at the back of the group, screaming at me, "Stick the knife in. Go on, you fucking coward. You useless cunt. Some fucking mate you are."

But all I can do is try and drag Oliver away from the violence going on around him, from the youths revenging his injury, and the girl sticking up for the harmless retard who lives down her street. My stomach turns at the blood seeping through Ollie's yellow jacket, but as I'm pulling him up by the shoulders I can hear him murmuring, "I'm all right, Marc. I'm all right, Marc. Just my arm. I'm fine."

"Oh, Ollie, man, why didn't you piss off when I told you? It's nowt to do with you, you daft, stupid, fucking hero twat. Could you not just run away?"

The street lads' ears must be more finely tuned than mine to certain sounds. One second they're piling into the prostrate figure of Emmanuel, the next they're off, scattering out of the estate, the girl with them, and they're all well gone before I hear the siren, never mind get a glimpse of the flashing blue lights. Emmanuel is left lying bloodied and unconscious in the road. Oliver is cradled in my arms, his blood streaming now over my chinos. Sam comes running from the house with towels under her arms, a roll of bandage in her hand. As we're trying to stem the blood I can see Mrs Dunn, hovering anxiously in her doorway, a hand up over her eyes. Sam shouts back at her. "He's all right, Mrs Dunn, just go in, he's sorted." But of course she keeps on coming, feeling her way down the path, half-blind, in her old dressing gown and slippers.

"I'll have to go to her," says Sam. She puts some of the towels under Ollie's head and leaves the rest with me. "Press down on the wound."

Ollie's eyes flicker open, watching me as I'm peeling off the sleeve of his soaked waterproof, and I have to disguise my shock at the mess under there. I wrap the towel tightly round his left arm, and start to wrap the bandage over it, but it gets tangled in seconds so I abandon that idea and concentrate on pressing hard on the wound as Sam instructed. I watch Oliver's face getting paler, but he summons up a wan smile when he sees me looking at him.

"Never a dull moment eh, Ollie?" He shakes his head, gives me a lopsided grin. Charlie Brown. I turn away to watch Sam helping Vera along slowly, one hand round her back, the other under her elbow. "Here's your mam coming, pal. Lucky you didn't get any blood on your new tee-shirt." His eyes are closed again, but he mumbles something I can't make out. "What you say, Ollie?"

He tries again. "N't tell her about La Frogs whisk..."

"I won't. Trust me."

The police siren wails as it turns into the close. Ollie opens his eyes wide and looks at me in surprise, as if he's been woken by an alarm clock and found me unexpectedly in bed with him. He takes a moment to recollect, then says lucidly, "Is me camera all right, Marc?"

I take a look past his shoulder, counting the bits on the road. "Hard to say. Is it still under guarantee?"

Ollie seems to consider this, blinking in perplexity, but as I'm waiting for him to answer he loses his spark again, dropping his eyelids and actually yawning loudly. "Me mam'll know," is the last thing he says before he slips out of consciousness, his pale face impassive in the on-off illumination of the flashing police light.

Sam arrives with Mrs Dunn in tow. Despite her age and infirmity, Oliver's mam hunkers down beside him, takes his head onto her knees and starts stroking his hair, whispering softly in his ear. Sam kneels down too, and picks up the bandage I dropped. She soon clears the tangle and, working rhythmically, wraps it tight round Oliver's arm.

Relieved of my responsibilities, my anxiety level rises. "What about the ambulance?"

"On its way," she assures me. How could I doubt? I glance over at Emmanuel, lying motionless in the road, and back again at Oliver, still pale in his sleep.

"Hope they're bringing two."

270

Before she responds she takes a hard, cold look at the pimp and drug dealer lying in his mess. "Who gives a fuck about him?" she says. She doesn't swear very often, my Sam.

A few yards down the street the doors of the patrol car open simultaneously and two police officers emerge. They scan the scene briefly, then start to walk unhurriedly towards us. Another Friday night on the estate, pissheads and villains at each other's throats. The three of us around Oliver are equally indifferent to their approach. We're looking beyond them, past their patrol car, following the line of street lamps to the entrance of the close, waiting for an arrival more vital.

THE END

Biography

David Williams grew up as one of seven children in a mining community in the North East of England, a childhood he has written about with humour and affection in his popular collection of short stories *We Never Had It So Good*, published by Zymurgy.

While pursuing a varied career in teaching, entertainments, marketing and management development, eventually leading to the formation of his own successful company, David has also been a prolific free-lance writer, with many plays broadcast by the BBC, books and plays published by top education publishers in the UK, Australia, Germany and Scandinavia, and many credits as a writer and format creator for popular TV and radio quiz and game shows. He has written and produced educational and training videos, DVDs and software. He is a member of the Society of Authors and NAWE. He often performs at public readings, workshops and seminars, including a collaboration with ex-Lindisfarne favourite Billy Mitchell in a readings and musical show called *Born at the Right Time*.

11.59 is David's first novel. It was a semi-finalist in the 2010 Amazon Breakthrough Novel Award, which attracts 10,000 entries worldwide. He is currently working on a novel about the relationship between father and son railway pioneers George and Robert Stephenson.

David Williams has been married to schooldays sweetheart Paula 'for years and years'. The couple have three grown-up children and two grandchildren. The drama in their life comes from following the fortunes, on and off the field, of their local football team, Newcastle United.